The Tide Don't Break

A Shelf Indulgence Novel

Kennedy Layne

Magnolia Ink

Published by Magnolia Ink
Statesboro, GA

First Edition, 2025
Revised, 2026

Cover designed by Sarah Conner, Davis Marketing

ISBN: 979-8-9935996-0-1

Printed in the United States of America

Contents

Epilogue

The Bonus Sessions

Content Warning

This novel contains sensitive subject matter that may be triggering for some readers. Please take care while reading.

<u>Topics addressed include:</u>

Mental health struggles

Suicide attempt

Suicide (off the page)

Bullying

Self-harm

Trauma

PTSD

Panic/Anxiety Attacks

Night Terrors (only mentioned)

Heart attack

Hospitalization and medical trauma

This story explores themes of healing, hope, and recovery—but it does not shy away from the darker moments that often come first. If you're in a tender place, I encourage you to prioritize your well-being and read with care.

Mental Health Resources

If you or someone you love is struggling, please know there is help and support available:

United States:

988 Suicide & Crisis Lifeline —

Call or text 988, 24/7, for free and confidential support.

988lifeline.org

International Resources:

befrienders.org — Global suicide prevention and emotional support.

Other Helpful Resources:

National Alliance on Mental Illness (NAMI): nami.org

The Trevor Project (for LGBTQ+ youth): thetrevorproject.org

You are worthy of help. You are not alone. Healing is possible—and your story is not over.

Dedication

For my sister—

My Disney bestie and forever Swiftie sidekick.

Thank you for being my built-in best friend, hype woman, and the one who always screams the bridge with me like our lives depend on it. You've loved me through every plot twist, meltdown, and "are you ready for it?" moment.

This story is for every midnight drive, castle countdown, and lyric that's ever made us feel seen.

Love you always, to Cinderella's castle and back.

Swear To Be Overdramtic & True

Dear Reader,

This story contains heartbreak, pain, healing, longing and second chances—but I promise
you this:

You will get your happily ever after.

Love wins in these pages.

No cliffhangers. No heartbreak endings. Just love—the kind that stays.

So breathe easy, cozy up, and fall in love.

You're safe here.

With Love,

Kennedy Layne

Honeyshore, Georgia

Bellamy County

Population: ~12,000

Est. 1803

Honeyshore isn't flashy, but it never pretended to be. Tucked inland along the winding bends of the Honeyshore River and pressed against the edge of Bellamy Marsh Nature Preserve, this Southern town clings to its roots like Spanish moss to the oaks. The streets are lined with weathered brick, soft porch lights, and family names etched into mailboxes for generations. There's no ocean breeze here—just the thick scent of mud, salt, and magnolia. It's the kind of place where teenagers cruise the bluff at night, and even the ghosts know your business.

Life in Honeyshore moves slow, marked by shrimping seasons, high school football rivalries, and the low hum of gossip over Sunday dinner rolls. It's sentimental, intimate, and a little bit stuck in the past. Some say the town holds onto its people too tightly. Others say it's the only place that ever felt like home. For those who left, coming back means facing everything they tried to forget. But in Honeyshore, time doesn't heal—it remembers.

Peach Cove, Georgia

Loblolly County

Population: ~25,000 (including students)

Est. 1733

Home of Magnolia Bluff University Est. 1901

Peach Cove is a bluff town with a heartbeat—part college charm, part coastal ambition. Situated near the Peach Bay, it's known for its leafy campus, seasonal tourism, and artsy edge that makes it feel just a little like Savannah but with a charm all its own. At its center is Magnolia Bluff University, where the brick buildings are ivy-lined, the bay breeze whispers through the rose garden, and students wear their maroon and navy with pride on Shark Nation Saturdays. The campus overlooks the water, a view that's seen friendships form, hearts break, and more than a few bad decisions under moonlight.

The town hums with movement—brunch spots, boutique shops, and late-night haunts like Sandytown Diner and The Cove House. Greek Row looks pristine, but the memories etched into its walls are messier. Peach Cove is where teens from places like Honeyshore come to reinvent themselves—to get a little lost before they find their way. Locals say Honeyshore's sweet but stuck. Honeyshore folks say Peach Cove's just a smaller Athens wannabe. But between tailgates, beach-weekend detours, and midnight drives to the Hopeulikit (pronounced *Hope You Like It*) Drive-In, Peach Cove becomes something more—it becomes yours. Until the real world calls you forward...or back.

Part One

The Reef Sessions

Playlist

♥

(Ali's Version)

"champagne problems" — Taylor Swift

"I Want to Hold Your Hand" — T.V. Carpio (from *Across the Universe* soundtrack)

"Pieces of Me" — Ashlee Simpson

"Save Me" — Remy Zero

"Love Myself" — Olivia O'Brien

"How Did It End" — Taylor Swift

"The Archer" — Taylor Swift

"Like Real People Do" — Hozier

"dorothea" — Taylor Swift

"All Too Well (10 Minute Version) (Taylor's Version)" — Taylor Swift

Vault Track:

"Because I Liked a Boy" — Sabrina Carpenter

Playlist

Dylan's Version

"The Boys of Fall" — Kenny Chesney

"Thunderstruck" — AC/DC

"Can't Help Falling in Love" — Elvis Presley

"Slow Dance in a Parking Lot" — Jordan Davis

"Body Like a Back Road" — Sam Hunt

"Take Your Time" — Sam Hunt

"Lay Me Down" — Sam Smith

"My Songs Know What You Did in the Dark" — Fall Out Boy

"Flatliner" — Cole Swindell ft. Dierks Bentley

"Single Saturday Night" — Cole Swindell

Vault Track:

"Chattahoochee" — Alan Jackson

Invisible

Ali

Ali stared at the blinking cursor on her laptop screen, praying it would type something brilliant on its own.

It didn't.

Dr. Mitchell's voice droned on at the front of the room—something about narrative tension and "writing from the wound," which, on any other day, Ali would've loved. But today her brain was cotton. She tapped her pen against her notebook, ignoring the mostly empty page in front of her and doodling a lopsided flower in the margin.

This was what she wanted. What she loved—words, stories, turning messy feelings into sentences that made people feel something. Her dad called it "fluff." Said she was smart enough to do something practical. Like accounting.

God, she'd rather eat glass.

A text buzzed on her phone.

Daisy:

> Lunch after class? I need to talk to youuuuuuu.

Ali smiled, already hearing Daisy's dramatic voice in her head. She was a hurricane in designer sandals—always talking, always sparkling, always pulling Ali into things she had no business doing. And Ali let her. Always.

She glanced at the clock—thirty more minutes. Just ten minutes, three times. That's how she always tricked her brain: break the time down, make it smaller, easier to survive. Ten minutes didn't feel so bad.

She shifted in her seat, the desk creaking slightly beneath her. Being the curviest girl in class always made her hyper-aware of the space she took up, especially in these old lecture hall chairs clearly built for someone with half her hips and none of her thighs.

Still, she sat up straighter and took a breath.

I'm here, she reminded herself. *I made it to MBU. This is not the junior college in my hometown. I'm doing the damn thing.*

And maybe—just maybe—one day her stories would take her somewhere bigger than her hometown of Honeyshore or Peach Cove (where MBU was located). Somewhere she didn't feel so...ordinary.

Ali beat Daisy to Sandytown Diner, their usual lunch spot. She picked a booth in the back and ordered a Coke Zero while she waited on her bestie. She wasn't sure when Daisy would actually get there since 12:30 meant like 1:15ish to Daisy, so she pulled out her Kindle to pass the time.

"I swear, if I have to hear one more time about her yacht named after a Kardashian, I'm going to drown myself in a whole gallon of those frickin' Celsius drinks she's obsessed with."

Daisy slammed her purse and backpack down on the bench seat across from Ali, startling the shit out of her in the process. Daisy's oversized sunglasses slid to the end of her nose, revealing the dramatic eye roll she'd perfected since middle school.

Ali stifled a laugh, putting away her Kindle. "You picked Kappa Nu. You knew what you were signing up for."

"Correction," Daisy said, holding up a manicured finger. "I picked Kappa Nu because I have taste. I did not pick this monster child for my Little."

Ali raised a brow. "She can't be that bad."

"She says 'supposably.' On purpose. Like it's a personality trait."

Ali snorted.

"She cried because she didn't get the peach Stanley cup in her bid basket. Then she tried to trade someone for theirs like it was the Hunger Games." Daisy leaned in, lowering her voice dramatically. "She also asked me what a GPA was. Or, as she called it, 'a gappa'".

"No."

"Oh yes. Oh! And after I explained what a **GPA** is...she said—and I quote—'Do we even have to worry about that if our dads donate enough?'"

Ali coughed on her soda, laughing. "She's a legacy, right?"

Daisy flopped back in her seat. "Of course she is. Her mom was president back when Kappa Nu was more interested in charm bracelets and diet pills than actual philanthropy."

Ali rolled her eyes but smiled. This was the part of Daisy she loved—the unfiltered drama, the way she could turn a trip to the local cafe into an episode of Real Housewives: Panhellenic Edition.

Ali always felt a little invisible next to her, but never in a bad way. Daisy sparkled enough for both of them.

"Oh! I talked to Dylan last night. His trip to Orlando was going even better than expected!"

Coach Busby had practically exploded with pride when Dylan got the invitation. Magnolia Bluff wasn't a giant school—they didn't get that kind of attention. Guys from their conference usually hoped for a decent showing at a regional Pro Day, maybe a film clip passed around if they were lucky. But Dylan? He got a private workout with the actual Orlando Tritons. That wasn't just big. That was unheard of.

She was so proud of him.

Ali tried to look unbothered, sipping her Coke Zero like her stomach wasn't tying itself into knots. But the name alone—Dylan McKenzie—was enough to stir up that stupid, familiar ache in her chest. Star quarterback, campus golden boy, Daisy's older brother. He was everything girls swooned over: tall, smart, quiet in a way that made you lean in when he talked. But what got to her wasn't all that. It was the way he looked at people—really looked. Like they mattered. Like they weren't just part of the crowd. And for a fleeting second, once or twice, she thought maybe he'd looked at her that way, too.

Of course, she knew better. Dylan had sworn off dating, said he was laser-focused on football and his grades. He wasn't interested in drama, parties, or the attention that came with his name. He barely talked to anyone outside of the team or his classes, and he definitely didn't notice quiet girls like Ali Presley—girls who stayed on the edges of the room, who were more comfortable writing about love than living it.

Daisy was now mid-rant about the horrors of organizing a Kappa Nu mixer with the swim team ("They smell like microwaved protein powder, Ali, I'm not exaggerating") when a shadow passed over their table.

"Well, if it isn't the social chair herself," a warm voice said behind them.

Daisy blinked, then screeched. "DYLAN?!"

Ali turned, and—holy crap.

There he was. Dylan McKenzie.

Even in a simple MBU navy tee, jeans, and backwards MBU baseball cap he looked like the posters in the Magnolia Bluff student store in real life—tall, broad-shouldered, and stupidly handsome. His dark hair was a little longer than she remembered. His face was tanner, jaw a little sharper, like he'd been living on energy drinks, protein bars, and stress.

But his eyes—those gray-blue eyes that light up the whole stadium—locked onto hers for half a second, and her heart gave a traitorous little skip.

"Surprise," he said, grinning as Daisy launched herself at him.

"What are you doing here? You weren't supposed to come back till Friday!"

"Coach asked me to come back early. Needs me to work with a red shirt—Busby said the guy's going through some things."

He hugged her with one arm, his duffel bag still slung over the other shoulder. "Figured I'd drop by and say hey before I hit the weight room. Followed by an all-nighter at The Pen". MBU's library, The Pennington Resource Hall.

The guy never rested. He'd always been afraid of becoming a cliché—just another "dumb jock." So, he worked his ass off to maintain a 4.0 while still being the best on the field. He didn't date, didn't drink, and when he showed up at fraternity parties or socials, it was mostly to keep things from getting out of control. He'd socialize, sure—but that was about it.

"Hey Dylan," Ali managed to sound normal. "Welcome back."

Dylan smiled—just a flicker, nothing major—but something about the way he looked at her made her entire body feel suddenly aware of itself.

"Thanks," he said. "You girls get into trouble while I was gone?"

"Well, I got Verruca Salt as my Little this year," Daisy whined. Dylan just laughed and shook his head.

"Y'all going to dinner Sunday night at mom & dad's?" he asked.

Daisy groaned. "Do we have a choice?"

"No," Dylan said, clearly enjoying it.

Daisy waved him off. "Go sweat. You're ruining my lunch with your jock vibes."

He laughed and turned to go, giving Ali one last glance over his shoulder and a wink before disappearing into the stream of students.

Ali let out a breath she didn't realize she'd been holding.

Daisy sipped her Diet Coke. "Anywhooo, you ARE going to the party at the Tau Delt house Saturday night, right?"

Ali choked. "Uh no. I'm good but thanks for inviting me anyway."

Daisy smirked. "Girl. You're so cute. Making it a question was just to be nice. You are definitely coming with me."

Ali looked away, stomach turning. She would rather just go to their dorm after the game & read or watch *The Vampire Diaries* for the 100th time. She hated all the Greek Row parties. Ali didn't fit in there, but she would go because Daisy wanted her there. At least it wasn't at the Trobes' house this time. She hated the jerks in Tau Rho Beta. And Dylan *was* in Tau Delta Epsilon, so at least she knew he would be there.

Delicate

Ali

Magnolia Bluff lived for game days. Honestly, the whole town of Peach Cove lived for Saturdays in the fall.

By the time the sun started to set, the entire campus pulsed with energy—students spilling out of dorms, tailgates cranking up music and maroon and navy flags fluttering in the coastal breeze along Main Street

A charred scent from the tailgate grills mixed with the briny aroma of boiling peanuts, all carried on the salty tang of air that always rolled in from the bay. Ali had grown up only 45 minutes away in Honeyshore, frequenting the campus every fall with her family for game days. But experiencing it as a student just hit different. Saturdays felt electric.

She stood on the edge of the student section at Russell Stadium—Stowers Field stretching out before her like a stage. The Reef, they called it. A perfect name for the sunken field surrounded by waves of seats and lights that shimmered like ocean spray. Every inch of the stadium buzzed with pride and anticipation.

Her maroon athletic skort hugged her hips just right, soft and stretchy and perfect for blending in. She'd paired it with an oversized navy MBU tee, tucked in casually at the front of her waist. Her blonde hair was twisted into a messy bun, wisps falling around her cheeks from the humidity. The only makeup she wore was tinted lip balm, and her go-to white tennis shoes were already a little dusty from the gravel lot. She didn't dress up for games—she never had. Athleisure was her comfort zone. Her armor.

Daisy, on the other hand, was a walking Pinterest board. Her little maroon dress hugged her perfect curves and flared just slightly at the hem. She'd paired it with white knee-high cowgirl boots and navy jewelry, her signature brunette, glossy waves bouncing as she flipped her hair. If she was nervous about seeing her brother play tonight—the home opener in his last season as a Shark—she didn't show it.

"I swear, every girl here wants to marry Dylan," Daisy said with a laugh as they made their way to their seats, weaving through a group of girls already chanting the fight song.

Ali forced a laugh and tugged on her tee a little, feeling self-conscious. "He's not even a player," she said, and then mentally cringed. "I mean, not *that* kind of player."

Daisy waved her off, too distracted to notice the flush rising in Ali's cheeks. "He's just so...disciplined. It's kind of intimidating, honestly. But clearly it works. He crushed it at the workout day, and now Coach Busby says the Tritons are seriously interested. Mom's already redecorating the guest room for his 'future ESPN interviews,'" she added with an eye roll. "Like Magnolia Bluff is known for producing pro athletes or something."

Ali knew better. Dylan wasn't just talented—he was focused, relentless, and painfully kind. He always held the door open. Always carried his own gear, even when other guys passed it off. He wasn't flashy, not really. Just quietly magnetic.

And he had no idea how many times she'd watched him from the bleachers like this, heart pounding, pretending she wasn't looking at all.

The Reef was packed and pulsing with electricity. The crowd was already on their feet, chanting in unison, "The tide don't break! The tide don't break!" It was a sound that could raise goosebumps—deep and thunderous, echoing through the night. On a clear evening like this one, you could hear it carry all the way across Magnolia Bluff and down into Peach Cove. It was magnetic. Unstoppable. The kind of feeling that lived in your bones.

Ali forced herself to watch the game, not *him*. Not the way he rolled his shoulders before the snap. Not the way his jaw clenched in concentration as he read the defense. And definitely not the way he pointed to the stands after a touchdown—probably for his parents, but her stomach flipped anyway.

"You want to walk over to Row with us afterwards?" Daisy asked, already texting on her phone.

"Maybe," Ali hedged. She hated frat houses; hated Greek Row altogether. Too loud. Too cramped. Too many people pressing into each other in hallways that smelled like beer and regret.

But Dylan would be there tonight.

And sometimes...he looked at her like she belonged there.

...Ready For It?

Dylan

The tunnel was shaking.

The stomping, the chanting, the drums —it all rolled together into a pulse pounding through Dylan's chest as he stood shoulder to shoulder with his team, cleats echoing on the concrete, helmet in hand. He bounced once, rolled his neck. Focused.

This was it. Season opener. Senior year.

He closed his eyes for a beat, soaking in the sound of The Reef just beyond the curtain of smoke and stadium lights. The chant had already started —"The tide don't break! The tide don't break!"— shouted by thousands and building like a storm. He had heard it for his whole life—growing up coming to MBU games. But here, in the belly of Russell Stadium, it roared.

The line surged forward. Coach Busby slapped his shoulder as they hit the break in the tunnel. Then they ran.

Dylan burst through the smoke and out into the blinding lights, into the thunder of Magnolia Bluff University. The crowd was a blur of navy and maroon. His name echoed somewhere in the mix, but he barely registered it.

This wasn't about him.

It was about the team. The school. The game. He'd worked his ass off for this moment—years of early mornings, late nights, no drinking, no distractions. No dating. Just discipline.

He jogged to the sideline, falling into formation with practiced ease, heart still hammering.

Then, out of the corner of his eye—just a glimpse.

Messy blonde bun. Navy T-shirt. Maroon skort.

Ali.

His stomach flipped. He hadn't meant to look for her, but he had.

He faced the field again, jaw tight, hands flexing at his sides.

Focus. You've got a job to do.

The clock was bleeding down—just seconds left.

The scoreboard showed a three-point deficit, the crowd's roar edging toward panic and hope all at once. Dylan wiped the sweat from his brow, helmet still off, breathing steady but fast. Every muscle was wound tight. This was the moment you dream about—or dread.

Coach Busby's voice cut through the noise, sharp and calm. "One play. Give it everything."

Dylan jogged back to the huddle, locking eyes with his teammates, their faces fierce and ready. He could feel the weight of the entire team—the hard work, the sacrifices—pressing down on him like the humid night air.

The snap was clean.

He dropped back, scanning the field through the clamoring noise, searching for an opening. The defense was swarming—desperate, relentless.

His heart pounded in his ears as he took the snap and stepped up, dodging a rusher's outstretched arm. The line held, just barely.

Time slowed.

He pumped his arm and launched the ball high, the Hail Mary sailing in a perfect arc toward the end zone.

For a heartbeat, the world held its breath.

The stadium lights caught the ball's gleam as it spiraled through the air—a fragile, shimmering thread between victory and heartbreak.

Then, chaos.

Players leapt, hands stretching, bodies colliding under the glowing night sky.

And in that chaos, Dylan's eyes found one thing—Ali's face in the crowd, wide-eyed, breath held.

The ball came down, tipped, caught—a game-winning touchdown.

The crowd exploded. "BLEED THE BLUFF!"—it was their victory rally cry. Captain Rip, the Southern pirate and Riptide the Shark were running into the end zone with MBU flags.

Dylan leapt into the air, hands lifted to the sky, adrenaline crashing through him like a tidal wave.

In that moment, everything else faded.

The fight. The discipline. The doubt.

Only the victory. Only the team.

And somewhere in the roar—a whisper of her.

The shower tiles were cracked in a few spots—reminders that the locker room hadn't been updated since long before Dylan set foot on campus. Still, nothing about it bothered him tonight. Not the busted faucet handles or the flickering fluorescent lights. Magnolia Bluff had just beaten the Eagles, their biggest conference rival, under the stadium lights, and every single hit, sprint, and call had been worth it.

He ran his hands through his wet hair, letting the hot water hammer over his neck one last time before cutting it off. His body ached in that satisfying way—bruised but not broken, worked but not worn out. Game nights like this felt like the reason he'd put in all the extra hours. The 6am lifts, the late-night film study, skipping parties and ignoring texts he didn't want to answer.

He was laser-focused. Always had been.

And tonight, it had paid off.

The locker room was alive with celebration—guys blasting music, slapping helmets, and shouting half-coherent chants. His teammates had doused Busby in Gatorade on the field. Dylan had ducked that mess on purpose. That was for the cameras, not for him.

He toweled off quickly, pulling on a pair of jeans and a gray MBU athletic tee, then layered his navy Tau Delta Epsilon zip-up over the top. His fraternity wasn't just some social flex for him—it was his place. His brothers were some of the few people he trusted, guys who understood the pressure without needing him to explain it. At the TDE house, he didn't have to be perfect. He just had to show up.

He slung his duffel bag over one shoulder and checked his phone.

Daisy:

> *Party at the House is already wild. You better hurry, Big Bro. I told Ali she HAD to go and you know she hates these things.*

He shook his head, smiling. That was Daisy. Forever the social butterfly.

Not that he minded the Ali part.

There was something about her—quiet but not timid, observant in a way most people weren't. She was soft around the edges, but sharp underneath. He'd noticed the way she shrunk in crowds, but never when Daisy was around. Like her best friend gave her permission to take up space.

He didn't know why he kept noticing her. But he did.

And now, apparently, she was coming to the party.

Dylan grabbed his keys from his locker, gave a few nods and back-slaps to teammates on the way out, and stepped into the night. The stadium behind him still buzzed with leftover energy, the kind that clung to your skin long after the final whistle. Music was already drifting from the frat houses on Row, bass thumping in the humid air.

He headed toward the TDE house, the porch lights glowing like a beacon through the live oaks.

Let the night begin.

Dylan leaned against the kitchen counter, a sports drink bottle in one hand, the buzz of the Tau Delta party pulsing through the house. Music from the living room blended with the sound of laughter and the occasional pop of a beer tab. His body was still loose from the post-game adrenaline, but his mind was wandering—until Daisy appeared in the doorway.

Her cowgirl boots tapped across the tile as she made her way in, dress swaying, concern written across her face.

"Hey," she said, nudging him gently. "Can I ask you a favor?"

He raised an eyebrow. "Sure. What's up?"

"It's Ali," Daisy said, brushing a piece of hair behind her ear. "I think she's freaking out. Like, she said she was going to head back to the dorm, but I don't think she really wants to. She just gets overwhelmed sometimes, you know how she is."

His heart gave a slow, deliberate thump.

Daisy glanced over her shoulder. "I tried talking her down, but she's halfway out the door, and honestly? I think you're the only one she might actually listen to. Can you...maybe just check on her?"

Dylan nodded before she even finished the sentence. "Yeah. Yeah, of course."

Daisy smiled, a soft, grateful look that reminded him of when they were kids. "Thanks, Dyl. She really likes being here. I just don't want her to leave because she got in her own head."

"I've got it," he said, already heading toward the front door.

Sparks Fly

Ali

The bass from the party thumped through the floorboards of the old Tau Delta house, vibrating up through Ali's sneakers as if her body was just another part of the beat. She stood near the wall, inching closer to the front door with each passing minute. Her fingers tugged at the hem of the shorts under the skirt part of her skort—again. They kept riding up, the clingy fabric twisting uncomfortably high on her thighs.

She crossed her arms. Uncrossed them. Crossed them again.

The air was heavy with the smell of beer, body spray, and too many boys in one space. Her messy bun was failing her now, strands falling loose and sticking to her neck, frizzing out in the humid coastal night. She swiped at them absently, blinking through the fog of noise and movement and too many eyes.

She shouldn't have come.

Daisy was off somewhere flirting with the starting kicker from the team. Daisy would be annoyed when she realized Ali was looking for a way out. Her chest felt tight. Like the walls were too close and the music too loud and the lights too sharp.

She was three feet from the door when she felt a hand wrap gently around her forearm.

She froze.

"Hey," Dylan said.

She turned. Slowly. His voice was soft and calm—completely at odds with the chaos around them. And he was holding out a red Solo cup.

"I figured you could use a Coke Zero," he said, grinning. "Not spiked. Promise."

She blinked at him, surprised.

"Dylan—"

"You were about to ghost," he said, stepping closer, his tone teasing but not unkind. "C'mon. We're not letting you escape that easily."

She gave a half-hearted smile and looked toward the door again.

"Five minutes," he offered, nodding toward the porch. "Just fresh air. I'll even keep an eye on your skort so it doesn't try to strangle you again."

Her cheeks flushed. "I'm not—how do you even know about that?"

"I have a sister. And eyes," he said, nudging her shoulder lightly. "You keep tugging at it like it owes you money."

That startled a laugh out of her. Just a small one.

Without waiting for her answer, he opened the front door and led the way outside. The porch was quieter, the cool breeze a welcome relief. He dropped down onto the wooden porch swing and patted the seat next to him.

She hesitated. Swallowed hard. That swing creaked under normal people. She wasn't sure she wanted to risk the embarrassment.

He caught the flicker of hesitation in her eyes.

"Ali," he said gently, "If I can bench three hundred pounds and sit on this swing without it snapping, I think you're good."

Her heart beat louder than the music now. But she gave in, slowly lowering herself beside him.

"There we go," he said, draping his arm casually across the back of the swing. "See? No structural damage."

Ali rolled her eyes but couldn't stop the smile tugging at her lips.

They sat like that for a beat—just the creak of the swing, the far-off sound of cheers from the backyard, and the faint smell of the bay drifting in with the breeze.

"You looked like you were having fun tonight," he said quietly. "Cheering and all that."

She looked at him sideways. "I wasn't exactly front and center."

"I noticed anyway."

Her stomach flipped. She took a sip of her Coke Zero to cover it.

"I'm glad you stayed," he added, his fingers brushing her shoulder lightly. "This party would've sucked without you."

And for once, she didn't try to deflect it with sarcasm or self-deprecation.

She just said, "Thanks."

The knock came just as Ali was slipping on her sneakers.

She froze, laces still undone, hair damp from the shower she'd rushed through ten minutes earlier. It was already 7:40, and she was going to have to haul ass to get to her 8am on time.

Daisy groaned from the bathroom, toothbrush hanging from her mouth. "Can you get that?"

Ali padded to the door and cracked it open.

Dylan stood there holding two iced coffees and a paper bag.

He grinned. "Morning. I come bearing caffeine and carbs."

Her heart did a full somersault. She blinked, momentarily stunned.

"I—uh—"

Daisy came up behind her, spitting toothpaste into a water bottle like it was an everyday occurrence. "DYLAN! Ugh, you're literally a hero. Is that cinnamon swirl?"

He handed her the bag. "Two cinnamon swirls and a ham and cheese croissant. I guessed."

Daisy gave him a quick hug and slung her backpack on without hesitation. "You walking us to class?"

"If you don't mind," he said, glancing once at Ali. "Thought I'd get some steps in."

Daisy was already halfway down the hall.

Ali, on the other hand, still hadn't moved. She could feel her pulse behind her knees. She tied one shoe. Fumbled the laces on the other. Then finally stood, brushing invisible lint from her biker shorts like that would ground her.

"Thanks for the coffee," she mumbled, taking the one labeled with a messy *Ally* on the side. They never spelled her name right.

He smiled, his eyes warm. "Of course."

But she couldn't look at him for too long. Not after yesterday...

They'd all crammed into Dylan's Jeep Wrangler for the drive to Honeyshore, the doors off and the radio blasting. Dylan drove. Daisy sat shotgun. Ali took the backseat.

She wasn't expecting him to keep checking the rearview mirror. Not like that. Not like she was the most interesting part of the trip.

Every time their eyes met, her stomach dipped like the road beneath them had disappeared.

At dinner, seated at the long, weathered table with fried chicken and cornbread, Dylan sat directly across from her. And she swore—swore—he kept brushing her knee with his under the table. It could've been an accident. Except it happened more than once.

And each time she'd look up, startled, he was already looking at her. Heat blooming in his cheeks. And something else too—something sharp and curious and unmistakably interested.

Daisy hadn't noticed a thing. She'd been too busy gabbing about her Communications class and asking if she could borrow Dylan's Jeep for the Jekyll Island trip next weekend.

But Ali had noticed everything.

She adjusted the strap on her backpack as they made their way down the sidewalk, side by side. Dylan didn't push, didn't tease. Just walked next to her, sipping his coffee like this was normal.

Like he hadn't been secretly flirting with her under his mama's kitchen table.

"Sleep okay?" he asked casually.

She nodded. "You?"

He smiled. "Eventually."

She nearly tripped on the curb.

Everything Has Changed

Dylan

The clang of metal echoed through the weight room later that afternoon, but Dylan barely registered it.

He stood at the squat rack, bar loaded, staring straight ahead like it might tell him what to do.

Sweat beaded on his brow, but it wasn't the set that had him off-balance—it was her.

Alison Katherine Presley.

Ali with the messy bun and the nervous hands. Ali who never made too much noise in a room, but somehow always pulled his attention like gravity.

He rolled his shoulders, shook out his arms. Tried to focus. Coach Busby always said the weight room was sacred—where the real work happened. No distractions. No excuses.

But his head was full of her.

He racked the bar after one lazy rep and sat on the bench instead, towel over his shoulders, heart thudding in that way it always did when he thought about her too long.

She'd looked like she wanted to disappear that morning when he showed up at her dorm. Even after Sunday—after all those looks they'd exchanged—she was still unsure. Still pulling at her sleeves and hugging her coffee like a lifeline.

He liked that she got nervous. Not because he wanted her uncomfortable—God, no—but because it meant she cared. Meant there was something under the surface she wasn't saying out loud.

But Ali wasn't like the girls who chased him after games or cornered him at frat parties with fake smiles and empty compliments. She was thoughtful. She watched people. She noticed the things most missed.

And she had no idea what she did to him.

He leaned forward, elbows on his knees, palms pressed together. He needed to tread carefully.

She was like a deer in headlights—wide-eyed and anxious, ready to bolt at the first sign of pressure. And he wasn't about to be the reason she ran.

He could still see her on the porch swing Saturday night, knees drawn together, arms crossed tight like a shield. But she'd let him sit close. Had even leaned into him for a minute when he draped his arm around her shoulders like it was the most natural thing in the world.

Because with her, it was.

And now?

Now he just had to figure out how to ask her out without scaring her off.

It wouldn't be some loud, public scene. No frat party, no crowd, no pressure. Just him and her. Maybe coffee after class. Or a walk on the marina dock where the student athletes stretched after runs.

Something quiet.

Something safe.

Something that felt like her.

He ran a towel over the back of his neck and leaned against the cool metal of the squat rack, heart finally settling into something steady.

Then it hit him.

The Cup & Chaucer.

That little second-hand book shop and coffee cafe on Main, tucked behind the old antique mall, where the floors creaked and the windows were always open just enough to let the smell of espresso and old paper hang in the air. Ali's favorite spot. He'd overheard her talking about it once—told Daisy she liked to go on quiet Sunday afternoons to sit in the back room with her Kindle and a large iced latte. Something caramel or vanilla, if he remembered right.

Daisy had rolled her eyes and said the place smelled like attic dust and regret.

But Ali had just shrugged and said, "Exactly. It's perfect."

He hadn't forgotten.

She liked slow spaces. Places where she didn't have to perform.

Which made it perfect.

No crowds. No music pulsing through her chest. Just a mismatched couch, a tiny two-person table, and books stacked in uneven towers. A quiet corner of the world where he could just be with her—no teammates, no sister, no eyes on them.

He could picture it already. Her legs tucked under her, fingers wrapped around her iced coffee, cheeks flushed from the walk. The way she'd look up through her lashes when she was trying to hide a smile.

He smiled to himself, slinging his gym bag over one shoulder and heading toward the showers. He had a plan now.

Not a big one. Not flashy. But it didn't need to be.

Because the truth was, he didn't want to impress her.

He just wanted to know her.

And if she'd let him—really let him—he'd make damn sure she knew she wasn't just some girl he noticed.

She was the girl he couldn't stop thinking about.

Fearless

Ali

The Cup & Chaucer smelled like espresso steam and paperbacks, the kind of place that settled in your bones and told your nerves to hush. The front room was buzzing with soft chatter, classic versions of pop songs playing quietly under the clink of mugs and the shuffle of worn sneakers on old wooden floors.

Ali curled her fingers tighter around her water as she made her way to the back room, her heart thudding like it had been running ever since she got the text during her 11am class. She had absolutely no idea what Professor Folkmore had lectured on today. She thought it was World War II, but it could have been the history of rock-n-roll for all she had paid attention today.

The little reading nook was mostly empty, just like she liked it—faded armchairs, a sagging green couch, and one tiny table by the window. She slid into the chair with the best view of the street and tried not to look at the door.

It still didn't feel real.

> *Hey*
> *Meet me at Cup & Chaucer after your last class*
> *I'll grab you that caramel iced thing you like*
> *—D*

He'd texted her this morning like it was the most casual thing in the world. Just one message, no punctuation, no emojis. But it had detonated in her brain like a firework.

She had stared at it for so long, blinking at the screen and rereading it like it might change. Like she'd imagined it.

He remembered her drink.

She'd never told him—not really. He must've overheard her ordering once. That one random Sunday she, Daisy, and Dylan had all ended up at the same table in the campus center. He hadn't even looked up from his notebook that day.

But clearly...he had noticed her.

Now here she was, sitting in her sacred spot—with him on the way—and her brain was short-circuiting. She tucked one leg under her, then untucked it. Smoothed her skort. Tugged it back down. Tried to sip her water but her throat was like cotton.

Was this a date? It didn't feel like a date. He hadn't said anything flirty.

But Dylan didn't do dates. Everyone knew that. And even if he did, he wouldn't go for someone like her.

Right?

She sighed and tucked a frizzy strand of hair behind her ear, heart leaping when the bell above the front door jingled.

And then there he was.

Baseball cap. Navy, fitted sweatpants. A heather gray Magnolia Bluff Football tee. Looking like he belonged on a billboard and somehow like he didn't know it.

Dylan McKenzie had just walked into her favorite quiet place.

And for some reason...he'd walked in for her.

He spotted her in the back room and smiled—wide and easy, like he did this kind of thing all the time. Like he wasn't the most talked-about guy on campus. Like her heart wasn't currently attempting a prison break in her ribcage.

Ali swallowed hard and pressed the condensation-slicked cup to her lips, pretending to be mid-sip. Casual. Cool. Normal. She even nodded a little like, *Oh hey, you found me,* as if she wasn't watching his every move out of the corner of her eye.

He stopped at the counter, leaned on it with his forearms like he had all the time in the world. Said something to the barista that made her giggle with a sickly sweet, "Maacccccc! You're too much!"

Good gawd.

Ali shifted in the deep armchair, crossing her legs and then immediately uncrossing them because she couldn't get comfortable. Her shorts were riding up again under the skort and she tugged at the hem, heart racing. She caught a glimpse of herself in the mirror over the bookshelf and immediately swiped a hand through her hair, trying to flatten the frizz the humidity had claimed.

It's just Dylan, she told herself. *It's* literally *Dylan.*

The boy who once punched his best friend in the face during her sophomore year in high school for calling her "pathetic" when she didn't have a prom date. Who'd been sent to the principal's office, got suspended for three days, and never even flinched when people asked why he did it.

Because, in his words, "You don't get to talk about her like that. Not ever."

He'd said it in the hallway, right in front of the vending machines. Right in front of her.

That was Dylan.

Not the star quarterback. Not Daisy's older brother. Just...Dylan.

But now he was walking toward her with two iced coffees in hand and a tilt to his mouth that looked suspiciously like he knew she was spiraling. She straightened in her seat, pulled her face into something resembling a smile, and tried—desperately—not to die.

"Hey," he said, sliding into the chair across from her like it was the easiest thing in the world. He passed her a cup. "I didn't know if you'd already grabbed one, but figured I'd play it safe."

"Thanks," she said, hoping her voice didn't come out all breathy and weird. "You were right."

His smile deepened. "I usually am."

And just like that, she was doomed.

They fell into easy conversation—like they always had. Laughing about how Daisy had spilled sweet tea all over the dinner rolls at Sunday supper, rolling their eyes at the sorority drama heating up on campus, and ranking the best iced coffee spots within a ten-mile radius like it was a scientific study.

It was comforting. Familiar. She could almost pretend her palms weren't sweating, that her pulse wasn't hammering behind her ribs every time he looked at her too long.

But somewhere between him making fun of her notebook tabs and her insisting he'd cry if he ever actually read *A Walk to Remember*, the air shifted.

He leaned forward, elbows on his knees, coffee cradled in his hands. "I like it here," he said, glancing around the room with its mismatched chairs and soft music playing overhead. "It feels like a break."

Ali blinked. "Yeah. That's why I come. No one really talks in here. It's like...everyone agrees to just be chill for a second."

His gaze dropped to his cup, then back up to meet hers. "I think I needed that. A break. From all of it."

She swallowed. "From football?"

He shook his head slowly. "From pretending like I don't know what I want."

The words hung there—heavy and completely out of place next to their earlier talk about croissant quality and first editions.

Ali froze, her fingers curling around her cup.

He didn't move. Didn't look away.

She could feel it. Whatever this was, whatever he was trying to say without saying it—it was real.

"Dylan..." she started, but he cut her off, soft and steady.

"You don't have to say anything. I just—" He exhaled, watching her. "You're not like anyone else. And maybe you don't see it, but I do. I have for a long time."

She sat there, unsure if her brain had short-circuited or if the world had just tilted a little off-center.

Because Dylan McKenzie was looking at her like she was something he'd been looking for.

And for once, she didn't want to run.

The weeks that followed settled into a rhythm that felt almost too good to be real.

A couple of evenings a week, just after her last class, Ali would head to The Cup & Chaucer. Dylan would already be there—usually in a tee and ball cap, tucked into the corner of the back room with two iced coffees and that lopsided smile he seemed to reserve just for her.

Their dates weren't flashy. Sometimes they barely talked—just shared a playlist and read side by side. Other nights, they stayed until the shop closed, deep in conversation about everything from their childhood memories together to their plans for the future. Dylan was prepared to be drafted in the NFL. He was ready, and he knew it. Ali wasn't as sure but knew she had to follow her passion for writing. She didn't know if she would be a published author, a content writer, or even a freelance copywriter but was confident the right place would find her when the time was right.

She started to look forward to these evenings with an ache in her chest, one that felt suspiciously like happiness.

By their third week, something had shifted again. It wasn't just easy anymore. It was charged. Quiet but electric.

That Friday night, as she walked with him to the parking lot behind the coffee shop, her steps were slower than usual. She didn't want it to end. She lingered at her car, one hand gripping her keys, the other stuffed in her hoodie pocket as she tried to think of something—anything—clever to say.

Instead, Dylan stepped forward.

He didn't ask. Just cupped her face gently, like she might spook and bolt if he moved too fast.

Then he kissed her.

It was soft and certain, the kind of kiss that didn't ask for permission but gave her every chance to pull away.

She didn't.

By the time he pulled back, her whole body felt lit up from the inside, like someone had flipped a switch she didn't know was there.

He rested his forehead lightly against hers. "Go with me tomorrow," he said, voice low.

She blinked, still catching her breath. "Where?"

"The party. At TDE. After the game." His eyes searched hers. "Come with me as my girlfriend."

Her breath caught. The word girlfriend echoed in her head like it was too big, too impossible.

But then he smiled again—that same quiet, grounded smile that made her feel like maybe she could be brave.

She nodded.

And for the first time, the world didn't feel scary at all.

It felt like she was going to say *"Yes"*. But then he saw the anxiety in her eyes and gently offered, "I'll tell Daisy."

She couldn't agree to that. Daisy was her best friend. She needed to be the one to tell her.

Ali gently shook her head and simply said "I feel like it needs to come from me."

She all but fell into her Chevrolet Malibu. And with a gentle smile and wave, she was off to face her best friend. She wasn't even sure what she was nervous for; it just felt like a weird line had been crossed and she was unsure of how Daisy would react.

Bad Blood

Ali

"Unreal. You really played the victim, didn't you? God, you're so manipulative it's disgusting. I...I just never thought in a million years he would fall for your stupid, pathetic, damsel act."

Ali stood frozen in the doorway of their dorm suite, stunned.

Daisy was livid—face red, voice shaking, rage spilling out like gasoline.

"What a joke," Daisy sneered. "You're a joke."

Ali blinked. "Daisy...I didn't—"

"God, you look like an oversized wallflower with stage fright. Say something already!"

But Ali had no words. Her throat felt like it had closed up. Daisy shoved past her, slamming the door hard enough to rattle the frame. Ali stood frozen, stunned. Her ears rang from the echo. Then finally—like muscle memory—her body moved. She went straight to her room, crawled under the blanket on her twin bed, and let the tears fall.

She cried until her chest ached, until her body took over—shaking, gasping, dry heaving sobs that left her breathless.

When it got to be too much, she stumbled to the bathroom. And there, in the harsh white light, she stared at herself in the mirror. Skin blotchy. Eyes wild. Arms wrapped around her middle like she could physically hold herself together.

She didn't want to hurt herself. Not really.

She just wanted the hurting to stop.

The ache. The shame. The way Daisy's words echoed like truths she'd always feared.

She sank to the floor, back against the cool tile, and buried her face in her knees. That was the first night she locked herself in the bathroom to fall apart.

She wouldn't tell Dylan.

She wouldn't tell anyone.

Not ever.

The weeks that followed were a blur of whispers, glances, and a thousand little wounds Ali couldn't prove—but felt all the same.

Daisy and her sorority sisters didn't let up. They just got more creative. Insults disguised as jokes. Exaggerated sighs when Ali entered a room. Group texts filled with side-eyes and gifs that weren't technically about her—but always arrived the second she walked by. Sometimes it was worse—overheard conversations in the student union, laughter that cut like glass, snide comments muttered just loud enough.

Ali adapted.

She started wearing long sleeves. Oversized sweatshirts. Layering her favorite Magnolia Bluff tee under zip-ups even when the coastal sun still burned into October. She wore rubber bracelets around her wrists and claimed it was a "throwback" trend. No one asked questions. They never do when you're quiet and smile enough to make them comfortable.

Daylight

Ali

She stopped going to parties. Dylan asked—he always asked—but she found reasons not to. "Too much reading," or "headache," or "just tired." She didn't tell him that the thought of stepping into another Greek house, another room full of girls who hated her just for existing, made her chest cave in.

So instead, he made new plans.

Drive-in movies where she could lean against his shoulder with a bucket of popcorn between them. Walks at the marina where he pointed out which boat he was going to buy her "one day when he signed his rookie contract." Late-night fries and milkshakes at the 24-hour diner she loved. And long, quiet hours in his dorm room—where they worked side by side or binge-watched *The Vampire Diaries* (even though he claimed to "hate drama" and "already knew who she'd choose"). He never complained when she hit pause for the fifth time to talk about Damon and Stefan. He just smiled, reached for her hand, and let her ramble.

Ali started avoiding her dorm suite. Only going back to sleep and shower. She'd wait until Daisy was gone before unlocking the door. Sometimes she stayed out past midnight just to be sure.

Dylan knew something wasn't right. He wasn't clueless.

He knew his sister didn't approve—and wasn't subtle about it. He just didn't know how bad it had gotten. Ali wouldn't let him.

She didn't want him caught between them. Didn't want to be the reason he pulled further away from his sister, no matter how awful she was being. So she smiled and told him everything was fine, and he let her. For now.

Then came the biggest game of the season.

Conference championship. Magnolia Bluff against a top-seeded rival. ESPN cameras. Stadium packed.

Ali watched the entire game from the front row in her oversized hoodie, her heart pounding every time Dylan stepped onto the field. He was unstoppable. Calm under pressure. Fire in his veins. And when the clock hit zero, the crowd erupted.

Dylan McKenzie had just led the Sharks to a conference title. They were bowl bound.

Everything after that felt like slow motion. The confetti. The roars. The players lifting him onto their shoulders. She was clapping, trying to blend into the celebration—when he spotted her.

He jumped up into the stands, weaving through the crowd, helmet still in one hand.

"Dylan—" she started, confused.

But then he reached her.

Grabbed her waist.

Pulled her in.

And kissed her.

Right there.

In front of the entire student section.

The camera crews.

The cheerleaders.

The world.

He kissed her like no one else existed.

And when he pulled back, she was breathless.

Stunned.

The stadium was screaming.

Someone on the mic said her name.

People were cheering.

Dylan just smiled and tucked her hair behind her ear.

"About time," he whispered.

And Ali...Ali didn't know how to feel.

Except safe.

And wanted.

And maybe, finally, seen.

She reached up to grab his neck and before she could chicken out, she mumbled "I love you."

Mine

Dylan

S he said *I love you*.

Right there in his favorite place in the world. The stadium he loved more than his own home. In front of the crowd. In front of half the damn country.

Alison Presley, the girl he had been low-key in love with since the day he was in 10th grade when she threw her leopard-print backpack in his Jeep, had just told him she loved him.

Then she kissed him again, whispered "I'll meet you at your dorm," like it was the most natural thing in the world, and slipped away into the crowd with her hood up and her cheeks flushed.

He was still standing there with his helmet in one hand and a stupid grin on his face when coach wrapped an arm around his shoulders and dragged him toward the tunnel.

The locker room was chaos.

Teammates yelling, spraying water bottles, slapping shoulder pads. Cameras from the local news station were everywhere. Dylan said all the right things—thanked his offensive line, gave credit to the team, said they "trusted the process." But inside? He was already gone. Already rewinding that kiss in his mind. Already hearing her voice again.

I love you.

Shower. Change. High-fives and hugs. The kind of post-game euphoria athletes live for.

And yet, as he walked toward the stadium parking lot under the sharp glow of floodlights, duffel bag slung over his shoulder, Dylan only had one thing on his mind: *get home to her.*

Then he saw Daisy.

Leaning against his Wrangler like she'd been waiting for hours. Hair curled. Lashes long. Wearing a slinky maroon dress he knew she picked just to stand out in the post-game crowd. She was scrolling on her phone like she didn't have a care in the world.

"Don't even say it," Dylan muttered as he walked up.

Daisy slipped her phone into her tiny designer bag. "Don't say what? That you're about to ruin your night by skipping the best party of the year for a girl who probably left twenty minutes ago?"

He didn't rise to it. Just yanked open his backdoor and tossed his gear inside.

Daisy crossed her arms. "You know she won't go. She never goes. She can't handle it. And I know you're playing house right now, but you're going to miss your entire senior year if you keep letting her drag you into her little emotional cave."

He slammed the door to the backseat shut. "You done?"

"Dylan, come on. Just show up for thirty minutes. Make an appearance. I saved you a drink and everything." She softened her voice, shifting into that sweet little sister tone she used when she was about to push just a little too far. "You know people are going to start talking. You're the captain, the QB—"

"I'm also a grown man," he said, jaw tight. "And the girl waiting in my dorm loves me. That's where I'm going."

Daisy's face flickered. "God, she's got you hooked."

He didn't reply. Didn't have to.

Because he was already getting into the driver's seat.

Already turning the key.

Already done listening.

He parked behind his dorm and took the stairs two at a time. His heart was pounding harder than it had during the final drive of the game. It was stupid. He knew she'd be there—she said she would—but still. The second he unlocked the door to his suite and saw her purse on the hook, he exhaled.

She was here.

And then—there she was.

When Dylan opened the door to his bedroom, he found her sitting on his bed, knees drawn to her chest, his hoodie swallowing her whole.

She looked up at him with wide eyes, her damp hair curling from a shower, her cheeks flushed like she'd been arguing with herself. Or maybe trying not to bolt.

"Hey," she said, voice too casual to be real. "I figured you'd take forever."

His heart flipped. "Hey, Ali."

He dropped his bag and walked toward her, slowly, like if he moved too fast she might vanish. She didn't. Her gaze tracked him like she couldn't help it.

When he kissed her, she sighed against his mouth like she'd been holding her breath all week.

They didn't rush.

They never did.

But this time, the slow burn was too much. He deepened the kiss. Her hands found the hem of his shirt, tugging it upward. He helped her pull it off and tossed it to the side.

Ali stared at his chest, cheeks flushing.

"You can touch me," he said, voice low.

Her fingers brushed over his abs, hesitant at first. He groaned softly, catching her wrists and kissing her knuckles.

When she pulled back and peeled off his hoodie, her body stiffened. She was down to her bralette and comfy shorts—bare skin and soft curves she was clearly trying to hide, arms folding around herself almost instinctively.

"I know I'm not—" she started, but he shook his head.

"Stop." He stepped in, gently catching her chin so she'd look at him. "You are the sexiest thing I've ever seen, Ali Presley. You always have been."

Her lip trembled.

"I mean it," he whispered, brushing a kiss to her cheek. "I've wanted you since sophomore year in high school. Every curve. Every inch. Every version of you."

She gave him a small, nervous smile—and then tugged her bralette over her head.

Dylan's breath caught in his throat.

She stood there—fully exposed, vulnerable and trembling—and it hit him like a tidal wave. Not just how beautiful she was, but what this moment meant.

"I haven't...um, I mean I've never," she whispered, barely audible, voice trailing off and eyes darting to the side.

He swallowed. "I know."

Ali's eyes searched his face. "Is that...okay?"

Dylan leaned forward, kissing the hollow of her throat, down to the swell of her chest. He let his hands trail reverently over her hips, her back, her thighs.

"It's more than okay," he said. "You're trusting me with this. I'm never gonna forget that, Ali. I swear."

When she nodded, he kissed her again—deep, slow, all tongue and heat and soft sounds. He guided her to his bed, laying her down gently, making sure her head rested on his pillow. He took his time—removing the rest of their clothes between kisses, his hands learning every soft dip and curve like he was memorizing a map.

She was shaking beneath him, not in fear—but in anticipation. And when he asked if she was sure, she gave the smallest but most powerful "yes" he'd ever heard.

He moved over her slowly. Worshipfully.

Her fingers clawed at his back when he entered her—carefully, inch by inch. She gasped, and he kissed the corner of her mouth, stilling to let her adjust.

"You okay?" he whispered, forehead against hers.

She nodded, eyes glassy. "You feel...so good."

Dylan let out a shaky breath and began to move.

They found a rhythm—soft, slow, bodies tangled. He whispered to her the whole time—telling her how good she felt, how perfect she looked like this, how much he loved her.

Ali's head tipped back. She moaned—quiet, raw, completely lost in the moment.

Her legs wrapped around him. Her hands gripped his shoulders. She moved with him now, less nervous, more sure.

And when she came—trembling, gasping his name—it nearly broke him.

He followed with a groan, his body shuddering against hers, burying his face in her neck as the world went quiet around them.

They didn't speak right away.

She clung to him like a lifeline, and he wrapped her in his arms, still inside her, breathing her in.

"I love you," she said again, softer now. "I've never loved anyone."

He kissed her shoulder. Her wrist. Her lips.

"I'm yours," he said. "All of me."

Haunted

Dylan

Sunday mornings usually meant recovery—ice baths, tape, team meetings. Today, it meant Ali.

She was still asleep when he woke up, curled against him, one leg thrown over his waist and her hair a tangle of gold across his pillow. Her bare skin glowed in the sliver of light coming through the blinds. His hoodie was half off one shoulder, his sheets twisted around her hips.

She looked like she belonged here.

And maybe she did.

He didn't move. Just stared at her for a while. Memorizing the curve of her nose, the faint freckles, the way she breathed steady and slow.

Eventually, she stirred. Eyes blinking open. Smile soft and sleepy.

"Hey," she murmured, voice scratchy with sleep.

"Hey," he whispered, pressing a kiss to her forehead. "You hungry?"

He made her a breakfast sandwich with extra cheese because she liked it that way, and she called it gourmet like he was a five-star chef. They curled up under in his bed, limbs tangled, watching *Gilmore Girls* because "If I have to pick between Rory and football, you're gonna lose, McKenzie."

He didn't mind.

He watched the show with one eye, and her with the other. She'd steal glances at him during the funny parts. Nudge his leg during the emotional ones. Their laughter filled the room like it was stitched into the air.

Later that afternoon, when the sun sank low and golden light spilled through the blinds, Dylan rolled over and kissed her.

Not rushed. Not desperate. Just slow, deliberate affection pressed to her lips like a promise. His palm cradled her cheek, thumb brushing the soft skin under her eye as if he needed to memorize her. Her breath caught—because even now, even after everything—they were still soft with each other.

This time, when he moved over her, she wasn't so nervous. He hovered just above, eyes locked with hers, and waited. For permission. For breath. For that silent, aching pull between them to rise up and swallow them whole.

Ali nodded, just once. And that was all he needed.

He sank into her with a groan, deep and low, the sound echoing against her ribs. She arched under him instinctively, gasping, her fingers tangling in the curls at the nape of his neck. His hips rolled slow and steady, drawing the tension tighter and tighter between them, but he never broke eye contact. Not once.

He kissed her like he meant it. Like every movement, every stroke, was a love letter only she could read. His hands roamed her sides, her waist, her thighs—worshipful, careful. She touched him back with more confidence now, less hesitation. Her fingers dragged across his back, nails scratching lightly, pulling him closer.

She whispered his name like a prayer. He said hers like a vow.

And when the heat crested and her legs trembled around his waist, Dylan reached down and laced their fingers together. Held her hand against the pillow as he quickened his pace, kissed the corner of her mouth, her jaw, the soft hollow of her throat.

"Let go," he whispered.

And she did—with a gasp and a cry, shattering beneath him as he held her tight and followed her over the edge with a groan that sounded like the breaking of something holy.

They lay tangled together afterward, sweaty and quiet and breathless.

His head rested against her chest, rising and falling with the rhythm of her breath. She combed her fingers through his hair, her other hand still locked with his. He kissed her collarbone, her sternum, the curve of her breast, and whispered against her skin.

"You're mine," he said softly. "You always were."

Ali didn't reply.

She just closed her eyes and held him tighter—because for the first time in her life, being wanted didn't feel like a burden.

She tucked herself under the covers and looked up at him like nothing in the world could touch them here.

He wished that were true.

But later, when she was in the bathroom brushing her hair, he sat on the bed, towel wrapped around his waist, and thought back to something he hadn't let himself focus on before.

When he kissed her wrist last night—slowly, sweetly—he'd seen it.

Scars.

Thin. Faint. Delicate.

But real.

At the time, he hadn't registered it. Not really. But something about it now—it wouldn't let go.

And when she came back to bed in one of his worn MBU shirts, he couldn't stop looking at her wrists.

She noticed.

"What?" she asked softly, crawling into bed beside him.

He forced a smile. "Nothing. You're just pretty."

She smiled and leaned into him, unaware of the storm beginning to stir in his gut.

He had to take Daisy to their parents' house for Sunday dinner—tradition, even when it sucked. Ali kissed him goodbye at the door, barefoot and smiling, telling him to drive safe.

The whole drive, he was quiet. Daisy was on her phone most of the time anyway, spewing gossip and half-listening to herself. At one point, she mentioned how Ali was "so weirdly clingy lately" and Dylan had to grip the wheel tighter to keep from saying something he couldn't take back.

At dinner, he pushed food around on his plate while his dad talked about bowl predictions and his mom tried to get Daisy to focus on anything but her sorority drama.

He kept thinking about Ali.

About the way she flinched sometimes, even when he touched her gently. The way she kept her arms covered, even when it was hot. The way she avoided the house parties lately. How she never went back to her own dorm unless she had to.

The scars.

He needed to ask her.

Needed to make sure she was okay.

Because something told him—deep in his chest, in that place where gut instincts live—that this wasn't just about his sister being a brat.

And if Ali was hurting, if something had happened...

He'd burn down the fucking world before he let her go through it alone.

You Are In Love

Ali

S he felt it before he even said anything.

Something in the air had changed. Dylan was still being Dylan—sweet, attentive, soft-spoken—but there was a weight in his eyes she couldn't name. Something heavy and too quiet.

They were curled up on his bed again. Sunday night had faded into early Monday morning, and she should've already gone back to her dorm to sleep before class. But she hadn't wanted to leave. Not after the kind of weekend they'd had. Not after she gave him everything.

So when he asked, his voice gentle but serious, her whole world tilted.

"Ali," he said, brushing her hair from her cheek, "Can I ask you something?"

She sat up slightly, her stomach turning. "Okay…"

He paused. Looked down. And then, with aching tenderness, took her hand in his and pushed her sleeve back just an inch.

"I saw it," he whispered. "Last night. The scars."

Her blood went cold.

Dylan's thumb hovered just over the faint lines across her wrist. He didn't press. Didn't push. Just looked at her with those heartbreakingly kind eyes.

"Is someone hurting you?" he asked. Then even more gently, "Ali…are you hurting yourself?"

Her breath caught in her throat.

And then everything shattered.

She turned her face, but he cupped her cheek and made her look at him. That was the worst part—he didn't look angry. Or disgusted. He looked wrecked.

Tears flooded her eyes before she could stop them. "I—I'm sorry," she whispered, her voice cracking like broken glass. "I didn't think—I didn't want you to know."

His arms were around her before the next sob could leave her throat.

She collapsed into him. Every part of her broke open.

It all spilled out—Daisy's words, the screaming, the names. The slamming doors. The cruel games her roommates played. The isolation. The quiet digs. The way it never stopped, not even when she hid.

She told him about the nights she'd lock herself in the bathroom just to feel like she could breathe. About how the blade had only come a few times. About how terrified she'd been, how lost. Every time it happened. She didn't know how else to make the pain inside to go away.

"I didn't want to die," she choked, "I just didn't know how to make it stop."

Dylan didn't speak.

He just held her tighter.

She felt something wet hit her temple—and realized he was crying, too.

His chest heaved with the weight of her pain. His arms around her didn't loosen, not even for a second.

They stayed like that for hours. Curled into each other in the darkness.

He didn't let her go.

Not once.

Not even when the sun rose and her alarm buzzed for her 8am class.

Not even when she tried to apologize for everything, again.

He just pulled her sweatshirt over her head, handed her, her sneakers, and quietly said, "You're not going to class today."

She looked at him, confused. "Then where are we going?"

He looked her dead in the eye. Calm. Certain.

"To health services," he said. "You're gonna talk to someone. I'll be with you the whole time."

She didn't speak. Didn't argue.

For the first time in weeks—maybe months—Ali didn't feel afraid of what came next.

Because he wasn't walking away.

He was walking her toward healing.

The waiting room smelled like hand sanitizer and stale coffee.

Ali sat stiffly in the oversized chair, her palms damp, fingers twisting the hem of her sweatshirt sleeves. Dylan hadn't let go of her hand since they walked in. Not when he signed her in. Not when she sat down. Not even now, as her knee bounced involuntarily and her throat tightened with every passing second.

She felt like everyone could see straight through her.

The girl who couldn't handle life. The girl who needed help. The girl who sliced her wrist open and then pretended like everything was fine.

Dylan leaned over and whispered, "You're doing so good, Al. I'm so proud of you."

Her chest ached at the sound of his voice—so warm, so solid, like he meant every word.

The nurse called her name and everything in her wanted to bolt. Her feet felt nailed to the floor, her breath coming too fast. But Dylan stood, gently tugging her up with him, steady and unflinching.

"I'll be right here when you come out," he promised, pressing a soft kiss to her temple. "Every step. Okay?"

She nodded. Or maybe she just blinked. It was hard to tell.

The psychiatrist's office was smaller than she expected, cozy even. A worn blue couch sat across from a desk with too many sticky notes. There was a tissue box in every corner. A soft lamp in place of harsh fluorescent lights.

"Hi, Alison," the woman said kindly. "I'm Dr. Stephenson. Come on in and make yourself comfortable, wherever feels safest for you."

Ali hesitated, then lowered herself onto the edge of the couch. She kept her arms crossed tightly over her middle, unsure of what to do with the weight of her own body in this space.

"Um, it's just Ali."

"It's nice to meet you, Ali.'

Dr. Stephenson didn't rush her.

She didn't pry.

She just asked questions gently—"How have you been coping lately?" and "What brings you in today?"

At first, Ali didn't say much. A shrug. A few mumbled phrases.

But the silence in the room didn't feel like judgment. It felt like an invitation.

And slowly, something cracked open.

She talked about the fighting with Daisy. About how she felt like she was constantly in the way. How she tiptoed around her own dorm room, afraid of doing anything wrong. How her world had become so small she couldn't remember what it felt like to feel okay.

She admitted she'd hurt herself.

And then, barely a whisper: "I didn't want to die. I just...didn't know how to make everything stop hurting."

Dr. Stephenson nodded, not startled, not alarmed—just grounded.

"I hear you, Ali. I'm really glad you came in today."

They talked for almost an hour. By the end of it, her chest didn't feel quite so tight. She wasn't okay, but she wasn't buried anymore either. There was a flicker of something else.

Hope, maybe.

When she came back out, Dylan stood up so fast he nearly knocked over the fake plant beside him.

She didn't even get a word out before he wrapped her in his arms.

And just like that, the crushing shame loosened a little.

"I'm proud of you," he whispered again, kissing the top of her head. "You did the hard part. We'll figure out the rest together."

Ali clung to him, and for the first time in a long time, she let herself believe that maybe—just maybe—she didn't have to do this alone.

After finals ended, she went home to Honeyshore for Winter Break. She drove herself. Dylan helped her load up her Malibu and kissed her with a fierceness she would never get used to. They would be in their hometown together, yet a world apart because of Daisy.

Ali spent the drive back home blaring Taylor Swift, singing about boys, mean girls, and feeling twenty-two.

And when she crossed over into Bellamy County, she felt a sigh leave her body as the stress from MBU faded away.

Ali talked to Dylan every single night before falling asleep. And they texted all day.

The week of Christmas, she had a sleepover at her cousin's house. Ashley was the youngest of four kids with three older brothers. Since Ali was an only child, and being they were only six months apart, they were more like sisters growing up.

The fireplace crackled low in Ashley's room, casting flickers of gold over the floral duvet they were sprawled across. A mostly empty bottle of Moscato leaned sideways on the nightstand, and half a bowl of kettle corn sat between them, the sweet-salty kernels now slightly stale.

Ali finally felt normal again.

Ashley lay on her stomach, twisting a ring around her finger, her dark blonde hair pulled into a lazy bun. "Okay, I've been waiting all night," she said, eyes dancing with curiosity. "You've got that *I'm holding a secret that might explode out of me* face. Spill. Everything."

Ali let out a breath, biting back a grin.

Then she told Ashley everything.

About Dylan.

About the looks that made her stomach flip. The coffee outside her dorm. The kisses at Cup & Chaucer. The night he kissed her on the field in front of thousands. The night she gave him her virginity. Her voice wavered a little on that part, but Ashley just smiled softly and reached over to squeeze her hand. Then she dished. Everything. Their first night together, the rushed sex in the shower before class some days, the slow love-making on Sunday afternoons, all of it. She finally had someone she could girl-talk with.

"I knew he'd fall for you," Ashley whispered, eyes gleaming. "He'd have to be brain-dead not to."

Ali laughed—really laughed—for the first time in what felt like weeks. But then the laughter faded, and her chest tightened.

She looked down at the wine glass in her lap. "Ash...it hasn't all been good."

Ashley sat up straighter, instinctively on alert. "What do you mean?"

Ali hesitated. Her fingers found the sleeve of her sweatshirt, twisting it nervously. "Daisy. When I told her...she just completely lost it."

Ashley's jaw tensed. "Define lost it."

Ali didn't sugarcoat it.

She told her about the screaming. The slurs. The cruel words that rang in her ears for days. The icy silence. The way Daisy had turned her entire sorority against her. She described what it was like to walk around campus feeling invisible and yet exposed all at once. Avoiding the parties. Pretending everything was okay when inside, it was anything but.

"I started hurting myself," she said quietly, voice barely audible.

Ashley's breath caught.

Ali swallowed hard, forcing the words to keep coming. "But I—I got help. Dylan found out. He didn't run away. He took me to health services the next morning. My doctor, she doesn't make me feel dumb or crazy. She got me in within a campus therapist and put me on a mood stabilizer & anxiety meds. I actually think...it's all helping. Dylan doesn't coddle me or anything. His strength is incomparable."

Ashley's eyes glistened, but she didn't let a single tear fall.

Instead, she cupped Ali's cheeks, thumbs brushing gently along her jaw. "You are the strongest person I know."

Ali shook her head. "I'm not."

"You are," Ashley said firmly. "You've been drowning and still managed to crawl towards the surface. That's strength."

Ali's eyes filled with unshed tears, a soft sob catching in her throat. She wasn't used to kindness landing so solidly. She hadn't had any girls to talk to.

Ashley wrapped her in a hug so fierce it knocked her wine glass over. "You ever feel that low again," she whispered fiercely, "I swear to God, I will drive three hours in my pajamas from Georgia U and sit on your bathroom floor with you all night if I have to. Screaming, bitching, tears, whatever—I'll be there. You're not alone in this. Not anymore."

Ali cried then—not from pain, but from relief.

And for the first time in a long time, she believed her cousin meant it.

They fell asleep under the blankets, mascara smudged, legs tangled, the empty popcorn bowl on the floor and soft music playing from Ashley's phone. And when Ali woke up the next morning, tucked into Ashley's bed with the sun warming her cheeks, she felt something she hadn't in months.

Safe. Whole. Content.

Christmas Tree Farm

Dylan

The FaceTime call with Ali ended hours ago, but Dylan was still lying on his childhood bed, staring up at the ceiling fan turning slow above him. The house was quiet now—his parents long asleep—but he couldn't settle. Not after the conversation he'd just had with Daisy.

He couldn't tell Daisy everything. That wasn't his story to share. But when she rolled her eyes at the mention of Ali again—when she made another snide comment about how Ali was "milking" her sadness for attention—he snapped.

"You've been a bitch to her, Daisy," he said. "She hasn't done anything to you except fall for someone who's your brother. Get over it."

Daisy had exploded, her voice rising with each accusation. "You're choosing her over me! You always used to have my back, and now it's like I don't even know you. You don't see how she's manipulating you?"

He didn't even finish the argument. He retreated to his old room. But he was still reeling. He couldn't stay here.

He grabbed his bag, sent an apology text to his parents—told them he had to get back to campus early to prep for the bowl game—and left. If he stayed, he might say something he couldn't take back.

Ali wasn't even at school yet—she was still at her parents' house until after Christmas—but he needed space from the toxicity. From Daisy. From the guilt that always followed him like a shadow when they fought.

He turned onto I-16 just before midnight, the hum of the road the only thing keeping him grounded. The silence in the car was thick, but his thoughts weren't quiet. They were all her.

Ali.

He just wanted to be where she was. Even if she wouldn't be on campus until next week.

The headlights cut through the Georgia night, the road stretching out in front of him like a lifeline. He wasn't even sure when the decision happened, just that one second he was headed back to campus and the next, he was pulling an illegal U-turn through the interstate median, aiming his Jeep north back toward Bellamy County, Honeyshore, and the Presley house.

It was after 1am when he pulled into their driveway. Lights still twinkled from a garland wrapped around the front porch. He sat for a minute, hands on the steering wheel, wondering if this was insane.

But then the front door cracked open.

Her dad stepped out in flannel pajama pants and a hoodie, squinting into the driveway. "Dylan?"

He climbed out, rubbing the back of his neck. "I'm sorry it's so late. I was headed back to school but—" He blew out a breath. "Ali doesn't know I'm here yet. I just...I didn't want to spend Christmas fighting with Daisy."

Mr. Presley didn't ask any more questions. He just nodded. "Guest room's made up. Come on in, son."

Ali shrieked when she saw him standing in the Presley kitchen the next morning, barefoot and holding a mug of coffee like he belonged there.

"Dylan?" she said. She was still in pajama pants and a sweatshirt, hair up in a messy bun, searching for some caffeine. "What are you—"

"I made a detour." He smiled, soft and boyish. "I missed you."

Her mom handed him a spoon without missing a beat. "You can stir. Ali's on icing."

Ali's heart flipped. She barely registered the explanation he whispered later—about Daisy, the fight, the drive—because by then she'd already pulled him into the pantry and kissed him hard enough to say *you're safe here.*

The whole day unfolded like something out of one of those cheesy holiday rom-coms she and Ash loved so much.

They watched *It's a Wonderful Life* with her mom, cuddled up on the couch under a red fleece throw. During *Miracle on 34th Street,* Dylan helped her press Hershey's kisses into peanut butter blossoms while Ali sang along to Christmas songs from the Alexa in the corner. And *Home Alone* had him laughing so hard she had to swat him with a kitchen towel.

He hadn't even realized how heavy he'd been feeling until he was surrounded by the soft domestic peace of the Presley home. Her dad grilling steaks out back, her mom sipping wine while Ali curled into Dylan's side on the couch, cookie tin balanced on her lap.

That night, as they sat curled up on the back porch under a blanket and next to the fire pit in the quiet Georgia neighborhood, Dylan finally realized:

This wasn't just the best Christmas he'd ever had.

It was the first time he truly felt like he was home.

King of My Heart

Ali

The house was quiet. The kind of quiet that only followed a day full of presents and pie and laughter. The kind of quiet that wrapped itself around everything like a thick winter blanket. Her parents had long since gone to bed. The fire downstairs had burned out. But her heart wouldn't settle.

Ali padded softly down the hallway, her fingers nervously curling around the hem of Dylan's hoodie she'd stolen earlier. She paused at his door, barely breathing. It was stupid, maybe—selfish. But she needed him. Not for comfort. Not to be held.

She needed all of him.

She eased the door open, and the glow from the moon cast soft silver over the bed where he slept, shirtless, a tangle of sheets wrapped around his hips. Her breath caught. God, he was beautiful. Golden skin, muscles stretched and relaxed in sleep, his mouth slightly parted.

"Dylan," she whispered.

He stirred, turning toward her voice. "Al?"

"I can't sleep."

His brows lifted, his voice husky from sleep. "Come here."

She stepped in without hesitation and closed the door behind her, locking it. The floor was cold against her bare feet, but the moment he sat up and reached for her, the chill vanished.

She climbed onto the bed, straddling him before he could fully register what was happening.

"Ali…" His voice held a question—but not hesitation. His hands came to her thighs instinctively.

"I want you." Her lips brushed against his jaw. "Right here. Right now."

His breath hitched. "We should be quiet—"

"Then make me," she whispered, and kissed him.

Her fingers raked through his hair as she rocked against him, already hard beneath her. The quiet gasp he made into her mouth sent heat spiraling through her. She reached between them, sliding her hand beneath the covers, under the waistband of his boxers.

"Ali…" he groaned, grabbing her hips. "You're gonna kill me."

She grinned into his mouth. "Promise?"

She lined them up and sank down onto him slowly, biting her bottom lip hard to keep from moaning out loud. Every time felt like the first time. Every inch of him made her body come alive. He filled her in every way—physically, emotionally, completely.

She moved slowly at first, grinding her hips as her nails dug into his chest. Searching for the right rhythm. Learning as she went. His hands tightened around her thighs, guiding her rhythm, but letting her lead. His eyes never left her face, watching every flicker of pleasure dance across her features like she was art.

"You're so goddamn beautiful," he breathed, voice rough. "I don't know how I got this lucky."

Her heart thudded harder at that. She leaned forward, riding him harder now, her hair falling around their faces like a curtain.

She was close. So close. But then—

Dylan's hands suddenly gripped her waist and flipped them, one swift motion that sent her back against the floor with a soft thump. He caught himself on his elbows so he didn't crush her, then slammed his mouth to hers to catch the scream building in her throat.

He drove into her deeper now, harder, muffling every whimper and cry with his kiss. Hitching a leg around his waist to fill her as deeply as he could. Her hands clutched his back, fingernails raking across his shoulders as she shattered beneath him. Her body trembled around his as wave after wave crashed through her.

He came seconds later, groaning low against her mouth, his whole body tensing as he buried himself to the hilt and held.

They lay there for a moment, tangled together on the floor, the only sounds their ragged breaths and the faint hum of the heater through the vent.

Dylan nuzzled her cheek and kissed the corner of her mouth. "Merry Christmas, Al. I love you, baby."

She smiled, her fingers tracing lazy circles on his back. "Best Christmas I've ever had."

The Moment I Knew

Ali

Ali had barely touched her strawberry lemonade.

The beach grill was packed—students shoulder to shoulder, pressed into booths and standing around pool tables. TDE guys sporting their letters. Kappa Nu girls in maroon, navy, and white. Everyone buzzing after the bowl game win. Shark Nation had officially taken over Myrtle Beach.

She was trying. Trying to smile, trying to breathe, trying not to flinch every time Daisy's laughter rang out from across the room.

Then the music started.

It was karaoke night, which usually meant cheesy duets or someone belting "I Will Survive" off-key. But when the opening beat of "Milkshake" dropped, Ali froze. She hated that song.

It wasn't just the song. It was who was on stage.

Daisy and three other Kappa Nu girls with matching bows in their hair stood at the mic. And they weren't singing the original lyrics.

They'd rewritten them.

Ali's name in the chorus.

"Ali's milkshake brings no boys to the yard
They're like, 'nah, not that broad
Damn right, they'd rather starve
She could feed a whole frat with her carbs"

Jabs about her weight in every verse.

Lines about "Thirst traps with no takers" and "How to land a man by crying at his feet."

Laughter erupted. Phones came out.

Ali couldn't breathe.

She scanned the room, wild-eyed, heart slamming in her chest. That's when she saw him.

Dylan.

Across the room near the bar, frozen.

His eyes locked on hers.

But he didn't move.

He didn't stop them.

And in that split-second, something inside her shattered.

Ali turned and ran.

Out the back door, into the cold, January night. Her feet hit the pavement, one after the other, not even noticing the tears on her cheeks until they blurred the road signs. She didn't stop until she was back at the hotel.

She grabbed her stuff. She grabbed her keys.

And she drove.

All the way home.

Back to Honeyshore.

Ali moved through the house like a ghost. Her parents were asleep. The quiet wrapped around her like fog.

She didn't want to die.

She just wanted the pain to stop. The humiliation. The ache that kept her chest in a vise.

The image of Daisy sneering. The sound of Dylan's silence.

She sat on the cool bathroom tile, shaking. The bottle of anxiety meds in her hand.

She hadn't planned this. Not really.

She just needed to sleep.

To forget.

To rest.

Tears dripped onto her wrist as she opened the bottle.

Heather Presley hadn't slept. Not really.

She and her husband had heard the garage door open. Then the code to the alarm system beeping as someone re-armed it.

Heather had climbed out of bed and peeked out the window to see Ali's car in the driveway. She'd waited a few minutes, figuring her daughter might need space. A bad night, maybe. She knew Ali had been off lately—quieter than usual, and harder to read.

But something had told her not to go back to sleep.

When more than fifteen minutes passed and Ali still didn't come say hello, Heather's gut twisted.

She slipped on a robe and padded down the hallway.

"Ali?" she called softly, tapping on her bedroom door. No answer.

The bed was made. Still untouched.

Heather checked the bathroom next.

When she opened the door, she didn't scream.

She couldn't.

The sound stuck in her throat.

Her baby was on the floor.

Unmoving. Pale. Her wrist resting limply across her stomach, the faded scars there like a scream she hadn't heard soon enough.

The open pill bottle was nearby.

"Ali!" Heather dropped to her knees, hands shaking as she touched her daughter's face. Still warm. Too warm.

Her voice cracked as she yelled for her husband. "Daniel! Call 911!"

Ali didn't respond.

Heather gathered her into her arms, rocking gently like she did when Ali was little and had bad dreams. "Stay with me, baby. Please stay with me..."

She didn't know what else to say.

She just held her daughter and prayed the ambulance wouldn't be too late.

This Is Me Trying

Dylan

He hadn't slept.

Couldn't eat. Could barely breathe.

The team left the grill not long after the party ended in disaster. Coach Busby knew something had happened, could tell by the look on Dylan's face when he'd finally caught up with him in the parking lot—ashen, silent, fists clenched so tightly his knuckles had turned bone white.

But it didn't matter.

Team travel was a legal obligation. They couldn't just let players disappear mid-bowl weekend. Especially in an entirely different state.

So Dylan sat stiff and hollow on the charter bus all night, replaying the scene on a torturous loop.

Ali, wild-eyed and humiliated. Her expression cracking into something he would never forget—panic, betrayal, despair—as she turned and ran.

And him, frozen.

Frozen like a coward.

Not because he didn't care.

Because he cared so damn much.

He had never seen cruelty like that, not even from Daisy. Not until that moment.

And Ali thought he was ashamed of her.

When he finally made it back to Peach Cove, he drove like a madman the final hour home. Called. Texted. Called again.

But Ali never answered.

Her phone started going straight to voicemail sometime around sunrise.

His stomach churned. He'd been praying she just needed space. That she was at home. Maybe crying, maybe angry—but safe.

But the Presley house was empty.

The porch light was off. The curtains were drawn. No cars in the drive.

It felt...wrong.

Panic clawed its way up his throat.

He drove to her aunt and uncle's house next, nearly blowing through a red light to get there. They might know where the Presleys were.

Ashley answered the door in sweatpants and a dark green Georgia University hoodie, eyes rimmed with red. She shouldn't be here. Should be in Macon at school.

He didn't even have to ask.

She just shook her head, and her voice cracked when she said, "She's at the hospital, Dylan."

He staggered back a step, like her words had slapped him.

"She came home last night. Aunt Heather heard the alarm go off and figured she just needed space, unsure of what was going on. But when they didn't hear from her after a while..." Ashley swallowed hard. "They found her in the bathroom. Pills. A lot of them."

His lungs locked up. He bent over, palms on his knees, trying to stop the world from spinning.

"She's alive," Ashley added quickly. "Stable. But in bad shape. She's not...she's not okay, Dylan. She's scared. Ashamed. She hasn't said much, but they're going to transfer her to a mental health facility in Savannah. Probably today or tomorrow. She's not in a place where she's safe to be alone."

He closed his eyes.

And the sob hit him so hard he nearly fell.

He'd never felt more helpless than when they told him *no*.

No, you can't go back there.

No, she's not taking visitors.

No, she's being evaluated.

No, unless you're immediate family.

But he didn't leave.

He paced the sterile lobby like a caged animal, pain simmering just beneath his skin. Eventually, Heather Presley emerged with swollen eyes and trembling hands. She didn't say much—just looked him in the face and nodded.

"I'm going to tell them you're family," she whispered. "Because you are."

The doors buzzed open. A nurse escorted him down a dim hallway painted in washed-out shades of green and beige. Everything felt wrong. Cold. Too quiet.

Then they reached her room.

And nothing in all his life—not football injuries, not fights with Daisy, not even watching Ali run out of that party—could've prepared him for the sight of her sitting cross-legged on a hospital bed in a pair of socks and a gown, pale and hollow-eyed, her hair in a messy bun, hands folded tightly in her lap like she was trying to hold herself together with sheer will.

He almost hit his knees.

She looked up when the door opened, and the breath left her body in one visible, shuddering exhale.

"Dylan..."

His name came out barely a whisper, like it hurt to say.

He stepped inside and closed the door behind him. He didn't move any closer, not yet. Didn't know if she wanted him to. But she didn't look away.

"Ali," he rasped.

A single tear slipped down her cheek. "I didn't think you'd come."

"I had to." His voice cracked. "You left, and I didn't know if you were—if I'd lost you. I was going out of my fucking mind."

Her lower lip trembled. "I thought you were ashamed of me."

"No." He crossed the room then. Dropped to his knees beside her bed like a prayer. "I was frozen. I was furious! I was trying not to lose it in front of the entire goddamn student body. But not at you. Never at you. I was ashamed of Daisy. I was ashamed I didn't stop it. But you?" He reached for her hand. "You're the only thing in my life I've ever been proud to love."

A sound cracked from her chest like a broken sob. She curled her fingers around his and let herself cry.

"I wanted to die," she whispered. "I didn't want to hurt anymore. Not from Daisy. Not from school. Not from the way people look at me like I don't belong. I—I can't keep trying to outrun it."

His eyes burned. "You don't have to outrun it. I'll carry it with you. I'll fight for you. I'll walk through fire for you, Ali, if you'd just—"

She shook her head. "It's too much, Dylan."

"No—"

"Yes." Her voice was firmer now, even though her eyes stayed wet. "I love you. God, I love you so much. But it's killing me. I almost died, Dylan. You can't ask me to go back to that place. To be her punching bag. To pretend that being with you doesn't make everything harder."

He closed his eyes. "You don't have to go back there. You don't have to deal with her. We can figure something else out. Please—"

Ali stood, gently tugging her hand away from his. She moved to the little table and held up a folded letter. When she turned, her shoulders were straight. Her eyes glassy.

"I'm going to Savannah," she said softly. "They've got a long-term program there. And I've already applied to transfer to Bellamy Community College in Honeyshore for the spring. I'm going to get my Associates Degree in Accounting. Something stable. Something quiet. My dad can help me since he's a senior partner at Whitestone, ya know."

"You're not quiet," he whispered. "You're the loudest thing my heart has ever heard."

She crumpled into his arms then, both of them weeping. He kissed her temple, her shoulder, her wrist—right over the scars that had started all of this. She touched his face like she was memorizing it.

"I'm blocking your number," she said. "Not because I don't love you. But because I do. Because I have to get better. I have to find out if I can be okay without anyone saving me. And you deserve someone stronger than me, Dylan. Someone who won't ever bring you down."

His tears soaked into her hair. "You already are someone worth saving."

Their kiss goodbye was quiet and endless and made of every word they couldn't say. Then she stepped back.

And Dylan walked out with his hands clenched, his heart shattered, and no idea how he was supposed to finish the semester & graduate when his entire world had just walked into a psych ward and he didn't know when—if—she was ever coming back.

Part Two

Ten Years Later: The Healed Sessions

Playlist

(Ali's Version)

"Lose You to Love Me" — Selena Gomez

"Liability" — Lorde

"You're on Your Own, Kid" — Taylor Swift

"Lover" — Taylor Swift

"The Alchemy" — Taylor Swift

"Look What You've Done" — Tasha Layton

"Thinking 'Bout You" — Dustin Lynch ft. MacKenzie Porter

"Overcomer" — Mandisa

"Fight Song" — Rachel Platten

"Sometimes" — Britney Spears

Vault Track:

"Anxiety" — Megan Thee Stallion

Playlist

❤

(Dylan's Version)

"Some Habits" — Cole Swindell
"Stay With Me" — Sam Smith
"Sex On Fire" — Kings of Leon
"Whatever It Takes" — Imagine Dragons
"More Than Miles" — Brantley Gilbert
"Burn" — Usher
"Stand By Me" — Ben. E. King
"Cover Me Up" — Morgan Wallen
"Good As You" — Kane Brown
"Unchained Melody" — The Righteous Brothers
Vault Track:
"Hall of Fame" by The Script ft. will.i.am

Invisible String

Ali

The A/C roared against the sticky Georgia heat, blasting her with the sharp scent of lemon-scented air freshener and something vaguely plasticky from the vents. Ali leaned her head toward the cool stream, her blonde waves fluttering slightly in it, as Taylor Swift sang about devils rolling dice and angels rolling their eyes on the radio. Fitting, it seemed. She gripped her sparkling, maroon clutch a little tighter in her lap as they took the interstate exit and began the slow climb toward Peach Cove.

The summer sun hung low in the sky, casting golden light across the trees. Long shadows of mossy oaks danced across the windshield. The further they drove, the more it felt like stepping into a time capsule—a place that had held some of her best memories...and her worst.

Someone in the back seat of Abigail's dark green Range Rover (thank God *she* didn't have to drive here) made a joke about sequins versus sneakers and the car erupted in laughter, but Ali only smiled faintly, eyes flicking to the familiar landmarks. Her stomach was tangled in nerves, excitement, dread, and something else—a soft ache that sat just beneath the surface. She hadn't been back here in a decade.

She blinked out the window as they passed the corner where Sandytown still thrived with students—the one she and Daisy used to haunt religiously. Her lips curved, unbidden.

"She cried because she didn't get the peach Stanley cup in her bid basket," Daisy had said once, dramatic and gorgeous. *"Then she tried to trade someone for theirs like it was <u>The Hunger Games</u>."*

Ali had nearly choked on her pimento cheese sandwich, laughing.

Daisy had always been the center of the room, confident and bold and unfiltered. And back then, Ali had loved basking in her orbit. Their friendship had been easy—until it wasn't.

The car turned onto Tide Drive, and something caught in Ali's throat.

Up ahead, Russell Stadium rose in the distance, its towering lights already glowing against the hazy blue dusk. The giant screen glinted in the sun, reflecting back the late summer sky. Her breath hitched.

The Reef.

That's what they'd called it. Everyone had. Students, locals, even the announcers during game broadcasts. It wasn't just a stadium; it was a whole ecosystem. A place of wild cheers, stomping feet, painted faces, and roaring pride in a sea of navy and maroon.

She could still remember the electric thrill of sitting in the student section pressed between Daisy and some girl from Daisy's sorority, waiting for Dylan's name to be called. The crowd had gone feral when he jogged onto Stowers Field, helmet tucked under one arm, the number 13 stretched across his back.

She'd never told anyone, especially not Daisy, how hard her heart had raced each time.

Now, a decade later, it felt like that same heartbeat was rattling against her ribs.

She'd see him tonight. She was almost certain of it. And she wasn't ready.

Not for his voice.

Not for those eyes.

Not for the ghosts she'd tried so hard to leave buried here.

The banquet hall glittered with soft gold lighting and floor-to-ceiling windows that overlooked Russell Stadium. Even in the off-season, the field glowed under the lights, every blade of turf crisp and green, like the game could start at any moment.

Inside, glass vases held floating candles and navy hydrangeas, and crisp white linens covered every table. The air was cool and perfumed with catering spices and designer cologne, buzzing faintly with alumni chatter and clinking glasses.

It was elegant. Expensive. Nothing like the undergrad formals of her memory.

Along the far wall, the silent auction drew a steady stream of attention. Some of the prizes were charmingly expected—gift baskets with wine and cheese, autographed memorabilia, a weekend retreat to Savannah, passes to the exclusive golf club on Hilton Head Island. But the centerpiece was unmistakable.

A framed teal Orlando Tritons jersey, the silver number 13 gleaming beneath the lights. Beneath it, a digital display glowed:

Donated by: Dylan "Mac" McKenzie, Magnolia Bluff U Class of 2015, Suma Cum Laude

Ali stared at it for one breath too long.

Mac.

He went by that now. Of course he did—NFL players didn't go by boring, studious names like Dylan.

Still, her eyes caught on the silver, stitched name across the back. *McKenzie.* Her stomach flipped. She hadn't seen him yet, not in person, but somehow his presence filled the room like he had already stepped inside.

The gala had been a safe idea in theory. She was here professionally, with her coworkers from the accounting firm in Honeyshore. It wasn't like she'd run into him face-to-face.

Right? He was definitely too important for her anyway. She would just avoid him—everything would be totally fine.

She turned away quickly, clutching her cherry blossom martini—her go-to cocktail—and made a beeline for the side of the hall, pretending to study a raffle display. Her navy sequin dress shimmered under the lights, catching flashes of movement with every step. The off-the-shoulder neckline gave it a trendy edge, but more importantly, it let her feel pretty while still covering the insecurities she wasn't ready to shed. The maroon jewelry and matching clutch added a rich pop of color—a quiet tribute to Magnolia Bluff's legacy hues. And then there were the shoes: maroon Adidas, clean and bold. She was a sneakers and tennis shoes kind of girl anyway, so tonight's theme was perfect.

The dress was technically a midi, but on her 5'2" frame, it grazed the tops of her shoes like a gown. She felt good in it. Strong. Present. But her heart still raced.

She wasn't here for him.

She wasn't the same girl who used to wait in the student section, heart pounding every time he touched the ball. She had built a whole new life.

So why did just seeing his name on a jersey make it feel like the floor shifted under her feet?

The soft hum of conversation filled the banquet hall as Ali stood near the tall windows, the glowing stadium lights spilling across the empty field below like a spotlight on the past she'd tried to leave behind. The night air was cool on the balcony where a few guests had already wandered, some going down to take pictures on the turf—laughing, snapping photos, reliving their college days in the glow of the floodlights. Ali's fingers tightened around her clutch as the glittering decorations caught the light, reflecting the sequins in the dresses around her.

The annual Sneakers & Sequins Gala. She had never gone before, but this year the cause was different. She was here for the new program the university was rolling out.

This was Magnolia Bluff University's world—a world she had walked away from ten years ago.

Still, she wasn't alone in this sea of sequins and nostalgia.

Ali exhaled and let herself be gently pulled back into the present by Abigail's animated voice beside her.

"Oh my God, that guy definitely just winked at you," Abigail whispered with a grin, bumping her shoulder playfully as she sipped from a glass of bubbly.

Ali laughed, the sound surprising even herself. "He was absolutely aiming at you," she said, lifting her cocktail "You're the one in the gold dress with legs for days."

"True, but you're the only one who matched your sneakers to your clutch," Abigail replied, nodding at Ali's maroon Adidas. "You've got the whole aesthetic down. Definitely main character energy."

Their coworkers from the Whitestone CPA office mingled nearby, swapping college stories, hashing out the upcoming football season, snapping selfies with the mascots—Riptide & Captain Rip, and making bids at the silent auction tables. The mood had shifted—lighter now that the drinks were flowing and the music softened to a background hum. "Banana Pancakes" played over the speakers, mellow guitar riffs drifting through the air like a memory. Ali let her guard down inch by inch, reminding herself of how far she'd come.

She and Abigail made their way toward the dessert table, dodging a pair of tipsy alumni reenacting their old cheer routine. For a moment, Ali let herself feel it: the joy, the ease, the way the soft lighting made everything look warm and golden.

Then the room dimmed slightly as a spotlight hit the stage. The background music faded into quiet.

"Ladies and gentlemen," came the smooth voice of Provost Kensington from the microphone at the podium, "Thank you for joining us tonight at the Magnolia Bluff University Sequins & Sneakers Gala. Your presence here honors not just our past, but the future we are building together."

Abigail leaned in. "Oooo, is it time?" she whispered excitedly.

Ali smiled, but her heart gave a quiet stutter. She knew what was coming.

"And now," Provost Kensington continued, "It is my great pleasure to introduce someone who has given so much to this university both on and off the field. A proud alumnus, a leader, and a changemaker...please welcome to the stage—Mac McKenzie."

The applause rose like a tide, and Ali froze.

He was here.

And he was walking toward the stage.

And there was nowhere left to hide.

And just like that, the air left her lungs.

I Almost Do

Dylan

"Mac, we'll be ready in about five more minutes," the provost's assistant announced, sticking her head in the door.

Mac. It had all started here in this stadium. His career. His nickname. His legacy.

It started when he was still playing at MBU—the local media needed something snappy—and it stuck. His family never used it. Neither did Ali, not that she used his name much at all anymore. Not since she walked away ten years ago.

He adjusted the cuffs of his jacket, half-listening as Kallie rattled off the event schedule from the corner of the VIP lounge. The room overlooked The Reef where the setting sun painted the bleachers in warm, copper light.

Kallie tapped her tablet. "Your speech is second, right after the provost's welcome. I already emailed you the updated script, but your version is better—more heart, less institution-speak."

He nodded, distracted, gaze drifting out the floor-to-ceiling window to the field where everything changed. His last game at Magnolia Bluff had been under those same lights. He'd thrown three touchdowns, won the Southern Coastal Conference MVP, and had Ali in the stands—her voice the only one he could always hear. She'd worn his hoodie over her dress that night, proud and beaming. Had told him she loved him. Had given him everything later that night in his dorm. He swallowed around the lump forming in his throat.

And then came the party a few weeks later after winning the bowl game.

His stomach tightened at the memory. The glow of victory was still warm when everything fell apart. Daisy. Her Kappa Nu sisters. That awful karaoke incident. He should've stopped them. He still didn't know why he froze, what made him hesitate. He was a stupid kid and was embarrassed by what Daisy had done. Ali misunderstood, taking his hesitation as shame of her. He still lived with the guilt.

He hadn't even known how bad it was. Not until the next day, when guilt set in like a slow rot. He should've protected her. Should've stood up. Should've left Myrtle Beach immediately—to hell with the university's rules.

But he hadn't. And by the time he got to Honeyshore, his life as he knew it was forever changed.

"Earth to Mac." Kallie snapped her fingers gently, smiling. "You good?"

He blinked, dragging his focus back to the present. "Yeah, sorry. Just thinking."

"About the speech or the donation?" she teased, setting the tablet down.

"Both." It was a lie, and she knew it. He was thankful for her friendship. She had been part of Daisy's "big family" at Kappa Nu, studying Sports Management and Business. They didn't really know each other because she was a couple classes above him, but he ran into her at Greek mixers and formals when he was still a Freshman. After going on to law school at Georgia University, she took on a full-time position at Summit Athletic Management in their Southern Division. Signing Dylan had skyrocketed her as one of their top agents.

Kallie tilted her head, softening. "You sure you're ready for this? It's a big moment."

"I want to do it," he said simply. "For Altman. For the guys who are still here. For the ones we never knew struggled, and the ones we may not know are struggling even now."

Kallie's expression shifted—proud, but thoughtful. "You're a good man, Mac. You've always cared more than you let on."

He shrugged. "Doesn't change the fact I couldn't fix it back then."

"No one expects you to fix the past," she said, voice gentle now. "But you're building something better going forward. That counts."

He looked out over the field again, trying to believe that. But all he could think about was the girl in the stands who once believed in him before anyone else...believed in him other than his ability to throw a football. The one person he wanted to see tonight, even if he knew she wouldn't want to see him.

And then it hit him—that feeling. That spark of presence.

He didn't know how, but suddenly, he *knew*.

She was here.

The crowd murmured politely as Dylan stepped up to the podium, the spotlight warming his features. His eyes scanned the room—faces blurred in the dim light, smiles polite, but none quite held his attention. Until, across the banquet hall by the windows, he saw her.

Ali.

She sat at a table with people he didn't recognize, a tall redhead whispering to her, framed by the glowing stadium lights, the sequins on her dress catching the gleam like tiny stars. For a heartbeat, everything else faded—the chatter, the music, the distant echo of a crowd long gone. There was Ali, the girl he'd loved and lost, looking just as striking as the day she pushed him away.

His throat tightened. Years of anger and regret tangled with something softer, deeper. He wanted to cross the room, to say everything and nothing at once. But the moment was fragile, charged—and all he could do was hold her gaze, silently asking if she was still there.

Dylan stepped up to the mic, stadium lights glowing beyond the tall banquet windows. He paused for a breath, voice quiet but strong.

"Thank you Provost Kensington. Good evening. First off, thank you for being here tonight—for showing up not just in sequins and sneakers, but with heart, with purpose, and with hope.

Six months ago, we lost a senior running back—a teammate, a friend, and a brother to so many—who struggled with battles most of us couldn't see. Altman Patterson was the kind of guy who lit up the field and the locker room. He ran with fire. He smiled big. And behind it all...he was hurting.

His passing shook us to our core. And it forced us to confront a painful truth: that mental health is just as vital to our athletes as physical strength. The weight of silence can crush even the strongest. We missed the signs. We missed him.

And now we carry that weight. But we're choosing to carry it forward. To build something better.

That's why tonight, your support means more than ever. The funds we raise tonight will go directly toward launching something we've been dreaming of—a new initiative we're calling:

Project AP: Above the Break.

Named in honor of Altman Patterson. And created for every student-athlete who's ever felt like they were treading water with no one on the shore.

This program will provide direct access to mental health resources—counseling, mentorship, early intervention, and education—designed specifically for the lives of student-athletes. Not just a hotline or a pamphlet, but real, ongoing support.

Because football teaches us about toughness. Teamwork. Resilience. But it also teaches us that sometimes, the bravest thing you can do...is ask for help.

We want our athletes to know: You are seen. You are heard. You are not alone. Not on this field, not at this school, not in this family.

So let this be our rally cry. Not just for Altman—but for every Shark who comes after him.

At the Bluff, the tide don't break.

We fight.

We finish.

We rise. "

The lights were warm on his face, but Dylan barely noticed. Applause washed over him, but his pulse was stuck on something else entirely. Her.

Alison Katherine Presley.

He hadn't expected her to come. Hadn't even dared to hope. But there she was—just like she used to be and somehow completely different. Her hair had changed, it was lighter now, no longer a dirty blonde. But it was definitely her. That energy. That gravity.

Kallie had warned him not to get distracted tonight. But the second their eyes locked across the room, he wasn't standing at a podium anymore—he was back at The Reef, heart pounding, scanning the bleachers for her smile.

"Magnolia Bluff gave me everything I never knew I needed—a team, a future...and a place to belong. Tonight, I get to give something back."

He nodded toward the screens flanking the stage. "We've got ten incredible live auction items lined up for you tonight in addition to the 4 tables of silent auction items in the back that y'all have been bidding on all night. All proceeds go directly to fund Project AP: Above the Break."

Applause again—louder this time, heartfelt.

Dylan cleared his throat. "Let's kick it off with something close to home." He gestured to the first item on the list: "Dinner for six at Coach Busby's lake house, with private film night on the dock." That got a laugh from the former players in the room.

He walked the crowd through the next few items: a weekend retreat at a vineyard near Athens donated by an alum, signed memorabilia from MBU's 2015 White Oak Bowl championship season, a local artist's one-of-a-kind painting of The Reef at sunset.

But it was the final item that made the room buzz.

"And for our final package," Dylan said, letting his smile tug just slightly wider, "I'm offering four box suite tickets to a home game with the Orlando Tritons—including full VIP access, a postgame meet-and-greet, and dinner in the team lounge. I'll be there. So will Kallie. She made me include her in the package."

The audience chuckled.

He looked out over the crowd, eyes scanning instinctively—though he tried not to. *Was she still watching?*

"I'm proud to offer this tonight," he finished. "Because this place—this school—made me who I am. And maybe if we keep showing up for each other, it'll make someone else whole again, too."

As he went to retreat from the stage, Provost Kensington stopped him and took to the mic. "On behalf of myself, AD Tracey Hamm, the MBU athletic department, and our student athletes, we would like to extend a heartfelt thank you to Mac for his generous donation to help found Project AP. He has graciously offered to match tonight's funds raised during the live auction."

Another round of applause erupted. Building to a standing ovation for one of their own.

He stepped back from the stage now, handing it off to the professional auctioneer brought in for the night—a fast-talking alum with a booming voice and a toothy grin who'd clearly done this before.

"Alright, folks," the man boomed, "Let's make some noise and open those wallets! First up, dinner and a movie with none other than Coach Busby!"

The crowd laughed and hollered. Dylan smiled, hands clasped loosely in front of him as he moved to the side of the stage, just out of the spotlight. Kallie joined him, iPad in hand, already tracking bids in real time on the donor app.

"Nice delivery," she murmured. "You didn't even look like you were scanning the room for her."

He shot her a look. "Subtle, Kallie."

She winked. "I'm pretty damn good at my job. I get paid to notice things, Mac. Nothing gets by me."

He rolled his shoulders back, trying to refocus. But it was impossible to shake the knowledge that Ali Presley was here—maybe watching. Probably avoiding him entirely.

The first few items went quickly, laughter and friendly competition bubbling through the crowd. The Coach Busby dinner racked up a respectable $3,500. The vineyard weekend went even higher, a bidding war between a pair of former teammates now married and clearly out to one-up each other. Dylan forced a smile for the photos, posed with a donor or two. But his eyes kept drifting.

The auctioneer's voice cut through again. "Now let's talk football. Let's talk the NFL. Let's talk box suite tickets to see the Orlando Tritons on their home turf—four of them. All access. Private dinner. VIP passes. And a night hosted by Magnolia Bluff's own Mac McKenzie!"

A cheer rose from the crowd.

Dylan gave a tight nod and stepped forward again, this time only for effect. He let the energy build.

"Do I hear two thousand?" the auctioneer called. "Yes—three? Four? We're at five now!"

Kallie leaned in. "You should smile. You're about to break eight grand."

He tried. "You think she's still here?"

Kallie didn't need to ask who he meant. She scanned the crowd casually. "Back left. Near the windows."

His breath caught. He didn't dare look. Not yet. Not while standing in front of hundreds of people.

"Nine thousand!" the auctioneer roared. "Do I hear ten?"

Another cheer. A chant started. "The tide don't break! The tide don't break!" A hand shot up near the stage.

"Ten thousand it is! Anyone going to top that?"

Silence for a beat.

"Going once...going twice..."

Dylan let his gaze drift—just barely. Just enough to catch a shimmer of navy sequin near the edge of the crowd.

Then someone shouted from the back "Fifteen thousand!"

Dylan's eyes shot to the back. Waving her brochure like she was at a rock concert, the redhead next to Ali. Ali was staring at her like she'd lost damn her mind.

"Going once...going twice," the auctioneer did one last scan. "Sold! To the lady in gold!"

"Thank you ma'am—and thank you, Mac McKenzie, for donating what just became our highest bid of the night!"

More applause. Flashbulbs. Kallie tugged him back toward the shadows as the auctioneer queued up the next item.

But Dylan wasn't listening anymore. Not to the bidding. Not to the music. Not to the well-wishers.

She was still here.

Ali.

And this night had just gotten a whole lot more complicated.

Don't Blame Me

Ali

"Oh my gawd Abigail! Have you lost your ever-loving mind!?" Ali whisper-shrieked to her bestie.

Abigail gave a casual shrug as she sipped her champagne flute, "Not at all. Girls' Weekend for Shelf Indulgence!"

"An NFL game is not a 'girls weekend Ab!"

"Ashley would disagree."

"She doesn't count. She like sprays her hair and paints her face when she goes to the Atlanta games. Also, I highly doubt she would give up one of her Sundays for the Tritons. You know she's a season ticket holder in Atlanta."

"Oh honey, she'll definitely give it up for you."

"This is not for me. I'm not even going."

"There's four tickets. Four book club members. It's a no-brainer. Discussion closed," Abigail declared, like she was an idiot or something.

The final cheer erupted as the auctioneer announced the last winning bid, and the DJ eased back in with something poppy and nostalgic—Gracie Abrams or maybe a cover of it. Ali couldn't tell over the buzz of laughter, clinking glasses, and the sound of people returning to mingling, but she could feel the shift. The party was back on.

Meanwhile, her ears were roaring. She was literally going to throw up. She couldn't believe Abigail bought those damn tickets to his family's suite. She made a mental note to tell Kellan to hide Abigail's Diet Cokes from her for a whole week.

She smiled politely at Abigail as she sipped the last of her cherry blossom martini. "Bathroom," she lied with a little wave of her clutch.

Abigail arched her brow knowingly but said nothing, just gave her a nod and turned back to chatting with a table of other donors. Abigail wasn't an alum, she went to Georgia U in Macon. And while she knew that Ali went through something while at MBU and dating Dylan, she obviously had never told her the whole story. She did not need to relive that moment ever again.

Ali didn't head toward the bathrooms though.

Instead, she veered toward the balcony doors, blending with a small crowd stepping outside to cool off. The air hit her like a breath—hot but breezy and a little salty, the lights of Russell Stadium glowing below like a memory you couldn't quite forget. She followed the edge of the balcony, heart hammering a little harder than she wanted to admit, before slipping quietly down the stairs that led to the field access.

It wasn't that she was avoiding Dylan.

Well...okay. Maybe it was exactly that.

She just needed air. Distance. Space from the eyes that might have seen her reaction during his speech—raw and real and a little too close to the truth she'd buried. The turf felt soft beneath her sneakers as she wandered onto Stowers Field. The Reef. Ten years later, and it still had magic.

She wrapped her arms around herself, looking up into the bright halo of stadium lights. Everything looked the same. And nothing did.

Behind her, the party was building to life. But she heard footsteps coming down the steps. Fast.

She didn't have to look.

She knew.

"Ali."

His voice reached her, soft but cutting through the quiet like a thread she'd once held too tightly. She tensed but didn't turn. Not yet.

Quiet footsteps, closer but now muffled by the turf.

"I was hoping I'd get a chance to—"

"Mac!" A high-pitched voice broke in, and she heard them before she saw them—two women, glossy hair and glossy lips, both in jewel-toned dresses that clung like they still lived on Greek Row. Two of Daisy's former sorority sisters. "Selfie with the MVP?" one giggled, already holding out her phone.

Ali turned just slightly and saw them intercept him, all teeth and nostalgia and perfectly filtered memories. Her stomach dropped.

Dylan—Mac—looked past them for a second. Toward her.

Their eyes locked.

Panic surged. She bolted, ducking toward the far side of the field where the shadow of the building gave her cover. Her sneakers didn't exactly make for a silent escape, but she moved fast, weaving around the edge of the structure like the old days when she knew every inch of this place.

But he was a football player.

And he still knew how to chase.

"Ali, wait—please."

She stopped cold.

Her back against the warm brick, eyes squeezed shut.

It was happening. After ten years.

The gravel crunched under Ali's sneakers as she twisted, intending to run, breath caught somewhere between a gasp and a curse, when he caged her in. He opened his mouth, whatever he was going to say, she really didn't want to hear it. She couldn't hear it. She panicked and her mouth was suddenly on his—urgent, familiar, devastating. His hands gripped her waist like he still knew exactly where she broke, and her body betrayed her completely.

Ten years. Ten years and still, this.

Her fingers threaded into his hair, pulling him closer like she hadn't once built her whole life around staying away from this exact moment. It wasn't sweet. It wasn't slow. It was teeth and lips and memories colliding under a Georgia sky that smelled like salt and pine.

When he pressed his forehead to hers and whispered her name—"Ali"— like it meant something again, that's when her heart finally buckled.

The heavy door swung shut above them, muffling the music from the ballroom. Ali barely registered the sound before Dylan was pushing against her—so close she could smell the warmth of bourbon and something sharply clean, like soap and stadium air.

"Ali," he breathed. Just her name, but it wrecked her.

She didn't answer. Didn't trust herself to.

Instead, she grabbed the lapels of his blazer and pulled him in like something primal had taken over. Their mouths collided in a kiss that felt like a fire alarm—urgent, loud, and impossible to ignore. He groaned softly against her lips, his hands finding her waist like they'd been waiting ten years for the chance.

"You shouldn't have come back looking like that," he murmured against her mouth. "You look like something I dreamed up."

"Shut up," she whispered, breathless. "Just—shut up and kiss me again."

And he did. Harder this time.

Her back scraped against the brick wall as his body pressed into hers. The heat of the masonry combining with the heat of their kiss, grounding her for a half-second before his hands were pulling up the hem of her dress. His fingers skimmed the skin of her thighs and she gasped, arching toward him.

He hissed in a breath. "Still so soft," he muttered. "You used to—God, I remember exactly how you sound."

"Don't say that," she warned, her voice breaking. "Don't pretend like this is still—"

But then his mouth was on her throat, and the rest of the sentence vanished. She tilted her head, letting him taste the curve of her neck, the hollow of her collarbone. He tugged her dress up higher, and she helped, hitching it until it bunched around her hips.

Her hands were just as greedy—pulling at his belt, unfastening his pants with more desperation than finesse.

"You're shaking," he said, touching her cheek.

"I'm fine."

"You're not."

"I don't care."

Something like pain flickered in his eyes, but it was gone just as fast. "Then let me make you forget."

And then he was pushing her panties to the side to push inside her—fast, deep, and so achingly familiar she could've cried. Her back arched, hands clawing at his shoulders as he moved, thrusting hard enough to knock her breath loose with every snap of his hips.

"Ali," he rasped, burying his face against her neck. "So fucking tight," he groaned. Then he was whispering in her ear, "Tell me this is real. Tell me you feel it too."

She didn't answer—not with words. She couldn't.

She just kissed him like he was the last mistake she'd ever make. He grabbed one of her legs and hitched it around his waist, and she held on like she might fall apart without him.

The sound of the party was a distant hum now—muted by the pounding in her chest, the soft grunt of his voice in her ear, the wet, heady sound of skin on skin.

And when she came—his hand slapped over her mouth to silence her screams—he followed, hips stuttering, breath ragged, and groaning her name.

They stood like that for a moment, tangled and trembling. The air between them thick with things unsaid.

She was still breathless, unmoving, when she heard a crunch on the gravel.

"Mac?" a woman's voice called. "Have you seen my phone?"

Ali froze. His hands were still on her hips. Her dress was still bunched.

He turned toward the voice. "Kallie?"

That was all she needed to hear.

Ali shoved away from him so fast she almost stumbled. Her dress fell back into place as she backed up a step, eyes wide, lips still parted.

"Ali—wait—" Dylan reached for her.

But she was already gone.

She was moving. Fast—shoving her way past the building, heart in her throat. Inside, the party spun by in streaks of light and sound, but all she could hear was her own pulse pounding.

Kallie. Of course.

She didn't know why she'd assumed he was here alone. Of course they were close—his friend, his agent. *Fuck, what if they were more?* Ali had just made herself the punchline in a story she swore she wouldn't rewrite. Not again.

The Archer

Dylan

The humid air hit his sweat-damp skin like a slap. He was still catching his breath, the sharp edges of reality rushing in all at once.

Then he saw it.

Ali's clutch.

It lay on the concrete like a forgotten piece of something sacred, small and glittering under the floodlight. He bent to pick it up, fingers shaking.

From the sheer panic rising in his chest.

She was gone.

"Mac!"

He turned as Kallie came around the corner, her white red-bottom tennis shoes shining. She looked polished, every hair in place, perfectly composed in a Tritons-branded cocktail dress. Until she got close enough to see his face.

"You okay?" she asked, scanning him quickly. Then her eyes dropped to the clutch in his hand. She stopped cold.

Kallie had known him long enough to recognize when something wasn't just a moment.

Her eyes softened. "She was here?"

He didn't answer. Didn't have to.

Kallie's brows drew in, and something passed between them—a silent understanding. She stepped forward, laying a gentle hand on his arm.

"You're supposed to be back inside," she said quietly. "Your photo op with the winners and the Chancellor—"

"That's not happening," Dylan said, voice gravel.

She glanced at the clutch again. "I figured."

Then she straightened, gave him a quick nod. "Go. I'll handle it. I'll say you got pulled away on a player emergency call or something."

He looked at her, grateful and tense all at once.

"She ran, Kay."

"Then run after her," she said. "Before she decides not to let you find her again."

He didn't waste another second. Didn't stop to think. He took off down the side of the building, cutting through the staff entrance and around the back lot, scanning every shadow, every exit.

"Ali," he called out—quiet but urgent.

Nothing.

The sound hit him before anything else. A soft, shaky gasp. Then another. Faint, like someone trying not to cry but losing the battle.

He froze. Turned toward it.

The lot was still full, cars glinting under low security lights. He moved slowly at first, heart thudding. Then he heard it again—a choked, muffled sob—and took off in that direction, rounding the corner of a dark green SUV parked near the edge of the lot.

There she was.

Curled in on herself behind the back tire. Knees pulled to her chest. Head buried. Her shoulders shook with each uneven breath as she tried—and failed—to keep the panic at bay.

Dylan's heart cracked clean open. *Fuck, what had he done?*

He crouched down fast but careful, keeping his voice low and steady. "Ali."

Her head snapped up, eyes wide and wet, her lips parted as if she couldn't decide whether to speak or just break apart.

"I've got you," he said, voice shaking. "You're okay. Just breathe."

She shook her head. Her hands trembled where they gripped her shins. She couldn't catch her breath.

He sat all the way down on the pavement beside her, not touching yet. Just being there. Being solid.

"You're safe," he said. "I'm right here. You're not alone."

She drew in a sharp, panicked breath—and he could see her fighting to stay in control, to keep the wave from cresting.

"Breathe with me," he whispered, drawing a slow inhale through his nose. "In...then out. Just like that. Come on, baby. In..."

Her chest hitched, but she tried. She followed him through one breath. Then another. Then she broke.

A sob ripped out of her and she lurched forward—straight into his arms.

Dylan held her tight, wrapping himself around her like a shield. He could feel her falling apart against his chest, and all he could do was hold on.

"You're okay," he whispered, again and again. "You're okay. I've got you."

And, to his amazement, she didn't pull away.

Illicit Affairs

Ali

The concrete was rough against her butt. Still, she couldn't move. Her chest felt too tight. Her head too loud.

She tried to count backwards. Tried to remember the grounding tricks from therapy. Name five things you can see. Four you can touch. Three you can hear—

The sound of cicadas somewhere nearby.

Two—

Footsteps. Quick, steady.

Then silence.

She didn't lift her head. She couldn't. But through the curtain of her hair, she caught a glimpse of worn gray New Balances stopping just inches from her curled-up body.

Her stomach dropped. Her throat burned.

No.

Please no.

Then he dropped into a squat, forearms braced across his knees.

"Ali."

Her name in his voice undid her. Low. Gentle. Shaky in a way Dylan McKenzie never was.

She was too scared to look up. Too scared to see the regret on his face. But if she ignored him...she couldn't do that to him. He didn't deserve that. So she peeked. Just barely.

His eyes were wide and terrified, scanning her face like he was trying to read her every thought, every hurt.

"I've got you," he said softly. "You're okay. Just breathe."

But she couldn't. Her lungs refused. Her brain screamed. Her fingers clenched at her dress like it could anchor her to something real.

He sat beside her—close but not touching—and started breathing, slow and deliberate.

"In...and out," he whispered. "You're safe. I'm here. You're not alone."

She wanted to tell him to leave. That she didn't want him to see her like this. That he should forget about what happened outside the building. That it meant nothing.

That *she* meant nothing.

That he didn't have to baby her or pretend out of guilt. He could just go back to the party. To that perfect woman waiting on him. His agent who looked like she should be walking the runway.

But the words wouldn't come. Just breathless, panicked gasps that sounded too much like crying.

Still, he stayed.

Matched his breaths to hers. Called her baby like he used to. Waited like he always did when she was scared—never pushing, never demanding.

Her heart shattered right there on the pavement.

She blinked, tears streaking hot down her cheeks.

Then everything cracked open.

She folded forward, collapsing into his arms like her body had decided for her. He caught her instantly. Wrapped himself around her like armor. His hands moved over her back, her shoulders, her hair. Soothing. Familiar. Safe.

"You're okay," he murmured into her hair. "You're okay. I've got you."

She didn't fight him. Didn't want to.

Didn't pretend she was fine.

Didn't pretend she didn't still needed him.

Didn't pretend that being held by him didn't feel like the first time she could breathe in years.

She didn't know how long they sat there—wrapped in the quiet hum of the parking lot, the cooling pavement beneath them, her body slowly unwinding from the grip of panic.

Eventually, her breathing steadied. The tightness in her chest loosened enough to let air in without pain. Her fingers unclenched from the fabric of her dress. She didn't move from his arms, though. Not yet. She couldn't.

Dylan shifted first, just enough to ease back and tilt her chin with the gentlest pressure from his fingers.

"Hey," he said softly, coaxing her gaze up.

But she kept her eyes down, or to the right, anywhere but on him. Her face was still blotchy, hot from the aftershock of the panic attack—and worse, from the embarrassment. She hated that he'd seen her like this. Again.

"Ali," he said again, firmer this time. "Look at me."

She did, finally. Briefly. Then her lashes dropped again, like her body betrayed her.

He stilled. And then she saw it—realization dawning in his eyes. The soft click of understanding.

"It's not just the panic, is it?" he murmured. "You're embarrassed."

Her lips parted, ready to lie. To deny it. But she was too tired. Too raw. So she just gave a tiny shrug, her cheeks flaming hotter.

He moved closer, ready to reassure her—his eyes already gentle, his voice gearing up to soothe.

But she cut him off.

"What about her?"

He blinked. "Who?"

"Cali," she said, "Or whatever."

A pause. Then he chuckled. Just a puff of air through his nose, but it was something.

"It's Kay-Lee," he said, smiling softly. "She's my agent. And one of my closest friends. Nothing more."

Ali arched a brow, skeptical. "You sure? She looked pretty comfortable following you around all night."

Dylan huffed. "She's actually half in love with my teammate, but they think they hate each other, so that's gonna implode one day."

Ali blinked. "Wait—seriously?"

He nodded. "I give it two months before someone throws a drink or they get married in Vegas."

A surprised laugh bubbled out of her before she could stop it. She covered her mouth, cheeks still pink, but it felt...good. Lighter.

His expression shifted—softer again. Reverent, even.

"There she is," he said, like he'd been holding his breath just to see her smile.

And for one fragile second, she let herself hold his gaze.

Let herself remember how much she used to love him looking at her like that.

Let herself wonder if maybe…he never really stopped.

Ali hesitated, chewing the inside of her cheek.

"Can I ask you something?"

Dylan nodded. "Always."

She looked down again, picking at a loose thread near her knee. "Did I…completely screw everything up?"

"What do you mean?"

"Like you know," she said quietly. "Back there. I shouldn't have—I just…I didn't know you'd follow me, and I freaked, and then you were you, and then it happened, and I ran, and—"

"Ali."

His voice stopped her. Steady. Sure.

"You didn't screw anything up."

Her eyes flicked to his again, uncertain. "You're not…seeing anyone?"

He shook his head. "No. There's no one."

She exhaled, tension loosening from her shoulders.

"And you?" he asked, casually at first. But his tone sharpened just slightly, revealing the truth under it. "Are you dating that guy you were with?"

She blinked. "What guy?"

"The Thor-looking motherfucker who held your arm all night."

She burst out laughing, caught so off guard she actually snorted.

"Jason?" she wheezed. "He's married to Ashley's brother. Lanier? He was in your grade in school. He was literally just keeping me grounded. Ash was worried about me coming tonight. We're all junior partners at Whitestone. I mean me and the group I'm with. We're all coworkers."

Dylan let out a relieved breath, shaking his head with a sheepish smile. "Well, good. I didn't like him."

"You don't know him."

"Doesn't matter."

Ali laughed again, this time softer, and nudged his knee with hers. "You really thought I was dating Thor?"

He grinned, his voice low. "Jealousy's a hell of a thing."

She smiled at that. A real one. And for the first time in a decade, it didn't ache.

"Jason is going to freak out when I tell him *Mac McKenzie* thinks he looks like freaking Chris Hemsworth."

Her phone buzzed in her lap.

She wiped her eyes quickly and glanced down. A text from Abigail.

Abigail:

> We're looking everywhere for you. You okay? Meet us at the car? We're thinking about heading back to Honeyshore— it's a long drive.

Ali sighed and showed Dylan the screen. "They're ready to leave."

He nodded, rubbing his hand across the back of his neck. "Yeah. I should probably get back inside. Duty calls."

But just as he started to shift up from his crouch, he paused and reached for her hand.

"I'm in town for a few days," he said, his thumb brushing over her knuckles. "Visiting my family. I have every intention of seeing you again."

Her breath caught. She opened her mouth to say no, to protect her peace, to tuck everything back in where it was safe. But something in his eyes—the steadiness, the softness—cut through the hesitation.

"I want to see you, too," she said, before she could change her mind.

She swallowed, fumbling for the next words. "I—um—I changed my number after the hospital. I just...I couldn't—"

"You don't have to explain anything," he said gently, already pulling his phone from his pocket and passing it to her. "Just put it in."

Ali stared at the unlocked screen, heart stuttering, before slowly typing in her new number. She handed it back, resisting the impulse to apologize again.

She stood up with him, brushing gravel from her palms. "You should probably head back separately. I can wait for my group here. I don't...really want my coworkers to see us walking up together."

Dylan's lips curved into a crooked grin, like he wasn't surprised in the least. "I get it."

She turned like she was about to walk away—but he caught her wrist.

And then he kissed her.

Firm and breath-stealing, his hand cradling her jaw like he still remembered exactly how she fit. She swayed into it, heart thudding against her ribs.

When he finally pulled back, he didn't go far. His lips hovered against hers, his breath warm.

"Goodnight, Ali," he whispered.

And then he was gone—turning, heading back toward the banquet hall, backlit by golden light and the weight of a thousand memories.

By the time she got home, the adrenaline had worn off and left her nerves frayed and buzzing.

She kicked off her shoes by the door, peeled down her dress in the hallway, and left a trail of clothes in her bedroom. The house was quiet. Ashley must be staying at Brant's place tonight. Good. She was too drained to talk.

The hot water stung at first, but then it soothed. Steam filled the space like a foggy cocoon as she lathered her skin, rinsed shampoo from her hair, and tried—really tried—not to think about his hands on her hips. His mouth against her throat. His cock pushing inside her.

She went through the motions of her routine. Moisturizer. Hair serum. Meds.

Her phone buzzed again—just Abigail checking if she made it home okay. Ali answered with a thumbs-up and a heart, then sank into bed.

She pulled up her Kindle app and opened the latest romantasy everyone was raving about. A smutty scene about a dark prince and a stubborn heroine and some magic-induced heat of the moment. Usually, she loved this part.

But tonight, the words blurred.

Because she could still feel him.

Dylan's hands on her waist. His mouth catching her gasp. His body, all hard muscle and desperation, pressing her against that wall like he'd been dying to do it for a decade. She'd never felt anything like that in her life. Not even in college. Not even back then.

It had been so long.

She hadn't been with anyone since him. Not really. Not all the way. Not like this.

She didn't trust easily. Didn't date seriously. She told her friends it was because she was busy. Focused. Selective. And all of that was true. But deep down, she'd always felt like if she moved on, if she gave herself to someone else—really gave herself—it would be a betrayal.

To him.

To what they had. To what they lost—because of her.

But damn...he felt so good tonight. Better than she remembered. Like her body had been waiting, quietly, for him all along.

Ali groaned softly and rolled to her side. One hand slipped beneath the covers to play with her nipples, the other into her panties.

She didn't tease herself. Didn't drag it out.

She was already wet. Already aching.

She slid two fingers inside herself, eyes fluttering shut. Her hips shifted. Her breath hitched.

In her mind, it was still him.

His mouth on her neck. His hand fisting in her hair. The low growl in his throat right before he'd thrust into her so hard the breath left her lungs.

Her fingers moved faster, building against the memory. The sharp press of his hips. The taste of his kiss. The way he looked at her like she was still everything.

She gasped his name.

"Dylan—"

And shattered.

Her back arched. Her toes curled. And she came hard, her cry echoing in the quiet bedroom, the sheets twisted around her thighs.

After, she lay still. Chest heaving. Heart pounding.

She didn't feel guilty.

Not anymore.

Just warm.

Just sore.

And maybe, for the first time in a long time...a little bit hopeful.

I Look In People's Windows

Dylan

Dylan keyed into his hotel room in Peach Cove, the temporary suite arranged by the university for the fundraiser. Clean, modern. Too quiet.

He shut the door behind him with a soft click, tossing the clutch Ali had dropped onto the small couch. He'd make sure she got it back tomorrow. His fingers had curled protectively around it the entire ride over, like it was some kind of stand-in for her hand.

He passed the bed, peeled off his blazer, tugged at the tight collar of his dress shirt.

Everything on him felt too tight.

Especially below the waist.

He checked his phone. Nothing.

Still, he stared at the screen like it might change if he willed it hard enough.

He wanted to text her. Just to see if she was okay. If she made it home safe. But he didn't want to push. Didn't want to crowd her.

So instead, he flicked on *Do Not Disturb,* set the phone facedown, and stripped.

One piece at a time.

Each article of clothing he shed left him more exposed than the last. His skin felt hot—like it was still lit up from her touch. His dress pants hit the floor and his boxers followed. He was already half-hard.

The moment he stepped under the water, a growl broke free from his chest.

He braced his hands on the tile wall, head bowed, water cascading over his shoulders and down his back. But no matter how hot the spray was, it didn't melt her from his mind.

Ali.

Her hair tangled in his hands. Her leg hitched against his hips. Her whimpers against his neck. The delicious sting of her hands pulling at his hair. The fucking wet heat of her—tight and slick and welcoming in a way that made his chest ache.

God, she'd felt so tight.

His cock twitched, hardening fully now. He groaned, deep and low.

He gripped himself at the base, stroking once, twice. Slow at first. Deliberate.

He hadn't been with anyone in...fuck. Too damn long. But tonight—her body had taken him like he'd never left. Like ten years hadn't passed.

He jerked his hand again, faster this time. The memory played on a loop.

The way she'd gasped when he'd slid into her. How her back arched. How her pussy squeezed around him like it didn't want to let go.

"Fuck, Ali..."

He pictured her—dress pushed up, nails digging into his shoulders and scalp as he drove into her again and again against the brick wall.

He bit back a moan.

Only thing he regretted was having to muffle her sounds. She used to cry out for him—his name on her lips like a prayer. And goddamn, he missed that.

His hips bucked into his hand, chasing the high that was already building, already burning.

He angled his head back under the spray, hand working his cock fast and desperate now, and let out a guttural groan as he came—hot, hard, and shaking.

"Ali—"

The name escaped in a broken exhale as pleasure tore through him. His free hand hit the tile wall to brace himself.

For a moment, all he could hear was the sound of water and his own breathing.

He stood there, head hanging, water washing away the evidence.

But not the ache.

Never the ache.

Not when it was her.

After the shower, Dylan threw on a pair of black boxer briefs and dropped onto the cool hotel sheets, muscles loose and spent, but his mind still a fucking riot.

He reached over to turn off the bedside lamp, then paused—remembering he needed to set his alarm. He was heading to Honeyshore early, and Kallie had a flight out of Savannah mid-morning. Even though she had her shit together ten times better than he did, he still liked checking in on her. It made him feel useful. Grounded.

He grabbed his phone. Turning off the *Do Not Disturb* setting.

Seven texts.

> Thank you for tonight.

> Not just the thing by the wall. But the panic part too.

> But also the thing by the wall. You felt amazing.

> And I'm glad you'll be in town.
> To catch up.

> Not for more wall things.

> But maybe that too.

> Also gawd sorry I'm rambling and blowing your phone up & you are probably asleep.

> Okay, goodnight.

He chuckled, warmth curling low in his chest. She was spiraling. Rambling in texts the way she used to in late-night study sessions with her legs folded under her and her lip between her teeth. He could see her, even now—freckled and flustered.

And God, he loved it.

He hit call before he could talk himself out of it.

It rang once.

Then again.

She answered on the third, voice quiet and cautious.

"Hey?"

He leaned back against the headboard, grin tugging at his lips.

"Stop spiraling, babe."

She sucked in a soft breath.

"Tonight was amazing," he said, his voice dropping, slow and deliberate. "You were amazing."

A pause. Then he added, with heat roughening every word:

"I haven't stopped thinking about your tight pussy all night."

She made a soft, shocked sound—half gasp, half giggle.

"Fuck, Ali," he murmured. "You wrapped around me like we were made for each other. You always did. But tonight? Goddamn. I've been hard for you since the second you walked into that hall."

Her silence was breathless.

He softened his tone, thumb brushing over the edge of the phone. "But also...thank you. For trusting me. For letting me be there. I know tonight was a lot. I'm not taking any of it lightly."

More silence on her end—except for a faint inhale, like she was trying not to cry again.

"I see you," he said, voice low and rough with truth. "All of you. Not just the parts I jerk off to in the shower, thinking about how you sound when you come. I see the girl who held it together when her whole world cracked."

That earned him a soft, watery laugh.

"I'll let you sleep," he said, not meaning it but knowing she probably needed it. "But we're not done, Ali. Not even close."

He waited for her to say something.

Anything.

There was a long pause.

He didn't push her. Just let the silence stretch, listening to the quiet sound of her breath on the other end.

Then, her voice—low, sultry, laced with something darker than teasing—came through the line.

"I couldn't stop thinking about it either," she said. "You. The way you felt. The way you filled me..."

Dylan's jaw flexed. He sat up straighter against the headboard.

"I came," she whispered. "Just now. Fingers soaked. Thinking about you slamming into me—how hard you fucked me against that wall like you'd never let me go again."

His hand fisted the sheets.

Ali exhaled, breathy and close to the phone. "I said your name. Loud."

Dylan sucked in a sharp breath, his head tipping back like she'd physically touched him.

"And now," she added softly, voice barely audible, "I think I can finally sleep."

A beat of silence. Then: "Goodnight Dylan." The whisper so soft he might've imagined it.

And she hung up.

Dylan stared at the screen, jaw tight, dick hard again, heart fucking racing.

He let out a long groan and dropped his head into his hands.

"Jesus Christ, Ali."

Alison Katherine Presley was going to be the death of him.

Gorgeous

Ali

The Netflix homepage idled in the background, the third time it had asked *Are you still watching?* ignored as white noise. Ali was curled up in bed, fuzzy socks on her feet, hair piled on top of her head, and her Kindle half-forgotten beside her.

She hadn't slept much. Not with the way Dylan's voice kept replaying in her head. That last, sinful whisper. The way her own name had fallen from his mouth like a benediction.

The front door creaked open, followed by the unmistakable sound of someone kicking it shut with their foot.

"It's just me and your cure for all things emotionally unhinged and hungover," Ashley called.

Before Ali could react, her bedroom door swung open and Ashley flopped dramatically onto the bed, two Zaxby's bags in hand. The familiar scent of chicken tenders and crinkle fries filled the air like a balm.

Ali blinked. "You brought me Zaxby's?"

Ashley grinned. "Duh. It's Sunday. You're hiding in bed. Jason said you disappeared to the bathroom for like half the night. That screams emotional hangover."

Ali laughed and shook her head. "I'm not hungover. I had, like, one drink."

Ashley paused mid-fry. "Wait. So you're in bed all day, red-faced, jittery, and Netflix-looped without alcohol as an excuse?"

Ali rolled her eyes, cheeks already flushing. "I wasn't in the bathroom."

Ashley narrowed her eyes like a cat sniffing out secrets. "You weren't?"

Ali hesitated. And that was all it took.

Ashley's jaw dropped, eyes gleaming. "You dirty little hussy!" She swatted Ali's arm with a pillow and squealed. "I knew it! You got laid, didn't you? That's why you disappeared. Who was it? Do I know him? Oh my God! Tell me everything."

Ali buried her face in her pillow and groaned. "I hate how well you know me."

"Start talking," Ashley said, flipping open the food bag and handing over the toast with a Zax sauce as a peace offering.

Ali sat up, cradling the buttery bread like a lifeline. "Okay. Fine. But you can't freak out."

"Please. Freaking out is my entire personality. Now spill."

Ali inhaled. "I went outside for air during the fundraiser. Just needed a break, and...Dylan followed me. He-"

"Wait a second sis! Dylan!?" exclaimed Ashley.

Ali ignored her and kept going. "He wanted to talk but I kinda jumped him..." Her face went crimson. "We had sex. Outside. Against the building."

Ashley gaped. "That's not just sex. That's cinematic."

Ali giggled, covering her face. "I thought I was going to have a heart attack. I literally almost had a panic attack in the parking lot afterward."

Ashley's smile faded, her tone softening. "Shit. Are you okay?"

"Yeah. I mean...I wasn't. But he found me again, and he talked me down. Sat with me on the pavement. Didn't push. He was so—him. Just steady and solid and sweet."

Ashley tilted her head, chewing slowly. "Dylan always was a good guy. Intense, but good. What else?"

Ali fiddled with the hem of her sweatshirt. "He told me he's in town visiting family for a few days. That he wants to see me. And then...I got home and couldn't sleep and I texted him."

Ashley raised a brow. "Risky."

"I know. I was spiraling immediately after. I was like, 'Oh no, what if he thinks I'm clingy or weird or—'"

"And?"

"And he called me. Told me to stop spiraling. Called me 'babe.' Said he hadn't stopped thinking about me. Except it was just like college. He was always so explicit"

Ashley squealed into her fist. "He talked dirty to you?!"

Ali nodded, cheeks burning. "Yes. But also somehow still gentle. Like he knew exactly what to say to make me feel sexy and safe at the same time. And I might've hinted that I...touched myself when I got home."

Ashley shrieked. "Ali! You left him with a verbal visual! You minx!"

Ali giggled into her hands. "I did! And then I hung up before he could say anything else. He let out this sharp inhale and I just—panicked and said goodnight."

Ashley rolled onto her back, laughing. "Okay, I take it back. You're not a hussy. You're a goddam legend."

Ali pressed the toast to her face and groaned. "I don't know what I'm doing."

"Yes, you do," Ashley said seriously, sitting up and nudging her with a fry. "You're doing what feels good. And for once, you're letting yourself have it."

Ali's eyes stung unexpectedly. "I think I want to see him again."

Ashley smiled. "Then you will. And if he hurts you—well, I'm a lawyer with access to a baseball bat and an encyclopedic knowledge of Georgia self-defense statutes."

Ali burst out laughing, nearly choking on a crinkle fry. "That's deeply unhinged."

Ashley grinned. "And legally sound. And I brought Zaxby's."

Ali leaned into her best friend's shoulder and smiled. "You're the best kind of insane."

Ali's phone buzzed.

She was halfway through folding a blanket from the couch, her hair messy from wallowing on the couch, when Dylan's name lit up the screen.

Dylan:

> Can I take you out sometime this week? Like...actually take you out. Not just...you know. Against a wall.

She snorted, cheeks instantly warming. "Unreal," she muttered, heart fluttering as her thumb hovered over her screen.

She typed:

Ali (unsent):

That sounds nice but I'm not really up for being seen out somewhere together.

Delete.

Ali (unsent):

I don't really do the whole going out thing. Like in public. Not with someone like you.

Delete.

Ali (unsent):

I want to. I do. But I'm just not ready for that yet. For what it would mean. How it might look.

Backspace. Delete.

She sighed, setting the phone down on the coffee table and walking away. She grabbed a Coke Zero from the fridge. Twisted off the cap. Took a sip. Came back and sat down, phone still glowing.

She took a breath and tried again.

> I'd love to see you, I'm just…nervous about being out together. Like, in public. After everything from college. It's been years, but some of that stuff still sticks, you know? I just need a little time to feel okay with all of that.

Her finger hovered over "send." She reread it three times. Bit her lip. Then finally tapped it.

A minute passed.

Then another.

> Hey. Thank you for telling me that….how about this: I pick you up, we drive around and look at the pretty houses on Mariner's Lane and Dockside Ave. You can wear sweatpants and judge everyone's landscaping choices. Then we grab something lowkey and eat it out at Bellamy Marsh Preserve. Sunset. Just you and me. No one else.

Her heart melted.

> You remembered the marsh?

> Still my favorite view I've ever had….well. One of them.

She bit her lip, smiling now.

> Okay. But I'm wearing biker shorts and bringing bug spray.

Deal. I'll be the guy in the Tritons hoodie pretending he doesn't know he's hot shit.

You're not pretending, McKenzie.

God, I've missed your mouth.

She slid onto her back, grinning like an idiot, phone still in her hand, heart racing for all the right reasons.

She was curled up under her throw blanket, half-watching *Ransom Canyon*, half-scrolling Instagram—but her mind was nowhere near the show or her phone.

It was still with Dylan.

The way he said, *"God, I've missed your mouth,"* was playing on a loop in her brain.

Her mouth.

She bit her bottom lip. Hard.

She'd never done that.

Not with him. Not with anyone.

She'd thought about it—gawd, she'd thought about it—but never actually followed through. Even back then, when things with Dylan had been intense and emotional and real...she hadn't been ready.

And after? After the hospital, after everything—she never really trusted anyone enough to go there again.

There had been guys. A few kisses. One or two whose hands had wandered. She let it happen, up to a point. Just enough to remind herself she was alive.

But she always stopped it.

Always backed off before things could go any further. Before clothes came off. Before expectations took over.

Ashley used to tease her about it, told her to "Just get laid already." Ali would laugh, brush it off, say she was busy or picky or not into hookup culture.

And now...after last night...after that wall...her whole body was buzzing with need.

She pressed her thighs together, lips parting instinctively as she remembered the way he felt—hard and hot, sliding deep inside her like he belonged there.

Her cheeks flushed.

She wanted to feel him again. Wanted to please him. Taste him.

Gawd, what would it feel like to have him in her mouth?

The thought made her stomach flutter and heat pool low. She didn't even know how to ask for that. Didn't know if she could say the words out loud. She wasn't bold like that.

But maybe...maybe she could give him a hint.

She sat up, grabbed her phone, and opened their thread.

Then she stared at the blinking cursor for a solid two minutes.

Typed. Deleted. Typed again. Deleted.

Finally, her fingers moved without her permission. And before she could talk herself out of it, she hit send.

> I keep thinking about what you said earlier. About my mouth.

> ...I think you'd like what it's been thinking about too.

Three dots appeared on the screen almost instantly.

Her breath caught.

She threw her phone across the couch and buried her face in her hands.

What did I just do?!

But her heart was racing in the best way.

Because this time?

She didn't want to back off.

Then her phone dinged. And dinged. And dinged.

She couldn't take it anymore. She lunged forward and snatched the phone up.

> Babe.

> You have no idea what you just did to me.

> I've been thinking about that mouth since I got in the car last night.

She clapped a hand over her mouth to muffle the squeal.

Another ding.

> Tell me what it's been thinking about. Or better yet...show me soon?

She barely had time to read it before another message popped up.

And just so we're clear—if "wall things" are now a category…I'm gonna need them on the regular. Like Tuesdays, Thursdays, and every day ending in Y.

Her hands flew to her face again, and she groaned into her palms, grinning like an idiot.

"Gawd, Dylan," she whispered, rolling onto her side and curling around the phone like it was a warm body. He was teasing her. Of course he was. But he liked it. Her wording, her honesty, her shyness and want tangled up together.

He liked her.

Ding.

Also, I think I left a handprint on that wall. Pretty sure we owe that building an apology.

Ali buried her face in the pillow and let out a breathless laugh.

Her fingers hovered over the keyboard.

My mouth's definitely been thinking about "wall things." But maybe…with a different wall next time? One that doesn't require public apologies?

She didn't send it.

Not yet.

Because her heart was pounding and her thoughts were racing and—

She wanted to savor this moment.

But not forever.

Because for the first time in a long time?

She wasn't scared of wanting more.

Her thumb hovered for only a second more.

Then—send.

"Omg," she groaned aloud the second it delivered, throwing herself back on the couch, eyes glued to the phone like it might explode.

She didn't have to wait long.

…Jesus, Ali. I'm trying to be good. But if you keep texting me like that, I'm gonna lose all sense of decency. You'll be blushing for days.

Her breath hitched. She covered her face with both hands, heat blooming across her cheeks, down her neck, between her legs.

> I'll pin you to any wall you want.

> Bedroom wall. Shower wall. Back of the closet door. Hell, against the fridge if that's what you need.

> Just tell me. I'll give you everything that mouth of yours is thinking about.

Ali let out a high, breathless sound and scrambled upright, pacing again.

Her pulse was doing cartwheels, her mind spinning with everything his words implied.

Fridge.

Closet.

Shower.

Bedroom. His bedroom.

Her knees nearly buckled.

Because that was the one she wanted most.

But she didn't know how to say it.

Not yet.

So instead, she typed something coy, with her lip caught between her teeth:

> I don't think I'm ready for a fridge yet…

Then— heart thudding— she added:

> But I think about your bedroom. A lot.

And this time?

She didn't throw her phone.

She held it tight.

And waited for what came next.

Closure

Dylan

Dylan was half-sprawled across the hotel bed, one arm behind his head, the other holding his phone like it might slip from his grip if he exhaled too hard. He hadn't taken his eyes off the screen since she sent that first message.

I keep thinking about what you said earlier.
About my mouth.
...I think you'd like what it's been thinking about too.

He'd practically groaned out loud. His cock had stirred instantly, twitching under the thin sheet. He hadn't even tried to hide his reaction—he was alone, and her words lit him up like a live wire.

But her last text?

I don't think I'm ready for a fridge yet...
But I think about your bedroom. A lot.

Fuck.

He sat up, running a hand through his damp hair. "Jesus, Ali," he muttered, the smile tugging at his mouth sharp and slow. His whole body felt like it was vibrating with want.

She didn't even know what she was doing to him.

Or maybe she did.

She was teasing him in the sweetest, shyest damn way—and it made him want her even more. Not just to touch her or bury himself inside her again. But to know her now. All the ways she'd changed. All the ways she hadn't.

He stared at her words again.

Your bedroom.

It knocked the air out of him a little.

Because that—that was a line. A soft one. Careful. But real. And honest. And she'd sent it anyway.

He swiped open his keyboard and started typing, slow and deliberate.

Dylan:

> You just say when, babe. The bed's big. The sheets are soft. And I promise—no one will hear you but me.

He hesitated.

Then added:

> I've been thinking about your mouth too. Ever since you wrapped it around my name last night.

He stared at that line, then hit send before he could overthink it. Because she deserved to know—he hadn't stopped thinking about her either.

And if she was really ready for more?

He was already halfway gone.

Sunday afternoon smelled like chlorine, charcoal smoke, and peach cobbler.

Dylan stood waist-deep in the pool, sunlight flickering off the water like shattered glass, arms stretched up as his niece screamed in delight.

"Ready?" he asked.

"THROW ME, UNCLE FYLAN!" She squealed with her sweet little lisp.

He launched her into the deep end with a laugh, and she hit the water with a cannonball splash that soaked his chest and the edge of his mama's rose bushes.

"Again!" she shouted, resurfacing with her goggles crooked on her face.

"You tryna drown me?" he teased, slicking back his hair. "Go catch your breath first, water bug."

Across the yard, his dad stood at the grill in flip-flops and an old Magnolia Bluff football tee, tongs in hand, flipping steaks with surgical focus. The scent of sizzling meat drifted through the air as his mama came outside balancing a tray with baked potatoes, sour cream, and a pan of her famous yeast rolls.

"Y'all better not let those babies get sunburnt!" she called as she set the tray down.

"They're lotioned up, Mama," Daisy replied, holding her youngest on one hip while sipping sweet tea with the other hand. Her wife, Laila, was stretched out on a lounger, sunglasses on, scrolling through something on her iPad.

Meanwhile, Dylan tossed a football to his nephew, who stood at the diving board, knees wobbly but grinning.

"Alright, buddy. You jump, I'll throw."

His nephew jumped, arms flailing, and Dylan lobbed the ball with perfect timing. The kid caught it mid-air and fell into the water with a triumphant splash.

"YESSS!" he screamed when he surfaced.

"Gonna draft you to the Tritons," Dylan said.

Hours passed in the way Sundays should—slow, warm, and full of family noise. After the kids had dried off and changed into pajamas, they all sat at the patio table. His dad served the steaks while his mama passed out plates like clockwork.

The table was full: laughter, teasing, seconds of cobbler.

And for a few rare, golden hours, it was easy to forget the rest of the world.

No interviews.

No NFL pressure.

No late-night texts from the girl who still made his pulse skip.

Just family.

After dinner, Laila wiped cobbler off sticky fingers and murmured something to Daisy about bedtime.

The kids hugged Dylan goodnight, squeezing his middle and asking if he was playing with them tomorrow too. When they disappeared inside, Daisy turned to him.

"You sticking around a little longer?"

He shrugged. "I can."

She smirked. "Cards? Or you scared?"

"Not scared," he said, already walking toward the house. "Just merciful."

Dylan stood at the kitchen sink, rinsing plates while the sound of cartoon lullabies echoed faintly from upstairs.

The air inside still carried the sweetness of his mama's peach cobbler, the tang of steak seasoning clinging to his fingertips. A summer breeze floated through the open window above the sink, lifting the sheer curtain and cooling the sweat still drying on the back of his neck.

He dried his hands on a dish towel and leaned against the counter, letting the quiet settle in.

It was strange how peaceful it felt here. He hadn't been home since the night he'd left Ali at Bellamy Memorial Hospital, and yet the house welcomed him like no time had passed. His sister and her family were also in town, visiting for a few days, so driving over after the fundraiser had just felt...natural. Right. The rhythm of family life picked up without missing a beat—the familiar chaos, the playful teasing, the long-running joke about how he still liked his dinner rolls drowned in butter, just like when he was six.

It should've felt like slipping back into something simple.

But his mind kept drifting.

To Ali.

To her flushed cheeks. That nervous lip bite. The texts she sent, the ones she almost sent, the ones she deleted and retyped. And the ones that made his entire body lock up in anticipation.

"About my mouth."

He let out a slow breath, jaw tightening slightly as the words replayed like a whisper against his skin.

He wanted her.

Not just physically—though God did he feel that, too. But more than that, he wanted to know what it looked like when she let go. When she trusted him with more than her body. When she didn't back off.

He could still see her pacing her bedroom floor, phone in hand. He didn't have to be there to picture it. He knew her. That quiet panic she had when her feelings got big. The way she second-guessed herself even when she already knew what she wanted.

But she'd hit send anyway.

That mattered.

He ran a hand through his hair and looked around the kitchen. Same linoleum floor. Same humming fridge. Same old-school salt and pepper shakers shaped like lighthouses his mama bought at Tybee one summer.

And yet everything felt different.

Because this time, he wasn't the same either.

Ten years ago, he let too much go unsaid. Let fear and family and unfinished sentences get in the way of something real.

But this time?

He wouldn't.

A creak on the stairs pulled him from his thoughts.

Daisy's voice followed. "Kids are down. Let's play, old man."

He pushed off the counter with a smirk. "Deal the cards, little sis."

But even as he followed her into the den, his mind was still somewhere else.

Half in the past. Half on her lips. And all the way gone.

"You're going down," Daisy said with a smirk. Her dark hair was up in a loose bun, and she wore an old Sharks hoodie over sleep shorts. "I've been practicing with tiny humans all year. I'm ruthless now."

He grinned, dropping into the chair across from her. "Bring it on, punk."

Daisy let out a surprised laugh, tossing a yellow card on the pile. "And also, don't think I didn't notice you dodging the baby monitor earlier. Afraid of bedtime meltdowns?"

He held up his hands. "I know better than to get in the way of your kids' wind-down playlist and a melatonin gummy."

They played in easy silence for a few rounds. Comfortable. Familiar. Like nothing had ever gone wrong between them. Like college hadn't happened. Like Ali—

He shifted in his seat.

"Y'know," Daisy said after a moment, not looking up from her cards, "You're quieter than usual."

He met her gaze across the table. "Just tired."

She nodded slowly, her expression unreadable. "Lot on your mind?"

A pause. "Yep."

She stacked a *Draw Four* on his pile. "Wanna talk about it?"

"Nope."

Another beat passed, and then she smiled—genuinely, not like it used to be when she was deflecting or guarding herself. "Okay."

And that was the deal, wasn't it? That was how they kept the peace. *Don't ask. Don't tell. Move forward.*

It wasn't perfect.

But it was something.

After a second game and a few beers neither of them really wanted, Daisy kicked her feet up on the chair next to his and said, "You seemed happy earlier. I haven't seen that in a long time."

He didn't say anything right away.

Because how do you explain to your sister that the thing she tried so hard to tear apart might actually be the only thing that ever felt like home?

Instead, he shrugged. "It's been a good weekend."

She studied him. "You seeing someone?"

His heart thumped once. Then twice.

"No," he said carefully. "Not really."

Not yet. But maybe...maybe soon.

Later, after several games and way too much trash talk they gave up playing. The coffee table was littered with cards, empty beer bottles, and the remnants of a half-eaten bag of Nerds Clusters. The TV played softly in the background—some random Food Network competition neither of them had paid much attention to—and the ceiling fan spun lazily above them, stirring the thick Southern air.

Daisy flopped sideways on the loveseat, feet tucked under her, a flushed grin spreading across her face. "You cheated," she slurred, pointing at him with exaggerated drama. "Nobody wins Uno and gin rummy unless they're a certified asshole."

Dylan chuckled, stretching his legs out in front of him. "Maybe you just suck."

She gasped, feigning offense, then snorted. "You're lucky I love you."

He leaned forward, gathering up the scattered cards. "And you're lucky I didn't let your kids gang-tackle you in the pool today."

"They did gang-tackle me," she said, eyes half-closed, her speech slower now. "That's why I have a bruise shaped like Lillie's elbow on my thigh. Worth it, though."

Dylan smiled, soft and real. These nights didn't happen often. Not anymore. And even with the haze of beer and sibling banter, he felt that weight in his chest—the quiet kind. The kind that came with growing up and apart and only sometimes finding your way back.

Daisy blinked slowly, then rubbed her face. "I'm drunk."

"Yup."

She laughed. "I'm gonna go crawl into bed with my very hot, very sober wife now."

"Good plan," he said, grabbing two bottles from the table and standing. "I'll clean up down here. Crash on the couch."

Her eyes opened fully. "You're not driving back to your hotel?"

He shook his head. "Too buzzed."

She nodded, serious for a second. "I'm glad." She stood, wobbled, and leaned in to hug him, her chin pressing against his shoulder. "Love you, Dyl."

He hugged her back tightly. "Love you too, Daze."

Then she was gone, stumbling up the stairs toward her old bedroom where her wife was already asleep. Her kids asleep in his old room.

Dylan stared at the quiet room for a long moment. The soft clink of bottles in his hands filled the silence as he walked them to the kitchen. He rinsed them out, set them in the bin under the sink, then came back and turned off the TV.

The house felt different at night.

Softer. Older.

He sank into the couch, kicked off his shoes, and laid back against the cushions with a sigh.

His phone lit up beside him—just a notification from a sports app.

But for a split second, his heart jumped, thinking it might be her.

Ali.

Her name alone made something thrum low in his chest.

He turned off the lamp, darkness settling around him. But even with his eyes closed, sleep wouldn't come right away.

Not when her voice was still in his head.

Not when his whole body still remembered the words she'd sent.

And not when his heart—after all this time—was finally starting to believe they might get it right

Dylan had just started to drift. Body heavy. Mind fighting off memory.

But something made him open his eyes.

Then he saw her.

Sitting on the loveseat, knees pulled to her chest, face streaked with tears.

"Daisy," he groaned, rubbing a hand over his face. "What's wrong?"

She flinched. "I'm sorry. I just...I couldn't sleep."

"Clearly."

She stared at him, glassy-eyed. "Do you ever think about her?"

He sat up fast. "Don't."

"I need to say it."

"We had a deal."

"I lied." Her voice cracked. "I've been lying since college."

He stood, shaking his head. "Nope. Not tonight."

But she surged forward, grabbing his wrist. "Dylan, please."

He tried to pull away. She held tight.

"Please."

He stopped.

Furious. Exhausted.

And maybe a little scared.

Daisy looked up at him with a face so full of shame he almost didn't recognize it. "I wasn't just mean to Ali because I was a bitchy little sister."

"Don't," he warned, voice hard.

She ignored it. "I was half in love with her."

He froze.

"I didn't realize it at first. Not fully. I just knew that she made me feel...seen. And safe. And warm in a way no one ever had. I wanted to be around her all the time. I wanted her to pick me first. But then she didn't."

Her voice cracked, trembling.

"She picked you."

Dylan didn't breathe.

"She picked you," Daisy repeated. "My fucking brother. Everyone picked you! Ali was mine! She was my best friend. She was supposed to be mine! And God, I hated her for it. I hated that she was happy with you. I hated that she smiled at you differently. I hated that she never looked at me that way."

"She didn't choose me to spite you Daisy."

"I know," she said. "But it still hurt like hell. And we lived in freaking South Georgia, Dyl. What was I supposed to do? Admit to the whole damn world that I might like girls—when I hadn't even admitted it to myself?"

Silence.

"I wasn't ready," she whispered. "So I turned it into hate. And jealousy. And sarcasm. I was spiteful and cruel, and I didn't know how to stop. And by the time I realized how far I'd gone, it was already too late."

He didn't look at her.

"But you know what kills me?" she said. "It wasn't even real love. Not like what I have with Laila. That's real. That's forever. What I had for Ali was just a crush. A stupid, painful, first-love kind of crush. And I let it destroy everything."

Still, Dylan didn't move.

"I just wanted you to know the truth. Finally."

He stayed frozen a beat longer, then muttered, "You don't get points for honesty now."

"I'm not trying to earn points, Dylan."

"Well, congratulations," he said, voice sharp. "You already did the damage. You got what you wanted."

"No, I didn't," she snapped. "You think I wanted to lose her too?"

"You never had her."

"I know that!" she yelled. "And then you didn't. Because of me!"

He flinched like she'd slapped him.

"I ruined it," Daisy said, breathing hard. "I know that. I live with that. Every day."

"I told you not to bring her up," he growled, eyes suddenly hot. "I warned you after Mimi died. I said if you wanted me in your life, you don't ever say her name again."

"I know."

"Then why—"

"Because I need you to forgive me."

He laughed bitterly. "It's not about me forgiving you."

"Then what is it about?"

"She tried to kill herself, Daisy."

The words slipped out like they'd been waiting years.

Daisy stopped breathing. "What?"

Dylan's jaw locked. "Shit."

"No. No, what did you just say?" She stepped toward him, voice trembling. "What do you mean?"

"I didn't mean to—"

"Dylan." Her eyes went wide.

He turned his back, hands on his hips, heart hammering.

"You knew she was in the hospital," he said tightly.

"No..." she whispered.

"It wasn't the flu. Or exhaustion. Or an eating disorder like you all gossiped about. It was a fucking bottle of anxiety pills."

Her knees buckled and she gripped the edge of the loveseat.

"I didn't know," she said, choking on the words. "I swear, Dylan. I didn't know."

"Well, now you do."

He didn't look at her.

Didn't want to see her face.

Didn't want to see the mirror of his own guilt reflecting back at him.

"I—I thought she just...went home," Daisy whispered, her voice cracking. "She never told me. You never told me."

"She almost died, Daisy."

"I didn't mean for—"

"She almost died," he said again, louder this time. "And I was there. Holding her hand. Not even knowing if she wanted me there. You weren't. No one was. Just me."

Silence settled heavy and thick.

Daisy didn't cry this time. She didn't speak.

She just sank into the loveseat, eyes vacant.

Dylan stood in the middle of the room, fists clenched, breathing hard.

Dylan was livid and exhausted at the same time. "Go to bed Daisy. We're done here."

He felt wrecked all over again.

And the worst part?

Ali still didn't know the truth.

Not about Daisy.

He didn't know if he wanted her to. He didn't want her to feel guilty. He knew how her mind worked.

Begin Again

Ali

Tuesday came fast. Or slow. She wasn't really sure at this point.

Ashley had half her head buried in Ali's closet, holding up options with a hum and shake of her head every few seconds.

Ali sat on the edge of her bed in a pair of soft biker shorts, chewing the inside of her cheek and trying not to spiral. Dylan had said comfy clothes.

"What about the book tee with the pink sleeves?" Ashley called out, holding it up like it was gold. "It's cute, it's you, and it's breezy enough if y'all end up outside at the Marsh."

Ali took it, fingers smoothing over the faded typewriter graphic and tiny stack of illustrated novels. "Okay," she nodded, voice quiet.

The truth was, oversized tees had always been her comfort zone. Not just because they were easy—but because they made her feel safe. Hidden, but still herself. Being plus-size meant that most days were already laced with too much thinking. Too much adjusting. Too much wondering if she looked like she was trying too hard, or not enough.

"Hair?" Ashley asked, already pulling out a brush.

"French braid?" Ali offered. "It's so freaking hot today."

Ashley grinned. "Perfect. Casual picnic princess. Dylan's gonna die."

Ali smiled, but her stomach flipped. She wasn't sure she was princess material. But maybe...maybe with Dylan, she didn't have to be anything more than herself.

Ali pulled the front door closed behind her, clutching her phone and a cold bottle of diet lemonade like they might somehow anchor her. Dylan's black Bronco was already in the drive, engine idling, windows down. He leaned his elbow against the sill, one hand on the wheel like a scene straight out of a dream she used to have ten years ago.

His sunglasses were pushed up into his messy brown hair, and when he saw her, he smiled slow and real—like seeing her made his whole day.

She bit the inside of her cheek to keep from smiling too hard back. "Hey."

"Alison Presley..." His voice wrapped around her like warm flannel. "You ready?"

"Sure," she said, climbing into the passenger seat and buckling up. Her oversized tee brushed her thighs when she moved, the soft fabric a comfort against the nervous flutter of her belly. She'd always loved this shirt—the pink sleeves, the stack of books. It felt like her. Safe. Easy.

Dylan pulled out of the drive and turned toward the historic district. "Thought we'd start with a little cruise," he said. "I wanted to see how Mariner's Lane is holding up."

The SUV rolled slowly down the shady strip where the water peeked through the trees and the Victorians stood proud with their wraparound porches and hydrangeas. Ali leaned toward the window, eyes soaking up every gable and gingerbread trim.

"This one was always my favorite," she murmured, pointing to a buttercream yellow house with blue shutters and ivy climbing the banisters. "It looks like a something from a storybook."

Dylan glanced over. "You said you wanted to write a romance novel set in that house one day."

"I did?"

He nodded. "You were eighteen. It was after Creative Writing. You rode home with me for the weekend because Daisy had a pledge thing going on. You made me slow down in the rain just to get a picture."

Ali's face flushed. "Gawd, I can't believe you remember that."

"I remember everything," he said simply.

She turned away, hiding the smile she couldn't fight. They passed Dockside Avenue next, the breeze thick with marsh salt and honeysuckle. It smelled like childhood and second chances.

After a bit, he looped them through a drive-thru, ordered her nuggets, fries and Coke Zero without even asking, and then drove them to Bellamy Marsh Nature Preserve. The gravel crunched under the tires as he pulled into a quiet spot facing the dock and water.

Ali pulled her legs up into the seat beneath her, crisscrossed and comfortable. "This is perfect."

He handed her the bag and drink. "Good. I kinda hoped it would be."

They opened their food with that easy kind of silence—the kind that didn't need to be filled. Birds skimmed the marsh grass in the distance, and frogs chirped somewhere deep in the cattails. And right there, with her Chick-fil-A sauce and bare legs under her tee, Ali felt more herself than she had in years.

"You okay?" he asked, looking at her like he could read every flicker in her brain.

She nodded. "I'm really glad I came."

"Me too."

They sat parked at the edge of Bellamy Marsh, the Bronco's windows down to let in the warm night air and the steady chorus of cicadas. The scent of salt and marsh grass drifted in, mingling with the faint hum of distant traffic.

Dylan leaned back, a grin spreading across his face as he launched into stories about his teammates—pranks gone wrong, locker room antics, and quiet moments that showed their real character. Ali laughed harder than she had in weeks, tears prickling at the corners of her eyes as his stories caught her completely off guard.

"I haven't laughed like this in forever," she admitted between gasps.

Ali took a breath and smiled shyly. "Sounds like some silly stuff Ashley gets our book club into. Shelf Indulgence. Sometimes we discuss books and drink cocktails. Sometimes it's Diet Cokes and corndogs or a Saturday morning iced coffee—or whatever fits the mood. Sometimes we just want to escape adulting."

Dylan's eyes twinkled. "Iced coffee, huh? You still into those caramel iced lattes?"

She nodded, a little embarrassed but pleased he remembered. "Absolutely yes. They're my weakness."

He laughed softly. "Maybe next time, I'll bring you one."

The two of them sat quietly for a moment, the gentle sounds of the marsh wrapping around them like a soft blanket.

Ali stole a glance at Dylan, the easy smile still lingering on his lips. The way he talked, laughed, the way his eyes crinkled—it all pulled at something deep inside her.

Her mind wandered back to their texts earlier, the way he'd said, "*God, I missed your mouth.*" She'd flushed just thinking about it then, but now, here with him, it felt even more electric.

She bit her lip, feeling a flutter of nerves and excitement. The thought of those words—and all the unspoken things behind them—lingered, making her heart race.

Dylan caught her gaze and raised an eyebrow, teasing. "What's got you all quiet?"

Ali smiled, a little shy, and shrugged. "Just thinking...about you saying you missed my mouth."

He chuckled, the warmth in his eyes deepening. "You should know, that's only the beginning of what I miss."

Her cheeks warmed, but she met his gaze steady. The night felt full of promise.

Ali's breath hitched, a blush creeping up her neck. "Oh yeah? Like what?"

He leaned a little closer, voice dropping low and teasing. "Like how good you were at those 'wall things' the other night. Got me thinking...you're full of surprises."

She bit her lip, heart pounding but daring to play along. "Is that so? Maybe I should show you a few more then."

His grin deepened. "Damn right, you should. Just don't be surprised if I get greedy."

Dylan, probably not wanting to push her too far, went back to talking about his life in Orlando. She paid attention, she did but she kept thinking about how badly she wanted her mouth on him.

Ali surprised them both when she leaned over and took his mouth with hers. His lids fluttered shut in surprise but then a soft groan and his hands fisted on her braid as he deepened the kiss.

He reached over and tried to pull her in his lap but she didn't move.

Ali's fingers trembled slightly as she popped the button on his khaki shorts. The reality of what she was doing hit her in a wave—hot, nervous, a little unsure.

She felt him watching her, his breath slowing, steadying, not with pressure, but with reverence. His voice was soft at first, coaxing.

"You don't have to," he said, brushing her cheek with his knuckles. "Not unless you want to."

She looked up at him from beneath her lashes, her voice barely a whisper. "I want to. I just...I've never—"

Dylan's expression softened, but there was still hunger in his eyes. "Hey. That's okay. I'll show you. You don't have to be perfect—just be mine."

He guided her hand with his, wrapping her delicate hand around him. She felt the weight and heat of him in her palm, her lips parting just slightly in surprise. He groaned, low and deep in his throat.

"Fuck, that's it. Just like that, baby."

Ali ducked her head, cheeks flushed, but when she leaned in and kissed the tip softly, Dylan hissed through his teeth.

"God, you're killing me." His hand pulled gently at her braid. "Use that pretty mouth, sweetheart. Let me feel those lips."

She hesitated, but his voice was steady and warm—filthy, yes, but laced with something deeper. When he used those explicit words, it didn't embarrass her; it emboldened her. Made her feel like a goddess in his hands.

"Open up for me. Just a little. There you go...good girl."

The praise lit something in her. She wrapped her lips around the head and flicked her tongue instinctively. Dylan's hips twitched, his hand tightening slightly in her hair, pulling at her braid.

"Oh fuck, Ali. You feel so good. Just a little deeper now—yeah, just like that. Slow and steady."

Her confidence grew with every moan that slipped from his throat. He kept guiding her, not rushing, just talking her through it.

"You're doing so good, baby. So sweet. Look at you—taking my cock like this."

Ali moaned softly against him, and the vibration made Dylan curse again.

"God, you don't even know what you do to me. You're so fucking sexy like this. That mouth was made for me."

She hollowed her cheeks, mimicking what he said, and when she looked up at him again, Dylan's head fell back against the seat.

"Fuck. You're a dream, Ali. My dream. Don't stop now, baby."

And she didn't.

His voice kept her steady. His dirty words fueling the fire inside her. And even though her heart was pounding, she'd never felt more powerful, more wanted.

When he warned her he was close, she didn't stop. She only looked up at him, silently telling him: *I want this. I want all of you.*

And Dylan, wrecked and shaking, could only whisper her name like a prayer as he came.

Ali wiped at her mouth with the back of her hand, cheeks flushed, heart pounding out of her chest. Her lips tingled, her throat a little sore, but all she could think about was the way he'd said her name—like it meant everything.

"Hey," Dylan whispered, his voice wrecked but warm. He reached down and cupped her face, gently tilting it up so she'd look at him. "Come here, baby."

She hesitated. She didn't want to make him uncomfortable. Worried she was too heavy for his lap. But he tugged incessantly. So she climbed awkwardly across the console, still a little unsure, until she was nestled against his chest. He tucked her under his arm, pressed a soft kiss to the top of her head.

"You okay?" he murmured. "Was that too much?"

Ali shook her head quickly, her voice still small. "No…I'm okay. More than okay. I wanted to."

He pulled back just enough to look into her eyes, thumb brushing under her lips. "You were amazing, Ali. So fucking beautiful."

She blushed, curling her fingers into the soft fabric of his t-shirt. "I didn't know if I was doing it right."

"You were perfect," he said without hesitation. "God, baby, I didn't want to stop you. You felt so good. You looked so good."

He kissed her again—this time soft, lingering, reverent. Not rushed or needy. Just full of quiet awe.

Dylan wrapped both arms around her, cradling her against his chest like something precious. "I've never wanted anyone the way I want you."

She melted into him, sighing as the warm evening air filled the Bronco. Outside, the cicadas still buzzed, the marsh was turning soft gold in the fading light, and the world felt far away.

"Does this…" she began, hesitating. "Mean we're…?"

He pulled her hand into his, threading their fingers together. "It means I'm not letting you go again."

Ali's throat tightened, but she nodded.

"Okay," she whispered. "Okay."

They sat like that for a long time—windows open, hearts open, her head on his shoulder, his thumb tracing circles against her thigh. Everything unspoken settled quietly between them, not needing to be rushed.

Because they had time now.

And this time, they weren't wasting it.

Ali stayed curled against Dylan's chest, her eyes watching the Spanish moss sway from the old cypress trees outside. The marsh shimmered in the fading light, all honey and shadow. His thumb kept tracing lazy circles on her thigh, grounding her in the moment—but also making her nervous.

Because she had to say it. Before they got too far. Before she got too lost in the warmth of him.

"Dylan," she said softly, pulling back just a little to look at him.

"Yeah?" he turned his head toward her, brows slightly furrowed, immediately picking up on her shift in tone.

She hesitated. Then looked down at their joined hands, her thumb brushing over his knuckle. "I'm...not ready to date you. Not out loud."

His jaw tightened slightly, and she saw him brace—just a flicker, but it was there.

"It's not you," she rushed. "I mean...geez, it's not. I like you. I want this. I just...I'm scared."

Dylan didn't speak right away. He nodded slowly, waiting, giving her space. Letting her fill in the silence on her own terms.

"In college," she said, voice catching. "After people found out. Daisy, her friends...everyone just turned on me. Like I was the villain. Like I wasn't good enough for you."

"You were always good enough for me," Dylan said fiercely.

"But nobody saw it that way," she whispered. "And I couldn't handle it. I let them make me feel small. Like I didn't belong with you. And I guess I never really stopped believing it."

He reached out, brushing a piece of stray hair behind her ear. "Ali..."

"I don't want the attention," she said, trying not to cry. "The whispers. The looks. People comparing me to whatever imaginary version of a girl they think you should be with. I—I know I'm not that."

"You're exactly who I want," he said. "I don't give a damn what anyone else thinks."

She smiled a little, but it was shaky. "I need time. I need to feel...strong in this. In us. Before it's anyone else's business."

Dylan let out a long breath, then leaned in and pressed his forehead to hers. "Okay," he said. "We'll do it your way. Whatever you need."

"You're not mad?"

"I'm mad people made you feel like you had to hide," he said, brushing his lips over her temple. "But I'm not mad at you. I'll wait. I'll protect this. And you."

Ali closed her eyes, letting the promise settle deep in her chest. It wasn't everything yet, but it was something real. Something steady.

She opened her eyes again and looked at him. "Just...don't stop texting me dirty things in the meantime."

He grinned, all dimples and heat. "I was planning on doubling down, actually."

That made her laugh—soft, a little teary, but real. She leaned in, kissed him slow and grateful, and finally let herself breathe.

Afterglow

Dylan

The next morning, Dylan pulled into the Rise and Grind parking lot and glanced sideways at Ali, sitting prim and proper in the passenger seat. Hands twisting together and pulling at her hemline. She looked like sunshine in her sleeveless Lilly Pulitzer dress—pink and green floral print, the kind that made her blue eyes look even brighter. A white headband pushed her hair off her face, her soft golden curls tucked behind her ears, and she had on little pearl earrings that probably came from her mama's jewelry box.

She was all buttoned-up Southern charm, but he knew what her mouth had done last night—and god, if that didn't mess with his head a little.

He was undercover in a baseball cap, brim pulled low and a MBU hoodie. He would probably pass out from heat exhaustion in it, but he wanted Ali to get coffee with him before he left town.

"You sure you're not gonna get coffee on your cute dress?" he teased, letting his hand brush her bare knee before she opened the door.

"I have Shout Wipes in my bag," she said, then added with a smile, "And backup shoes in my desk. I'm not new at this."

They stepped inside the café, the air cool and filled with the smell of espresso and baked goods. She tucked into his side just slightly, almost unconsciously, and he loved the quiet way she leaned into him in public—like maybe she wasn't ready to hold his hand across town, but she wanted to let him know she was his.

They waited in line, and Dylan took the opportunity to poke at her nerves.

"You always this weird the morning after? That's changed since college."

Ali blinked up at him, startled. "I'm not being weird."

"You're being shy. It's cute."

"I have a meeting at nine," she deflected, smoothing the front of her dress like it might suddenly wrinkle.

He leaned down and whispered, "You're glowing."

"I'm not."

"You are."

"Shut up."

"You look like someone who had her mouth full last night."

She gasped, eyes wide. "Dylan."

He bit back a grin. "Just saying."

She swatted his arm and finally laughed, her whole face softening. That sound always undid him.

They were next in line when the door opened behind them. The bell jingled, light and cheery, but his body stiffened before he even turned around.

Voices.

One in particular. His hand immediately went to her back. Protective instincts taking over.

"Well damn," Daisy said sweetly behind them. "This is unexpected."

Ali froze beside him. She didn't turn. Didn't speak. Her hands clutched the strap of her purse so tight her knuckles went white.

Dylan turned slowly, shielding her with his body.

Daisy stood a few feet back, sunglasses propped on her head. Laila beside her blinked, not yet realizing what she'd walked into.

Ali stepped forward to order, her voice too quiet to carry. Dylan stayed close, paid without letting her reach for her card, and handed her the latte.

Then Daisy spoke again.

"Ali."

Ali didn't look up.

"Ali, please. Just for a second—"

Dylan rounded on his sister, his voice low and firm. "No."

Daisy blinked. "I wasn't—"

"I said no. Don't do this. Not now. Not here."

Ali finally turned, shoulders back, chin trembling. "I have to get to work."

She said it like she was trying to keep from shaking. Like if she just stayed on script—coffee, commute, meeting—she'd be fine.

Dylan stepped between them. "We're leaving."

Daisy looked like she might cry. "You're not even going to let me say anything?"

"Not to her." His voice was sharp. "If you want to talk to me, you know how to find me. But you keep her out of it."

Laila stayed silent, watching all three of them like someone who'd just stepped into the middle of a play without knowing the script.

Dylan took Ali's elbow gently, leading her out the door. She let him.

They didn't speak until they reached the Bronco. He opened her door, helped her in, then got behind the wheel and just...sat there. Letting her breathe.

She stared out the window, coffee untouched in her lap. "Well," she said, voice hoarse, "that was fun."

He glanced at her. "You okay?"

"I don't know."

"Want me to drive you to work? I've got time."

She gave him a tiny nod. "Yeah. I just kinda need my car."

"Can Ash pick you up later?"

"Okay, yeah. Or I'll get Abigail to drop me off at home."

He reached over and laced their fingers together on the center console. She didn't let go.

Dylan pulled up to the curb outside the pastel-bricked building where Ali worked, his Bronco idling in the loading zone as early morning traffic streamed by. She'd been quiet the whole ride, fingers absently tracing her cup, her coffee untouched.

He hated seeing her retreat like that. Hated how fast she curled into herself when the past showed up and demanded space she didn't owe it.

"I'm sorry," he said, finally breaking the silence.

Her eyes lifted. "It's not your fault."

"I still hate that it happened. She shouldn't have come over."

Ali nodded but didn't speak.

Dylan leaned over the console. "She's leaving today. Headed back to Atlanta. With Laila and their kids."

That seemed to land. Her shoulders dropped half an inch.

"I wouldn't have brought you there if I thought she'd show up," he added. "I meant what I said. You come first."

Ali looked at him then, eyes big and glassy, like she was trying to believe him.

He reached up and tucked a strand of hair behind her ear, then rested his palm lightly on her cheek. "Hey."

"Hmm?"

"I'm proud of you," he said softly. "I know this morning sucked, but you handled it the best you could."

Ali blinked fast. "You always say the right things."

"Only when it's true."

She gave him a wobbly smile, then reached for the door handle.

"Wait," he said, voice low.

She turned, confused, just as he leaned in and kissed her.

Not a polite goodbye peck. Not a quick, closed-mouth thing.

A long, slow, lips-parting, breath-stealing kiss.

The kind that made time slow down.

The kind that made her melt toward him, hand bracing against his chest, lips soft and sweet under his.

The kind that said *you're mine*, without rushing her for more.

When he finally pulled back, his voice was rough.

"Text me when you're done today. I'll be back soon. I promise."

She nodded, dazed. "Okay."

He grinned. "And drink your coffee, Al. It's the antidote to your little weird vibe you have going on," he teased her.

She laughed a little, rolling her eyes. "There's no weird vibe. And I forgot to grab a straw," she finished, rolling her eyes.

"No problem, babe." He leaned across the car and grabbed a straw from the glove compartment, "I got you."

He watched her walk up the steps in her little dress and headband, confident again, like maybe the kiss helped her remember who she was.

Two meetings, three spreadsheets, one very weird office birthday cake. Survived.

You?

Stopped by my parents this morning to see my family before leaving town.

Interstate chaos, but I made it to Daytona. Just stopped to get gas.

Still thinking about that goodbye kiss though

Oh, that wasn't a goodbye kiss. That was a "please don't make me walk into the office feeling lonely" kiss.

Also…random question. Who's Laila?

Laila?
Daisy's wife. Why?

Wait—Daisy's married…

…to a woman?

I didn't know that.

And they have kids?

Yeah. For about five years now. They adopted three years ago. A brother and sister. Liam and Lillie.

Wow. I had no idea.

I don't mean that in a mean or like gossipy way—I just never heard anything about her life after I left MB. I guess I just didn't care what she did after I left.

You're not being gossipy. It makes sense you'd be surprised. It was a shock to me too at first, but Laila's really good for her. Grounds her.

I'm glad to hear that. It's just…a lot to process, I guess.

Yeah. There's a lot about Daisy that people didn't see back then.

Was she angry with me? For not seeing her? I mean, was it kind of my fault?

No baby. I won't let you think like that. Nothing was your fault. Just because things may have been more than we realized doesn't erase what you went through. I want you to know that.

Thank you.

It means a lot, honestly.

I've spent a long time wondering if anyone else remembered how bad it really was.

And I still don't want to talk to her.

I remember.

And I hate that I didn't do more to stop it.

But I'm here now. And I'm not going anywhere.

I'm still getting used to letting myself believe that…but I know.

And you never have to do something you are uncomfortable with. Not ever. One day at a time, Al.

He smiled at the screen, thumb hovering for a second before he finally locked it and tossed the phone into the passenger seat. The pump clicked behind him, the tank full. He returned the nozzle, slapped the gas cap shut, and climbed back into his Bronco, the familiar creak of the leather seat grounding him.

He could've flown back from Savannah—everyone asked why he didn't. But it was only five hours to Orlando. Less if traffic was light. And truthfully, he loved to drive. The rhythm of the interstate, the solitude of his vehicle, the silence between playlists and pit stops—it gave his mind room to settle. Reset.

The sun was high now—hot, relentless. Daytona heat had its own kind of bite, different from the coastal softness of Peach Cove and Honeyshore. He wiped his palm across his brow, cranked the A/C, then reached for his phone again—it felt like a Brantley Gilbert kind of moment.

"More Than Miles." Of course.

The guitar licks filled the cabin as he pulled back onto I-95, merging into traffic with one hand on the wheel and the other on the gearshift. He popped the sunroof open, letting the sky pour in. A long stretch of I-4 still lay ahead, but the road didn't feel heavy.

Ali's words—*I'm still getting used to letting myself believe that*—kept looping in his head. He wasn't going to rush her. But he wasn't going to let her go again, either.

The wind whipped through the open roof as he sped south, Orlando-bound, the chorus bleeding through the speakers and his chest.

By the time Dylan hit the outskirts of Orlando, the late afternoon sun had dipped into that golden stretch that made everything look a little cinematic. He turned off Brantley, letting the silence settle again as downtown came into view through the windshield. Home.

He pulled into his garage just after six, the Bronco rumbling to a stop. The house was cool and quiet inside—just the way he liked it after a few days of constant conversation. He tossed his bag on the entry bench, grabbed a sports drink from the fridge, and dropped down onto the couch. A few unread texts blinked on his screen, but he bypassed them and dialed the one number he knew would expect a check-in.

"Kallie," he said when she picked up. "Just got in."

"You alive?" she teased. "I figured you'd text from the road like a normal human, but I guess we're doing this the old-fashioned way."

"I'm a man of tradition," he deadpanned.

"Uh-huh. So? How'd it go?"

Kallie's voice was casual, but he heard the edge beneath it. She'd seen him that night. Seen Ali. Seen what it had done to him.

Dylan leaned back into the cushions, letting his head fall against the back of the couch. "It went..." he exhaled. "Better than I expected. Fundraiser went above our projected goal. Everyone clapped. I didn't trip over the podium. You were there, remember?"

Kallie snorted. "Not what I meant and you know it. I left you alone out there for a reason, Mac. What happened after I covered for you?"

He closed his eyes for a second, fingers tightening around the neck of his water bottle. "She was in the parking lot. Behind someone's SUV, sitting on the pavement. Could barely breathe." His voice dropped, almost reverent. "I found her. Talked her down."

Silence stretched between them, but not uncomfortably.

"And since then?" Kallie asked gently.

"We've been...talking." A pause. "Seeing each other." Then, a faint smile tugged at his lips. "More than talking, really."

Kallie's hum was laced with amusement. "So, she's not a ghost anymore."

"No." That part came out without hesitation. "She's real. Still the most genuine person I've ever met. Still funny. Still gorgeous. And still way too good for me."

"Dramatic much?" Kallie teased. But then she softened. "I'm glad, Mac. Truly. You were...lost for a long time. I think I forgot what you sounded like when you were grounded."

He let her words settle. They both knew the version of him that came out of college wasn't the same one she met when he was a Freshman. Football had saved him. But it hadn't healed him.

"She's scared," he admitted quietly. "Worried about what people would say. About going public."

Kallie hesitated. "And what do *you* want?"

Dylan didn't flinch. "Her." Then softer: "In whatever way she'll let me have her."

After the call ended, Dylan tossed his phone onto the coffee table and stretched out on the couch. For all the emotion he'd carried on the drive home, the house now felt...still. Like it was waiting with him.

Eventually, curiosity got the better of him. He leaned forward, grabbed his phone again, and thumbed through his unread texts. One stood out—Rocky, his teammate and longtime friend.

Rocky:

> Yo. Fourth of July. Our place. Naomi's already planning the whole damn thing—red, white, and bougie. You in?

Dylan smirked. He could already picture Naomi, looking like Vivica A. Fox's clone, going all out with themed drinks, an inflatable waterslide, and probably a sparkler choreography that'd make the halftime show jealous.

Rocky and Naomi had been his people from the moment he was drafted. They were the kind of couple who reminded him what stability looked like—ride-or-die, no drama, just constant love and brutally honest advice.

He tapped out a reply.

> Depends. Might be back in Honeyshore.

The bubbles appeared instantly.

> Honeyshore?? Mac, you never go home. What's in Honeyshore?

Dylan paused, staring at the screen.

Then typed.

> Something I should've never left behind.

He didn't even have time to lock his screen before his phone lit up again—this time with an incoming call from Rocky. *Of course.*

Dylan sighed, chuckled under his breath, and answered.

"Jesus, Rock, you couldn't just text?"

"You drop *that* bomb and expect a *text* reply?" Rocky's voice boomed, already loud and amplified by the telltale echo of speakerphone.

"Hi Mac!" Naomi chimed sweetly in the background. "We want details. Who is she?"

He dragged a hand down his face, leaning his head back on the couch cushion. "Y'all are too much."

"No," Rocky said, mock-stern. "You're too much. You're over here talking about *something you should've never left behind,* like you're a damn country song. Spill it."

"Yeah," Naomi added. "You sound like a man who's been *wrecked.* I know that tone."

Dylan laughed despite himself, trying to sidestep, heat creeping up his neck. "It's not like that."

"Bullshit," they both said at the same time.

Naomi continued, "You've barely looked twice at anyone since you got drafted. And now you're skipping parties, driving home, disappearing off the grid for a weekend—don't act like we're not gonna put two and two together."

He paused, then said carefully, "It's someone from back home. From college."

"Oooh," Naomi whispered like she'd just opened a good book. "A college sweetheart."

Rocky groaned. "Damn, Mac. This is serious."

"I didn't say that," Dylan replied quickly, though his voice lacked conviction. "We're just...catching up."

"Right," Rocky deadpanned. "And I'm just a tight end."

Naomi laughed, and Dylan could hear the clink of a wine glass in the background.

"Look," he said, running a hand through his hair. "It's complicated."

"Then we'll let it slide *this once,*" Naomi said, all warmth. "But if this turns into something real, we get to meet her."

"And approve her," Rocky added.

Dylan snorted. "Thanks for the support. Real subtle."

"You're welcome," Naomi sang.

Rocky added, "Just don't forget—Fourth of July. If you're around, we're throwing down. If not, you better have a damn good excuse. And MBU mystery princess is on the list now."

"Got it," Dylan said, smiling now.

"And Mac?" Rocky's voice dropped low. "If she's the real thing...don't screw it up."

Dylan's heart knocked hard in his chest. He didn't say anything.

He didn't have to.

Guilty As Sin

Ali

Ali had just crawled into bed, Kindle still propped open on her lap, when her phone buzzed. Her heart did a little jump at the contact name.

Dylan

She debated letting it ring but answered after a beat, biting her lip to hide the smile in her voice.

"Hey."

"Hey yourself," he said, voice already low and smooth. "Did I wake you?"

"Nope. Just finished reading a chapter. And by chapter I mean a particularly spicy scene."

"Oh yeah?" He chuckled. "Am I gonna have to start competing with fictional men now?"

She snorted. "Please. You already won that war back in college."

There was a pause, followed by a grin in his tone. "That sounds dangerously close to a compliment, Presley."

"Maybe I'm feeling generous."

"Good," he drawled. "Because I've been thinking about you all damn day."

Heat flushed her cheeks. "You always this charming after a drive home?"

"Nah," he said. "Just after I spend ten hours wishing I had your thighs draped across my lap again."

"Dylan..."

"Mmm. There she goes. That little breathy voice you get when you're embarrassed but turned on. Still my favorite."

Ali rolled onto her side, pressing the phone closer. "You shouldn't say things like that."

"Why not?"

"Because you know I'm gonna start overthinking everything again."

"Nah," he said gently. "No spiraling tonight. Just you and me."

She was quiet for a moment, her voice barely a whisper when she said, "What are you thinking about right now?"

"Honestly?" His voice dropped another octave. "I'm thinking about how soft you sounded the other night. When you whispered my name with your mouth full."

Ali inhaled and buried her face in her pillow.

"Dylan."

"Ali. Don't go shy on me now," he teased, voice honeyed heat. "I want you to think about it, too. About how good you made me feel. About how fucking proud I was of you."

Her breath caught.

"I could hear it in your voice," he continued. "You wanted to please me. And baby...you *did.*"

She didn't know what possessed her to say it, but the words slipped out before she could stop them.

"I want to do it again."

His sharp inhale crackled through the line. "Yeah?"

"Uh-huh."

He groaned softly. "Then don't make me wait too long. Because next time...I'm going to take *my* time."

Ali squeezed her thighs together, biting her lip.

"Goodnight, Ali."

"Goodnight, Dylan."

"...Sweet dreams, baby."

She hung up with a stupid grin still spread across her face.

She'd been staring at the same page for over an hour.

The book was good—great, even—but her brain wouldn't settle. Not when every time she blinked, she could still hear his voice in her ear. The things he'd said. The way he'd said them. It was like her body was still tuned to the exact frequency of his voice.

She sighed, flipping the page even though she hadn't absorbed a single word. The soft glow of her Kindle illuminated the room, casting faint shadows across her ceiling.

She should sleep. She had an early meeting. She'd already brushed her teeth and double-checked the alarm and fluffed her pillow five times. But her brain wasn't cooperating.

Then her phone buzzed on the nightstand.

Her heart jumped.

> You awake?

She bit her lip, pulse quickening. She reached for the phone.

> Yeah. Still up. Can't sleep.

Three dots appeared almost instantly.

> Me neither. I tried. I even made tea like an eighty-year-old man.

She smiled in the dark.

> Did it help?

> Not even a little. Kept thinking about that call. And how I was semi-hard just hearing your voice.

She dropped the phone on her chest for a second, palms pressed to her burning cheeks. *Gawd.*

The screen dimmed and she scrambled to tap it back on. Her thumbs hovered over the keyboard, then—

> You're not supposed to say stuff like that when I'm trying to be good.

> Oh, Al. You have no idea how bad I want to ruin that plan.

Her thighs clenched under the blanket.

She swallowed hard and set the phone beside her for a second, staring at the ceiling like it could help her breathe normally again.

But it was no use. The mental replay of his voice—low and rough, teasing and tender—was already running wild through her mind.

She grabbed the phone again, heart in her throat.

> Dylan, Seriously. You CANNOT say things like that when I'm lying here in just a t-shirt and panties.

She hesitated after hitting send. Her whole face flushed. *Gawd, did I just say that?*

The three dots blinked. And blinked.

Then:

> You're really trying to kill me, huh?
>
> Are you touching yourself right now, baby?

Her breath caught. She was warm all over. Squirming.

She bit her lip and typed slowly.

> No…but I've been thinking about it since you said my voice turns you on.

There. Honest. Bold—for her.

> That's because it does.
>
> You don't even have to talk dirty. Just whisper my name like you used to and I'm done.

Her hand drifted down, the ache building now that her mind had permission to go there. Her pulse thundered in her ears as her fingertips grazed the hem of her old tee—slid under it.

She whimpered softly.

The phone buzzed again.

> Tell me what you're thinking about.

She pressed her thighs together again, curling onto her side.

> You. Against that wall again.
>
> How hard you kissed me. How your hands were everywhere.
>
> How good you felt when you were inside me.

Three dots. Then a pause.

Fuck. Ali…call me now. Put the phone on speaker. I need to hear you.

Her breath hitched. Her whole body lit up.

She stared at the phone. Chewed her lip.

Her finger trembled as it hovered over the green button, heart pounding like a drum in her chest. But the way he asked, well told her—*"Put the phone on speaker. I need to hear you."*—something about it made her feel brave.

She tapped *Call* and brought the phone close, switching to speaker and laying it on the pillow beside her.

It only had half a ring.

Then—

"Hey, baby," Dylan said, voice low and warm, rough like gravel and sleep. Like she'd dragged him out of a dream where he had his mouth on her and didn't want to let go.

Ali's whole body shivered.

"Hi," she whispered.

Silence settled for a moment—thick, intimate, crackling with want.

"You touching yourself, baby?" he asked.

Her thighs clenched. She shook her head instinctively, then realized how pointless it was.

"Not yet," she breathed.

"Why the hell not?" His voice dipped, deeper now. Slower. That Southern rasp curling around every word like heat off pavement. "You just told me you were thinking about the wall again. Don't you want to feel good?"

"I do…"

"Then let me show you how good you can make yourself feel."

Ali exhaled shakily, her body already buzzing just from the sound of him.

"Take your shirt off," he said. "Now."

She obeyed, sliding her hands under the hem and tugging it over her head. Cool air kissed her skin. Her nipples were already tight, aching.

"It's off," she whispered.

He groaned softly. "God, I wish I could see you. Bet you're so fucking pretty right now."

Her cheeks flushed.

"Lie back," he said. "Nice and slow. Get comfortable. I want you spread out for me."

She leaned back into the pillows.

"Are you there?"

"I'm here," she whispered.

"Good. Now I want you to pinch those nipples for me."

Her fingers trembled as she obeyed. The jolt of sensation stole her breath.

"Gawd, Dylan…"

"There she is," he murmured. "That feel good?"

She nodded. "Yeah."

"Roll them a little. Gentle at first. Then harder."

Ali gasped, hips twitching as the pull of pleasure spread between her thighs.

"Now," he said, voice turning to velvet, "slide your other hand down. Nice and slow. Over your stomach, between your thighs."

She moved without hesitation now—needy, breathless, desperate to feel what he was giving her.

"Inside your panties?" he asked.

"Yeah," she whispered. "I'm already wet."

"Fuck," he groaned. "Push two fingers in. Let me hear what you sound like when you do it."

She whimpered the moment she breached herself, the stretch of it almost too much after thinking about him all day.

"There you go," he said, voice wrecked. "Nice and slow. In and out. You feel that?"

"Yes…"

"That's all you, baby," he said. "That's how good you make yourself feel. For me. Just from my voice."

Ali moaned, her fingers moving in a rhythm now, her other hand still teasing her nipple. Her body felt like fire under her skin.

"Rub your clit with your palm," he instructed gently. "Don't rush. Make it last."

Her hips rocked. She bit her lip to keep from crying out.

"Are you close, baby?"

"Yeah," she gasped. "Dylan, please…"

"You sound so fucking perfect," he growled. "I wish I could see you. I'd hold your thighs open and watch every second. I'd kiss you right there. Taste you until you couldn't take anymore. But right now, I want you to give it to me. Let go for me."

She whimpered, fingers moving faster now, everything building, tightening.

"That's it," he whispered. "Come for me, Ali. Let me hear you."

And she did.

With a cry that broke open in her chest, she came hard, her body shuddering, her voice tangled with his name.

The world spun, then stilled.

Her breath came in gasps. But Dylan didn't speak right away.

He just *stayed*.

There. Steady. Warm. Silent in the softest, most loving way.

"Still think that kiss was just for goodbye?" he teased, voice gentler now.

She laughed, still flushed and trembling. "That was *so* not a goodbye kiss."

"Damn right it wasn't."

She smiled, eyes fluttering closed. "I miss you already."

He exhaled like her words had wrapped around his ribs.

"Then don't go." Dylan didn't hesitate. "I'll stay on the phone with you all night."

Ali smiled at the ceiling, the sound of his breath on the line anchoring her in a way nothing else could. She curled onto her side, one arm tucked under the pillow, the other draped around her phone like it was a tether to him.

They talked about her book club—how Raleigh Ann *hated* the spicy fantasy they just finished but Abigail was obsessed. About work, too, and how her client's idea of submitting "supporting documentation" was a handwritten sticky note and a Twix wrapper.

She rambled until her voice got slower. Sleepier. She couldn't stop yawning.

"Still with me, babe?" Dylan's voice came through, a low hum in her ear.

"Mhm. Just resting my eyes," she mumbled.

"I'll talk. You just listen, okay?"

She hummed again in agreement, letting his voice wash over her. He told her about a rookie on the team last year who thought almond milk came from brown cows. About Rocky's kid accidentally setting off the sprinkler system at the stadium with a toy lightsaber. She giggled softly, lips curving as she burrowed deeper under the blankets.

Then a beat passed. A shift in tone.

"Can I ask you something, babe?" Dylan asked, voice soft but steady through the phone.

Ali rolled to her back, blinking at the ceiling as her heart picked up speed. "Yeah?"

A pause.

"How long has it been for you?"

Her breath caught. "What do you mean?"

"You know what I mean."

She exhaled, trying to laugh it off. "Why? Trying to calculate my stats like one of your game recaps?"

"Ali."

She didn't answer, fingers toying with the edge of the blanket.

When the silence stretched, she cleared her throat. "How long has it been for you?"

He didn't hesitate. "Over a year."

She blinked. "Seriously?"

"Yeah. Why?"

"I don't know." She tugged the blanket higher. "You're a professional football player. It's just...hard to believe."

He snorted, not amused. "So that makes me a man-whore?"

Ali winced, the weight of her own words crashing into her. "No—I didn't mean it like that. I'm sorry."

He didn't say anything right away.

She rushed to fill the space. "Can we just forget it? It doesn't matter, right?"

"It matters to me," he said gently but firmly. "Ali, I was inside you a few nights ago. You were so goddamn tight it nearly broke me. And then later, when you said you'd never given head before..."

Her cheeks flamed.

"I'm not trying to embarrass you," he added quickly. "I just want to understand. I want *you* to trust me with the truth."

Her eyes welled unexpectedly, her chest aching with pressure she couldn't name.

"Ali?" he said again, quieter this time.

She let out a long breath. "I haven't been with anyone since you."

His breath hitched.

"I've kissed guys. Let them touch me. But I always pulled away before it went further. I just...I didn't trust anyone like I trusted you. And I didn't want anyone else to have *that* part of me."

She paused, eyes fixed on the ceiling as a tear slid down her temple.

"You were too important. What we had was too big. I couldn't take it and...and give it to someone else just to feel something again."

Silence.

Then his voice, thick with something he wasn't hiding: "Jesus, Ali."

"I know it's weird—"

"No. Baby, no. That's not weird. That's...fuck, that's beautiful. And devastating. And I don't deserve to be the only one you've ever trusted with that."

She bit her lip, tears slipping freely now.

"But I am so goddamn honored that I was."

Ali turned on her side, pressing the phone tighter to her ear, like maybe it could close the miles between them.

"I think part of me always believed...if I waited long enough, maybe we'd find our way back."

"We did."

And with that, she smiled—soft and sleepy and safe. "We did."

Right Where You Left Me

Dylan

The phone call ended, and Dylan lay in the darkness, his heart still racing from the sounds of Ali's breath, her voice soft and hushed as she let him guide her through bringing herself to an orgasm. She'd admitted it, in the quietest whisper, just as the tension faded between them: she hadn't been with anyone else.

No one but him.

The words settled deep inside him, heavy with meaning. A claim. A connection. It sent a wave of possessiveness rushing through him, but it's not just that. It's something deeper. Something more essential. He's not the only one still holding on, and the thought of leaving it all unresolved gnaws at him.

Dylan stares up at the ceiling, the weight of the night pressing on his chest. He doesn't know how long he lies there, staring into the blackness, but the minutes bleed into hours. By 3 AM, the thought is clear: *I'm going to Honeyshore. Right now.*

There's no doubt anymore. No second-guessing. Training Camp's still weeks away, and he can't waste another day. His mind races with the desire to get to her, to surprise her, to remind her just how much she means to him. She's always had his heart, but now, more than ever, it feels like he's been holding back—stuck between fear and wanting something real.

Dylan swings his legs over the edge of the bed, his feet hitting the cool floor. He stands in the dim light of his room, the world outside still dark, still quiet, while the adrenaline buzzes through his veins. Without even thinking, he grabs his phone and starts booking the flight. Savannah. Early morning flight. He'll get there in a few hours, rent a car, and drive to Honeyshore.

He's doing this. No hesitation. No playing it safe.

By 4:30 AM, he's out the door, the hot air hitting his face as he slides into the Uber. His heart pounds, but it's not fear—it's anticipation. The world's still asleep, the streets empty as they head toward MCO. He doesn't know what to expect once he gets to Honeyshore. He doesn't even know how Ali will react. But it doesn't matter. All that matters is that he's with her.

The ride feels too quick, but by the time he pulls up to the airport, Dylan's nerves are still buzzing, just underneath the surface. He grabs his bag from the trunk, steps into the terminal, and heads straight to his gate. He can't believe he's doing this. But then again, he can't believe he left her yesterday.

By now, the sun has fully risen, casting a warm light across the highway as Dylan drives through the rolling fields of Georgia. It's almost 8:00 AM. He's getting closer. His stomach churns with anticipation as he rolls into the outskirts of Honeyshore.

He picks up his phone, fingers trembling slightly as he scrolls through his contacts. Ashley Palmer, Ali's cousin and best friend, pops up on the screen. She's an attorney, tough as nails, and someone Dylan knows won't sugarcoat anything. If anyone can help him pull off this surprise, it's Ashley.

He hits dial and watches the road ahead as the phone rings.

The line picks up after a couple of rings.

"Dylan McKenzie, if you're calling me before 9 AM, somebody better be dead or proposing." Ashley's voice is warm but professional—she's already at work, probably in the middle of something important.

"Ash," he says quickly, trying to sound casual but failing to hide the nervousness in his tone. "Listen, I need your help."

There's a slight pause, and Dylan can almost hear the raised eyebrow through the phone.

"Help? With what? What's going on?" Ashley's voice has that sharp edge of a lawyer who's already prepared for something complicated.

Dylan inhales deeply, steadying himself. "I'm on my way back to Honeyshore."

Ashley's initial skepticism is clear in her response. "You just left yesterday Dylan. What's up?"

Dylan laughs a little, his hands tightening on the wheel. "I know, I know. But I couldn't stand it, Ash. I've got to do this. She still has my whole heart. But I'm...I'm nervous. I don't want to freak her out."

Ashley's silence stretches between them for a moment, and then, to his surprise, she sighs, a soft exhale of a breath that shows she's giving it some thought.

"I've seen how much she's been smiling the last few days, Dylan," she admits quietly. "I know some of what's been going on between you two, and...she's been happier. I'll help you, but you've got to be careful. If you show up at her office like a dramatic rom-com scene, she'll lose it. She won't handle it well. Trust me."

Dylan's stomach does a flip at her words. He's not trying to be dramatic, but he *is* trying to be bold. "Right, okay no office...so, what do you think?"

Ashley doesn't hesitate. "Let's ease into it. You check into your hotel in Honeyshore, and then I'll meet you at Kroger. We'll get everything you need to make her dinner. It'll be casual, and she won't feel like you're throwing her a curveball. I'll make sure we pick out all her favorite stuff, too."

Dylan nods to himself, even though Ashley can't see him. It makes sense. He can already picture Ali's face lighting up at the thought of him cooking for her. "That sounds perfect," he says, the relief in his voice obvious.

Ashley's voice softens, a hint of warmth behind her words. "One thing, though. She's still allergic to papayas. Don't forget that."

"Got it," Dylan says with a chuckle. "No papayas. Thanks, Ash. I really appreciate this," Dylan says, feeling more at ease as they talk through the details. "I want it to be perfect."

"No problem," Ashley replies, her voice now steady and confident. "I'll stay away from the house tonight. I'll crash at Brant's place, give you two some space. I'll give you the code to our door, so you can beat her home. Just make sure you're not...overwhelming her, okay?"

"I won't," Dylan promises, his heart swelling with gratitude. "Thanks again, Ash. I owe you one."

"No, you owe me like ten," she teases, but there's affection in her voice. "But I'll let you have it for free since I'm 100% Team Dali. Always have been."

Dylan smiles to himself as he ends the call. His heart races as he gets closer to Honeyshore. This surprise, this dinner—it's his chance to show Ali everything he's felt all these years. No more waiting. He's finally going to make his move.

Labyrinth

Ali

Ali grips the steering wheel tighter as she makes her way home, her eyes flicking to the rearview mirror every few seconds, even though there's no one behind her. Her mind races—too many thoughts crammed into a single space. She hasn't heard from Dylan all day. Not a text, not a call. Nothing.

Did I say too much last night? Was I too much?

She gnaws on her bottom lip, trying to push the thought away, but it lingers. She'd been so honest, so raw with him about how she hadn't been with anyone since him. Her pulse still raced at the memory of how vulnerable she felt saying those words out loud. And now, as the day stretched into the late afternoon, she feels the weight of it all—of her feelings for him, of her fear of scaring him away.

She knows she shouldn't feel this anxious. She's a grown woman. But it's Dylan. And for some reason, with him, it always feels different. Like maybe, just maybe, this time could be *real.*

Had I been be too clingy...

The thought makes her wince. After last night's phone call, where she'd practically bared her soul and literally let him listen to her pleasuring herself, she didn't want to come across as needy or desperate. So she hasn't texted him today. She'd resisted the urge to reach out But now, as the minutes drag on, that familiar anxiety churns in her stomach.

She can't help herself. She pulls out her phone, unlocking it and scrolling to Ashley's name. *Maybe she'll know what to do.*

Ali hesitates for a moment before hitting send, typing:

The "too soon" feels ridiculous as soon as she types it. She's overthinking again. But she can't help it. Every time she tries to make sense of what's between her and Dylan, the uncertainty creeps in.

As she pulls into the driveway, she sighs in frustration, her eyes scanning the empty spot where Ashley's car usually sits. *Of course, she's not here right now.*

A heavy sigh escapes her lips. She could really use someone to talk to, but Ashley's not home. Ali turns off the engine, staring blankly at the steering wheel for a moment.

She's tired. Summer at the firm isn't slow—it's tax extensions, mid-year reviews, and clients who think "quick question" means an hour of unpaid work. Her brain is fried from numbers and niceties, her shoulders sore from carrying everyone else's bottom line. Her mind exhausted. She doesn't even feel like dealing with the texts or the anxiety or whatever's going on between her and Dylan right now. She just needs a shower. A minute to clear her head.

The humid air hits her as she steps out of her white Grand Cherokee and heads inside.

Her phone buzzes in her hand. She doesn't check it, though—she can't. The weight of the day is too much, and right now, all she wants is to feel the warm water wash away the tension. She walks toward her bathroom, the uncertainty of the day still hanging over her.

The sound of the water still echoes in her ears as she steps from the shower and wraps her hair up, staring at her reflection in the mirror.

A few stray tears streak down her face, leaving damp trails against her skin. She's embarrassed—*so embarrassed*—that she let herself get carried away with Dylan last night, that she let him talk her through such an intimate, vulnerable moment. And now, this. The silence. The waiting.

Why did I let him do that?

Her chest tightens as she recalls the phone call, the way his voice had guided her, calm and steady, through the waves of desire, and how, at the end, she'd been so honest with him, telling him she hadn't been with anyone else. That she'd only ever had sex with him.

Why did I say that?

She never wanted to admit it, not to herself, let alone him. But last night, in the midst of everything, it had slipped out. And now, she felt exposed. *Too much.*

Ali's breath catches as the weight of it all crashes down on her. The phone call had felt like such a connection, like a moment where they were really *there* with each other. But now, as the tears start to trickle down her cheeks, she feels foolish.

Why had I let him push me? Why had I let him into that part of me so easily? And now, he's gone quiet. She hasn't heard from him since, and the silence eats at her. *Did I scare him away? Was I too much?*

With trembling hands, she grabs her towel from the bathroom hook and wraps it tighter around her body as she walks into her bedroom, her steps slow, heavy. The weight of the day still lingers—work, the anxiety, and now, her emotional mess. She crosses the room and sits cross-legged at the edge of her bed, her fingers curling into the fabric of her towel.

I'm such an idiot.

Her phone buzzes again, the vibration on her nightstand sending a small shock through her. She glances at it, but the moment feels too fragile. She doesn't want to look. Not yet. Not until she's figured out how to fix whatever it is she's messed up.

Her shoulders slump, the tears still streaking down her cheeks as she stares at the floor, feeling the weight of everything, the vulnerability, the desire, and the fear of rejection. Her heart aches—not just for Dylan, but for herself.

She wonders if this is how it always goes. She gives so much of herself, and then it's always the same: a moment of connection followed by a silence that feels louder than anything.

Ali wipes her face quickly, feeling embarrassed even in her own space. She feels like she should have known better, like she should have held back. But how can you hold back from someone who already knows *all of you?*

Ali's phone continues to ring, the vibrations on the nightstand relentless. Each buzz echoes in the quiet of the room, a reminder of the one person she's trying so desperately to ignore. Dylan. She won't pick up. She can't. Not now. Not when everything feels so raw.

Her hands tremble slightly as she wipes away the last of the tears, but they keep coming. She doesn't want to be weak. She doesn't want to seem desperate. *What the hell am I even doing?*

And then, as if the universe decided it had other plans, she hears it. That voice—so familiar, so *him*—cuts through the stillness.

"Are you going to answer me or not, babe?"

Ali jerks upright, her heart lurching in her chest. She hadn't heard him come in. But there he is.

Dylan.

He's standing barefoot in the doorway, his phone held out toward her like a lifeline. The concern on his face is immediate, his brow furrowed as he takes in the sight of her, still sitting on the edge of the bed, the towel barely clinging to her body, eyes red from crying.

For a moment, neither of them speaks. Time seems to slow. Ali's pulse races as the shock of seeing him so suddenly sends a wave of heat to her face. She doesn't know what to do with the mix of emotions crashing through her—the confusion, the relief, the vulnerability that she's never been able to hide when it comes to him.

Before she can say anything, Dylan's across the room in a few long strides, his arms wrapping around her. He doesn't wait for her to respond. He just pulls her into his lap, sitting on the edge of the bed, his body warmth immediately surrounding her.

"What happened?" he asks, his voice softer now, filled with concern as his hands gently cradle her face. His thumb wipes away the remnants of her tears, his eyes scanning hers, trying to understand the pain that's settled in her expression.

Ali can't hold back anymore. She lets out a shaky breath, her chest tight as she tries to pull herself together, but the tears start again. She doesn't want to cry in front of him—not like this—but it's impossible to stop.

"I—" She falters, her voice breaking. "I thought...I thought you were done with me. I thought I scared you away."

Dylan's face softens, a deep sadness in his eyes. His hands move to her back, rubbing soothing circles as he pulls her in closer.

"Hey," he murmurs gently, pressing his forehead to hers. "No, you didn't scare me away. I'm sorry for making you feel like you had to carry all this by yourself. I...I should've texted you. I shouldn't have left you hanging."

He cups her face in both hands now, looking at her like she's the only thing in the world that matters. "I'm not going anywhere, Ali. I never was. I'm sorry for making you doubt that. I just...needed to see you. To be here."

Ali's breath catches in her throat, his words soothing the sharp edges of her anxiety, but the weight of it all is still there. She leans into him, seeking comfort in his embrace. *How did he know? How did he always know when she was on the edge?*

"Dylan," she whispers, her voice still fragile. "I thought I'd...said too much. I told you things I haven't even told myself."

Dylan's eyes soften, and he presses a gentle kiss to her forehead. "You've never said too much to me, Ali. You've always been enough, always. I just...I didn't know how to fix things until now."

Dylan held her close, his hands gently stroking her back as they sit in the quiet of the room. The only sound is the soft rhythm of their breathing, steadying as the tension between them begins to ease.

He takes a deep breath, gathering his thoughts before speaking. "I didn't mean to hurt your feelings, Ali. I swear. I just...I didn't know how to do this without screwing it up. I was trying to surprise you."

Ali shifts slightly in his lap, her face still buried against his chest as she listens to him. Her hands, which had been clenched in the fabric of his shirt, slowly relax. His words, as simple as they are, are exactly what she needs to hear.

"I—" Dylan pauses, letting the words sink in. "I had this whole plan, you know? I talked to Ashley this morning. She helped me figure it out. I was so wound up about getting everything right, I didn't know how to tell you I was coming."

Ali lifts her head slightly, meeting his eyes, still unsure but listening intently. Dylan's gaze softens as he continues.

"I thought about calling you, but...I didn't want to spoil the surprise. I was so damn nervous. I literally planned this at 3am. I'm used to being all in control, but with you...it feels different. I wanted to get it right."

He shifts slightly, the words coming easier now, like a weight lifting from his chest. "So, I was outside at the grill, trying to get things ready for dinner. I thought you'd be home soon, but you were already in the shower before I even realized you'd come in."

Ali's brows furrow in confusion, her lips parting as she listens. Dylan chuckles softly, the sound warm but a little nervous.

"I called you, trying to tease you, to get your attention," he admits, a sheepish smile tugging at his lips. "But when you didn't pick up, I...I came looking for you, I didn't expect to find you here, looking like...well, like you were just having the worst time."

His voice softens, his hand brushing a stray lock of hair from her face. "I never meant to hurt your feelings, Ali. Never. I was just so wound up about everything going perfectly that I lost track of what really matters."

Ali's heart clenches as she listens to him. The way he explains himself—honest, sincere—finally makes sense. Her stomach knots with relief, but she still feels the sting of the earlier silence.

"I should've been more open with you," Dylan says, his voice low and apologetic. "I wasn't trying to ghost you. I swear, that wasn't it."

Ali sits up a little more, her fingers curling around his shirt. "You don't have to explain, Dylan. I...I get it now. I just—", she hesitates, swallowing hard. "I thought I messed things up. I thought maybe you didn't want me anymore."

Dylan's expression softens further, and he shakes his head quickly. "No. Never that. I've always wanted you, Ali. You're it for me. I just...got ahead of myself"

Ali gazes at him, the rawness of his words making her chest tighten. "I just want this to be real, you know?" she whispers, her voice thick with emotion.

"It is real, Ali," Dylan replies, his voice steady. "I'm here. I'm not going anywhere. I've never been more sure of anything in my life. But I'm sorry for making you doubt that."

He pulls her back into his arms, the moment feeling like the calm after the storm. Ali sighs, resting her head against his chest once more, feeling the weight of everything ease as Dylan continues to hold her, offering the reassurance she's been longing for.

Ali pulls away from Dylan's chest slowly, feeling the cool air of the room hit her flushed skin. Her heart beats in her throat, anticipation building as she looks into his eyes. There's something different now—something raw, a deep longing that neither of them can hide.

The moment feels surreal, but it's also right. The way his gaze never leaves her, the warmth of his touch, the way his breath hitches the second she shifts in his lap. She straddles him gently, her thighs pressing against him, and for the first time tonight, she feels fully *present*.

Ali pulls the towel wrap off her hair, letting the strands fall free, and watches Dylan's eyes darken at the movement. She can feel the heat radiating between them, the tension pulling tighter with every second.

Slowly, she shifts again. The shift in dynamic makes her pulse race faster. She leans forward just enough to press her lips softly to his, barely a touch, testing the waters.

Dylan's hands grip her waist, pulling her closer, his lips parting as he deepens the kiss. She feels him everywhere—his warmth, his desire, the way he holds her like he's afraid to let go.

False God

Dylan

He feels her—her warmth, her softness, the way she melts against him. Every inch of her is a perfect fit. His heart races in his chest as the desire for her consumes him, the world outside them fading into nothing.

God, she feels so good.

His hands slip from her waist to her back, pulling her even closer, his body aching for more. Her skin warm against his, and as their kiss deepens, Dylan can't help but groan against her mouth, tasting the sweetness of her and the heat that builds between them.

"Ali," he murmurs, his voice thick with need. He pulls back just enough to look at her, his hands trailing down her sides, savoring every curve, every inch of her. "You're perfect, you know that?"

Her breath catches, her chest rising and falling with each shaky inhale. She's beautiful—so beautiful—and Dylan's mind goes blank, focusing only on the woman in front of him, the way she makes him feel, the way she's breaking down every wall he's built around himself. He can't get enough of her.

He slides his hands to the curve of her hips, his fingers tightening as he lifts her slightly, bringing her closer. Her lips part in a soft gasp, her eyes flicking up to meet his, full of trust and longing.

"Tell me, Ali," he says, his voice low and rough, the hunger for her undeniable. "Tell me what you want."

Her eyes darken, her hands moving down to his chest, trailing down his abs to the waistband of his jeans, pulling his shirt over his head. "I want you. All of you. Right now."

Fuck.

Before he can even register what she's doing, she's already tugging the towel from her body, leaving herself completely exposed. Dylan's breath hitches, and without a second thought, he stands up, his hands moving quickly to strip off his jeans and boxers, letting them fall to the floor in a rush. Then he pauses.

Fuck, I took her without a condom the other night. What the hell was I thinking?

He moves quickly, grabbing a condom from his bag. As he walks back to the bed, his stomach tight with guilt, Ali's calm voice stops him.

"I'm on birth control, Dylan," she says, her eyes meeting his. "For the PCOS. Just like in college. We're safe if you don't want to use it."

He releases a breath, heart pounding with anticipation. He just takes a moment to look at her. She's breathtaking—her skin glowing, her body soft and perfect in every way.

Without hesitation, he lays back on the bed, pulling her gently with him, guiding her on top of him. He can feel the heat radiating from her, the slight tremble in her body. He watches her, his hands brushing her hair out of her face as she hovers above him, the anticipation making his chest tighten.

Dylan watches, his breath caught in his throat as she lowers herself onto him, her body trembling with nervousness and hesitation. He can feel the tightness of her, the way she pauses, taking him in slowly, adjusting. His hands find her hips, helping guide her down as she inches closer, her eyes flicking up to meet his for a moment of reassurance. Then, as her body sinks fully onto him, the feeling of her tightness takes him over, her movements slow but greedy, like she can't get enough. The way she moves—desperate but controlled—drives him wild, his hands tightening on her hips as he feels every inch of her. She's perfect, and he can't get enough of the way she's taking him.

"You're perfect," Dylan whispers, his voice low, husky with need. "Everything about you. Your pussy...baby, it's made for me. Made for me."

Ali's breath hitches, her body shuddering at the words. Dylan smirks, feeling her reaction inside her, his own body reacting to how tight and warm she feels around him.

"I can feel it," he growls, his hands moving to her hips, pulling her down onto him with more force, making her gasp. "Every time you move, I can feel your pussy tightening around me. When I talk to you like that, I feel you clench. You love it, don't you? You love hearing me talk to you like that."

The words hit her like a wave, and for a brief moment, she just stares at him. Her body shifts against him, her pulse quickening, her breath catching as she finally exhales, her hands gripping his chest for support. She looks down at him, her voice a little shaky, full of both embarrassment and undeniable desire.

Ali's breath hitches, her face flushing a deep red as she lifts her head to look at him. Her voice is small, unsure, a little embarrassed. "I...I do. But I don't know...it feels so...filthy."

Dylan's hands grip her waist, his thumbs brushing over her skin as he pulls her closer, urging her to relax into it. "Don't be embarrassed, baby," he says, his voice low and soothing, even as desire sharpens it. "You feel it, I can see it. Don't hide from it. Tell me what you feel. Tell me what you want."

"It feels so good, Dylan," she whispers, her hips moving instinctively against him. "Better than my fingers...so much better. So fucking good. I...I need more."

Dylan's breath hitches at her words, his body tightening with desire. He knows exactly what she's asking for, and he's more than willing to give it to her. Without hesitation, he flips them gently, guiding her onto her back with a soft but firm grip. His hands move to her legs, pulling one up around his waist, his cock already straining with need as he shifts between her thighs, ready to slide deeper.

She moans softly, her eyes locking onto his as he begins to move inside her, the heat of her tightening around him. He slides in slowly, letting her feel every inch, the stretch of her walls surrounding him, squeezing him. His body burns, but he holds back, letting her adjust to him, feeling her tightness clench as she tries to take more.

He stops, his breath coming in sharp gasps, feeling her so perfectly wrapped around him. He hangs on by a thread, fighting the urge to push deeper as she shifts beneath him, her body reacting to every movement. He waits, giving her time, knowing how much she wants him, how badly she needs this.

"Tell me when you're ready," he murmurs, his voice thick with desire, his hands gently stroking her skin as he waits for her to give him the signal to move again.

Ali's breath is ragged, her eyes locked onto his as her hands move to his chest, her nails scraping lightly over his skin. She smirks, a glint of raw desire in her gaze.

"Stop holding back, Dylan," she growls, her voice low and filled with urgency. "I'm not going to break. Fuck me. I want you—all of you."

The words hit him like a jolt of electricity. She's not holding back anymore, and neither is he. Dylan leans down, pressing a bruising kiss to her lips as he moves his hips, driving deeper into her, the feel of her tightness almost too much to bear.

Ali moans into the kiss, her legs tightening around his waist, urging him to go faster. "God, yes," she whispers against his mouth, "Fuck me harder, Dylan."

The command in her voice is too much for him to resist. Dylan moves faster, his hands gripping her hips as he pushes deeper, hearing the way she cries out in pleasure with every thrust. The sound of her words, her filthy encouragement, sends him spiraling.

"You're so fucking perfect, Ali," he groans, his voice rough, each thrust harder than the last. "Your pussy feels so fucking good on my cock. Like a goddam wet dream come to life."

Ali's body trembles beneath him, her nails digging into his back as she moves to meet him, desperate for more. "Yes, Dylan. You're the only one who makes me feel this good. Take me. Make me yours."

The filthy words, the rawness between them, drives him insane. Dylan pushes himself harder into her, feeling her walls tighten around him with each stroke. "God, Ali," he growls, "You're so fucking filthy. And I love it."

Dylan's hands grip her...one in her damp hair & one clenching her thigh tightly, as he watches her struggle to hold back, her breath hitching with every thrust. He can feel the tension building in her, her body trembling beneath him, but he needs her to let go.

"Come on, baby," he growls, his voice low and commanding, the urgency in his words adding to the raw heat between them. "I know you're holding back, but I need you to come for me. Right fucking now."

Ali's eyes meet his, her face flushed with desire, her lips parting as her hands dig into his shoulders. She's close, he can feel it, and he's not going to let her hold back any longer. "I don't want it to stop Dylan. It's so good."

"Don't you dare hold back, Ali," he commands, his voice rough with need. "Let go for me. I want to feel you come around me, feel your pussy tighten as you fall apart. I want to hear those sweet cries I've missed so damn much."

Her body shudders, her hands clutching at him desperately as she finally lets go, the sound of his name filling the air as her orgasm crashes over her. Her walls tighten around him, pulling him deeper as she comes, and Dylan can't hold back anymore.

"Fuck yes," he groans, his own release following quickly as he moves harder, deeper, feeling the way she wraps around him, her body completely undone. "That's it, baby. You're so fucking good Ali."

Dylan pulls out of her slowly, feeling the loss of her warmth, but he doesn't go far. His chest rises and falls with a deep breath, the weight of the moment still pressing on him. He moves quickly, pulling the covers back, a protective instinct rising in him. Without a word, he gently guides Ali into his arms, wrapping her tightly in the sheets as he pulls her close.

Ali rests her head against his chest, and he feels the slight tremor in her body as she melts into him. Her breathing is slow, but uneven, and he knows it's because she's still processing everything. He runs a hand through her hair, his thumb brushing softly over her cheek as he holds her, his body instinctively shielding her from any vulnerability she might feel.

"God, you were so good," he whispers into her hair, pressing a kiss to the top of her head. "So perfect, Ali."

Her body relaxes further against him, her fingers curling into the fabric of the sheet, and for a moment, it's just the quiet sound of their breathing. Dylan holds her, not wanting to let go, the weight of everything they've shared hanging between them like a quiet promise.

They lie like that for a few moments—quiet, content, still tangled in each other—until suddenly, Ali shifts slightly, and her eyes flutter open.

"So, what did you grill for us?" she asks, her voice a little hoarse but playful, a soft smile pulling at the corner of her lips.

Dylan laughs softly, the sound full of warmth and affection. He leans down, kissing her forehead gently. "You're worried about dinner right now?"

Ali looks up at him, her expression teasing. "What? I'm hungry."

Dylan chuckles again, his heart swelling with the ease of their connection. "I'll make you whatever you want, baby."

Starlight

Ali

The sun filtered through the windows, the day still young and full of promise as they made their way toward Tybee Island. Ali sat in the back seat of Abigail's SUV, squeezed beside Ashley while Raleigh Ann rode up front. The conversation was light, the laughter easy, the kind of chatter that flowed freely when it was just them—books, life, inside jokes.

It was comforting.

She loved these girls. Trusted them more than anyone else in the world. After everything that happened in college, they'd been her solid ground. Her chosen family. Abigail, Raleigh Ann, and Ashley were the only ones she let close.

Still, despite the ease between them, there was a flutter of nerves low in her belly.

Ali glanced out the window, back toward the gray Wagoneer Dylan had rented. He was driving, Brant up front with him. Kellan in the back seat. He'd promised to keep a low profile today—baseball cap pulled low, laid-back clothes—but just knowing he was out there, that he might be recognized, made her stomach twist.

She knew she was probably being silly. This was supposed to be a fun, relaxing day. But that old anxious voice wouldn't shut up.

"You good over there?" Ashley's voice pulled her out of her thoughts.

Ali looked over to find her cousin watching her with an amused smirk. "Yeah," she said with a shrug. "Just...nervous."

Ashley raised a brow. "About Dylan?"

"He promised to stay low key," Ali said. "But I still don't know how I feel about people seeing him. With me. Y'know?"

Ashley grinned, already teasing. "Sis, there's no reason to stress. It's just us."

Ali laughed softly but the nerves didn't quite leave. "I just don't want him to be hassled. I'm used to keeping my life...private."

From the front seat, Abigail met her gaze in the rearview mirror. "Girl, it's a beach day. You're overthinking it. We're here for you."

"Exactly," Raleigh Ann added, twisting the cap off a bottle of water. "We're all family sis. No one's looking twice at us."

The drive was easy, the winding road giving way to coastal views and tall sea grass, until they pulled into the sandy lot at South Beach. The sun was warm but not unbearable yet, and the quieter stretch of sand they'd chosen was perfect—peaceful, removed from the tourist crowd and pier noise. Just the sound of waves and a few families setting up for the day.

The guys took the bulk of the gear—tent poles, beach chairs, the heavy cooler—while the girls grabbed their bags and the lighter stuff. Ali caught sight of Dylan lifting the cooler like it weighed nothing, his forearms flexing beneath the loose sleeves of his t-shirt.

She couldn't help the glance. He noticed, of course. His eyes found hers, and he gave her a slow, private grin that made her stomach flutter. Then he turned back to the task at hand, setting up the tent with practiced ease.

She and Ashley pulled their chairs into the shade, settling in with their Kindles, sunglasses, and suntan lotion. The sea breeze danced around them, the morning still gentle. They talked idly—the girls falling easily into conversation about books and gossip while the three guys got a bocce ball game going nearby.

Ali leaned back in her chair, letting the sun warm her legs as she listened to the friendly bickering over who was winning. She didn't need to open her eyes to recognize Dylan's voice—it was always the one that cut through, steady and teasing, easy.

When she finally did glance over, Dylan was mid-throw, his movements smooth and confident. His cap was still low, but he looked over at her and caught her watching. He smiled again, that same quiet one that made her chest feel too full.

Eventually, everyone broke out lunch—sandwiches, chips, and cold drinks from the cooler. Ashley passed her a Mike's Hard Lemonade (pineapple flavor, her favorite), and Ali twisted the cap off with a soft hiss. Sweet. Cold. Perfect for the heat creeping in.

They ate and laughed, teasing each other about book recs and old beach trip memories. For the first time in a long time, Ali felt entirely safe. Like maybe it was okay to let her guard down.

After lunch, the guys started tossing around a football. The water shimmered like glass, sunlight dancing off it in flashes. It looked too good to resist.

"I'm going in," Ali said, glancing over at Ashley.

"Me too," Ashley replied, already brushing sand off her legs.

The two of them headed toward the shoreline, the sand hot beneath their feet. But just as Ali reached the edge of the water, Dylan's voice stopped her.

"Ali."

She turned to find him walking toward her, his expression soft, steady.

"Wait."

Ashley raised a brow but kept walking, giving Ali a knowing smile before disappearing into the surf.

Dylan reached her and brushed his fingers gently against hers. "Let's go together," he said.

She hesitated. The nerves bubbled back up, coiling in her stomach. But when he looked at her like that—like she was the only thing on the beach that mattered—she nodded.

He led her into the waves, slow and patient, the cool water licking at her calves, then her knees.

Eventually, the water dipped no higher than his waist—him being a foot taller—but on her 5'1" frame it rose to her chest, making her feel small and unsteady in all the ways she only ever did around him. He turned toward her, hands sliding to her hips with easy, familiar possession, heat pulsing through the thin barrier of water between them.

"Wrap your legs around me," he said, low and rough, like the suggestion was meant for her ears alone.

She went still, cheeks flaming, every nerve sparking. *What if I'm too heavy?*

But Dylan noticed. Of course he did.

"You're not too heavy," he said, voice quiet but firm. "You're perfect, Ali. I've got you. Don't worry about anything but being with me."

She swallowed hard. And then, slowly, she moved. Her legs wrapped around his waist, arms looping around his neck as he lifted her with ease. He held her effortlessly, like she weighed nothing. Like she belonged there.

And maybe she did.

The water moved around them, cool and calming, but all she could feel was him—his body, his heat, the sure grip of his hands on her thighs.

"See?" he murmured. "I've got you. You don't need to worry."

"I'm trying," she whispered, but a smile curved her lips.

His answering smile was soft but filled with heat. "Good," he said, drawing her closer.

They stood there, wrapped in each other, the waves rolling gently around them. Her forehead brushed his. His cap cast a soft shadow over his eyes, and she reached up, pressing the lightest kiss to the skin just beneath the brim.

Dylan's breath caught.

His hands tightened on her legs, but he didn't move. Didn't rush.

Ali leaned back just enough to meet his gaze.

And then she kissed him.

Slow at first. Lingering. His lips were warm and soft, tasting like salt and sun and everything that made her ache for more.

He kissed her back—deeper now, hungrier—but still careful. Still holding her like she mattered.

When she pulled away, breathless, he looked at her like she was made of sunlight.

"Fuck, Ali," he said, voice thick with want. "You have no idea how much I want you right now."

Her fingers brushed the edge of his cap, pushing it back just enough to see his face clearly.

"I think I do," she whispered, grinning.

He grinned back, that slow, familiar pull of his mouth that made her heart skip.

And then he kissed her again.

And everything else—waves, beach, time—just faded.

Sweet Nothing

Dylan

Dylan pulled back, his breath ragged as he forced himself to stop. *Fuck*. His chest tight, every muscle in his body screaming for more, but he knew he had to stop this before it got out of hand. They were at a public beach, for God's sake. The reality hit him hard—there's no privacy here, no way to let go like they could in the quiet of her place.

He gripped Ali's thighs gently as he eased her down, the need to hold her close still gnawed at him. The water cooled his heated skin, but it did little to calm the desire still coursing through him. He looked down at her and wished the world would stop spinning for just a moment longer.

"Let's get out of the water," he murmured, his voice thick with tension, guiding her toward the shore.

They walked slowly, Dylan's feet sinking into the wet sand with each step, his pulse still quick, the moment they just shared lingering in the air. Acutely aware of her body against his, the way she fit perfectly in his arms, but he forced himself to focus on the waves, the sand, anything to ground him. *Not now*, he thought trying to calm the storm inside him.

But then a young voice broke through his thoughts. "Excuse me, sir?"

Dylan's eyes snapped to the boy standing a few feet away, a small, scruffy kid—maybe twelve years old—holding a football and a sharpie. The boy looking at him with wide, eager eyes—the kind of look that comes from someone who's just met someone they admire.

Dylan's heart sank, and his body stiffened involuntarily. This is exactly why he needed to pull back. He's not alone. And as much as he's been fighting the urge to lose himself in

Ali, he knows he can't be a dick to a fan, especially not to a kid who's probably dreaming of being in his shoes one day.

He forces a smile, but it's harder than usual. His gaze shifts to Ali, who's standing quietly by his side, her expression unreadable, before turning back to the boy. Dylan takes a deep breath, trying to ease the frustration that pulses through him. "Yeah, of course, kid," he says, trying to keep his tone light. "What's your name?"

The boy grins, visibly relieved. "Kason," he says. Dylan takes it with a steady hand, quickly signing the football with his signature. The kid's eyes nearly sparkle as he thanks him.

"Thanks so much!" Kason exclaims, hugging the ball to his chest like it's the greatest thing in the world.

Dylan stands up, brushing the sand from his knees, offering Kason a quick pat on the shoulder. "No problem, Kason! Have fun kid."

As the boy runs off, clutching the signed ball, Dylan takes another deep breath, looking down at Ali. She's still standing there, her quiet presence a calming anchor, watching him with a mix of amusement and something deeper. He meets her eyes, a small smile tugging at his lips, though his mind is still elsewhere.

He squeezes her hand lightly, trying to regain his composure. "Well, that was…something."

Ali's lips quirk in a soft smile. "Yeah," she says, a teasing lilt in her voice. "Guess you're not as incognito as you thought, huh?"

Dylan chuckles softly, shaking his head. "Guess not," he mutters. But deep down, he knows he's not here for the fans, not today. He's here for her.

Dylan watches Ali, his chest tight with an unfamiliar anxiety. It's not about the kid—it's about her. He's worried about how she'll feel. He promised to do things her way, to keep things low-key, but he couldn't ignore the kid. He couldn't turn him away. It was just a quick interaction, but the guilt eats at him. He doesn't want to upset her, especially not when she's made it clear that she values their privacy.

His eyes search her face, looking for any sign of disappointment, but she just stands there, calm and steady, her hand still gripping his. He can feel the tension in his shoulders, the worry gnawing at him. He never wants to do anything that would make her feel uncomfortable, or push her too far into the spotlight when she's been so careful to keep things private.

"I didn't mean to...I just..." Dylan trails off, unsure how to even explain the rush of emotions that led to him signing that ball. "I promised I'd do it your way. But I didn't want to be a jerk to him. He's just a kid, Ali."

Ali looks at him for a long moment, her eyes soft but steady. There's no judgment there, only understanding. She squeezes his hand, her touch light but full of reassurance.

"Dylan," she says, her voice gentle, "You did the right thing. You're not a bad person for being kind to a fan, especially a kid who looks up to you. You didn't do anything wrong."

Her words settle into him, softening the weight that had been pressing on his chest. Dylan feels the tension leave his body as she gives him a small, comforting smile, squeezing his hand gently.

"I know you promised to do it my way," she continues, her voice steady and calm. "But I don't want you to feel like you have to hide who you are. I'm not upset."

Dylan exhales, the relief washing over him, but a part of him still feels uncertain. "You sure?" he asks, his voice almost hesitant, needing to hear it from her again.

Ali nods, her hand still holding his. "I'm sure. You're just being you, Dylan. And that's the person I want everyone to see. I'm with you, okay?"

Dylan finally smiles, the tightness in his chest easing. His eyes search hers, feeling the weight of her reassurance, of her trust in him. "Thanks," he says quietly, his voice thick with gratitude. "I just want to do right by you."

"You are," she whispers, her voice soft and full of affection. "Always."

As they walk back to the group, hand in hand, Dylan feels a quiet, sudden realization hit him.

I still love her.

The thought is jarring, and it hits him so fast, he almost falters. His heart tightens, but he knows better than to say it out loud. He can't freak her out. Not yet. Not when everything between them is still fragile, still new.

Instead, he squeezes her hand, offering a small smile. He won't say it, but he'll show her. He's determined to show her just how much she means to him.

Ali smiles up at him, the trust in her eyes making his chest tighten. They walk back to the tent, the warmth of the sun still on their skin, both of them quiet but comfortable. And for the first time in a long while, Dylan feels like things might just be exactly where they're supposed to be.

Cruel Summer

Ali

The stifling Georgia heat wraps around Ali the moment she steps out of the car, the humidity making it feel like the air itself is thick and heavy. The Fourth of July in Georgia is a reminder of how hot summer can be, especially this late in the season. The sun beats down relentlessly, but it's the heavy air that makes it hard to breathe.

Ali glances at Dylan, feeling a wave of nervous excitement. She's glad to be here with him, but the thought of being around her extended family makes her stomach flip. It's not the first time he's met them, but it's been a long time.

She adjusts her "Party Like It's 1776" shirt, paired with simple navy biker shorts, the cool fabric offering little relief from the sweltering heat. Her white Hokas are practical for the occasion, though she's not sure they'll survive the heat of the day. Dylan's dressed more casually, too—navy shorts with flags on them, and a red Southern Tide tee.

She carries a fruit tray designed to look like an American flag, the colorful arrangement of blueberries and watermelon an obvious nod to the day's celebrations. They make their way up to the front door, and Ali feels Dylan's hand at her back, steady and reassuring. It's a gesture that calms her nerves more than she wants to admit.

As they reach the door, it swings open, and there's Ashley, standing with her typical easy smile, her arms wide in welcome.

"Finally! Took you two long enough," Ashley teases, her voice carrying that familiar warmth. "I mean I literally left y'all like over an hour ago."

Ali laughs, the tension in her chest easing. "We were stuck in traffic. You know how it is..." Ali trails off, fighting back a blush. She definitely was late because of traffic. Definitely not because Dylan had her bent over the kitchen counter, fucking her brains out while she tried to make the fruit tray. Traffic. Yep, that was the reason.

Ashley grins knowingly. "I know the feeling. Six blocks is a hell of a drive," she comments with a wink. "You both look good, though."

Ali turns crimson, glancing at Dylan. He clears his throat. "Ash, you know you're my favorite, right?"

Ashley laughs, a playful glint in her eye. "Look at that—American flag fruit. Y'all are too cute. C'mon everyone else is here already." She steps aside, and they walk into the house.

Inside, the smell of hamburgers on the grill wafts through the air, and the sound of people chatting and laughing fills the house. Ali's eyes scan the room for familiar faces. Her family—well, mostly Ashley's immediate family—is already gathered in the living room and kitchen. Ashley's parents were bustling in the kitchen, prepping something that smelled like butter and garlic, while Ash's three brothers lounged in the living room, locked in an intense zombie apocalypse game on the Nintendo.

Jason walked up with a grin and pulled Ashley into a tight squeeze. "So, I finally get to meet my number one fan?"

He turned to Dylan, extending a hand.

"I'm Jason—though apparently I go by 'Thor' in your house."

Dylan laughed out loud as they shook hands. "Thor *does* wield lightning. Gotta respect the most badass Avenger."

And just like that, the tension coiled in Ali's chest starts to ease.

The heat wraps around Ali as she and Dylan step out into her parent's backyard later, the air thick with humidity and the smell of grilled food. The backyard is bustling with energy, filled with the sound of family chatter, laughter, and her little cousins splashing in the pool. It's one of her favorite holidays, and while there's an excitement in the air, there's also an undeniable weight hanging over Ali. She can feel the tension in her chest pulling back in, the nerves she's tried to ignore all day.

As they walk further into the yard, Ali's eyes catch her parents standing near the grill, their smiles wide as they spot her. Her mom, Heather, steps forward first, arms open wide to embrace her daughter. The hug is tight and warm, a familiar comfort that makes Ali's heart swell despite the nervous energy humming through her.

But as Heather pulls away, it's Dylan that her parents focus on next. Ali watches as her mom's eyes soften, and then, without hesitation, she pulls him into an embrace, just as tight as the one she gave Ali. Daniel, too, steps forward, clapping Dylan on the back with a firm but loving touch.

The warmth of their welcome is immediate, and despite the tension Ali's been holding in her chest, she can't help but smile. She watches them, standing there for a moment, feeling the weight of how much things have changed—how much time has passed since Dylan last stood in this backyard, back before everything had fallen apart, back before she had nearly lost everything.

Ali can tell Dylan feels it, too. She sees the way he stiffens for just a second before he relaxes into the embrace, returning the gesture with a tenderness she hasn't seen in him before. He's not the same man he was when everything fell apart in college, but in this moment, it feels like they're both stepping into something new. Something *healed*.

Heather pulls back first, her hands resting on Dylan's shoulders as she looks up at him with a softness in her eyes that makes Ali's chest tighten. "It's so good to see you, Dylan," she says, her voice thick with emotion. "I've been praying for you. You're family, you know that."

Dylan nods, his throat tight. "I know," he says quietly, his voice low, but full of meaning.

Daniel claps him on the back again. "We missed you, son. It's good to have you back here with us."

Ali feels a rush of warmth flood her chest at the sight. It's been so long since they were all in this space together, and despite the ghosts of the past lingering, she can feel the love, the family bond that's always been there.

After a moment, Ali steps forward, standing next to Dylan, and it's as if everything has shifted back into place. There's healing in the air, a sense of peace that she never thought she'd feel in this house again.

As the evening cools, the group heads to the marsh for the fireworks. Dylan takes Ali's hand, the simple touch grounding her as the excitement buzzes around them. Ashley leads the way, her voice full of energy, and Ali can't help but smile at the chaos of her extended family.

Once at the marsh, they set up near the water, the atmosphere quieter and more peaceful. Dylan pulls Ali down to sit between his bent legs, wrapping his arms around her waist as they settle in for the fireworks show. The first explosion lights up the sky, and Ali leans back into him, the sound and colors filling the night.

Dylan's warmth surrounds her, and for a moment, everything fades. It's just the two of them, watching the world light up in bursts of color. Ali smiles, resting against him, as the tension of the day slips away.

The drive back to Ali's house feels different—quiet, intimate. The others have all gone their separate ways, and Ali and Dylan are alone, the car filled with the soft hum of the engine and the occasional sound of crickets outside the window. The Mike's Hard Lemonades still buzz in her veins, making her feel lighter, a little tipsy.

She's aware of every inch of Dylan beside her, the warmth of his body next to hers, the way he's casually driving, but every time he glances over, his eyes soft and patient, her heart skips. She can feel the pull of him, the chemistry between them turning into something she can't ignore. It's different now, the way she's feeling—vulnerable, needy, and she's not sure how to push it aside.

Her fingers brush his on the center console, a silent invitation. Dylan's gaze flicks to her, his lips curling into a small, knowing smile. He doesn't say anything, but the tension is thick between them.

"I'm not sure how much more of this I can take," she says quietly, her voice soft but laced with the need she's been holding back all day. The alcohol makes her words bolder, her body warmer, the desire for him more urgent.

Dylan's grip on the wheel tightens just slightly, but his voice remains steady. "We don't have to rush, Ali. We can take our time."

She leans closer, her hand finding his, squeezing it gently. The moment the car pulls into the driveway, she feels the heat in her chest intensify, the drive having only built the pressure between them. The house is quiet.

Ali looks over at him, the desire in her eyes clear. "I need you, Dylan," she says, her voice breathless with the weight of what she's feeling.

So It Goes...

Dylan

Her back hit the door with a soft thud, the cool wood a contrast to the heat rolling off Dylan's body. His mouth claimed hers—desperate, hungry. His hands framed her face, then slid lower, gripping her thighs.

He grips to lift her, wanting the feel of her thighs wrapped around his waist but she pushes back.

"Babe, please," he whispered against her lips, his voice rough. "I bench press more than you weigh. Just trust me."

Ali hesitated, just for a second—still not used to being handled like something someone wanted. But she didn't look away. His eyes didn't leave hers.

She nodded.

Dylan's hands flexed under her thighs, lifting her with ease. Her legs locked around his waist, her arms looping around his shoulders. He walked them to the nearest wall, pinning her there, his lips crashing into hers again, then dragging down her jaw, his breath warm and ragged as he kissed the curve of her neck.

"God, you smell amazing," he murmured, tongue tracing the place just beneath her ear. "Like sunscreen and strawberries."

Ali gasped when his teeth grazed her pulse. Her head tipped back, fingers clutching the collar of his shirt.

He tugged at the hem of her oversized tee. "Need this off. Need you."

She let him pull it over her head, her cheeks flushing as she sat there in just her bra and her shorts. Dylan let the shirt drop to the floor, then stilled, just for a second, eyes drinking her in like a man who'd spent a decade starving.

"You're so damn beautiful," he said, breath catching.

Ali didn't look away. Not for one second.

Dylan adjusted his grip and carried her down the hallway. Ali clung to him, skin flushed, heart hammering. There was no urgency now. No frantic hands or stolen heat like earlier today when he'd bent her over the kitchen counter. This was different.

He nudged her bedroom door open with his shoulder and stepped inside, moonlight catching the edge of the comforter. Ali's arms tightened around him as he stopped at the foot of her bed.

Gently, he set her down, his hands sliding from her back to her hips, not rushing. Just...touching. His hands lingering at her waist. Her skin was warm—flushed and soft—and her breathing was already uneven.

He took a step back to look at her. Just look.

Ali stood in front of him in her pale pink bra and those tight biker shorts he'd been thinking about since she climbed into the passenger seat of the SUV that morning. God help him, he'd nearly pulled off the road when she adjusted them over her thighs.

"You good?" he asked, voice low, thumb brushing her side.

She nodded, wide-eyed and pink-cheeked, but not looking away.

He took his time, unhooking her bra and peeling it off, then letting his fingers run along the edge of her shorts.

"Earlier..." he said, watching her face, "That was need. This is something more."

She shivered.

He dropped to his knees.

He needed her to feel this. To feel him. Not just his body but all the years between them—what he'd wanted to say, what he still couldn't say, not yet. So he kissed the curve of her stomach, just above the waistband, then the inside of her thigh. Her hand found his shoulder, her fingers curling into the fabric of his shirt.

"Can I take these off?" he asked.

She nodded—slow, hesitant—and he took that as permission. She had her bottom lip tucked between her teeth. Carefully, reverently, he hooked his thumbs under the waistband and started to slide her shorts down.

In college, she would've covered herself the second they were off—turned away, tugged a blanket up, blushed so hard it made his chest ache. But now...she stood still, shaking slightly, but she let him look.

The fabric peeled down over her thighs, catching at her knees before slipping off entirely. He tossed them aside, then pressed a kiss to the inside of her thigh, just above her knee.

She stood in front of him in just her panties.

He bit back a groan.

"Ali..." His voice caught. His hands rested on her hips, fingers flexing. "I want to taste you."

Her eyes widened.

He watched her, carefully. "You always got so shy back in college. I didn't want to push."

Her breath hitched. She looked down at him—him on his knees, shoulders broad, eyes dark with heat and something gentler beneath. Her lips parted.

"I..." she whispered, swallowing. "You sure you want to?"

He smiled, slow and devastating. "I've never wanted anything more."

Her fingers trembled where they hovered near her stomach, and he reached up, catching one in his hand. Brought it to his mouth and kissed her knuckles.

"What if I don't like it?"

"Then you just say 'stop', baby. I've got you. I promise."

"Let me, sweetheart," he murmured, lips brushing her skin. "Just say yes."

There was a long beat.

Then, barely audible: "Yes."

That was all he needed.

Dylan leaned forward and pressed a kiss right over the center of her panties. Her knees buckled slightly, and he caught her, guiding her down until she was sitting on the edge of the bed, legs open just enough for him to fit between.

He ran his hands up her thighs again, slower this time, then hooked his fingers into the waistband of her panties and looked up at her once more.

"You still with me?"

Ali nodded, lips parted, pupils blown wide. "Yeah."

He peeled the last piece of fabric down her legs and tossed it behind him.

She was already trembling. He eased her down to lie on her back.

Dylan ran his hands up the outsides of her thighs, fingers spreading to cup the softness of her hips. He kissed one, then the other, letting his lips linger on her skin, before he dipped his head and finally tasted her.

Ali gasped, hips jolting at the first slow drag of his tongue.

"Easy," he murmured against her, voice thick with restraint. "I got you."

He kissed her again—open-mouthed, patient—taking his time as he explored every inch of her. His hands anchored her thighs as he licked her softly, rhythmically, learning what made her whimper, what made her curse under her breath. She was already wet, already coming apart for him, and he hadn't even taken off his shorts.

Dylan groaned low in his throat, the sound vibrating against her as he licked deeper, slower, savoring her like she was the only thing that had ever mattered. He pulled back just enough to breathe, his mouth slick, his breath hot against the inside of her thigh.

Then he slid his hands higher and pushed her legs wider—gentle, but firm—urging her to give him more. To open for him.

"Yeah," he rasped, eyes locked on hers. "Just like that. Let me see you, baby."

Ali whimpered, her head falling back, one hand tangled in his hair, the other gripping the sheet like she needed something to hold on to.

Dylan took her in—every inch of her spread open for him, glistening and perfect—and felt his control fracture at the edges.

"Fuck," he muttered, his voice wrecked. "You taste so sweet. Like heaven. Like you were made for this."

He dipped his head again, licking through her folds with slow, filthy precision. Her thighs trembled around him.

"I could eat this pussy all night," he murmured, his tongue dragging over her with maddening patience. "So wet for me. You feel that?"

Her hips jerked, a breathless gasp tumbling from her lips.

He smiled against her.

Yeah. She felt it.

He pressed two fingers inside her, pumping slowly, curling just right.

"This pussy's perfect," he growled. "Tight, warm...fuck, I missed this. Missed you."

His lips closed around her clit again, sucking just enough to make her cry out. He loved every damn sound she made.

"Don't hold back, Ali," he whispered between licks. "Wanna hear you. Wanna taste you when you fall apart on my tongue."

Her whole body shook—hips lifting, thighs closing in around his head as he pushed her closer and closer to the edge.

"That's it, baby," he groaned, his voice rough and raw. "Give it to me. Let me drink you in."

Slut!

Ali

Ali's legs were trembling.

She couldn't remember how to breathe—couldn't remember anything, really, except the wet heat of Dylan's mouth between her thighs and the way her name sounded when he moaned it against her skin.

Good. Lord.

Her fingers were tangled in his hair, not tugging, just holding on. Anchoring herself to the only solid thing in the room: him.

He licked her again, slow and filthy, and she gasped.

"Fuck, baby," he rasped, voice deep and dark and unsteady. "You taste so sweet. Like heaven. Like you were made for this."

The words hit her like lightning.

Her body arched without permission, a sharp cry slipping from her lips.

Nobody had ever talked to her like that. Not without making her feel like a punchline afterward. But Dylan...he sounded like he meant every filthy word. Like her body was something sacred. Something his.

"I could eat this pussy all night," he murmured, licking her again, slower this time. "So wet for me. You feel that?"

Ali's breath hitched, her hips stuttering against his face.

"Yes," she whispered, cheeks burning. "Oh my gawd yes."

He groaned, and she felt it—felt it—all the way through her.

"This pussy's perfect," he growled, fingers stroking deep inside her now. "Tight, warm...fuck, I missed this. Missed you."

Her eyes fluttered shut, everything too much. Too good. The heat. His mouth. The way his voice made her ache.

She didn't know whether to cry or come.

Maybe both.

"Don't hold back, Ali," he whispered between licks. "Wanna hear you. Wanna taste you when you fall apart on my tongue."

Gawd.

She couldn't stop the moan that ripped from her throat, couldn't stop her thighs from shaking as he sucked her clit into his mouth like he meant it.

She wasn't thinking anymore. Just feeling.

"Dyl—" she gasped. "Oh gawd, I—"

"Come for me," he groaned, voice wrecked. "Let me feel it."

And she did.

She shattered—head thrown back, body arching, every inch of her unraveling under his mouth, his hands, his words. He didn't stop, didn't let up, just held her right there while wave after wave rolled through her.

Ali didn't feel shy. Or hidden. Or afraid of her body. She never felt that way with Dylan.

She felt wanted.

She felt worshipped

Then Dylan's arms were around her—solid, sure, there. Lifting her off the bed.

"I got you," he murmured, voice thick, one hand cradling her hip, the other sliding up her spine.

She leaned into him, still trembling, her breath catching against the crook of his neck. Her thighs were slick, her skin on fire, and her brain wasn't entirely convinced that orgasm hadn't split her into pieces.

"You good?" he asked, lips brushing her temple.

Ali nodded, too breathless to speak.

He turned her gently, guiding her to face the bed. She went with him, pliant, dazed. His hand stayed firm on the small of her back as he leaned her forward, until her hands met the edge of the mattress, and she folded over it—knees locked, back arched. He lifted each leg placing her knees on the bed. Had her kneeling on it, leaning in her forearms. Open and exposed for him.

The position should've made her self-conscious, but it didn't.

Not with him behind her. Not with his body heat wrapped around her like armor. Not with the way he pressed a kiss to her shoulder, soft and reverent.

"You're so fucking sexy like this," he breathed against her skin, kissing lower, toward the curve of her spine. "Still shaking."

She felt him step back just enough to push his shorts down, the sound of fabric hitting the floor making her toes curl. Then his boxer briefs. She didn't need to look—she felt him. The heat of him. The sheer want radiating off his skin.

And when he stepped forward again, bare now, hard as stone and throbbing behind her, she gasped.

"Feel that?" he asked, voice rough, his palm smoothing down her back. "That's what you do to me, Ali."

Her whole body ached for him—open, throbbing, ready.

He kissed her again, right between her shoulder blades, and then rested his hands on her hips.

"I'm not gonna rush this," he said, voice shaking now too. "But I need to be inside you, baby. Right now."

Ali nodded, moaning low. "Please."

Ali braced herself against the bed, her breath coming in shallow waves. Dylan's hands flexed at her hips, thumbs dragging slow, grounding circles into her skin like he could soothe her and stake his claim all at once.

Then he shifted closer.

She felt the thick press of him at her entrance—hot, hard, already pulsing with restraint.

He slid in with one deep, slow thrust, filling her so completely it punched the air from her lungs. Her fingers fisted the comforter. She swore the earth tilted.

"Fuck," Dylan groaned, head dropping to her shoulder. "You feel so good, baby. So fucking tight."

He gave her a second to adjust—hips rocking in shallow rolls, one hand sliding up her back to her shoulder, the other pressing into the curve of her waist. Holding her there. Keeping her.

And then he started to move.

Long, deep strokes. Deliberate. Possessive. Like he was carving his name into her body from the inside out.

Ali moaned, the sound broken and desperate.

"Been dreaming of this pussy for ten fucking years," he rasped, picking up pace. "And it's still mine."

She cried out, body jolting with every thrust, every word.

"You hear me, Ali?" he growled, thrusting deeper. "You're mine."

"Yes," she gasped. "Gawd—Dyl—"

He reached down and wrapped his hand gently around her throat—not squeezing, just holding. Anchoring her.

"Say it," he demanded, breath hot at her ear. "Say you're mine."

Her head dropped, body clenching around him. She was so close again, the pressure building fast.

"I'm yours," she choked out, her voice barely a whisper.

Dylan snarled—snarled—and drove into her harder, deeper, making her legs shake.

"Louder."

"I'm yours!" she cried out, voice breaking, throat raw. "I'm—oh my gawd—I'm yours, Dylan!"

"That's right," he groaned, fucking her harder now, like he was chasing the words down into her soul. "Mine. Always fucking mine."

Her climax slammed into her like a wave, ripping through her body in hot, shattering pulses. She screamed his name, her entire world narrowing to the feel of him inside her, around her, claiming her.

And then he followed.

With a guttural curse and her name on his lips, Dylan thrust deep one last time, his whole body shaking as he emptied into her, hips grinding, breath wrecked.

Still holding her like something precious.

Like something his.

Dylan didn't let her go. Not even for a second.

Daylight

♥

Dylan

The moment her body went limp, trembling and spent against the bed, he wrapped his arms around her waist and eased them both down, gently lowering her to the mattress. He stayed close, skin flush against hers, his chest to her back, his breath still ragged.

Ali whimpered softly, her eyes fluttering closed as she melted into the sheets.

"Shh, I got you," he whispered, pressing a kiss to her shoulder, then another to the back of her neck. "You did so good for me, baby. So good."

She made a tiny sound at that—barely a hum—but it made his chest ache.

He could still feel the echo of her around him, the way she'd clenched when she came, screaming his name like it belonged to her. And it did.

It fucking did.

He reached for the blanket at the edge of the bed and pulled it up over both of them, then wrapped himself around her. One hand found her thigh, gently stroking the soft skin there. The other settled on her stomach, fingers splaying wide, grounding her. Letting her know he wasn't going anywhere.

Not tonight.

He kissed her again, slower this time. "You okay?"

Ali nodded into the pillow. "Mhm."

He held her tighter.

She needed this part—always had. He remembered the way she used to go quiet after they'd made love in college, curling up so small under the covers like her body didn't quite belong to her again yet. Like she needed time to come back into it.

And he gave it to her. Every time.

He buried his face in her hair and just held her.

But even in the silence, the thoughts started creeping in.

I have to leave tomorrow.

Training camp was starting back up. Rookies were coming in. Peterson wanted him in pads by Wednesday. Kallie had been texting nonstop about the charity shoot he'd already rescheduled once. His agent was patient—but not that patient. And Dylan had been ignoring half a dozen reminders from the team about logistics and press appearances.

He'd already put everyone off for two weeks. Because of her. Because the second he saw her again, the second she let him back in, he couldn't pull away.

But time was up. Reality was calling.

And he fucking hated it.

Ali stirred slightly, pressing herself back against him like she could sense the shift in his mind. Like she knew he was drifting, even if his body hadn't moved an inch.

"Dyl?" she mumbled.

"I'm here," he said instantly, kissing the curve of her shoulder. "Just thinking."

She didn't answer, but she didn't pull away either. Her hand found his on her stomach and laced their fingers together.

He swallowed hard.

Tomorrow could wait a few more hours.

Tonight was hers.

Dylan couldn't sleep.

Ali was warm in his arms, her back pressed to his chest, her breaths deep and steady. Her hair smelled like coconut and summer, her skin still soft with heat from earlier. He'd held her all night, barely letting her shift without chasing her in the sheets.

But it wasn't restlessness keeping him up.

It was her.

It was the quiet way she'd curled into him like she belonged there.

It was the soft hitch in her breath when he told her she was his.

It was the ache in his chest knowing he had to leave in a few hours—and the impossible pull not to.

He kissed the back of her shoulder, barely a brush.

Ali shifted in her sleep, her body instinctively pressing closer. He ran a hand down her side, slow and careful, fingertips skimming the curve of her waist, her hip, her thigh. She let out a soft sigh.

"Ali," he whispered.

She stirred. "Mm?"

He slid his hand lower, between her thighs, and found her already warm, already yielding. She gasped softly, her hips shifting in invitation.

Dylan kissed the back of her neck, then her shoulder. "Turn over for me, baby."

She did, slow and languid, her eyes blinking open to meet his in the moonlight.

He settled between her thighs, bare skin brushing hers, his cock already hard and throbbing, but he didn't rush. He just looked at her.

"You're so fucking beautiful," he said, voice thick with sleep and something heavier.

Ali reached up and cupped his jaw. "I missed this."

"I missed you." He leaned down and kissed her—slow, deep, sweet. The kind of kiss that undid him more than any orgasm.

He lined himself up and pushed in slowly, carefully, watching every flicker in her eyes as her mouth dropped open, as her back arched just a little. She wrapped her legs around his waist, pulling him closer, deeper.

"Gawd," she whispered, breath catching. "Dylan..."

He set a rhythm—gentle, deliberate. Rocking into her like they had all the time in the world. No rush. No pressure. Just this. Her gasps filled the room, soft at first, then sharper as he angled his hips just right.

Her hands clung to his back, her nails digging in slightly when he hit that spot that made her legs tense around him.

"You feel so good, Ali," he murmured, lips brushing her jaw. "So soft. So fucking perfect."

She whimpered, her voice barely a breath. "Don't stop."

"I won't," he promised, kissing her again, holding her face in his hands like she was breakable and his all at once. "I'm right here."

And he made love to her like that—slow, deep, unrelenting. Until her soft moans turned into cries. Until her eyes squeezed shut and her body shuddered around him. Until she came again, clinging to him like she never wanted to let go.

And only then, with her trembling beneath him, did he let himself fall too.

Silently. Completely.

Right into her.

Come Back...Be Here

Ali

Ali stirred at the sound of the dresser drawer sliding shut.

The room was still dim, painted in soft gray-blue light from the sliver of dawn pushing through the blinds. Her body was heavy, warm, still humming from the way he'd woken her hours ago—tender, slow, so deep it had made her cry out his name until her voice broke.

She reached out instinctively, but the space beside her was cold.

Her eyes fluttered open.

Dylan stood across the room, shirtless, a pair of jeans zipped but unbuttoned as he slipped socks into his duffel. His back was to her, all wide shoulders and tense muscle. His movements were careful. Quiet.

He didn't want to wake me.

Her chest tightened.

She watched him for a moment—his hand brushing over the toothbrush he'd left on her sink, the way he folded his sweatshirt instead of cramming it in. He wasn't just leaving. He was trying to leave gently.

And somehow, that hurt worse.

"Hey," she rasped, voice still coated in sleep.

Dylan froze.

Then he turned, eyes soft and apologetic as he crossed back to her side of the bed.

"I didn't mean to wake you," he said, crouching down beside her. He reached up and brushed her hair back from her face. "I was trying to let you sleep."

Ali blinked up at him. "What time is it?"

"Little before six." His thumb dragged gently across her cheekbone. "I've got an eight-thirty flight."

Right. Of course.

He'd told her last night. She just didn't want to believe it.

She swallowed hard, throat tight. "You were just gonna sneak out?"

He shook his head. "No. I was gonna kiss you before I left. I swear."

Ali nodded, but the ache in her chest only grew.

Dylan exhaled and leaned his forehead against hers. "I don't want to go."

"I know."

"I've got training this week. Kallie's been on my ass. And Peterson wants me back for drills this week."

She nodded again, her fingers finding his. "I know, Dylan."

He kissed her, soft and lingering, like he didn't want to let go.

"I'm gonna text you when I land," he murmured. "I'm gonna call you tonight. And tomorrow. And every day until I see you again."

Ali smiled, small and sleepy. "Okay."

"I'm serious," he said, voice rough now. "This doesn't stop because I have to leave. You and me? We're not over."

"I know," she whispered. "I believe you."

Dylan pressed another kiss to her lips, then to her forehead, then finally stood.

Ali watched him finish packing through blurry eyes, heart heavy but full.

Because for the first time in ten years, she wasn't afraid of what came next.

It had been a month since Dylan left.

Thirty-one days.

But he hadn't missed a single text.

Not one call.

Every morning, without fail, her phone buzzed before her alarm even had a chance to go off—*Good morning, baby. Hope you slept okay. I miss you.* Then came the call. His voice, deep and rough with sleep, telling her about the protein shake he was choking down or how Rocky had already started trash talking before sunrise drills.

And every night?

He called again—right as she was climbing into bed, her hair in a messy bun, her oversized T-shirt slipping off one shoulder. He always waited until she was under the covers. Always asked how her day was. Always teased her in the best ways. Some nights ended with whispered moans and shaky goodnights. Other nights, they talked until she drifted off to sleep.

It didn't feel like a routine. It felt like *home*.

Ali sat cross-legged on her couch, her Kindle open in her lap but untouched. Her eyes drifted to her phone screen for the third time in as many minutes, the last message from him still sitting there:

> You looked so fucking pretty in your little sundress today. That photo should be illegal. Call you after film session—it'll be later than normal. Get in bed without me.

She smiled, heart warm and gooey in her chest.

He'd sent it around 8 p.m., right after she'd posted a pic from brunch with the girls. Nothing fancy—just mimosas and waffles and her in that lemon-print, sleeveless Lilly dress she used to second-guess herself in. She hated her arms. But Dylan? Dylan had replied like it belonged on the cover of *Vogue*.

Ali leaned her head back against the couch and exhaled.

She missed him.

More than she thought she would. More than she'd let herself admit—even now.

Not just the sex—not the way he made her body feel like a prayer—but the way he saw her. The way he made her laugh. The way he never let her go to sleep without reminding her that she mattered.

Her phone buzzed again, and her heart jumped.

> Ten minutes. Don't fall asleep on me, Presley.

Ali grinned. It was after 10 already.

> Not a chance.

She hit send, then pulled the fabric of his old Magnolia Bluff football tee up to her nose and breathed him in.

Ten minutes.

She could wait.

But only just.

Ali startled awake at the sound of the front door slamming.

Hard.

She blinked, disoriented, her heart thudding as her eyes adjusted to the dim, warm light of the living room. The TV was still glowing with the Netflix screen saver, her Kindle splayed open on the cushion beside her. Her phone, face-down on her stomach, buzzed one more time before going silent.

The front door opened again—slammed again—followed by the unmistakable sound of heels being kicked off and a sharp voice muttering, "I swear to God if he ever says that shit to me again—"

Ali sat up, groggy and confused. "Ash?"

Ashley appeared in the hallway, barefoot and red-faced, her purse sliding off her shoulder. "Brant is a literal fucking child."

Ali blinked. "Wait—what time is it?"

"Almost midnight." Ashley threw her purse down and let out a frustrated breath. "Sorry. I didn't mean to wake you. I just needed to get out of there."

Ali's heart dropped.

Dylan.

She grabbed her phone and turned it over—six missed calls. Two texts.

> Babe? You fall asleep?

> Ali, you okay? I'm getting worried.

She cursed softly under her breath and texted back as fast as her fingers would allow.

> I'm okay. I'm so sorry. I fell asleep on the couch. Ashley just got home and she's upset. I need to be here with her tonight. I'll call you in the morning. I love you.

She stared at the screen for half a second longer, then locked the phone and set it face-down on the cushion beside her. Ashley deserved her full attention right now.

Her chest ached—not with guilt, exactly, but with that low, gnawing feeling of *I didn't mean to let you down.*

"Ali?" Ashley's voice cracked a little from the kitchen. "Do we have any wine?"

"Coming." Ali pushed herself off the couch and padded barefoot toward her cousin, her best friend.

Ashley needed her now.

And Dylan would understand.

He always did.

Jump Then Fall

Dylan

Dylan stared at the phone.

And stared.

The screen dimmed, but he tapped it once to bring it back. Read the message again.

I'm okay. I'm so sorry. I fell asleep on the couch. Ashley just got home and she's upset. I need to be here with her tonight. I'll call you in the morning. I love you.

His thumb hovered over the screen, but he didn't type anything back yet.

He just...sat there.

In the dim glow of his bedroom, with the hum of the A/C rattling in the corner, he sat straight up in his bed and read the message for the fifth time.

She said *I love you.*

Not a flirty "love ya" or a "k love you bye" kind of thing. No emojis. No softener. Just those three words, plain and quiet like they didn't carry weight.

But they did.

To him, they always had.

He rubbed the back of his neck, his jaw tightening. It wasn't that he didn't believe her. God, he wanted to believe her. But she'd been sleepy. Rushed. Distracted. Probably slipped into old habits. Her best friend was hurting, and Ali always showed up for the people she loved—even when it cost her something.

Had she even realized she wrote it?

He'd been so careful. So fucking careful. Letting things build. Letting her feel safe. Letting her take the lead when she needed to. Because the last time he'd told her he loved her, she'd broken down and told him goodbye.

This felt different.

This *was* different.

Still, he didn't text back right away.

He let the weight of it settle. Let himself feel it. The ache of not hearing her voice tonight. The sweetness of those three words. The uncertainty wrapped inside them.

She might not have meant to say it.

But she'd said it.

And whether she knew it or not—he'd been hers the whole damn time.

He finally picked up the phone, stared at the screen once more, and typed slowly.

> Sleep tight, baby. I'll be here when you're ready to say it out loud.

He paused. Then sent one more text:

> I love you too.

Crazier

Ali

Ali blinked awake to the pale gray light of morning and a dull ache behind her eyes. The sweetness of the Red Moscato always left her with a headache.

Thank you very much, Diabetes.

Her head rested against the sidearm of the couch, her body curled awkwardly in the same spot she'd been in for hours. Her neck was stiff. Her shirt, wrinkled. Somewhere across the room, Ashley was snoring softly beneath the throw blanket Ali had tucked around her after they'd polished off two glasses of red wine and a half-eaten pint of mint chocolate chip.

Everything from last night rushed back in slow motion—the slammed door, Ashley's teary rant about Brant and the baby voice he used in arguments (which was, yes, as horrifying as it sounded), the way Ali had shifted gears instantly. From aching to hear Dylan's voice...to being the friend someone needed.

She reached for her phone on the coffee table and unplugged it from the charger.

Twenty-seven notifications. Group texts. Work emails. A DM from Abigail. Probably a meme or a Reel about the Night Court or the Inner Circle—one of their favorite fandoms.

And two messages from Dylan.

She tapped it without thinking.

> Sleep tight, baby. I'll be here when you're ready to say it out loud.

> I love you too.

Ali sat bolt upright.

Oh my gawd.

Her heart launched into a sprint, like it was trying to leap out of her chest and run straight to Florida.

No. No no no. I didn't—

She scrolled up.

Read her own text again.

I love you.

Shit!

She groaned inwardly.

She hadn't even realized she'd said it. It had just…slipped out. She'd been flustered and tired and trying to reassure him. Trying to keep it simple. Familiar. She used to say it all the time, back when they were kids playing house in a dorm room.

But that was ten years ago.

And now?

Now it was real. And she'd said it first.

Without thinking.

Without meaning to.

And he'd said it back.

Ali dropped the phone onto her lap and stared at the ceiling like maybe it would open up and swallow her whole.

"I'm an idiot," she whispered.

Ashley stirred from across the room. "You're not an idiot. You're just in love."

Ali looked over, wide-eyed. "You read my texts in your sleep?"

Ashley sat up slowly, her hair wild, one eye barely open. "No. But I know that look. That's the *Dylan-just-broke-my-brain-with-one-sentence* face."

Ali groaned and buried her face in her hands.

Ashley smirked.

Ali (unsent):

Okay so I know I said "I love you" last night and I think I might have blacked out emotionally?? I didn't even realize I said it until I woke up and saw your text. But I did mean it. I think. I mean—no, I do. Gawd, this is already a disaster. I should not be allowed to text before coffee. Please don't freak out.

Her thumb hovered over send.

She'd typed it. All of it. The truth, messy and earnest and terrifying.

But her chest clenched and her stomach flipped, and at the very last second—backspace.

She deleted the whole thing. Every word.

"Coward," she muttered.

Ashley made a noise that might've been an agreement or just a yawn.

Ali sighed and stared down at the screen again, trying to will herself to be brave. To just text him back, like a normal human being in a healthy, grown-up relationship.

And that's when it happened.

The typing bubble appeared.

Her stomach dropped straight through the couch.

Oh my gawd.

He was typing.

She froze.

Did he see her typing bubble and realize she was wigging out? Could he feel it through the screen? Was he about to say it was too soon? That he needed to slow down? That she'd scared him off?

Then the message appeared.

> Stop spiraling, sweetheart. I know you love me. It's okay. I've got you. And I love you too.

Ali blinked.

Her breath caught.

She read it once. Twice.

And then her whole body melted into the cushions.

She let the phone fall to her chest, hands over her face, eyes burning for no good reason except maybe he always knew what she needed before she did.

He didn't tease.

He didn't question.

He just held her.

Even from hundreds of miles away.

And somehow, in that moment, the fear cracked open—and love slipped in like sunlight.

Ali wiped at her eyes with the sleeve of Dylan's T-shirt and sat up a little straighter, the phone still warm on her chest. His message glowed back at her like it knew it had unraveled her.

Stop spiraling, sweetheart. I know you love me. It's okay. I've got you. And I love you too.

She let the words sink in again.

She hadn't ruined it.

He wasn't scared.

He knew—and instead of running, he pulled her closer.

Her fingers trembled as she unlocked her phone and tapped out a reply.

> You always know when I'm spiraling. It's unfair. And deeply annoying. And also the only reason I'm not currently crying into a throw pillow.

Pause.

Then she added:

> I meant it. I love you. So much. Even when you're miles away. Even when I'm a mess. Maybe especially then.

She hovered for half a second. Then hit send.

Her message was barely delivered when the screen lit up again.

> Can I FaceTime you? Only if you promise not to freak out. Just wanna see your face for a minute.

Ali let out a soft laugh, wiping under her eyes again. Of course he would ask. Of course he'd *know* she might need a second to steady herself.

She texted back:

> You're annoying. And yes. Gimme 30 seconds. Gotta move to my room before I cry in front of Ashley.

She pushed herself off the couch, as Ashley let out a sleepy *hmmph* from the couch, and hurried toward her room with the phone cradled to her chest like it might disappear if she wasn't holding on tight. She climbed into bed, tucked the comforter over her legs, and pulled her messy bun through the top of her scrunchie to fix it.

Then hit **Accept**.

Dylan's face filled the screen— hoodie collar up around his neck, that sleepy grin tugging at his mouth.

"Hey, sweetheart," he said, voice warm and low.

Ali melted instantly. "Hey."

He stared at her for a second, his expression soft. "You okay?"

She nodded. "Better now."

"You sure?" His brow creased.

"Yeah," she whispered, smiling. "You saying 'I've got you' kind of short-circuited my brain, so...yeah."

He laughed. "Good. That was the goal."

She leaned her head against her pillow, the tension easing from her chest. "I think I'm just gonna spend the day vegging out with Ash. After last night..."

He nodded. "Sounds like a solid plan. Reruns and recovery?"

"Exactly." She smiled. "Probably something chaotic and nostalgic. Like *Hannah Montana* or *Cadet Kelly.*"

Dylan smirked. "As long as you promise to send me a picture of you both wearing face masks and eating Oreos out of the bag."

"You're asking for a lot, sir."

He grinned. "I miss your face."

She looked down for a second, cheeks warm. "I miss yours too."

A long beat of silence passed between them—comfortable this time. Full.

"I'll let you rest," he said gently. "Call me tonight?"

"Obviously."

He winked. "Love you, Ali."

Her throat tightened again—but it didn't scare her this time.

"Love you too."

The screen went dark as the call ended, and she exhaled, curling onto her side just as Ashley shuffled down the hall and peeked into her room.

"You decent?"

Ali laughed. "Barely."

Ashley climbed in beside her with zero hesitation and tugged the blanket over them both. "*Hannah Montana* or *High School Musical*?"

Ali didn't even blink. "*Hannah Montana.* Season one. Chaos and bad wigs."

Ashley grinned. "You're my soulmate."

They pressed play and let the old theme song fill the room, warm and bright and perfectly nostalgic.

Superman

Dylan

D ylan adjusted the backwards ball cap on his head and shoved his phone into his pocket, trying not to smile too hard.

He was still riding the high from that early morning FaceTime—Ali in bed, sleepy and beautiful, whispering *love you* like it wasn't the most important thing he'd heard in years.

His chest hadn't stopped buzzing since.

"Bro," Rocky said, bumping his shoulder as they stepped through the hospital's glass doors. "You've got that *I-just-got-a-love-letter-or-a-lap-dance* face. Which was it?"

Dylan rolled his eyes. "Neither. Shut up."

Rocky just laughed, holding the door for a nurse as they made their way down the brightly colored hallway. The Orlando Tritons had done regular visits with the children's hospital for years—selfies, high fives, autographs, stuffed mascots. Dylan never missed a chance to show up. Not just because it mattered to the team, but because it mattered to *him*.

And this morning, it mattered even more. He was grounded. Clearheaded. Still wearing the warmth of Ali's voice like armor.

A tiny hand tugged at his hoodie before they made it to the playroom.

He looked down.

A girl in purple princess pajamas grinned up at him, cheeks still round with baby fat and one of those IV stands rolling at her side.

"Are you the football guy?" she asked, eyes wide.

Dylan crouched down to her level. "I might be. Depends who's asking."

She giggled, hugging her IV pole closer. "I saw you on TV. You jumped over that guy like *whoooosh*!" She lifted one arm like she was flying. "That was awesome."

Rocky barked out a laugh behind them. "He practices that in front of mirrors."

"I do not," Dylan muttered, then turned back to her. "What's your name?"

"Emma," she said proudly. "And this is Tempest." She patted the IV stand lovingly. "She helps me feel better. She's also the Tritons' dragon, but I let her live here now."

Dylan blinked, then grinned so wide it hurt. "That's the best thing I've heard all day."

Emma beamed. "She used to be named Sparkle Bug, but then I saw Tempest on your team's coloring book."

"Smart call. Tempest is way tougher."

"She *breathes lightning*," Emma whispered like it was a secret.

Rocky leaned over. "So do I after team chili night."

"Gross," Emma said, wrinkling her nose.

"Exactly," Dylan said, tossing Rocky a glare. "You're gonna traumatize the poor girl."

Emma just laughed—bright, loud, full of life—and Dylan felt something loosen in his chest. This was why they came. This was the good stuff. Forget the interviews and the cameras. This? This mattered more than any highlight reel.

They were almost to the end of the hallway when a voice called out from one of the rooms.

"Hey—hey, McKenzie!"

Dylan turned, and Rocky followed his gaze to a lanky teen propped up in a hospital bed. He wore a beanie over a bald head and a worn Magnolia Bluff University hoodie that looked two sizes too big. His IV drip was slow, steady, and hooked behind him like a shadow, but the grin on his face was electric.

"Man, no way," Dylan said as he stepped inside. "You a Shark?"

The kid's smile stretched wider. "Will be soon, if chemo doesn't slow me down."

Dylan blinked hard and stepped up to the side of the bed. "Hell yeah. What's your name?"

"DeShawn," the teen said, pride swelling in his voice. "My uncle went there. I've got Shark Nation in my blood. Can't wait to see a game at The Reef."

Rocky whistled low. "You're aiming for the big leagues, huh?"

"Damn right I am," DeShawn said, adjusting the IV line without missing a beat. "I already know what dorm I want, and I've got a playlist for my move-in day."

Dylan couldn't stop smiling. "You're more prepared than I was."

DeShawn tilted his head, studying him. "You still keep in touch with Coach Busby?"

Dylan nodded. "Every few weeks. He still cusses like a sailor and calls me Prime Time but yeah."

"That's so sick." DeShawn's voice lowered, more serious now. "I watched that old clip the other day. The final drive against Gulf Coast. You hurdled that safety and threw the ball to the ref like a mic drop."

Dylan barked out a laugh. "You did *not* just call it a mic drop."

"It was though," DeShawn said, eyes sparkling. "That's the moment I knew I wanted to go there."

Something shifted in Dylan's chest. That game felt like a lifetime ago—but somehow it still lived in people. In kids like DeShawn, who were already dreaming bigger than the room they were stuck in.

Dylan reached out, offered a fist bump. "We'll save you a seat in Shark Nation, alright?"

DeShawn bumped his fist back, grin returning. "Make sure it's on the fifty."

The Mexican restaurant sat on a quiet corner in downtown Celebration, all colorful tilework and string lights, with a menu laminated against spilled juice and queso drips. Dylan slid into the booth across from Rocky and Naomi just as their youngest plopped a tablet on the table and immediately opened a *Paw Patrol* game at full volume.

"Volume, Zo," Naomi said without looking, nudging a paper cup of apple juice toward her daughter. Zoey turned it down to a merciful level and stuck her tongue out before focusing on her screen.

Rocky raised a chip like a toast. "To hospital visits and children who name their IV poles after mascots."

Dylan grinned, still riding the high from earlier. "Tempest had a big morning."

Naomi laughed softly, but her eyes flicked toward him with that quiet perceptiveness Dylan had never quite learned how to dodge. She handed their older son a set of headphones before reaching for her sweet tea.

"So..." she said, too casually. "Ali."

Dylan's hand paused halfway to the chip basket.

Rocky just leaned back with a satisfied smirk. "Here we go."

Naomi ignored him. "You've looked like a man permanently texting someone for four weeks straight. Either it's her or you've got a secret *Candy Crush* addiction."

Dylan snorted. "It's her."

"And?" Naomi pressed, stirring her drink like she wasn't watching his every micro-expression.

He glanced down at his plate, then back up—shoulders easing in that slow, quiet way he rarely allowed outside of his own house.

"She told me she loves me," he said.

Naomi blinked. "She did?"

"She didn't mean to." He scratched the back of his neck, voice softer now. "It just...happened at the end of a text. She was tired. Distracted. Didn't even catch it at first. But when I told her, she didn't backpedal. She meant it. Sent it in writing, too."

Naomi's face shifted, something gentle in her smile. "And how are *you* feeling about it?"

He didn't answer right away. His gaze moved to Zoey, still laser-focused on her tablet, and then to the sidewalk outside the big front window—families strolling past boutique shops and a bubble machine sputtering in the town square. Celebration had a way of feeling like a snow globe town, charming and surreal.

"I've never been more sure of anything," he said finally. "Not in my whole damn life."

Rocky let out a quiet breath. "Well, damn."

Naomi reached across the table and gave Dylan's hand a light squeeze. "Good. She's good for you. You've been lighter lately. Softer."

Dylan smirked. "Don't let the team hear that."

"They already know," Rocky muttered. "You've been humming in the locker room. I thought you had a head injury."

Naomi rolled her eyes. "Ignore him. I'm happy for you."

Dylan nodded, a smile tugging at the corners of his mouth. "Thanks. I think I'm finally where I'm supposed to be."

Today Was a Fairytale

Ali

The sky outside had shifted from soft blue to dusky lavender, the last light of day melting behind Ali's blackout curtains. Inside her bedroom, the glow of the TV cast flickers across the walls, the air thick with the scent of popcorn, lip balm, and the faintest trace of peppermint lotion from earlier.

Ali and Ashley were still piled under the comforter in their pajamas—Ali in one of Dylan's old shirts and fuzzy socks, Ashley in her "Get In Loser, We're Going Snacking" set from Etsy. At some point, the throw blanket from the couch had migrated in, and now it was tangled around both of them like a fleece burrito.

The end credits of the *Hannah Montana* season one finale scrolled across the screen.

Ashley exhaled dramatically. "Okay. Miley's officially lied to too many people, and I need something with singing and high-stakes talent show drama."

Ali cracked open one eye. "You're thinking *Camp Rock,* aren't you?"

Ashley looked insulted. "When am I *not* thinking *Camp Rock*?"

Ali grinned. "Sold."

Ashley backed out of Disney+ with the precision of someone disarming a bomb. "*Camp Rock* one. We do not acknowledge the sequel."

Ali reached for her phone and opened the DoorDash app. "We need sugar. And fries. Maybe a quesadilla. Something with a shocking number of carbs."

"Root beer float," Ashley said, pointing at nothing in particular. "From that diner place."

Ali was already typing. "I'm getting the cookie skillet. Don't fight me."

"As if I'd ever fight a cookie skillet ."

By the time the trailer montage started to play and Demi Lovato looked dramatically at her reflection in a pond, the order was placed, their stomachs growled in anticipation, and Ashley was full-on harmonizing with the intro music like she was auditioning for *The Voice: Pajama Edition.*

Ali laughed and curled deeper into the blanket. The day had been nothing but fleece and feel-good chaos, and honestly? She needed it. She hadn't touched her email, hadn't brushed her hair since 10 a.m., and hadn't once let herself overthink Dylan's last message.

Okay, maybe once.

Twice.

But she was proud of herself for mostly chilling. Ashley had a way of making the noise quiet, of anchoring her in a way few people could.

The doorbell rang, and both of them sat up like feral raccoons.

"Skillet cookie," Ashley said reverently.

Ali grabbed the tip envelope from the nightstand. "Let's go, baby."

By Thursday afternoon, the sugar high had faded and the emails were relentless.

Ali sat at her desk, eyes glazed as she stared at a spreadsheet she'd opened four times and still hadn't updated. Her office was quiet except for the low hum of the air conditioning and the faint tapping of someone's keyboard down the hall.

Her phone buzzed across the desk, flashing

Dylan

She smiled before she even picked it up.

She may have added the cute heart emojis next to his name in her contacts in the middle of Joe and Demi's duet the other day—Ashley had clutched her heart and declared it "a spiritual experience." Ali, overwhelmed by feelings (and sugar), had edited his contact mid-chorus.

No regrets.

She snatched it up like it might disappear.

"Hey, you," she said, already smiling.

"Hey, baby," came his voice—low, rough, and just the right kind of smug. "You busy?"

"Only emotionally. What's up?"

She could hear him smile. "I'm coming to see you this weekend."

Her brain short-circuited. "Wait—what?"

"I miss you, Ali. Like…it's getting bad. I almost kissed my phone screen last night."

Her stomach did a full somersault.

"I had to bribe Kallie with brunch and promise I'd finish a promo shoot early next week," he went on. "But she cleared my schedule. I'm flying in Friday."

Ali leaned back in her chair, the breath whooshing out of her like someone had opened a window in her chest.

"You're really coming?"

"I'm really coming. I need you, sweetheart. I want a weekend of nothing but you. Pajamas and bad TV and me holding you so tight you forget what loneliness ever felt like."

She bit her lip, her voice small but full of warmth. "You already do that. Just by calling."

"Yeah, well," he said, his voice thick now, "It's not enough. I need to see your face without a screen between us."

Ali blinked hard at the sudden sting behind her eyes. "I'll stock up on junk food and cozy blankets."

"And I'll bring you breakfast in bed. Every damn morning."

"You are *so* lucky I love you," she whispered.

"I really am," he said softly. "See you tomorrow, baby."

They stayed on the line for a few more seconds—quiet, connected, not needing anything else.

When she finally hung up, the spreadsheet was still blank. But her heart was full.

She sat there for a moment after the call ended, staring at her phone, her lips still curved in a stunned little smile. Then her fingers started tapping—light and restless—against the desk, her mind already racing ahead.

She could wait for him to Uber from the airport. Let him come to her.

Or…she could take a half day, drive to Savannah, and be there the second he stepped off the plane.

The image hit her so fast and so clear—Dylan in arrivals, baseball cap pulled low, that slow grin breaking across his face when he saw her—that she was already on her feet.

Screw the spreadsheet.

She *skipped*—literally skipped—down the hallway in her sandals, earning a bewildered look and a muttered "everything okay?" from reception. She wasn't even embarrassed. Just laughed and waved.

As she passed Jason's office, she popped her head in, "Follow me, Thor."

Abigail's office door was cracked. Ali knocked once and pushed it open.

Abigail glanced up from her monitor, brows lifting. "Why do you look like a Hallmark movie just threw up on you?"

Ali grinned. "He's coming. Tomorrow. I'm taking a half day and picking him up at the airport."

Abigail blinked once. "Dylan?"

Ali nodded, bouncing on her toes like a child announcing Christmas came early. "I want to be there when he lands. I don't want to waste a single second."

Abigail let out a full-body gasp and jumped from her chair. "YES. Go. I'll cover everything."

"Actually—take the whole day," Jason chimed in from behind her. "Get a blowout in the morning. Spray tan."

Then he paused. "Scratch that—no spray tan. He'd mess it up before it dried."

"We don't care what you do," Abigail added, "just go be cute and happy."

Ali laughed, hugging herself. "Y'all are the best."

"We know," they said in unison.

"Now get out of here before I cry from how disgustingly romantic this is. I need to call Kellan and remind myself I have the best husband in the world. Except for the week he hid my Diet Cokes."

She narrowed her eyes, deadly serious. "Don't think I've forgotten about that."

Ali cackled. "Justice for caffeine."

"Exactly," Abigail said, waving her off. "Now go. Be in love. Be annoying. I fully support it."

Ali blew her a kiss and turned down the hallway, practically floating.

She tried walking normally back to her office, heart pounding, already mentally planning her outfit, her playlist, and—priorities—her wax.

The second she stepped back into her office, she grabbed her phone and started texting at lightning speed.

> Hi Saylor! I know it's last minute but pleasssse tell me you have an opening by some miracle today! I need to be smooth, confident, and emotionally stable by tomorrow. Prioritizing the first two but would really love all three.

She hit send and flopped into her chair with a dreamy sigh, spinning in a slow, contented circle. Her reflection in the black computer screen looked flushed and happy.

God, she missed him. And tomorrow, she wouldn't have to.

> GIRLIE POP! One of my regulars just canceled for 2pm—probably got back with her situationship again. Come on in. I'll have the good numbing spray and a heating pad waiting. PCOS girlies stick together. We suffer…but make it.

Ali snorted so loudly she nearly dropped her phone. She texted back a string of heart emojis and a *"You're a lifesaver"* before marking the appointment in her calendar with six exclamation points.

Tomorrow couldn't come fast enough.

Dress

Dylan

D ylan grabbed his duffle from the overhead bin the second the seatbelt light dinged off, muttering a quick thanks to the flight attendant as he moved toward the front of the plane. His heart was already racing, thumping out a beat that had nothing to do with altitude.

He cleared the jet bridge and headed straight for the rental car counter, weaving through the sleepy little Savannah airport with practiced efficiency. Cap low, hoodie up, head down.

No lingering. No stopping. Just get through, get to the car, get to—

Then he saw her.

Bright pink. Wavy blonde curls. Bottom lip caught between her teeth as she scanned the arrivals area like she was searching for someone who might already be looking at her.

Dylan froze mid-step.

Ali.

His chest tightened, and a grin broke across his face before he could stop it. That *was* her. She was here. Waiting for him.

And holy *hell*—those shoes.

His gaze dropped automatically, eyes widening at the sight of her short legs wrapped in strappy, towering, six-inch sandals that did things to him he wasn't prepared for in public.

His girl who hated heels. His girl who once tripped wearing kitten wedges at a semi-formal and declared "Gravity is a myth perpetuated by thin people."

She was in full Barbie bombshell mode. He was semi-hard from thirty feet away.

She had to have borrowed them from Abigail. Had to. No way she owned shoes like that.

But she was wearing them. For him.

And that made him want to do very, *very* unholy things the second they were alone.

Then she spotted him.

Her eyes locked on his, wide and shining and full of something that hit him straight in the damn chest.

She looked like she was about to run—like she wanted to—but then her gaze flicked downward, just for a second, and he saw the exact moment she remembered the heels.

Ali Presley in six-inch sandals wasn't built for a sprint. But damn if she didn't start a determined fast-walk anyway, like she couldn't stand one more second of distance between them.

It was the cutest thing he'd ever seen.

And it completely undid him.

Dylan didn't think. Didn't hesitate. He *took off*—breaking into a sprint across the terminal floor, ignoring the curious looks and the startled airport staff and the fact that he was definitely going to get stopped by security if he kept this up.

She barely had time to gasp before he was there, dropping his duffle with a *thud*, cupping her face in his hands, and crashing his mouth against hers like he'd been starving for it.

Ali melted into him, arms winding tight around his shoulders, her body going soft and desperate in all the ways he loved.

He grabbed her hips, lifting her effortlessly, and she wrapped her legs around his waist like it was second nature. Like she'd been waiting for this moment as long as he had.

"Hi," she whispered between kisses, breathless and a little teary.

Dylan held her tighter. "Hi, baby."

And then he kissed her again—right there in the middle of baggage claim, with her legs around him and her shoes dangling and the world spinning a little too fast.

He kissed her like it had been years. Like he hadn't just seen her face on FaceTime last night or heard her sleepy voice that morning. Like she was oxygen and he'd been drowning since the moment he boarded that plane.

Ali's legs tightened around his waist, her lips still parted, breath shallow against his cheek.

They might've stayed like that forever—wrapped up in each other, floating above the marble floors of the Savannah airport—if not for the soft but firm sound of someone clearing their throat.

Dylan blinked and turned his head slightly.

A security guard stood a few feet away, hands politely folded in front of him, a mildly guilty look on his face like he hated to ruin the moment.

"Afternoon, sir," the guard said gently. "Ma'am. Sorry to interrupt, but…if you could just, uh, move things along? We're still in a public area."

Dylan felt Ali's body jolt with a tiny laugh against his chest.

He nodded quickly, adjusting his grip on her and lowering her back to the ground—carefully, mindful of those skyscraper heels.

"Right," Dylan said, clearing his throat and giving the guy an apologetic smile. "Sorry about that."

"No trouble," the guard replied with a barely-there grin. "Just…maybe save the leg-wrapping for the parking lot."

Ali buried her face in Dylan's chest, clearly mortified. He just laughed, tugging her in close with one arm while grabbing his duffle with the other.

"Come on, Trouble," he whispered into her hair. "Let's get you outta here before I forget there are laws."

Dylan merged onto I-16 with one hand on the wheel and the other resting casually on Ali's thigh, his thumb brushing over the hem of her dress. She hadn't stopped talking since they pulled out of the airport parking deck, and he wasn't complaining. He'd missed her voice. The way it sped up when she was excited. The way she waved her hands around—even when buckled in—to really *emphasize* a point.

"…and then Ashley said it wasn't that deep, but Abigail nearly launched her Kindle across the room because apparently *it was* that deep, and now we all have to reread the chapter with fresh eyes," Ali said, gesturing wildly. "Anyway, I think we're picking a new book next week, but we're split between a dark academia murder thing or something spicy with pirates, which feels like emotional whiplash but also kind of on brand for us?"

Dylan smiled, keeping his eyes on the road but soaking up every word. "Spicy pirates, huh?"

"I mean, it's probably just pirate-adjacent," she said with a shrug. "Like, seafaring rogues with a trauma kink and a moral compass buried somewhere under the tattoos."

He huffed a laugh. "You sound into it."

"Look, I'm not saying I have a type…" She shot him a sidelong glance and smirked. "But if you got a gold earring and a ship, I wouldn't hate it."

"I'll make a few calls. I bet Captain Rip could hook me up" he teased, giving her thigh a squeeze.

She giggled and leaned her head back against the seat, her curls catching the sunlight streaming through the windshield. "God, I missed you."

He glanced over at her, heart squeezing in his chest. "Missed you more."

She reached out and toyed with the sleeve of his t-shirt. "Also, Abigail and Jason completely cleared my schedule today and told me to take the whole day off. I was just going to do a half day, but they bullied me out the door and told me to go get a blowout. Then Ab threatened me with emotional violence if I showed up at work today."

"She's solid," Dylan said.

"She *is*. So I was thinking…" Ali lit up again, turning in her seat. "We should take her a six-pack of Diet Cokes as a thank you. She's still holding a grudge over Kellan hiding hers in the garage that time, so I feel like it'll hit. Grab a coffee from Rise & Grind for Jason."

"Done," Dylan said easily. "Want to write her name on each can in Sharpie like an offering?"

Ali laughed, reaching over to squeeze his arm. "I love you."

"I know," he said with a grin, kissing the back of her hand. "You told me."

They stepped inside, the door clicking shut behind them with a soft thud.

Ali bent down, already reaching for the ankle strap of one of the sandals Abigail had loaned her—six-inch torture devices, no matter how cute they looked.

But Dylan's hand shot out, catching her wrist.

"Don't," he said, voice low and rough behind her.

She straightened slowly, brows lifting. "Don't what?"

He looked her up and down, and the heat in his gaze was enough to make her knees wobble—*especially* in the damn heels.

"Don't take them off," he said again, stepping closer. "It would be a crime to get you out of that dress before I've had you in it. And those shoes?" His voice dipped darker. "Baby, I've been semi-hard since the airport. You're not going anywhere."

Her breath caught. "They're not even mine."

"I don't give a fuck if they belong to Abigail, Cinderella, or the Queen of England," he murmured, crowding her gently against the wall. "I want them on when I make you scream."

Her stomach flipped. "Dylan..."

He kissed her then—deep, hungry, full of that quiet desperation they'd been sitting in for weeks. His hands slid down her waist to the curve of her ass, fingers digging in as he pressed her back, hips already tight against hers.

"You feel how much I missed you?" he whispered, grinding just enough to make her gasp. "You know how crazy I've been thinking about this body? About *you*?"

Her fingers tangled in the front of his shirt, anchoring herself. "You're not playing fair."

He kissed along her jaw, down to her throat, dragging his mouth slow and hot. "Wasn't planning to."

So High School

Ali

He pulled back just enough to look at her—really look at her—his hands still gripping her hips.

"You remember the wall at the fundraiser?" he murmured, voice gravel-dark. "Been thinking about that for a month."

Ali's knees buckled slightly, her back pressing against the cool wall behind her.

Dylan smirked like he *felt* it.

"I'm starting to think I have a thing for you and *wall things*."

"You're ridiculous," she whispered, breath catching as his hand skimmed up her thigh beneath the hem of her dress.

He slid his hand higher, fingers tracing over the edge of her panties—lace, damp, and ruined for anyone else.

"You wore these for me?" he asked, his mouth brushing hers.

"Maybe" she said, breathless.

His growl was low and guttural as he hooked her leg around his hip, her heel dragging across the back of his thigh. The angle made her breath hitch.

"I'm not going to make it to the bedroom," he rasped. "Not with you looking like this. Not when I've been hard since *Savannah baggage claim*."

He shifted, freeing himself just enough to press the thick, hot length of him against her through the lace. Her hips jerked, and he groaned, forehead pressed to hers.

"Tell me you want it here," he said. "Tell me you want me to fuck you right against this wall."

"I want it," she whispered, shaking. "God, Dylan, please."

And then he was pushing her panties aside and sinking into her—deep, hard, *home*—with a moan that sounded more like a prayer.

She cried out.

His hands framed her face, his thrusts slow and deep and devastating. "You feel that, baby? How wet you are for me?"

She whimpered, digging her nails into his shoulders, the wall solid at her back, his body even more so in front of her.

"Fuck," he breathed, "I missed you so bad. You're mine, Ali. Say it."

"I'm yours," she gasped. "Yours. Always."

Her back hit the wall over and over with the rhythm of his thrusts—deep and deliberate, like he was trying to etch this into her bones. She clung to him, breath shaky, the heels giving her just enough height to take all of him while he worked her body like he owned it.

Which he did.

Every. Damn. Inch.

"Look at me," he whispered against her mouth. "Eyes on me, baby."

She did. And what she saw in his face—pure awe, raw hunger, that dark, desperate need—made her whimper.

"You are so fucking beautiful," he rasped, voice almost breaking. "You have no idea what you do to me."

"Dylan..."

"I mean it," he said, sliding one hand down to grip her thigh harder, opening her wider for him, grinding deeper. "I think about this every night. About how perfect you feel. How perfect you *look* when you fall apart."

She was close—*too* close—but he wasn't letting up. Not yet. He slowed the pace just enough to keep her right on the edge, her entire body twitching with need.

"Please," she gasped, nails digging into his shoulders.

"I know, baby," he groaned, sweat beading at his temple. "I know you're right there. But I want to *see* it. Want to feel you go wild for me. Let me hear those pretty noises. Let me wreck you."

He dipped his head, kissing down her throat, licking at the sweat-slick skin just below her jaw. "You're mine, Ali. You've always been mine."

Her body clenched hard around him and her head drop back with a cry. "Dylan—*oh gawd*—I can't—"

"Yes, you can," he said fiercely, lips at her ear. "Come for me. Now."

She shattered. Her thighs trembled around his hips, her heel digging into his back as she came hard—pulse fluttering, voice breaking on a sobbed moan of his name. Her whole body tightened around him like she didn't want to let go, and he didn't stop moving, thrusting through it like he needed to feel every second of her falling apart.

"Jesus *fuck*," he growled, bracing a hand above her on the wall. "That's it, sweetheart. That's my good fucking girl."

She was still pulsing around him—tight, wet, perfect—when his control snapped.

He let out a strangled groan, deep in his chest, and slammed into her one last time, burying himself as deep as her body would take him. His hips stuttered as he came, eyes squeezed shut, forehead pressed hard to hers.

"Fuck, *Ali*—" he gasped, holding her like she might slip away, like the only thing keeping him tethered to the world was being inside her.

Her name fell from his lips like a prayer, a curse, a thank-you whispered to the universe for bringing her back to him.

His thighs trembled with the force of it, breath ragged against her cheek as he spilled inside her, hips grinding in slow, broken circles until he had nothing left.

Nothing but her.

They stayed tangled together—his body flush against hers, her back still pressed to the wall, her breath mingling with his. Her heel dug into his thigh, and his hands roamed slowly over her sides, like he wasn't ready to let go just yet.

He pulled back just enough to meet her eyes. His gaze was heavy-lidded, his voice rough from everything they'd just done.

"Abigail's never getting those heels back."

Ali blinked, then laughed—soft and breathless and still a little dazed. "They're loaned, not stolen."

"They are *claimed*," he said, dragging his thumb gently along her jaw. "You're never taking them off around me again."

She rolled her eyes but the smile stayed. "You've got a whole thing now, don't you?"

"Damn right I do," he muttered, leaning in to kiss her again—this one slower, sweeter, all tongue and tenderness and too many weeks apart. "My girl. My heels. My wall."

Ali made a scandalized sound, eyes wide. "Oh my *gawd*—you read *Iron Flame*?"

Dylan grinned, not even pretending to be ashamed. "Only the parts with Xaden making Violet throw lightning and forget her own name."

She snorted, head dropping to his shoulder. "You are *unbelievable.*"

"Tell me I'm wrong," he said, carrying her toward the hallway. "Dark, broody man. Wall sex. Tactical use of shadows. Sounds familiar, doesn't it?"

She giggled into his neck. "You're insufferable."

"And yet," he said, stopping just long enough to nudge her bedroom door open with his foot, "You're still clinging to me."

The bathroom filled quickly with steam, fogging the mirror and softening the edges of the world. Dylan stood behind her under the spray, water cascading down their tangled bodies, his hands never far from her skin.

He washed her gently—fingers sliding over her thighs, her shoulders, her scalp—as if memorizing every part of her all over again. She leaned into it, boneless and safe, her cheek resting against his chest as he rinsed the suds from her hair.

Neither of them said much, but the silence was full. Full of touches and soft kisses, of murmured *you okay, baby?* and whispered *I missed you too much* when her arms circled his waist.

By the time they climbed into bed, Ali had traded the heels for fuzzy socks and Dylan had pulled on a pair of low-slung sweatpants. Her hair was damp and braided over one shoulder, and she was curled into his chest like she was built to fit there.

"Comfy?" he asked, brushing a hand down her spine.

"Mmm," she hummed. "You're warm."

They lay like that for a long while, letting the softness settle in around them—just skin, and sheets, and the clean scent of soap between kisses. HGTV played quietly in the background.

Eventually, Dylan shifted, propping himself on one elbow to look at her.

"Hey," he said, voice a little shy for a man who'd just taken her against the entryway wall. "Wanna go on a date with me tonight?"

She blinked, amused. "You're here for twelve seconds and already planning an outing?"

He grinned. "You'll like this one."

Her brow arched. "Hit me."

"Flashback Friday at the Hopeulikit Drive-In. Double feature. *Clueless* and *10 Things I Hate About You.*"

Ali gasped like he'd offered her front-row Taylor Swift tickets. "*Shut up.*"

"I would never," he said solemnly. "I saw it on the schedule earlier this week and called to make sure they had our usual spot open."

Her eyes softened. "You remembered our spot?"

He leaned down to kiss her temple. "It's where I fell in love with you the first time, Al. Of course I remembered."

She swallowed hard, her fingers curling around the edge of his shirt. "You're gonna make me cry."

He smiled against her hair. "Then I'm definitely doing something right."

Ali popped a Raisenet into her mouth and leaned her head against Dylan's shoulder, her eyes flicking between the screen and the sky behind it—deep indigo now, scattered with stars.

Being back in Loblolly County felt strange. Not bad exactly. Just...weird. Like slipping into an old cardigan she hadn't worn since college. A little too familiar. But Dylan sitting beside her—his arm draped over her shoulder, his fingers idly stroking the curve of her bicep like he couldn't not touch her—that made it feel different.

Old and new all at once.

This was the man she should've been here with all along.

The crack of a windshield being smashed pulled her focus back to the screen just in time to see Kat Stratford backing into the jerk's car with perfect precision. *Oops.*

Dylan chuckled under his breath. "Still one of the greatest scenes of all time."

She nodded, smiling around a mouthful of popcorn. "It's cathartic. Like a feminist war cry in Doc Martens."

He leaned closer, his breath warm at her temple. "You ever do anything like that?"

She gave him a look. "I'm a rule follower."

"That wasn't a *no.*"

Ali grinned. "Okay fine. I once sharpied *karma's real* on a Trobe's bathroom mirror after he ghosted Daisy."

Dylan turned to look at her, impressed and amused. "Wait, *Trobe's*? As in...Tau Rho Beta?"

She nodded, eyes still fixed on the screen. "Right across from the downstairs keg fridge."

He laughed, low and surprised. "Damn. Remind me never to get on your bad side."

But she didn't laugh this time. She kind of paused, fingers curling in the hem of her dress as she cleared her throat. "Daisy was still in my life ya know. She was in a daze, was wrecked. I just—" She shook her head. "I wanted to do *something*."

Dylan's expression softened, the edges of his teasing melting away. His arm tightened around her shoulders, warm and steady. "Of course you did."

Ali shrugged, but the pressure in her chest loosened just a little. The memory still stung, but saying it aloud—with *him*—took some of its bite away.

"Anyway," she said after a beat, nudging him lightly, "I stand by it. He deserved it."

"Hell yeah, he did," Dylan murmured, pressing a kiss to the top of her head. "Remind me to order you a pack of Sharpies for emergencies."

She laughed again, more genuine this time, the ache fading into something softer as Kat strutted off-screen and the next scene rolled. And just like that, the past felt a little more bearable. A little less sharp. Because Dylan was here, beside her, making space for every part of her—even the broken pieces.

Dylan

Onscreen, Bianca Stratford hauled off and decked Joey Donner across the jaw, and the crowd erupted—both in the movie and in a few parked cars nearby. Dylan grinned, but his focus had already drifted.

Ali was curled up beside him in the passenger seat, legs tucked under her, one bare foot pressed against her thigh. Her flip-flops had been abandoned within the first five minutes of them pulling in. She was leaning in closer as the movie went on, her cheek practically on his shoulder.

He could feel the rise and fall of her breath. The warmth of her body. The faint scent of whatever lotion she used—coconut, or something like it. He wanted to bottle it. Bury his face in it.

She shifted slightly. "I have to pee," she whispered.

He turned, brows lifting. "Now?"

She gave a sheepish little smile. "I didn't want to interrupt the movie, but I can't hold it."

Dylan gave her a look. "You want me to walk you?"

"You don't have to—"

"I'm walking you."

She rolled her eyes affectionately, but she was already gathering herself up. He slipped out of the Grand Cherokee and came around to her side just as she was stepping down, shoes back on, her dress brushing against her legs. She tucked her hair behind one ear, fingers catching on a knot from the wind.

They rounded the corner past the concession stand and dim porch light, where the restrooms sat quietly, a few couples milling nearby with sodas and candy.

"I didn't want to miss the poem," she added softly, slowing as they reached the wall.

Dylan leaned against the stucco, hands in his pockets. "You've got time. Movie magic's on our side."

She glanced at him, eyes soft. "Wait here?"

"Always."

She gave him one of those crooked little smiles—the kind that made his chest tighten—and disappeared through the bathroom door, leaving him with the echo of her steps and the scent of coconut.

He let his head fall back against the wall and blew out a breath. Something about this night felt like closure and beginnings all at once. The kind of night he'd once dreamed about when everything had gone to hell. And now?

He was here. She was here. And it was better than he ever imagined.

The quiet buzz of the drive-in faded beneath the soft music from the movie and the occasional rustle of popcorn bags. Dylan leaned against the stucco wall just outside the women's restroom, scrolling his phone aimlessly—Ali had been inside for less than two minutes.

That's when he heard it.

"Mac? *Mac McKenzie*, is that you?!"

His head jerked up.

Fuck.

Walking toward him, stilettos clacking across the concrete like some kind of omen, was Jenna Hawthorne—one of Daisy's old sorority sisters. Bleach blonde, way too tan, and still wearing that same glossy-lipped smile he remembered from Magnolia Bluff.

He hadn't seen her in a decade. And he could've gone another ten without fixing that.

"Jenna," he said, straightening up, trying to keep his voice even. Calm. Not draw attention.

But she was already closing the gap, squealing as she threw her arms around his neck in a full-body launch that left him stunned and stumbling half a step back.

"Oh *my God*, it *is* you! You look *exactly* the same," she purred, still hanging off him like she had a claim.

Dylan stiffened, jaw clenched. "Hey, uh...yeah. Hi."

She pulled back, eyes raking him with open appreciation. "God, Daisy used to *brag* about you all the time. I haven't seen you since the Tau Delt formal—remember that night? I still have the pics."

Before he could reply, she spun toward the guy waiting nearby—some dude in boat shoes and a neon polo. "Babe! *This* is Mac McKenzie. Daisy's brother. Played at Bluff, now he's in the NFL!"

The guy blinked, eyes widening with immediate recognition. "No *way*. The Tritons, right?"

Dylan gave him a tight nod, trying not to look like a cornered animal. "Yeah. That's me."

And then his stomach dropped.

Ali.

Any second now, she was going to walk out that door and see this. This sorority reunion clinging to him like it was 2014 again. And there wasn't a snowball's chance in hell he was letting Jenna's presence ruin their night. Not when Ali had come so far. Not when he *finally* had her back.

He shifted slightly, forcing a smile. "Hey, it's great seeing you guys. Really. But I'm here with someone and—"

"Oh come *on*, just one selfie?" Jenna was already digging in her purse, gloss catching the light. "Daisy will *die* when she sees this."

His jaw ticked. "Not a good time, Jenna."

She blinked, thrown by the shift in tone. "Jeez. Still intense, huh?"

He didn't answer. Just glanced at the bathroom door, praying for a few more seconds before Ali came out and saw this trainwreck unfolding.

He needed to get this girl away. Now

Too late.

Dylan's stomach dropped as the bathroom door swung open and Ali stepped out, still tugging down the hem of her oversized T-shirt dress, flip-flops popping. Her hair was a little wild from the car ride, her cheeks flushed from laughing just ten minutes ago. But the second her eyes landed on Jenna—with her arms still draped around Dylan's shoulders—something in her face shifted.

He moved instinctively, wanting to close the distance, to grab her and walk the hell away from this mess before it got worse.

But Jenna spotted her first.

"Oh my *God*," she gasped, eyes lighting up—but not in a nice way. "Wait. *Ali Presley*? You're still around? We thought you, like, moved out of the country after that night in Myrtle Beach."

She giggled. Fucking giggled.

Dylan's blood ran cold. "Don't start, Jenna."

But Jenna just smiled sweetly, tilting her head with faux innocence. "Are you two...here together?"

He opened his mouth to answer, but Ali's voice cut clean and quick across the parking lot.

"No. We just ran into each other earlier," she said, crossing her arms tightly over her chest. "He's visiting family in Honeyshore."

Dylan's heart stopped.

Jenna blinked. "Oh," she said with a sugary nod. "That makes *so* much more sense."

He turned to Ali, trying to catch her eye, trying to *understand*. But she wouldn't look at him. Her arms stayed locked in place, like armor.

"Well, that's *adorable*," Jenna added, linking her arm through her boyfriend's. "Good seeing you, Mac. And...Ali. You look...God you look the same." The tone made it sound like an insult.

Dylan didn't say a word as they walked off, Jenna's laughter still floating on the humid air.

Silence wrapped around them like a fog. Ali's arms stayed crossed, her lips pressed tight. She didn't reach for his hand. Didn't say anything.

And Dylan?

Dylan was *wrecked*.

His pulse thudded painfully as they walked back to the Jeep. Every step pounded with the same thought: she still didn't want him.

Not really.

After everything they'd shared. The whispers. The *I love yous*. The promise of more. The fucking *heels*.

And yet, when it counted—when someone from their past showed up—she acted like he was a stranger.

She hadn't just denied him.

She'd *erased* him.

He gripped the steering wheel as they reached the car, jaw tight, chest hollow. She climbed in without a word. Didn't even look at him.

Dylan stared out, his fists clenched in his lap.

She still couldn't claim him.

Worse—she still wouldn't *let herself* be claimed.

And fuck if that didn't break him clean in half.

Dylan didn't say a word as he pulled out of the drive-in.

Didn't look at her.

Didn't ask if she was okay.

Didn't turn the music on like he normally would, filling the silence with something easy and familiar. The quiet between them stretched thick and suffocating.

She was still curled into the passenger seat, arms crossed, eyes on the window like she was trying to disappear into the trees lining the backroads of Loblolly County.

He gripped the wheel tighter, knuckles bone-white.

This wasn't how it was supposed to feel. Coming back here with her...it was supposed to be full circle. Sweet. Maybe even healing. Instead, it felt like a fucking rewind button he couldn't stop hitting.

Dylan let out a slow breath, steadying himself. His voice, when it came, was quiet. "I'm taking you home."

Ali didn't answer. Didn't argue. Just gave a small, almost imperceptible nod.

He looked back at the road.

What the hell was he supposed to do now?

Fly back to Orlando and pretend like everything was okay? Like he hadn't just watched the woman he loved pull away from him like loving him out loud was something to be ashamed of?

Like he hadn't seen her protect herself first—again—by throwing up walls she swore were gone?

He'd promised himself this time would be different.

She *said* it would be.

And yet...

Dylan blinked hard, jaw tight. This wasn't about public validation or some macho claim. It wasn't about Jenna or Daisy or the past.

It was about *her* still not believing she was worthy of being loved in the light.

Not just in whispers. Not just in bedsheets and beach kisses and secret texts.

But in front of the world.

And now he was driving her home, back to her safe little bubble, and wondering what the fuck he was supposed to do when she looked at him like a risk instead of a constant.

He didn't want to leave.

Didn't want to stop fighting for her.

But damn if he wasn't tired of waiting for her to believe in what they had the way *he* did.

They walked in without a word.

The click of the front door shutting echoed louder than it should've, like punctuation on the kind of silence that had nothing to do with peace.

Ali hovered by the entryway, arms still wrapped around herself. Dylan didn't look at her. Couldn't. Just followed her silently to her bedroom.

He crossed to where he'd dropped his duffle earlier and reached for the handle.

"I think," he said quietly, eyes on the bag, "It's probably better if I grab a hotel tonight. We can talk tomorrow."

She gasped.

It wasn't dramatic. It was tiny—choked and barely audible—but he heard it like a siren.

"No—Dylan, please—" Her voice broke as her hand flew to her mouth, tears already spilling down her cheeks.

He turned around slowly.

Ali was crying, full and raw, trying to speak through the rush of panic. "I didn't mean it like that—I wasn't trying to hide you—I just...I froze. I panicked. I didn't want her to hurt you or twist anything or—"

"Ali," he said, holding up a hand. Not sharp. Just quiet. Measured. "Breathe."

She tried, but it hitched. Her shoulders shook with the effort. She wiped at her eyes with the back of her hand, hiccupping through it.

Then—a soft knock at the bedroom door.

Dylan slowly crossed the room, his footsteps quiet on the hardwood. He opened the door just a crack.

Ashley stood on the other side, her expression drawn with concern. "I heard—"

"I've got it, Ash. Thanks," he said, calm and steady, no heat in his voice. Just tired. Anchored.

Ashley glanced past him to Ali, whose face was blotchy and wet and whose fingers trembled at her sides. Ali gave the smallest wave, her lips pressed tight.

Ashley hesitated, but nodded once and stepped back. "Okay. Just holler."

Dylan closed the door gently behind her. Then turned back to Ali.

He took a long breath.

Then another.

And finally—*finally*—he sat on the edge of the bed. Far enough to give her space. Close enough to show he hadn't walked out yet.

"Okay," he said. "Talk."

He watched her for a long moment. The hiccupping breaths. The way her fingers twisted in the hem of her t-shirt dress. Her eyes, rimmed with red but locked on his like she was begging him not to go—not yet.

So he didn't.

He waited.

Finally, she spoke.

"When I was in the hospital," Ali said, her voice barely above a whisper, "They diagnosed me with Borderline Personality Disorder. I didn't even know what that meant at the time. I just...I thought I was broken."

Dylan didn't move. Didn't breathe too loud. He just listened.

"I've spent years in therapy trying to understand it. To manage it. To *live* with it. And I have. Mostly. But there are still triggers." Her voice cracked, but she powered through. "Fear of abandonment is one of them. And tonight...Jenna? *She* was the trigger."

She swallowed hard, voice trembling.

"I saw her and it was like I was twenty again. Weak. Ashamed. Disposable. And you—*you*—you're the only good thing I ever had from that time in my life, and I panicked. Because the second she looked at me, I felt like I didn't deserve you."

Dylan's chest tightened.

Ali's hands balled into fists in her lap.

"I've worked so damn hard to move forward, Dylan. I swear. But trauma's weird. It's sticky. And sometimes it shows up before I can catch it. Tonight...I messed up. I *know* I messed up. And by the time I realized what I was saying, I couldn't figure out how to fix it without making it worse."

She let out a shaky breath.

"I wanted to protect us...but I made you feel like I was ashamed. And that's not true. It's the opposite, actually. I've never loved anyone the way I love you."

Dylan's jaw clenched as he stared down at his hands. When he finally spoke, his voice was low.

"You built a wall between us tonight," he said. "And it was just as solid as the one I count on every Sunday to protect me."

Ali flinched.

"But, I'm still sitting here," he added softly.

She looked up.

"I'm still here," he repeated. "Because I know what trauma can do. I've seen it. And I know it doesn't mean you don't love me. But, baby…you've *got* to let me stand beside you. Not behind you. Not hidden. Not like a damn secret."

Ali nodded, tears spilling again. "I want that. I really do. I just…sometimes the fear wins before I even know it's fighting me."

Dylan leaned forward, forearms resting on his knees.

"Then we fight it together."

She let out a tiny, disbelieving laugh through her tears.

Dylan reached for her hand.

"You're not broken, Ali. You're *fighting*. And I can work with that. I just need you to stop shutting me out when things get scary. Let me be scared with you."

Her hand squeezed his. Tight. Desperate.

"I'm sorry," she whispered.

"I know," he said.

Then he reached out and gently pulled her into his arms—slow, deliberate, like giving her time to resist.

She didn't.

She melted into him, breath shuddering, face tucked into his neck. And Dylan closed his eyes.

For a moment, he just held her. Let the silence settle. Let the weight of everything they'd just said start to shift—just a little. But even as her sobs softened, something sharp still sat in his chest. A wound he hadn't dared touch in years.

"I need to tell you something," he murmured, his voice low and rough. "Something I've never said out loud. Not even to Daisy."

Ali didn't move, but he felt her breath catch against his skin.

"I was traumatized too," he said. "That night…when they wouldn't let me in the hospital to see you. When they told me I wasn't family, that I had to wait. I thought—"

His voice cracked. He swallowed hard. "I thought you were already gone. And I hadn't even said goodbye."

Her fingers clutched at his back like she could take the words away, but he kept going, voice steadier now.

"For a solid year, I had night terrors. Panic attacks. I'd wake up gasping, thinking I was too late. I got help—campus health started it, and after I got drafted, the Tritons put me in touch with a team psychologist. I worked through it. But, baby…" He pulled back just enough to look her in the eyes. "You did abandon me. Back then. And I get it. I know why now. I know it wasn't to hurt me. But it broke me anyway."

Tears welled in her eyes again, brimming, silent.

"And tonight, when you said we weren't together—when you wouldn't let yourself say I was yours?" He let out a breath, thick with emotion.

Ali let out a soft sound—a mix between a sob and a gasp. Her hands cradled his face now, trembling.

"I'm not trying to punish you," he added, gently. "But I need you to know—I'm scared too. I've loved you every day for ten years, and I don't think I can survive losing you again."

Ali didn't speak. She didn't have to. Her eyes were wide and shimmering, mouth parted like she wanted to say something but couldn't find the breath. Couldn't find the strength.

So Dylan just leaned forward again, pressing his forehead gently to hers.

They stayed like that.

No more confessions. No fixing. No unraveling the past.

Just breath.

Just the quiet.

Her fingers slowly unclenched in his shirt. His hand slid up her back, holding her close, not to keep her—but to let her stay.

He felt her heartbeat slow against his chest. His own body ached with exhaustion, but not just from the day. From the years. From everything they were finally letting themselves feel.

No tidy endings. No whispered promises.

Just rest.

"I'm not going anywhere," he whispered finally, lips barely brushing her temple.

And then he settled them in the bed, pulling the comforter over them both as he laid back with her in his arms.

Still here. Still his. Still hers.

For now, that was enough.

When her breathing evened out, warm and steady against his chest, Dylan knew she was asleep.

She didn't let go of him.

Not completely.

Her fingers stayed curled in his shirt, like if she loosened her grip, he'd vanish. And maybe...part of her still believed that.

He stayed still for a long while, staring at the ceiling in the dark. His mind wouldn't shut off. Not after everything she'd said. Not after everything he'd finally said back.

He reached for his phone off the nightstand, careful not to jostle her, and angled the screen away from her face. The light burned at first. Then he opened Safari.

He typed: **Borderline Personality Disorder.**

Then: **Fear of abandonment BPD. How to support someone with BPD. Loving someone with BPD.**

He scrolled in the dark, devouring every word in silence. The clinical definitions. The symptoms. The stigma. The pain behind it all. The strength it must've taken for her to sit on that bed and say it out loud.

She'd been trying. Every day.

He swallowed hard, his chest tight.

He ordered a book on Amazon about being in a relationship with someone who suffers from BPD that he kept seeing recommended.

He couldn't fix this for her. He knew that. But he could learn. He could meet her there. Not just in the good moments—but in the panic, the spirals, the dark. Because she deserved someone who wouldn't flinch when the fear crept in.

And dammit, he was going to be that person.

But, Daddy I Love Him

Ali

Ali blinked awake to warm light and an even warmer body wrapped around hers. Dylan's arm was heavy across her waist, his face pressed into the back of her neck, his breath steady and soft. For a few blissful seconds, there was nothing but the rhythm of his breathing and the muted hum of birds outside.

Then came the ache behind her ribs.

Last night came flooding back—Jenna, her panic, Dylan's duffle, the suffocating sobs, the truth. Her stomach turned, but before she could spiral, his arm tightened.

"You okay?" he mumbled, voice rough with sleep.

She nodded, then shook her head. "Kind of?"

He kissed her shoulder gently. "We can talk."

So they did. Wrapped in sheets and sunlight, they talked.

About BPD. About how hard she's worked to regulate and unlearn all the instinctual fears, the catastrophizing. She admitted that sometimes, it still felt like a war inside her head—fighting the voice that said she was too much, not enough, destined to ruin everything.

Dylan listened.

Then Dylan told her about therapy. About the first time he sat across from a counselor on campus, arms crossed and jaw locked, not knowing where to start. How it took months to even say her name without his chest seizing up. How he tried to deny the PTSD diagnosis. How it was scary and confusing for him. But, how he stuck with it anyway—first out of necessity, then because it actually started to help.

He told her about the breathing techniques that calmed his spirals. The nightmares that still came sometimes, but less often now. The guilt he'd carried. The fear. The work he'd done so he could love her without letting that fear control him.

Ali listened.

She squeezed his hand, tears stinging behind her eyes—not from sadness, but from the quiet awe of being seen like this. Loved like this. Not in spite of the mess, but through it.

They sat with it all. No judgment. No rush.

And when it grew too heavy, Ali shifted the energy the way she always did—with a breath and a bit of light.

"So," she said, nudging his chest. "Pancakes and emotional maturity? Or pancakes and farmer's market?"

He cracked a smile. "Can we do all three?"

Downtown Honeyshore buzzed with a slow kind of life on Saturday mornings. Booths lined the squares with local honey, homemade soaps, fresh bread, and succulents in painted pots. A troubadour played covers of early 2000s songs, and toddlers squealed over kettle corn and cheese straw samples.

Ali wore a breezy white dress and her favorite crossbody. Her Golden Goose shoes comfy and worn in. Dylan kept a low profile in a navy baseball cap and sunglasses, but still looked like a walking billboard for hot boyfriend energy in his soft teal T-shirt and gray sweatpants.

He carried the reusable tote like it weighed nothing, full of peaches, sourdough, and some overly expensive jam Ali had absolutely been upsold on.

"You're such a sucker," Dylan teased, leaning in close as they walked past a flower stand.

"I like being romanced by artisanal preserves," she said, biting back a smile. "Let me live."

They paused at a corner booth draped in wildflowers, and Ali pulled out her phone. "Smile," she said, already snapping the pic.

Dylan raised an eyebrow. "We're doing selfies now?"

"We are when you look this good in natural light."

He kissed her temple before she could pull away.

Back at the house, Dylan ducked into the shower, whistling something that might've been "Love Story" while Ali curled up in her bed with her phone.

She scrolled to the picture she'd taken earlier—Dylan's arm slung around her shoulder, both of them squinting slightly in the sun, cheeks pink, eyes soft. It wasn't perfect. But it was real.

Her thumb hovered for a second, then she opened Instagram.

First: a college photo. Her in a Magnolia Bluff crewneck, leaning into Dylan in his uniform on the field after a win, both of them flushed and younger.

Second: the one from the market. Ten years later. Older. Softer. Still them.

She typed the caption quickly, then hit post.

He's still the only one I'd let call the plays.

From the 50-yard line to forever.

#DaliForever #FellForYouTwice #MyAlways #StillMyFavorite #WorthTheWait #QuarterbackedMyHeart #SharkBaitToSeaDate #TheTideDidntBreakWithUs

Honeyshore, GA

She set the phone down and curled into the comforter, her heart doing cartwheels.

Maybe this was what healing looked like. Messy. Imperfect. But real. And—finally—shared.

Ali had barely set her phone down when she heard the unmistakable sound of Ashley squealing from the hallway.

"Sisssss!" Ashley's voice echoed through the house, followed by the sound of her socked feet pounding against the hardwood.

Ali barely had time to sit up before Ashley burst into the room, launching herself onto the bed like a human cannonball, phone clutched in one hand and eyes wide with excitement.

"Omg, I'm so proud of you!" she practically shouted, bouncing on her knees and holding her phone out like it was glowing. "You *posted!* Like, publicly! With *words!* And his *face!*"

Ali laughed, her cheeks warming. "Oh my gawd, Ash. You act like I just proposed or something."

"No, no, no," Ashley said, flopping down beside her with a dramatic sigh. "This is bigger. This is, like, soft-launching your entire *healed era*. This is giving vulnerability. This is giving *main character energy*. I'm obsessed."

Ali rolled her eyes, but her heart fluttered. "Okay, *relax*. It's not that big a deal."

Ashley grinned. "Ali Presley, this is your Super Bowl. Let me have this." Ashley's phone buzzed in her hand, and her eyes lit up.

"It's Abigail!" she said, already accepting the FaceTime call before Ali could protest.

The screen lit up with Abigail's perfectly curled red hair and a raised eyebrow. "Okay *excuse me*," she said, grinning. "Are we not going to talk about the fact that my best friend just broke the internet with her soft-focus football thirst trap?"

Before Ali could respond, Abigail clicked something on her screen.

"Hold, please—merging in Raleigh Ann."

A beat later, Raleigh Ann's face popped up in the corner of the screen, her eyes wide. "Y'all. *Y'ALL.* I had to pull over. I was crying in the Starbucks drive-thru."

Ali groaned and pulled a pillow over her face. "Oh my gawd."

Ashley yanked the pillow away, laughing. "Nope. You don't get to hide. You gave us permission to be *feral* the minute you captioned that photo with feelings."

Abigail was already nodding. "I mean...*'from the 50 yard line to forever'*? That's practically a sonnet. I'm printing it on a sweatshirt."

"I'm making it my next phone background," Raleigh Ann added. "Do we think Dylan will autograph it?"

Ali rolled her eyes, but she couldn't stop smiling. Her cheeks hurt, and her chest ached in that warm, full way that only the people who knew every broken piece of her could bring out.

"I hate all of you," she said, wiping at her eyes and laughing.

"You love us," Ashley said, throwing her arm around Ali's shoulder.

"Obviously," Abigail said, smirking. "And we love you back. And also—*that post?* That man? Ali, babe...you won. Like, in life. That's your man!"

"And your cleavage looked amazing," Raleigh Ann added.

Ali snorted. "*Thank you.*" The screen erupted in giggles, and for the first time in a very long time, everything felt exactly right.

Miss Americana & the Heartbreak Prince

Dylan

Dylan scrubbed the towel over his hair, water still dripping down his chest as he stepped into the steam-filled bathroom. He grabbed his phone off the counter, intending to check the time—and maybe shoot his mom a text to tell her about those honey sticks from the farmer's market.

Instead, a red notification banner caught his eye.

@ali.kat1995 tagged you in a post.

His brows pulled together.

She rarely posted. And if she did, it was usually a dog meme or something about her book club yelling over fantasy fan casts.

He swiped it open.

And froze.

It was a side-by-side.

On the left—a photo from college. One he remembered down to the minute. He'd just won the homecoming game, and Ali had been waiting by the tunnel, cheeks flushed and hair windblown. He'd barely let her speak before tugging her into his arms. Someone had caught the kiss—her smile against his mouth, her hand curled into his jersey.

On the right—the photo from this morning. Her in that blue and white sundress, him in his faded Tritons tee. They were both squinting in the sun, smiling, cheeks pressed close together. Her hair was wild and she looked so damn happy.

He didn't move for a solid five seconds.

Then he exhaled—low and long—his heart thudding like a drum in his chest.

"Shit," he whispered, a grin tugging at his mouth. He rubbed the towel down his neck and stared at the post again, heart swelling. "She really did it."

His girl. His Ali.

She hadn't just said it.

She showed the whole damn world. His heart squeezed tight.

He could hear the girls in the bedroom through the bathroom door—laughter spilling out like a champagne cork had just popped. Ashley's voice was unmistakable, and Ali's giggles followed.

His phone buzzed again.

Rocky:

> BRO. Tell me that post is real and I didn't hallucinate it mid this *Bluey* marathon. Naomi is going to have a meltdown when she sees this.

Kallie:

> MAC! Pick up your damn phone.

Daisy:

> Okay fine, this made me smile. A lot. You look happy, Dyllie. I'm glad. ▯

(Replying to Daisy):

> Appreciate it, but call me Dyllie one more time and I'm telling the kids you used to eat dry Ramen like chips.

(Replying to Rocky):

> She's it, man. Always was. Now quit grinning like a Hallmark grandma and text me the film schedule for the week.

Incoming call—

Kallie.

He ignored it.

Again—**Kallie, calling.**

A third time.

Dylan sighed and finally accepted it.

"About damn time," Kallie's voice came through, breathless like she'd sprinted through her penthouse. "I've been trying to reach you for fifteen minutes. Did you see it? Do you understand what just happened?"

Dylan leaned against the wall, towel slipping a little lower as he scrubbed a hand through his damp hair. "Yeah," he said, voice thick. "I saw it."

"You're tagged, McKenzie. On *Instagram*. That's public. That's not just a soft-launch anymore—that's a *hard commit*, babe."

"I know," he said. And he did. He felt it in his chest like gravity.

"You okay?" Kallie's voice softened.

He smiled, small and real. "I'm more than okay."

"Good," she said. "Because your entire fanbase is already feral in the comments. But screw them—she did this for *you*, M. That girl just told the world you're hers."

Dylan glanced toward the door again, where the laughter kept bubbling over like it couldn't be stopped.

"She's always been mine," he said quietly. "Now she's just not hiding it."

Dylan opened the door to the bedroom just in time to see Ashley kiss Ali on the cheek and bounce off the bed like she'd been launched, the other two girls still squealing through the FaceTime call as she darted out, phone in hand.

The door clicked shut behind her.

Ali blinked up at him, still flushed and glowing, a blanket bunched around her legs.

He didn't say anything at first.

Just stood there in the soft light of her bedroom, his hair damp, towel riding low,, looking at her like she was his entire world.

She looked nervous and unsure. He wasn't having that shit.

Dylan held up his phone.

Ali tilted her head.

He didn't speak—just smirked faintly and tapped the screen, thumb clicking "Share to Story."

A second later, her phone buzzed.

She looked down at the screen—and there it was.

@mac_mckenzie13 reposted your story.

Her breath caught. When she looked back up, he was already walking toward her. Slow. Intentional.

"You know you broke the internet just now, right?" he said, voice low and teasing as he set his phone down and dropped onto the bed beside her.

She shrugged, eyes soft. "Only the parts I care about."

Dylan leaned in, pressing a kiss to her jaw. Then lower, to her neck. "You're dangerous when you're confident."

"I'm dangerous anyway," she murmured, threading her fingers through the ends of his curls. "You're just now catching up."

He huffed out a laugh, but it faded as he shifted, gently rolling her onto her back and hovering above her. "I'm staying, by the way," he said, voice barely above a whisper. "Until Monday morning."

Her heart stuttered. "You are?"

He nodded. "I'm not ready to let go of this yet. Of you."

She reached up, fingers tracing the line of his jaw. "You don't have to let go."

"I know," he murmured, brushing his lips over hers. "That's the whole point."

He kissed her again, deeper now. Slower. His hand slid beneath her shirt, tracing the curve of her waist, her ribs, like he needed to memorize the map of her all over again.

They didn't rush. Not this time.

Every movement was a promise—quiet and tender and achingly reverent. The way he kissed down her body like he had all night. The way he whispered her name into her skin like it was a secret just for them.

Ali clung to him, breathless, eyes glassy, her body arching beneath his as they moved together. And when he finally pushed deep and still, holding her gaze with his own, she knew—without question—this was what coming home felt like.

They stayed wrapped in each other afterward, limbs tangled, hearts steady.

She rested her head on his chest, drawing lazy circles on his skin, and smiled. He was here. And for once, so was she.

August

Ali

August flew by.

Ali spent her days texting Dylan between answering whiny emails from clients trying to write off country club memberships and scrambling to wrap up quarterly filings. His texts were constant—sometimes playful, sometimes filthy, sometimes just a sleepy selfie from the training facility with a "miss you" that derailed her focus for the rest of the afternoon.

Camp had him up before sunrise most days, and the pre-season schedule was already heating up, but he still found time to call her every night. Sometimes it was from the backseat of a car headed to a team dinner. Other times, it was from his hotel room with his hoodie pulled over his head, asking what she had for lunch like it was the most important question in the world.

And even though the season was closing in fast, every message felt like a promise: *I'm still here. I'm not going anywhere.*

She was standing barefoot in her kitchen, nursing an iced coffee that had long ago melted into a watery mess, when her phone buzzed.

Dylan:
You got a sec, baby?

She smiled, already moving toward the living room to plop onto the couch.

Always. What's up?

Her phone rang almost immediately. She answered on the first ring.

"Hi," she said softly, already smiling wider.

"Hi," Dylan replied, that deep, syrupy voice curling in her chest like honey. "You busy next weekend?"

Ali scrunched her nose, mentally scrolling through her calendar. "Not that I know of. Why?"

"The season opener's next Sunday," he said. "Home game. Big deal. New uniforms...the whole thing."

She could hear the smile in his voice.

"Abigail's got those suite tickets," he added. "The ones she won at the fundraiser? I was thinking...if y'all are free, maybe the four of you could come down for the game?"

Ali's heart did that soft fluttery thing it always did when he included her people. "You want us in the suite?"

"I want you with me," he said. "Where I can find your face in the crowd and feel a little less like the world's watching."

She melted into the cushions, warm all over.

"Ya'll can come Friday," he added. "Make a weekend of it."

Ali hesitated.

"I know you hate driving," he said gently. "That's why I'm offering this too—stay with me. All of you. I've got room. Plenty of it."

She blinked. "Wait, you want me...and Abigail and Raleigh Ann and Ashley? In your house?"

"I can handle four women and an army of hair products. I'm a grown man," he teased. "Besides, Naomi says it builds character."

Ali laughed. "You're seriously okay with us crashing your space?"

"I'm seriously counting down the days until you're in it."

Her cheeks flushed as she tucked her legs under her. "You sure?"

"Completely. I want you here, Ali. In my world. At my games. In my house."

She exhaled slowly, smiling at nothing.

"Okay," she whispered. "We're in. Cross your fingers that Ash isn't already going to Atlanta. But I'm in either way."

Ali ended the call and tossed her phone onto the couch, grinning like she was twelve and someone just told her the Jonas Brothers were coming to prom.

"ASHLEY!" she hollered. "Get in here, emergency!"

Ashley appeared in the doorway, mascara wand in hand. "What? What happened? Is Dylan okay? Are *you* okay?"

Instead of answering, Ali was already pulling up her phone and starting a group FaceTime. Abigail answered first, immediately suspicious.

"You're flushed," she said. "What did he do? Are we mad or excited?"

"Excited," Ali said, bouncing slightly. "Just wait—Raleigh Ann's joining—"

"Already here," Raleigh Ann chimed in, settling into her desk chair. "Why do y'all always FaceTime during work hours? I'm not even mad, I just want to understand."

Ali waved her off. "8am is not work hours Raleigh Ann. At least for the non-teaching world. Okay. So Dylan just called. He wants us to come to the *season opener* next weekend. Like, all four of us. The suite tickets from the fundraiser."

Ashley squealed and dropped onto the couch beside her. "YES. Do I wear my cute Tritons tee or save that for the tailgate?!"

"It's Sunday," Ali added quickly. "Kickoff is at one."

"Long weekend vibes," Abigail said approvingly. "I'm packing my comfiest hangover outfit."

Ali paused, biting her lip. "Also...he invited us to stay with him. Like, at his house. Friday through Sunday."

Raleigh Ann's eyebrows flew up. "The whole crew? Mac invited *us* to *his* house?"

"He said he has extra space," Ali said with a little shrug. "And that I hate driving. Which...accurate."

"Honestly, I'm shocked he's letting all of us disrupt his NFL player sanctuary," Ashley said, smirking. "That is like sacred space. He's in love."

Ali flushed deeper, chewing the inside of her cheek. Then—

"Wait. Okay, this is dumb, but...am I just assuming I'm sleeping in his bed? Like—is that weird? Should I offer to bunk with one of y'all? Would that be weird? Oh gawd—"

All four of them burst out laughing.

"Ali," Abigail said, wheezing. "You think we're driving five hours just to snuggle with *you*?"

Ashley threw a pillow at her. "Girl. If you even try to sleep anywhere but wrapped around that man, I'll stage an intervention."

"You're the *girlfriend*," Raleigh Ann added. "You go in the boyfriend bed. We'll manage with guest rooms, or whatever. Just tell us if we need to bring earplugs."

Ali covered her face, groaning. "I hate y'all."

"You love us," Abigail said smugly. "Now send the group chat the dress code for the suite. I need to know how hot I can reasonably look around professional athletes while married."

The road shimmered in the late morning sun, and the inside of Abigail's Range Rover felt like the warm, glittery core of a girl-powered supernova. Taylor Swift's *Blank Space* blasted from the speakers, windows cracked just enough to keep the air moving as they crawled through yet another stretch of I-95 traffic.

Ali sat up front, one leg tucked under her and the other bouncing with nervous energy. Her sunglasses slid down her nose as she glanced at the clock for the sixth time.

"Y'all," she said, twisting to look at the others. "We've been in this same stretch for, like, twenty minutes."

"Welcome to Georgia," Abigail muttered, tapping the steering wheel. "Where time slows down and so do the minivans."

"Can I request a snack handoff?" Raleigh Ann called from the back. "I think my blood sugar's low and my tolerance for Ali's pre-boyfriend nerves is even lower."

Ashley cackled and passed over a half-opened bag of sour gummy worms and a protein bar. "This car is 90% estrogen and 10% Target snacks."

"Sounds like heaven," Ali murmured, grabbing a Diet Coke from the cup holder and cracking it open. The fizzy hiss made her sigh like it was medicinal.

Shania Twain's *"Man! I Feel Like a Woman"* came on next and all four of them screamed like they'd summoned it.

By the second verse, they were full-on belting, windows down now and harmonies questionable at best. Abigail beat the steering wheel like a drum, Ali flung her hair out the window, and Ashley threw up her hands in a dramatic air guitar solo.

Somewhere near Jacksonville, after the singing gave way to giggling and hair fixes, the real planning started.

"Okay," Raleigh Ann said, leaning forward between the seats like she was orchestrating a military operation. "So, what's your entrance plan? You walking in like a romcom heroine or what?"

Ali groaned. "Can't I just exist?"

"No," Ashley said immediately. "You're a girlfriend now. Like a literal NFL WAG. Of a *quarterback*. There's an art to the entrance."

"She needs to be a little late," Abigail said, nodding sagely. "Fashionably delayed. Like, *oops, I got distracted looking hot.*"

"And you better wear those sandals again," Raleigh Ann added. "The ones that made Dylan look like he was about to propose in the airport lobby."

Ali blushed furiously. "I hate y'all."

"We love you," Abigail corrected, glancing sideways with a grin. "And you deserve a stadium entrance. You already won the game, babe."

Ali stared out the window, heart fluttering somewhere between nerves and excitement. Her Spotify queued up the next song—"Enchanted". She let herself lean into it, the lyrics washing over her, soft and dreamy and so ridiculously on brand it almost made her laugh.

She texted Dylan a picture of the road ahead with:

> almost there <3

A bubble popped up almost instantly.

> I've been pacing for twenty minutes. Drive faster.

Ali smiled down at her phone, stomach flipping like it always did when it came to him. God, she couldn't wait to see him.

Ali's phone buzzed just as they took the exit off I-4 to Dylan's house.

> Change of plans.

> Rocky and Naomi invited us for dinner. Super casual. Steaks and kid mayhem. They said "Bring the Instagram girl."

Ali snorted, thumb flying.

> That's me. A coastal influencer now. Do I need to wear linen?

> Only if it's wrinkled and off-white. Bonus points if you say "mouthfeel" at least once.

Ali bit her lip to stifle a grin.

> You want us to come straight there?

> Nah. Come to the house first. I want you to myself for at least twenty minutes.

Her stomach flipped, heat rising in her cheeks. Abigail didn't even pretend not to notice.

"You're blushing," she said. "Did lover boy send a sext or a dinner invite?"

"Both," Ali muttered, sliding her phone face-down onto her lap.

Ali's heart did a little skip as Abigail's Range Rover turned off the main road and onto a quiet, palm-lined street. Everything in Lake Nona looked pristine—golf courses like green velvet, sleek sidewalks curved between fountains and sculpted hedges, and houses that looked like something out of *Architectural Digest.*

"This is where Disney villains live when they retire rich," Ashley muttered from the back seat, eyes wide behind her sunglasses.

Ali gave a breathless laugh, but her pulse wouldn't settle. The closer they got, the more real it felt. This was Dylan's world now—polished, expansive, private. She wasn't sure if it made her want to swoon...or throw up.

"This one," he'd texted earlier, along with his gate code and a photo of the driveway. Big white stucco, tall windows, bronze hardware, and a wraparound porch with fans turning lazily overhead. Florida luxury at its most laid-back.

As Abigail eased into the circular drive, Ali's stomach gave a nervous twist. His Bronco was parked out front. This time, there was no hiding behind sunglasses or "keeping it lowkey."

"You good?" Abigail asked, cutting the engine.

Ali nodded, but her fingers gripped the handle a little too tight. "He lives here."

Ashley smirked. "And he wants *you* here."

Raleigh Ann leaned forward from the back. "Now get out of this car and go knock the wind out of your man."

Ali took a deep breath and pushed open the door, stepping down onto the stone drive. The air smelled like citrus trees and fresh-cut grass. She smoothed her dress, adjusted her tote on her shoulder.

Then the front door opened—and there he was. In sweatpants, a tee that clung to his chest, and bare feet on the porch like some kind of barefoot *GQ* ad. His grin hit her like sunshine.

She didn't even realize she was smiling until her cheeks started to hurt.

Lavender Haze

Dylan

Dylan pushed open the front door and stepped aside, grinning as four pairs of flip-flops and sneakers padded into the entryway like it was the damn season premiere of *House Hunters: Book Club Edition*.

"Okay," he said, motioning with both arms like a tour guide. "Welcome to Casa McKenzie. Make yourselves at home. Shoes optional, fridge stocked, and please don't judge me for the six unopened Amazon boxes in the mudroom."

Abigail whistled. "Damn, Dylan. You didn't tell us you lived in a catalog."

He grunted.

Ashley dropped her duffel and immediately made a beeline for the living room. "This rug? I'd commit crimes for this rug."

"Appreciate that," Dylan said, catching Ali's eye with a crooked smile. She blushed faintly and tucked her hair behind her ear.

God, he'd missed her.

He showed them around—kitchen, pool, media room, the guest wing that could sleep a small army—and tried to play it cool even though every cell in his body was screaming *get her alone*. It had been weeks. She looked unfairly good. Like sunshine and slow kisses and trouble he'd gladly get into twice.

But they'd barely gotten to say more than a hello. And all her friends were here.

Once the grand tour ended, they ended up back in the kitchen, everyone either perched on stools or leaned against the island, eyeing the welcome snacks.

"So..." Dylan said, as casually as he could muster. "If y'all want, I can have a car take you to Disney Springs for a few hours. Hit some shops, get food, maybe check out the bar at the Boathouse..."

Ali's brows lifted in amusement, but before she could speak, Abigail let out a very pointed *snort*.

"Oh. *Ohhhh*." She straightened, hands on hips. "You really thought we wouldn't notice? That you were gonna shoo us off like toddlers to a Disney mall while you two played house?"

Ashley cackled. "He's literally blushing."

"I'm not blushing," Dylan muttered, running a hand over his jaw and trying not to look as guilty as he felt. "I just figured you might want some girl time. I was being polite."

"You were being horny," Raleigh Ann said sweetly.

Dylan opened his mouth, then closed it again, then sighed. "Okay, yeah. That too."

Ali laughed behind her hand, and that sound alone made him feel like the luckiest bastard on the planet.

"Look," Abigail said, grabbing a slice of pineapple from the charcuterie tray. "We *are* going to Disney Springs. Because I love shopping and the margaritas there are actually elite. But just know we're letting you win. This is charity."

"Deeply appreciated," Dylan said, deadpan.

Ali walked over, nudged his side with her hip, and whispered just loud enough for him to hear, "You're not slick, quarterback."

He grinned, tilted his head, and murmured back, "Didn't say I was."

The front door clicked shut, followed by the sound of retreating laughter and Ashley's voice yelling something about *needing churros immediately or she'd die.*

Dylan didn't move. Not for a beat.

Then, slowly, he turned toward her.

Ali stood barefoot in the kitchen now, her sundress swaying just slightly as she leaned back against the island. Her fingers played with the edge of the counter like she was deciding whether to run or stay. But her eyes...those wide, blue eyes were locked on him like she knew exactly what he wanted.

And she wanted it, too.

"Finally," he said, voice low.

Two strides and he was on her, crowding into her space, hands on her hips, thumbs pressing against the soft fabric of her dress like he needed to ground himself before he lost it.

"You've been driving me insane since you stepped out of that car."

"Abigail's mini dress," she whispered, grinning as his hands slid up her sides. "Not really my size. But she talked me into it. Said it would buy me some extra points."

"It bought you a one-way ticket to getting ruined against my kitchen counter," he muttered, dragging his mouth along her jaw.

Ali gasped softly as he nipped her earlobe.

"I missed you," she said, suddenly quiet again, sincere.

He pulled back just enough to look at her. "Yeah?"

She nodded, biting her lip. "Every day."

Dylan let out a slow breath, pressing his forehead against hers. "Me too."

His hands moved to the small of her back, tugging her flush against him.

"I've got you for the whole weekend," he murmured. "And baby, I'm not wasting a single second."

He kissed her then—slow, deep, and possessive. Like they hadn't been apart. Like this was their life now. No missed calls. Just them.

Ali sighed into it, arms winding around his neck as he lifted her to sit on the edge of the marble counter.

He pulled back just enough to say, "We've got time. No rush."

But the look in his eyes told her exactly how much he *wanted* her.

And the way her knees fell open beneath his hands told him she felt the same.

She was already breathless when he kissed down her throat, her skin warm and tasting faintly of coconut and nerves.

"Fuck, baby," he groaned against her collarbone. "You have *no* idea what you do to me."

Her thighs clenched around his waist, pulling him in, her sundress bunched high on her hips now. His hands roamed over her, greedy, reverent—squeezing her hips, dragging his palms up to cup her breasts through the thin fabric.

Ali gasped, arching into his touch.

"You don't have to hold back," she whispered, voice shaking but sure. "I don't want soft right now."

He pulled back just enough to meet her eyes, pupils blown, cheeks flushed.

"Say it baby."

"I want you to fuck me, Dylan." Her voice cracked on his name. "Right here."

It lit something in him—hot and primal.

He reached down, dragging her panties off her thighs and tossing them to the floor, then unbuttoned his jeans with one hand, his other hand already stroking through her slick folds.

"Already so wet for me," he rasped, thumb circling her clit, watching her hips jolt. "You don't even know what that does to me."

She whimpered, hands fisting his shirt.

"You wore that dress for me."

"Yeah," she breathed.

"You sat on my stool all smug, knowing I couldn't touch you yet."

She nodded, frantic now.

"You thought about me bending you over the counter, didn't you?"

A soft, wrecked sound escaped her lips. "Yes. Yes, Dylan—please."

He lined up and thrust into her in one slow, deep stroke that punched a moan from her throat. Her nails dug into his shoulders, mouth falling open.

"Jesus Christ," he groaned. "You feel like heaven. You're always so fucking tight for me."

He pulled back, then slammed into her again, his hips snapping forward with a rhythm that made the kitchen echo with every filthy, wet sound between them.

She was whimpering now, chanting his name under her breath.

"Tell me how it feels," he growled, fucking her harder. "Tell me who's making you feel this good."

"You," she cried. "God, yes, Dylan—I'm so close—"

He reached between them, thumb pressing into her clit again. "Then come for me, baby. Right now."

Her orgasm slammed into her like a tidal wave, body tensing, legs shaking around his waist, mouth open on a sobbed curse.

And Dylan watched it all.

Her eyes fluttering. Her body unraveling. Her walls tightening around his cock as she came apart for him.

He didn't last much longer.

"Shit, Ali—I'm gonna—fuck—"

He buried his face in her neck as he came deep inside her, hips jerking through it, hands gripping her thighs like they were the only thing tethering him to the ground.

They stayed like that for a moment, tangled and breathless.

Ali ran her fingers through his hair, gently.

Dylan groaned, brushing a kiss to her shoulder.

Our Song

Ali

The smell of grilled steak hit Ali before they even rang the doorbell.

"Okay, but if I get trampled by children, I expect someone to bring me dessert in the hospital," she muttered as Dylan squeezed her hand.

He laughed, kissed her temple. "Noted."

Rocky answered the door barefoot, holding a kid upside down by the ankles.

"Heyyy! Look who finally made it! Come in, come in—Naomi's threatening to burn the corn if I don't help, but I told her the grill's a sacred space."

"Hi, Aunt Ali!" Zoey yelled from behind his legs, launching forward and hugging Ali's knees before running off mid-giggle.

Ali blinked. "Did she just call me Aunt Ali?"

Dylan smirked, placing his hand on the small of her back as he guided her inside. "Yeah. Naomi started it. Figured it was easier than explaining 'Daddy's teammate's girlfriend who he talks about constantly.'"

Inside, the house was full of warm light and louder laughter. Naomi waved from the kitchen, apron on over a tank top and leggings, a wooden spoon in one hand and a baby monitor in the other.

"You must be Ali," she called. "Come in, sit, I'll pour you something cold!"

Ali smiled, suddenly shy. "Thank you for having me."

Naomi grinned and reached into the fridge, pulling out a can with a flourish. "Got something just for you—sparkling lime water, no sugar. Mac gave me a heads-up."

Ali blinked, a little taken aback. "Oh...thank you."

Naomi just winked, setting it on the counter with a glass of ice.

Rocky passed by again, this time with the toddler on his shoulders. "I told you she was real!"

"Barely," Naomi quipped.

Ali snorted, relaxing as the energy of the house wrapped around her like a blanket. Kids racing down the hallway. Cartoons playing on low volume in the background. Dylan casually moving through the space like he belonged here—like *they* belonged here.

At one point, he helped the oldest set the table and Zoey insisted on sitting next to "Aunt Ali." Naomi winked at her across the table like they were already friends.

And as dinner started, laughter and crumbs everywhere, Ali looked around the table and felt her chest ache in the best way. This was chaos. This was joy. This was the kind of life she never let herself imagine before. And somehow, she was in it.

Ali rinsed a plate in the sink, laughing softly at something Zoey had said during dinner, and passed it to Naomi, who was towel-drying beside her. The kitchen had mellowed—kids sprawled on the living room floor with a movie on, Rocky and Dylan half-watching from the couch, deep in some conversation about Miami.

Naomi glanced over, a soft smile playing on her lips. "You're good with them, you know. My kids."

Ali snorted. "They're easy to love. And Zoey's got the best one-liners I've ever heard from a seven-year-old."

"She's a menace," Naomi said affectionately. "But she gets it honestly."

Ali grinned. "It's sweet, though. All of it. Your family."

Naomi set a plate aside and leaned a hip against the counter. "Took work to build it. The real kind, you know? Communication, therapy, deep breaths...Costco snacks in bulk."

Ali nodded, sensing the weight behind her words.

"You ever want kids?" Naomi asked gently, not prying—just present.

Ali paused, fingers still under the warm water. "I think so. Maybe. With the right person. But it's complicated. My body doesn't always cooperate thanks to the PCOS, and I guess I'm still learning to trust myself. But Dylan...he makes me feel like I could have anything. Like it wouldn't matter what the road looked like, just that we're on it together."

Naomi's expression softened. "He's different with you. It's not just the smiling and phone-checking. It's the stillness. He's steadier."

Ali swallowed the lump in her throat and laughed lightly, trying to ease the emotion. "You're really gonna make me cry in your kitchen, huh?"

Naomi bumped her shoulder. "Please don't. We just wiped the counters."

They both laughed. Then Naomi tilted her head. "You mentioned a book club earlier, right? Shelf Indulgence?"

Ali lit up. "Yeah! Me, Abigail, Ashley, and Raleigh Ann. We read a little of everything, but we mostly talk about men and our deep love for fictional ones."

"Sold," Naomi said immediately. "Do you allow long-distance honorary members?"

"We encourage them," Ali grinned. "But fair warning—we're on a spicy hockey romance kick this month, and Raleigh Ann gets *very* passionate about book boyfriends."

Naomi grabbed her phone. "Add me to the group chat immediately."

Naomi finished wiping down the last bit of counter space and leaned her elbows on the island, watching Ali with soft, curious eyes. "Can I ask you something a little personal?"

Ali glanced up, brow raised. "Sure."

"You mentioned PCOS earlier. I've got it too. Diagnosed after Zoey, but the symptoms were there way before. It took forever to get someone to listen." She rolled her eyes. "I thought I was losing my mind for years."

Ali blinked, a beat of surprise flashing in her expression. "Same. I didn't get diagnosed until I was twenty-four. Irregular cycles, fatigue, brain fog, the weight stuff...it always felt like people thought I was just lazy or dramatic."

Naomi nodded, fierce and immediate. "God, yes. And the guilt. Like you're failing at something everyone else seems to do easily."

Ali bit her lip, her voice quieter now. "And then BPD on top of it..."

Naomi's face stilled—open, but gentle. "That's...a lot."

"I was diagnosed in college," Ali said softly, wrapping her fingers around the dish towel like an anchor. "I didn't even know what it was before then. Just that I felt *too much* all the time. Like any tiny emotional crack was the end of the world. Especially abandonment. It was—" she paused, swallowing. "It was hard on Dylan. On me. I spent years learning how to manage it. Therapy. Medication. Self-awareness. But there are still days I don't trust myself to get it right."

Naomi didn't hesitate. She reached over and gave her hand a squeeze. "You don't have to get it perfect to be worthy of love. And the fact that you *are* doing the work—that's everything."

Ali's eyes shimmered with unshed tears. "I think I spent a long time believing no one could love me *with* all that. That I was too much work."

Naomi shook her head. "Mac's face when he looks at you? That's not a man who's overwhelmed. That's a man who feels lucky."

Ali smiled shakily. "Thanks. I think I'm finally starting to believe that, too."

They stood in the stillness for a moment longer, nothing loud or heavy, just a quiet knowing between women who had fought hard to feel whole.

Then Naomi tapped the counter lightly. "Okay. Now that we've trauma bonded, can we please go find dessert? I hid a tray of brownies from Rocky and I'm ready to share."

Ali laughed, wiping her eyes. "God, yes. Brownies and book club initiation. You're one of us now."

I Think He Knows

Dylan

She was wearing his shirt.

An old Tritons tee—navy faded soft from a hundred wash cycles, the neckline slouchy, sleeves rolled up just a little over her swimsuit. It hung loose and low on her, knotted at the waist, but he knew exactly what it was. One of the first freebies from his rookie year.

And damn if it didn't hit him square in the chest.

He paused for a second at the gate, the smell of chlorine and sunscreen wafting on the warm breeze, the girls spread out around the pool like they were on spring break. But it was her that had his full attention. Legs dipped in the water, hair piled on top of her head, face tilted toward the sun. Like home. Like everything he'd missed.

She looked up, eyes squinting against the light, and smiled.

And just like that, he couldn't feel the weight of the pizza boxes anymore.

He'd always worn his shirts and hoodies a little big. Even back in college. Said it was for comfort, but truthfully? It was for her. Always for her. He liked knowing she could disappear into something of his when the world got loud. That she could wrap herself in something that smelled like him and maybe feel safe.

Safe. Loved. Wanted.

Hell, maybe even *kept*.

She didn't know that, and he didn't need her to.

But the way her fingers absently tugged the hem down when he walked in?

Yeah. She was his. Whether she said it out loud again or not.

He set the boxes on the outdoor table and raised an eyebrow. "Thin crust, extra cheese, pepperoni on half—because apparently Raleigh Ann has beef with pepperoni. Medium crust with sausage because Ali's picky as shit about pizza."

"I *literally* said it gives me heartburn," Raleigh Ann called from a lounge chair, not even looking up from her book.

"Same thing," Dylan muttered under his breath, smirking as he turned back to Ali.

"I am picky. But I know what I like."

She was standing now, walking over in that slow, swaying way that always made his brain short-circuit. The tee hit mid-thigh, her swim skirt barely visible, her cheeks a little pink from the sun.

She stepped close—too close—and gave him a once-over like she was judging an outfit. "You look proud of yourself."

He shrugged, grinning. "I bring offerings. I should be worshiped."

Ali snorted. "Oh please. You bring carbs and suddenly you're a god?"

"To be fair," Abigail called from the water, "He brought *multiple* carbs. That counts for something."

Ali reached for a slice and took a slow, dramatic bite—eyes locked on his like she was *daring* him to say something. "Well, your holiness...we thank you for your sacred delivery."

He chuckled, low and warm, and leaned in so only she could hear. "Careful, Presley. You keep looking at me like that, and I'm gonna make you eat that pizza in my lap."

She choked on her bite.

And it was absolutely worth it.

Dylan adjusted his laptop on his desk in his office, angling the camera so the sunlight from the back windows wasn't blowing out the screen. His hoodie sleeves were pushed up, hair still a little damp from the pool earlier. The smell of sunscreen and pepperoni lingered faintly in the air.

Kallie's face popped up first, her brunette curls pulled into a high knot, glasses perched low on her nose. "You look suspiciously happy. Where are you, McKenzie?"

"Home in Lake Nona," he said, leaning back on the stool. "Girls are outside..."

"Good. We've got Coach Peterson joining in a sec."

Right on cue, the Adrian Peterson's square filled the screen—stern face, ball cap, and a Tritons polo.

"Mac," Coach said with a curt nod. "Kallie said you wanted to talk schedule?"

"Yeah," Dylan said, voice steady. "Just wanted to put it out there before things get too packed. I'm planning to split my off-days time this year. I'll still be based in Orlando for team obligations, but when we're not in full schedule mode, I'd like to spend part of the week in Georgia."

Coach's eyes narrowed just slightly. "Distractions?"

"No, sir. That's why I'm saying it now. I'll still be doing everything I'm supposed to—film, lifting, conditioning. Hell, I've already scoped gyms near Honeyshore, can drive to MBU if needed, and I'll be on campus here the rest of the week for practices and team events. Nothing's changing on my end when it comes to the Tritons."

Kallie raised a brow. "You're not trying to pull a Brady and start practicing from the beach, right?"

Dylan smirked. "Nah. But if y'all see me on a paddleboard throwing spirals, don't be surprised."

Coach grunted, which was basically his version of a laugh.

"Just keep your priorities straight," he said. "You've been focused and sharp. I don't care where your home base is when you're off, as long as your head stays in the game."

"It will," Dylan said firmly. "I just...want to be able to breathe a little, too."

Kallie's voice softened. "You deserve that."

Coach nodded again. "Then we're good. Anything else?"

"Not today," Dylan said. "Appreciate you."

Coach Peterson's screen blinked out, and Dylan reached for his water bottle, twisting the cap just to do something with his hands.

Kallie didn't log off.

She tilted her head, watching him through the screen like she could read every thought. "So...you're really doing this, huh?"

He nodded. "Yeah. I mean...I'm not retiring. Not going anywhere. I just—" He scrubbed a hand over his jaw. "I need the space. And I want the time."

"To be with her?" Kallie asked softly.

"To be myself," he said, then cracked a faint grin. "But yeah. Her, too."

Kallie leaned back in her chair. "Walk me through the plan."

Dylan sat forward, more focused now. "Right after the season ends, I want to spend the full off-season in Georgia. At least until camp opens back up in July. Honeyshore's got enough space for me to train, lift, throw. I've got film access. I can drive to Savannah or even Jacksonville if I need to link up with other guys."

"You're thinking full-time from March to July?" she clarified.

"Yep. I'll come back to Orlando when I need to, but otherwise, I'm posted up there."

"And you'll still do your workouts? Diet? Promo obligations?"

"Absolutely," he said. "We can frontload media stuff in March and keep everything else virtual or on weekend trips."

Kallie paused. "You do know this'll stir up some whispers, right? Everyone's gonna think she's the reason."

"She *is* part of the reason," Dylan said without flinching. "But I'm not going rogue. I'm planning ahead. I've given this more thought than anything in years."

A small smile tugged at her lips. "You love her."

He didn't even hesitate. "Yeah. And I'm not hiding it anymore."

Kallie exhaled slowly, then nodded. "Okay. We'll build it in. I'll send over a rough schedule and run logistics by media and ops."

"Thanks, Kay," he said, the weight of months—maybe years—finally starting to lift.

She pointed a finger at the camera. "But if I catch you skipping workouts to float around Tybee on a paddleboard with your girlfriend, we're gonna fight."

Dylan chuckled. "Fair."

"Now go outside and kiss the girl already," she said, closing the Zoom with a wink.

He shut the laptop, heart steady, and stood.

This wasn't temporary anymore.

This was the beginning of something permanent.

The Man

Ali

She hadn't stepped foot in a football stadium since 2015.

Not since the bowl game that ended everything. The night that split her open and swallowed her whole.

But now...she was here.

Not in the same stadium. Not the same team. Not the same girl.

The Tritons' arena was a different beast entirely—modern, towering, built like a monument to speed and spectacle. The buzz of energy was palpable even in the early part of the day, with fans already lining up at vendor carts and tailgating in the lots. Navy and teal flags snapped in the breeze, the team logo shining from giant LED screens. And the moment she stepped through the VIP entrance, her breath caught in her throat.

It hit her all at once.

The green of the field. The roar of distant cheers. The towering walls of the stadium seats that felt like they could swallow her if she let them.

Her fingers clenched a little tighter around her clear Stoney Clover crossbody bag, knuckles pale.

Ashley bumped her gently with her hip. "You okay?"

Ali nodded before she spoke. "Yeah. Just...it's been a long time."

Ashley's expression softened and she linked her arm through Ali's as they walked together toward the suite level. "I know. But this time? It's different. This isn't the past."

Ali's smile was tentative, but it grew.

She smoothed the skirt of her navy and teal dress—one Ashley had found online from a boutique that screamed "soft game day glam" in the product description. It cinched her waist and fluttered just enough to make her feel pretty. Confident, even.

And the shoes? A pair of barely-worn, six-inch sandals she'd borrowed—*stolen*—from Abigail.

She had confessed the whole "wall" moment to her, flushed and breathless in her office. Abigail had smiled and told her that keeping the heels was non-negotiable.

"Claim your wins," she'd said, "Even if they start with a pair of shoes."

Now she was wearing those shoes in a stadium she never thought she'd walk into. Not as someone's secret. Not as a half-healed wound. As his.

The suite was glass-walled and wide open, with plush seating and a panoramic view of the field. Everything gleamed—sleek and high-end, just like everything else in Dylan's world now.

But the first thing Ali noticed wasn't the view or the rows of catered food.

It was Dylan's mom.

"Ali!" Carolina McKenzie stood up with a smile that reached her warm hazel eyes, arms already open.

Ali's breath hitched as she stepped forward. It had been ten years since they'd last seen each other. But Carolina wrapped her in a hug like no time had passed at all.

"You look beautiful, sweetheart," she whispered.

"Thank you," Ali managed, hugging her back. Her voice caught, so she blinked hard to keep the tears at bay. "So do you."

Dylan's dad gave her a gentler, quieter smile and a firm but affectionate side hug. "Glad you're here, Ali."

She nodded. "Me too."

Then she saw her.

Kallie.

The tall, striking brunette was standing by the windows, a drink in hand and sunglasses perched atop her head. And when she turned, her signature smirk curved—not smug, but knowing. Like she remembered everything from the fundraiser too. Including the moment Ali had bolted like Cinderella without the grace.

Ali flushed instantly, heat rushing to her cheeks.

But Kallie didn't tease. Didn't so much as raise a brow. She just walked forward like they were old friends.

"Ali," she said smoothly, her voice warm and confident. "Glad you made it." Then, with a playful grin, "We've upgraded a lot since that fundraiser."

Ali laughed, tension breaking in her chest. "I guess so."

Kallie leaned in and dropped her voice just enough to make Ali feel like she was in on something. "Don't worry. No awkward mentions of wall-related departures. Ancient history."

Ali snorted before she could stop herself. "Thank you."

"You're welcome. Come meet the others—there are a few friends of the team in here today. Players' families, a couple of board members." She looped her arm through Ali's like they were already on the same page. "Let's make you look like you've been doing this your whole life."

Behind them, Ashley mouthed **"Oh my god I love her"**.

Ali grinned.

Maybe she was still a little nervous. But with Dylan on the field, his people in her corner, and her girls at her back—she didn't feel small anymore. She felt ready.

Ali sank into one of the padded armchairs, crossing her legs and letting the cool blast of air conditioning wash over her. The stadium was buzzing below, a blur of teal and navy and flashing lights, but up here in the suite, everything felt surreal. Private. Luxurious.

Raleigh Ann plopped down beside her with a plate full of sliders and nachos. "Okay, I need to marry a football player immediately. Why didn't you tell me it was like *this*?"

Ashley leaned over the bar, sipping a club soda like it was champagne. "I feel like we're in an episode of *Real Housewives: Tritons Edition*." She looked at Abigail. "You brought your big sunglasses, right?"

"Obviously," Abigail said, adjusting her oversized frames dramatically. "We came to slay and stay hydrated."

Ali laughed, sinking a little deeper into the chair. She kicked off her sandals—Abigail's beloved donation to the cause—and curled her legs beneath her. "This feels fake."

"It's not," Abigail said with a nudge. "This is your life now, remember? The tight end's girlfriend. Or kicking guy. Or whatever position Dylan plays. Sports aren't really my thing. I only know what a tight end is because of Taylor Swift and TMZ."

Ashley rolled her eyes. "He's the quarterback, Ab."

"Well, he's *clearly* winning."

They all dissolved into giggles again, drawing a fond glance from Kallie, who was chatting with Dylan's parents near the buffet.

Ali leaned her chin on her fist, watching the field as the pre-game graphics lit up the jumbotron. Her chest tightened—not with anxiety this time, but with something warmer. Hope.

She was here. With her people. Watching her person. And for the first time in years, it didn't feel like the past was waiting to ambush her. It just felt like the beginning of something new.

The Alchemy

Dylan

The roar hit him like a wave—loud, hot, and electric.

Dylan stepped through the tunnel, the field exploding in front of him, the Tritons banner rippling in the breeze. Tempest, the sea dragon mascot, was already hamming it up on the sideline, tossing a football into the crowd as fireworks flared overhead.

But Dylan only had eyes for one spot.

The suite.

He couldn't *see* her exactly—not through the tinted glass and flood of color—but he *felt* her up there. He always did. Just knowing she was here had every nerve ending buzzing.

His cleats hit the turf with a familiar rhythm, his helmet tucked under one arm. This was the moment he'd dreamed about as a kid. The season opener. Sold-out crowd. National broadcast. But for once, the pressure didn't sit like a weight on his shoulders. It felt more like fuel.

He was grounded. Steady.

Loved.

A teammate slapped his back as they jogged out, music thundering through the sound system.

"You ready to wreck them?" Rocky called out, grinning as he adjusted his gloves.

Dylan smirked. "Born ready."

They made their way toward the sideline, the camera already in his face as the announcer boomed his name. He nodded at it with practiced ease, raising one arm for the crowd, but his mind was still upstairs—in that suite, with the girls who screamed louder than anyone, with *her*.

He could almost hear her voice, soft but fierce.

You've got this.

Yeah, he did.

Because she was here.

Because he wasn't running anymore.

Because this time, he knew who he was playing for.

Dylan's spiral arced high and clean, dropping perfectly into Rocky's hands in the end zone. Touchdown.

The crowd roared again.

He barely registered the chest bump from a teammate, the thud of shoulder pads, or the camera trailing him down the sideline. He was locked in.

Second quarter, and they were already up by two TDs.

But even as the game surged forward—another first down, another brutal hit he danced around—his mind kept tugging toward the suite.

At halftime, he jogged toward the tunnel, his jaw clenched, his body on fire in all the right ways.

"Don't let up," Coach barked as they passed. "You're not done yet."

Dylan didn't intend to be.

The Tritons took the win.

Final score: 34–17.

He shook hands at midfield, traded words with the opposing QB, then found himself surrounded by flashing cameras and booming voices.

"Mac!" a reporter called. "Incredible season opener. How does it feel to come out this strong in front of a home crowd?"

Dylan ran a towel over his face, catching his breath. "It feels good," he said, grinning. "The team came out hungry. We've been building chemistry all off-season, and today was just a taste of what we can do."

Another question flew at him, something about new offensive strategies, but his eyes caught on movement behind the reporter.

Kallie.

And just behind her—Ali.

He blinked. And then his whole body stuttered.

The shoes.

Her legs were bare, tan, and toned in that navy and teal dress he hadn't seen yet. But it was the *sandals—those* sandals—that stopped his heartbeat.

His lips twitched upward even as he tried to stay focused.

"You good?" the reporter asked.

Dylan cleared his throat. "Yeah—uh—just spotted my lucky charm," he said smoothly, nodding toward the sideline.

Kallie smirked behind her sunglasses. She knew exactly what she was doing.

And Ali?

She waved. And blushed. And he couldn't wait to get to her.

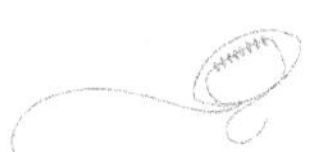

The house was still, the kind of post-game quiet that settled deep in his bones.

Ali's suitcase stood by the door with the other girls' bags. They had to get back to Georgia. They all had work in the morning.

Ali stood by the kitchen island, sipping water from one of his protein shaker bottles and wearing his navy Tritons hoodie over her dress. The heels—*those* heels—were now abandoned beside the stool where she'd slid them off with a groan and a muttered, "Dylan better appreciate my sacrifice."

He leaned against the doorframe, just watching her. "I more than appreciate it babe. I would thank you properly, but you have to leave. I'll be sure to make it up to you on the phone when you get home tonight."

Soft, flushed, windblown from the day. Hair clipped back now, mascara just slightly smudged, cheeks still pink.

She looked up and smiled—sleepy and so full of love it almost hurt.

"You were amazing today," she whispered, like it was still a secret. "Everyone around me was cheering for you like crazy."

He walked over and cupped her cheek, brushing his thumb gently under her eye. "You were all I saw."

She leaned into the touch.

"I'm glad I came," she said. "I was scared. But it felt good. Right. And maybe a little weird."

"Because of the stadium?" he asked.

She nodded. "Because of...everything. But I think I made new memories today."

He kissed her forehead, then her lips. Slow. Like he had all the time in the world.

"I hate that we have to head out soon," she murmured against his mouth.

"Me too," he said. "But, I'll be back soon. Or you'll be here again. We'll figure it out."

Her fingers slipped under the hem of his hoodie, resting against the skin of his lower back. "I just don't want to lose this. Any of it."

He tipped his forehead against hers.

"You won't," he promised. "You *won't*. Not this time."

And for a while, they just stood there—her in his arms, his heart beating steady again, both of them silently holding on to the moment before the world outside pulled them back into motion.

End Game

Ali

Ali sat cross-legged on her bed, laptop open, the soft hum of her ceiling fan the only sound in the room. A cold Diet Dr. Pepper sat sweating on her nightstand, and her inbox was open beside a dozen tabs of job listings.

Accounting positions near Orlando.

She'd typed it in half an hour ago. The results blinked back at her now, a blur of CPA firms and corporate listings that didn't mean much yet. She clicked through one, then another, scanning benefits and qualifications, but nothing quite clicked.

Still...her heart knew what she wanted. She wanted to be with *him*.

Dylan's life was in Orlando. His teammates, his season, his rhythm. And maybe she couldn't rewrite the past—but she could build something new alongside him now. She wanted to find her own footing, not live in his shadow, but *with him*. Not miles away.

She stared at her phone for a moment, then opened her contacts and tapped Kallie's name.

It rang twice before a smooth, no-nonsense voice answered. "This is Kallie."

Ali's voice was a little breathless, unsure. "Hey, it's Ali Presley. I hope this isn't a bad time."

"Not at all," Kallie said, her tone instantly warmer. "I was wondering when you'd call. What's up?"

Ali exhaled a nervous laugh. "I, um...I was wondering if you might be able to help me look for a job. In Orlando. Accounting or finance, preferably. And if you maybe know someone who could help me find an apartment..."

There was a beat of silence. Then Kallie's voice, gentle but sharp with understanding.

"Does Mac know?"

Ali shook her head, then realized Kallie couldn't see her. "Not yet. I wanted to…I guess I wanted to make sure it wasn't just a fantasy before I said anything. I'm not doing this *for* him. I'm doing it *for me*—but yeah, I want to be near him."

Kallie's smile was practically audible. "I respect the hell out of that."

"I still want to be independent," Ali added quickly. "I don't want to just…become Dylan's shadow, you know?"

"You won't. You're too damn smart for that."

Ali smiled, the tension in her shoulders easing.

"I've got some names I can send you," Kallie said. "And I'll ask around about apartments. You'd be surprised how many boutique firms in this town would fight for someone with your credentials. You're licensed in Florida too, right?"

"Yeah. Dual-state certified since last year."

"Even better," Kallie said. "Send me your resume tonight, and I'll make a few calls tomorrow."

Ali blinked back tears. "Thank you. Really."

"Don't thank me yet. Wait until you see what downtown rent looks like," Kallie said with a laugh. "Talk soon, Presley."

As the call ended, Ali set her phone down and leaned back against her pillows.

She wasn't sure when—or how—she'd tell Dylan.

But for the first time in a long time…the future didn't scare her.

Ali had just settled in at her desk with a fresh cup of coffee—her favorite mug, chipped at the rim and reading *"Accountants Make It Count"*—when her phone buzzed.

Kallie:

> Check your email. I found someone you need to talk to.

Ali's stomach flipped. She nearly sloshed coffee onto her keyboard as she set the mug down and opened her inbox. There it was—an email forwarded from Kallie with a short, clipped message at the top:

"Ali, This is Camden Vaughn. Managing partner at Vaughn & Ellis, downtown Orlando. Smart guy, good firm. Boutique-size but with a strong client roster. He's intrigued. Interview is Friday at 11. Dress like a badass. — K."

Ali blinked at the screen, rereading the words.

Interview. This Friday.

The email below was short and professional—Camden thanking her for her interest, asking if she'd be willing to set up a preliminary meeting on Zoom. It wasn't just real now—it was *happening*.

She clutched the phone to her chest, the kind of giddy nerves bubbling up that made her want to laugh and cry at the same time.

Her fingers hovered over her screen before she typed:

> Kallie. Are you magic? Be honest.

The reply came almost immediately:

> Nope. Just extremely well-connected and slightly terrifying when I need to be. You've got this. Let me know if you need anything before Friday.

Ali exhaled, heart racing, then tapped open her calendar.

Now she just had to figure out:

1. What to wear,

2. How to tell Dylan, and

3. How not to puke from excitement and nerves at the same time.

Ali adjusted her laptop camera for the third time and smoothed the front of her blouse. She'd kept it simple—a pale blue top, soft waves in her hair, and light makeup that said *"I am a competent professional who also gets eight hours of sleep and drinks green juice."* Lies. But polished ones.

She took a deep breath and clicked the Zoom link.

It loaded with a soft chime, and a man appeared on screen—mid-40s, sharp suit, salt-and-pepper hair, and an easy smile.

"Ali, hi! Camden Vaughn. Thanks so much for hopping on today."

"Of course. Thank you for meeting with me," she said, praying her voice didn't sound as shaky as she felt.

He dove right in, asking about her resume, her accounting work, and how she handled client relationships. The questions were fast but fair, and Ali held her own. Camden's expression didn't shift much—but she caught the slight lift of his brow when she described streamlining one of her firm's reconciliation processes.

They were deep into a conversation about long-term goals when she heard the front door creak open.

Dylan's voice floated down the hallway. "Babe?"

Ali froze. She didn't answer—just sat a little straighter and hoped to god the mic didn't pick him up.

"...and we really value independence in this role," Camden continued. "Our team is tight-knit, but we don't micromanage."

Ali smiled and nodded, ignoring the soft footsteps drawing closer.

Dylan peeked his head around the corner, brows pulling together. *Question mark face.* She widened her eyes and waved him off under the desk.

He mouthed something—*Are you okay?*—but she ignored it, forcing her attention back to the screen.

"Sorry," she said quickly. "Small house."

"No worries," Camden chuckled. "Mine's not much bigger. Last week my toddler walked in naked during a partner call."

Ali let out a breath of laughter. "That makes me feel slightly better."

Camden smiled. "Listen—I like your energy. Kallie vouched for you, and I trust her judgment. I'd love to schedule a follow-up and talk about what a role could look like with us."

Ali blinked. "Really?"

"Absolutely. You've got great instincts. And frankly, we're overdue for someone with your mix of precision and warmth."

"Thank you," she said softly, heart pounding.

"Talk soon," he said, and the screen blinked to black.

Ali exhaled hard and slumped back in her chair. Her phone buzzed immediately—

Kallie:

> Well??

Ali grinned down at it but didn't get a chance to type. A shadow passed the door.

Dylan leaned against the frame, one brow raised. "Sooo...what was that?"

She looked up at him, suddenly flushed. "What?"

"You waving me off like I was about to interrupt a nuclear summit."

Ali bit her lip.

He stepped closer. "You gonna tell me what's going on, or...?"

She hesitated.

Then—"Maybe."

He squinted at her. "Did you just *job interview hide* from me?"

Ali grinned. "Possibly."

Dylan crossed his arms, mock-serious. "Is this a secret mission or am I allowed to be excited?"

Her face softened. "It went well. There's gonna be a second interview."

Dylan's expression shifted—surprise, then pride, then something almost reverent.

"You're incredible," he said. "You know that?"

She blushed. "I'm trying."

He crossed the room in three long strides and pulled her up into a hug.

"You're not trying," he murmured into her hair. "You're doing it."

She felt guilty about not telling him her plan, but she wasn't ready yet.

This Is Why We Can't Have Nice Things

Dylan

"**I** got the job."

Dylan looked up from his protein bar, not fully processing her words at first. Ali was glowing—her cheeks flushed, eyes wild with excitement, bare feet bouncing against the kitchen tile. One of his old Tritons crewnecks swallowed her frame, the sleeves pushed to her elbows as she waved her phone in the air like it owed her rent.

"What job?" he asked cautiously.

"The one I interviewed for. Vaughn & Ellis. Kallie set it up. It's official—I start in two weeks."

He blinked, a grin forming before he even meant it to. "Holy shit, baby. That's amazing."

"I know!" she beamed. "It's full salary, full benefits, and the location is perfect. And it's small enough that I won't get swallowed up, but established enough to be taken seriously."

He crossed the room and wrapped his arms around her waist, lifting her briefly off the ground before kissing her temple. "I'm so proud of you."

She melted into him, laughing, but something was off. A beat too long. A hesitation in her shoulders. When she pulled back, she wasn't meeting his eyes.

"Wait..." He stepped back slowly, hands resting on his hips. "Kallie set it up? Where is it?"

"Here. I mean. Orlando."

His brows drew together. "You're moving here?"

"I was hoping to. I already talked to Kallie about apartment listings. Just something small and affordable. Close to the office."

His heart thudded once. "When were you going to tell me?"

"I'm telling you now."

"No, you're telling me after the fact," he said, his tone flat. "You already had the interview, started looking for places, called Kallie. You were making moves without me."

Ali bristled. "Because I didn't want to get your hopes up if it didn't work out. And I didn't want to make you feel like I was just following you like some lost puppy."

"Ali, come on. You think I'd feel that way?"

"I think you don't realize how hard it was for me to make this decision. To move. To start over again."

He ran a hand over his jaw, tension humming through his chest. "And I could've helped you with all of it. If you'd let me in."

"I *am* letting you in—now."

His phone buzzed once on the counter. *Daisy.* He ignored it.

"You always do this," he said. "You protect me from things that don't even need protecting. I've never asked you to prove your independence to me."

"I'm not proving anything," she shot back. "I'm trying to build something for myself. Something stable."

Buzz.

Daisy again.

"And what—we're just supposed to figure out logistics later? You're going to live across town and text me when it's convenient? Pretend this is some casual long-distance thing when we're five miles apart?"

She stared at him, wounded. "You're twisting this."

Buzz.

Daisy. Third call.

He let out a growl of frustration and grabbed the phone. "Daisy, now's not a good time—"

Her voice came fast and broken. "Dylan." She was crying, frantic. "It's Dad— he had a heart attack. They rushed him to Bellamy Memorial. It's bad. Please—please come."

Silence hit the room like a crash.

Ali stepped forward. "What happened?"

Dylan's jaw clenched. "I'm coming," he said into the phone. "I'll be there soon."

He ended the call without waiting for a response, then looked up—numb and hollow.

Ali was already moving. Grabbing her keys. Her shoes. Her purse. "Let's go."

He didn't argue. He couldn't.

Soon You'll Get Better

Dylan

Ali hadn't said much for the last hundred miles—not since he told her Daisy had been crying when she called. Not since the moment her knuckles turned white on the steering wheel, and she floored it to ninety on I-95 like the road might dissolve beneath them if she slowed down.

She didn't even flinch when he begged her to slow down. Just whispered, "I've got you," and kept going.

Now, as she pulled into the parking lot of Bellamy Memorial in under five hours, her hands finally began to shake. She threw the car into park, turned to look at him with glassy eyes, and said, "Go. I'll catch up."

He didn't wait for more. Didn't grab his bag. Didn't fix his hair or check his phone. He just ran.

The ER doors slid open with a hiss, the scent of antiseptic hitting him like a punch—cold, clinical, and all too familiar.

He hated hospitals.

Especially this one.

He shut his thoughts down fast. He couldn't let the ghosts creep in. This wasn't about the past.

This was about his dad. Now.

"Dylan McKenzie," he told the nurse behind the desk. "My dad. Talmadge McKenzie. He was brought in—"

She nodded. "Family's in Room thirteen. Straight back, last on the left."

He didn't thank her. Didn't breathe. Just walked—fast, then faster—until he reached the door. It was cracked open, the fluorescent light bleeding out into the hall.

He pushed it open and froze.

His mom was sitting in one of the plastic chairs, her face pale, but composed and she was holding Talmadge's hand. His father looked smaller in the hospital bed—oxygen hooked to his nose, monitors blinking quietly. Daisy sat in the corner, her knees pulled to her chest, tear tracks staining her cheeks.

The second she saw him, she was up.

"Dyllie." She flung her arms around his neck, sobbing again.

He held her tightly, his throat closing. "What happened?"

"They think it was a blockage," she whispered, wiping her face. "He collapsed outside the bank. A guy in the parking lot did CPR until EMS got there."

His mom stood then. "They've stabilized him," she said, her voice calm but raw. "But he's not out of the woods yet."

Dylan crossed to the bed and took his father's free hand. "Hey, Dad," he said softly, voice cracking. "You picked a hell of a way to get everyone back in town."

His phone buzzed softly in his pocket.

He almost didn't check it—couldn't bear the thought of more updates or condolences or anyone trying to make this feel normal. But when he saw her name, his heart squeezed.

Ali:

> Hey baby, they won't let me in because I'm not family. I'll be in the waiting room when you need me.

He stared at the screen for a long second, thumb hovering.

Not family.

God, that stung more than it should have. Not because it wasn't technically true—but because the idea of her out there, alone, just a few doors away, felt wrong. It felt backwards.

She'd just driven four and a half hours with laser focus, a full tank of adrenaline, and her heart in her throat. For him. For all of them.

And now she was being kept behind glass like she didn't belong.

He looked over at Daisy, and then to his mom, still clutching his dad's hand.

Then he stepped into the hallway and typed out a reply.

> You're my family. I'll be there in 2 minutes.

He hit send and started walking—fast. She was curled into the corner of the waiting room, hoodie pulled over her knees, hair twisted up in a messy clip. As soon as she saw him, she stood—eyes wide, worried, but steady.

He didn't say a word. Just crossed the room and pulled her into his chest, holding her tight enough to stop the shaking in his hands.

"I'm here," she whispered into his shoulder. "Whatever you need."

"I need you with me," he murmured.

And that was it.

He laced their fingers together and led her back through the ER doors. No one stopped them this time.

Carolina looked up as they entered, her expression softening the second she saw Ali.

"Oh, sweetheart," she said, stepping forward and wrapping her into a hug. "Thank you for coming."

Ali hugged her back gently. "Of course."

Talmadge was still resting, hooked up to monitors, pale but stable. Dylan watched Ali's face shift, her worry folding deeper. Then his gaze flicked to the chair in the corner—Daisy, half-curled, phone in hand talking to Laila.

She glanced up at the sound of the door. Her eyes landed on Ali, then flicked to their joined hands.

Daisy gave a slight wave. No words. Just the kind of quiet gesture that said: *I see you. I'm still figuring it out.*

Dylan didn't push. There'd be time for more later.

For now, he squeezed Ali's hand and led her to the space beside him—right where she belonged.

The machines hummed softly beside the hospital bed, a rhythmic reminder that time was still ticking—and that his dad was still here. Dylan exhaled slowly, sinking deeper into the stiff hospital chair, hands laced behind his neck as he stared at the worn tile floor.

Talmadge had drifted in and out for most of the afternoon, but now his eyes were open. Not sharp, exactly, but focused. Present.

Dylan leaned forward, resting his arms on his knees. "I gotta tell you something."

His dad gave the faintest lift of his brow—permission.

"We were arguing," Dylan said. "When Daisy kept calling. I was…frustrated. Confused. I almost didn't answer." His voice cracked slightly. "I was just standing there like a jackass. She wanted to move to Orlando for me and I threw it in her face because she didn't ask me to help her."

Talmadge's lips pressed into a thin line. He didn't speak yet, but he was listening. Dylan could feel it.

"I love her, I do." Dylan said. "Ali. And I meant it when I said I want to build a life with her. But she didn't tell me she was job hunting. Or that she'd called Kallie. Or that she was thinking about moving there. I found out after the fact, like it was already decided. And it caught me so off guard, I didn't react the way I should've. I got defensive."

His chest ached with the memory—her teary explanation, the shock in her eyes when Daisy's call finally forced his hand.

Talmadge shifted, slow and careful. "You mad that she made a plan without you, or scared she made one with you in mind?"

Dylan blinked, startled.

His dad gave a tired little shrug. "Sometimes love makes people run forward before they're ready. Sometimes fear makes people freeze. You two always did both."

Dylan dropped his gaze, teeth working at the inside of his cheek. "I think she's scared to believe it's real. That we're real."

"Then prove it," Talmadge said simply. "You're good at showing up, son. Just don't wait until she's gone again."

Dylan swallowed hard. "I won't."

A beat passed. Then another.

"She's good for you," his dad added softly. "Even I can see that. And I've been half-dead for three days."

That pulled a quiet laugh from Dylan, the kind that hit square in the chest.

"Yeah," he said, smiling faintly. "She is."

The cafeteria smelled like coffee and bleach—comforting in a weird, institutional way. Dylan scanned the rows of mostly empty tables, eyes locking on the familiar blonde head tucked low over a paper-wrapped lunch.

Ali.

She was alone at a two-top near the window, picking at a spinach wrap like it had personally offended her. Her hair was pulled into a messy ponytail, and her water bottle sat beside her phone, screen dark.

Dylan's chest squeezed.

He walked toward her, slow but steady, the ache of everything from the last few days rising and falling with each step. She didn't notice him at first—until his shadow crossed the table.

Her eyes lifted, wide with something like surprise.

Before she could speak, he bent and kissed her.

Gently. Fully.

Not rushed or desperate. Just...sure.

Her hand curled around his arm, anchoring herself to him.

When he pulled back, her eyes were glassy.

"I'm sorry," he said softly, crouching beside her now, hands warm on her knee. "For the fight. For not listening better. For not realizing what it took for you to even want to do all of this."

Her lip trembled. "Dylan—"

"I mean it," he cut in gently. "You didn't have to drive through the night or call my friends or keep showing up like you did. But you did. And I've never felt more...known. More loved."

She blinked fast, breath shaky. "I was scared you'd think I was just chasing after you. That I didn't trust you to choose me."

He shook his head, gaze locked on hers. "Ali, I chose you ten years ago. And again against that fucking wall . And again when you drove me all the way here. And again every time I open my damn eyes. I don't need a big announcement or perfect timing. I just need you."

She gave a soft, watery laugh. "You sure? Because I come with snacks and baggage."

"Good," he smiled, thumb brushing her cheek. "I'll carry the bags if you share the snacks."

Then, feeling a little embarrassed, he cleared his throat, "And I'm a hypocrite because I made plans to split my time in Georgia and didn't tell you." He admitted, cheeks burning, eyes averted.

She laughed. Actually laughed out loud at that. And leaned in again, forehead against his. They stayed like that for a long, quiet moment—his hand on her knee, her fingers laced in the sleeve of his hoodie. Breathing each other in. Holding on.

It wasn't flashy.

But it was everything.

Clean

Dylan

The door swung open and when he glanced up he saw his sister. She half smiled but detoured to a table against the wall.

Dylan crossed the cafeteria in slow strides, trying to figure out what the hell he was going to say. He hadn't had a real heart-to-heart with since the night after the fundraiser. Since before everything started to shift.

She didn't look up when he approached. Just stared down at the lid of her coffee cup like it had answers.

He eased into the chair across from her, bracing his elbows on the table.

But before he could speak, there was the soft scrape of another chair.

Ali.

She sat down beside him, not across. Not separate. Her shoulder brushing his, her presence like a warm blanket around his spine.

She didn't say anything right away—just slid her fingers into his under the table and gave a gentle squeeze. A quiet anchor. Her other hand stayed in her lap, fists loosely curled. Her smile was small, shaky, but real. Meant for both of them.

Daisy finally looked up.

Her gaze flicked to Dylan, then to Ali. Something unreadable passed through her expression. Guilt? Regret? Maybe just exhaustion.

Dylan swallowed, his thumb brushing over Ali's knuckles. "Hey," he said softly.

Daisy let out a breath that almost sounded like a laugh. "This feels weird."

Ali gave a tiny nod. "Yeah. It does."

"But not bad," Daisy added, her voice barely above a whisper.

They sat there for a moment—just three people tethered by too much history and still learning how to hold it all.

Dylan leaned back slightly, still holding Ali's hand. "We don't have to figure it all out right now. But maybe...we could start."

Daisy looked at them again. Then nodded.

"Yeah," she said. "Maybe we could."

Ali shifted slightly, still holding Dylan's hand. She glanced at Daisy, her voice quiet but steady.

"How are your kids?"

Daisy blinked at her, caught off guard.

Ali offered a small smile. "Dylan talks about them all the time."

That made Daisy's eyes soften. "Yeah?" Her lips twitched like she wasn't sure whether to smile or apologize. "They're good. Liam's a little obsessed with dinosaurs right now. And Lillie...she's basically a tiny dictator in a princess dress."

Ali let out a soft laugh. "That sounds...kinda perfect."

"It is," Daisy said, and for a moment, there was peace in her eyes. "Tiring. But perfect."

Dylan squeezed Ali's hand, grateful she asked. Grateful Daisy answered.

No digging. No pain.

Just the start of something better.

Mary's Song

Ali

Ali wiped her damp forehead with the back of her hand and took a long look at the box in her arms—labeled *Kitchen Things (aka coffee & wine)* in Ashley's messy handwriting. It was the last one. The final piece of her Honeyshore life, tucked inside a borrowed trailer hitched to the back of Dylan's Bronco.

Her heart fluttered and squeezed all at once.

This was really happening.

She was moving in with him. Not visiting. Not splitting weekends. Not dreaming from five hours away. Actually living with the man she loved in a place they'd already started turning into home.

Dylan's voice floated from the yard—something about making sure her Kindle charger hadn't gotten packed with the bathroom stuff. She smiled. Of course he remembered that. Of course he cared that much.

Behind her, the front porch of her little white rental was packed with bodies—Ashley in tears, Abigail dabbing her eyes, and Raleigh Ann dramatically fanning her face like it was a funeral.

"Y'all are so annoying," Ali mumbled, blinking back her own tears.

"Oh please," Abigail sniffled. "You cried watching the *Camp Rock* reunion on Tik-Tok."

"That's because Joe and Demi meant something to a generation!" Ali snapped, setting the box in the trailer.

Ashley barreled down the steps and threw her arms around her cousin. "You better call every day. Every. Damn. Day."

"I will."

"If he hurts you—" Raleigh Ann started.

"He won't," Ali said quickly. "He's...he's it for me. Y'all know that."

"We do know that," Abigail said, walking up with a small six-pack of Diet Cokes. "And we're proud of you. For being brave. For choosing love." She smirked. "And for letting him buy that bougie-ass bed for y'all."

Ali laughed through a tear. "I mean...it is beautiful."

The girls laughed with her, then pulled her in for one last group hug.

And when Dylan walked up behind her, sliding his arm around her waist and pressing a kiss to her temple, not one of them blinked.

Ashley narrowed her eyes at him though. "We mean it. Bodily harm."

"I believe you," Dylan said, raising his hands.

Ali glanced up at him, her heart thudding wildly.

This was it.

A new city. A new job. A new chapter.

And her favorite person by her side.

"I'm ready," she whispered.

Dylan kissed her again, softer this time. "Let's go home."

Two cars. One driveway. A whole new life.

Ali's tires crunched over the pavers as she pulled in behind Dylan, her fingers still wrapped around the wheel like she needed the grounding. Her Grand Cherokee came to a slow stop beside his Bronco, the trailer hitched behind it swaying ever so slightly as it settled.

He climbed out first, stretching like he'd been driving cross-country and not just five hours down the interstate. She watched from her spot for a second, the way he turned to look at the house—and then over at her. That grin. That stupid, heart-stopping grin.

Her heart squeezed.

Their driveway.

Their house.

Their future.

She stepped out, the Florida heat sticky against her skin, her sundress clinging to her thighs. The same house she'd visited just a few weeks ago—now filled with boxes labeled *bathroom stuff* and *Ali's books (do not touch)* and *blankets I never use but refuse to get rid of.*

He met her halfway, hands landing on her hips like it was muscle memory.

"This is real now," he murmured, voice rough from the drive and maybe from the weight of what this meant.

She nodded, blinking fast. "It's not just a weekend."

"Nope."

"It's not temporary."

He shook his head. "Not even a little."

She exhaled, relief and nerves tangled up in one long breath. "Okay. Let's do this."

Dylan kissed her forehead gently, then pulled back and looked toward the trailer. "We're really about to test your organizational skills, Presley."

Ali laughed, swatting at his chest. "Please. You'll be thanking me when you can actually find your favorite hoodie."

"I won't need it," he said, brushing her hair back. "You'll be here."

Her throat tightened. "Yeah. I will."

And with that, they turned toward the house—their house—ready to start the next chapter, one step, one box, and one shared closet at a time.

Epilogue

♥

<h1 style="text-align:center">Paper Rings</h1>

<h1 style="text-align:center">Ali</h1>

It wasn't *officially* their first night in the house, but the house was *officially* unpacked. Finally! You couldn't get more official than that.

She didn't rush.

Didn't even speak.

Just let the hem of Dylan's oversized Tritons tee fall to the floor and stood still in the glow of the bedside lamp—bare, flushed, already aching.

Her heart was thudding so hard it hurt, but Dylan? He just looked at her like a man undone. Still sitting at the foot of the bed in his black boxer briefs, one palm sliding slowly down his thigh like he was trying not to lose it.

"Jesus, Ali," he rasped, voice wrecked. "You're gonna kill me."

She stepped between his knees, cupped his jaw, and kissed him slowly—soft at first, then deeper. His hands skimmed up the backs of her thighs, over her ass, then up her spine, anchoring her to him. He sucked in a breath when her fingers dipped into his waistband, but when she went to straddle him, he shook his head.

"Uh-uh," he whispered against her mouth, standing to switch their places. "Lay down, baby. Let me take care of you."

"Dylan…"

"Ali." He crawled between her legs, pushing her gently down into the pillows, spreading her open with quiet reverence. "You're mine. Let me show you."

She was already wet—he could see it. Feel it. But he still took his time, dragging his mouth over her stomach, her inner thighs, the curve of her hips like he needed to savor every inch of her.

And then his tongue found her clit.

Ali gasped, her back arching as her fingers shot to his hair. "Oh—my—gawd—"

He chuckled low, and the vibration made her moan louder.

"You always taste so fucking sweet," he murmured, licking slow and deep, tongue curling just right. "I've missed this. Missed making you come apart."

Her thighs started to tremble. "Dylan, I can't—please—"

"Yes you can." He slid two fingers inside her and crooked them just right, groaning against her. "You're so damn tight already. Let go for me, baby. Right now."

She came hard—hips jerking, thighs clenched around his shoulders, his name tumbling from her lips like a prayer. And he didn't stop until she was twitching beneath him, begging him to.

When he finally pulled away, his mouth was slick, his eyes dark and wild.

"You okay?" he asked softly, crawling up her body, kissing her neck.

She nodded, breath still shaky. "Better than okay."

"Good." He grabbed himself, hard and thick and throbbing, guiding the tip against her entrance. "Because I'm not even close to done with you."

He guided himself inside her—slow and deep—groaning at the feel of her.

Ali gasped, head falling back, her body arching to take more.

They moved together in that slow, desperate rhythm—like they'd waited a decade for this one night. No rush. No words at first. Just the sounds of skin and breath and soft, broken moans in the shadows of their new bedroom.

Then Dylan's forehead touched hers, and his voice cracked—raw and reverent.

"I love you," he whispered. "God, I love you, Ali."

Her hands clutched his back, her legs tightening around his waist. "I love you too," she breathed. "Always."

He kissed her—deep and slow—before pressing in harder, faster, their bodies syncing like muscle memory. Like fate.

And when she came again, clenching around him, calling his name, he held her through it—murmuring against her neck, "That's it, baby. I've got you. Always."

He followed right after, burying his face in her shoulder with a ragged groan, her name the only thing on his lips.

They stayed like that for a while—bodies tangled, breath still catching. The world felt soft around the edges, like it had exhaled with them.

Dylan rolled onto his side, pulling her with him so they were nose to nose, still connected, his hand tracing lazy circles on her back.

Ali blinked up at him sleepily, her fingers brushing the curve of his jaw. "So...this is our bed now."

He grinned, all slow and wrecked. "Our bed. Our house. Our life."

She smiled, heart so full it almost ached. "Think we'll get used to it?"

He kissed the corner of her mouth, then her cheek, then her temple. "Never. I want every day with you to feel just like this. Like the first time I knew I'd never love anybody else."

Ali let out a soft sigh and nestled closer, her head tucked under his chin, legs intertwined.

Outside, the world was quiet. Inside, her whole world was wrapped around her.

How You Get the Girl

Dylan

The lights inside the Superdome were blinding.

Dylan McKenzie stood in the center of it all, sweat still slick on his brow, confetti falling like a waterfall of glitter around him. The Tritons had done it. Super Bowl champions. He could barely hear over the roar of the crowd, but it didn't matter.

His heart was thundering louder than anything else.

He held the MVP trophy in his right hand, still in disbelief. It felt weightless in his grip—because the only thing that mattered was standing thirty yards away in the front row, with tears streaming down her cheeks and a hand clutched over her heart.

Ali.

She was glowing. In a navy and teal dress, the same sandals he'd claimed months ago as his. Her hair loose in waves, her mouth trembling with joy. He'd seen her look at him with love a thousand times. But this—this was something else.

Something that changed everything.

The reporter said his name, tried to ask a question, but Dylan was already moving. He turned toward the mic. Toward the cameras. Toward her.

And then he did it.

Dropped to one knee, right there on the turf, MVP trophy at his side. Pulled a small velvet box from the taped edge of his cleat and opened it.

The crowd gasped. Then fell silent.

"Ali Presley," he said, voice steady, sure. "You've been my peace, my storm, my favorite everything since the day we met. You've waited. You've healed. You've loved me when you didn't have to. So now I'm asking—will you marry me?"

Her hands flew to her face. Her knees buckled.

And then—she nodded. Hard.

"Yes," she sobbed. "Oh my gawd, yes!"

The crowd erupted. His teammates swarmed. He barely felt the slaps on his back or the cameras flashing from every direction.

He felt her.

Ali launched herself into his arms, and he caught her midair like she was made for that exact moment. His hands cradled her back, the ring still pressed between them, and his mouth found hers.

"You're mine," he whispered.

She nodded against him. "Always was."

In the biggest moment of his life, Dylan didn't just win a ring.

He gave one away.

They skipped the afterparties.

No champagne-soaked banquet halls or velvet ropes. No media circuit or club table to celebrate the biggest win of his life. He'd smiled through the press conference, dodged Rocky's teasing, and passed his MVP trophy off to the Tritons' equipment guy with a wink and a, "I'll get it later."

Because there was only one thing he wanted.

Ali.

Now she was standing in the middle of their hotel suite—naked except those *fuck-me* sandals, her eyes full of something that made his knees weak all over again.

"How about some wall things for the MVP?," she murmured, voice soft and teasing.

His grin was slow and sinful. "Abso-fucking-lutely baby."

She stepped toward him, hands drifting up under his shirt, tugging it over his head. He let her, drinking in the way she looked at him—like she couldn't believe he was real.

"Fiancé," she whispered, testing the word.

He groaned. "Say it again."

She pressed her palm to his chest, fingers splaying over his heart. "My fiancé."

Dylan's breath caught. "God, I love you."

Then she dropped to her knees.

The air left his lungs in a rush. She looked up at him through thick lashes, her fingers already undoing the zipper of his pants. He brushed a hand through her hair gently, reverently, until she took him in her mouth and he forgot how to breathe entirely.

"Ali..." he rasped, hips stuttering forward. "Fuck, baby..."

She sucked him slow and deep, one hand curling around his thigh, the other pressing flat to his stomach to keep him grounded. But nothing could anchor him now. Not when she was loving him like this. Not when her eyes flicked up and he could see it—the joy, the possession, the promise.

His hand trembled as he reached for hers and kissed the ring now sitting on her finger. Right there on the hotel room floor.

"My fiancée," he whispered, like a vow. "Mine."

She released him with a soft pop, her voice wrecked and breathless. "Yours."

He groaned and gently threaded his fingers through her hair, holding her there, thumb brushing her cheek. "Open up for me again, baby. Just like that," he murmured, voice low and rough. "Wanna feel that pretty throat take all of me."

She obeyed, lips parting, eyes locked on his. He eased back into her mouth, guiding her pace, slow and deep.

"Fuck," he whispered, hips flexing. "So warm. That mouth was made for me."

Her throat fluttered around him and he nearly lost it, groaning through clenched teeth.

"You feel that?" he rasped, barely holding on. "That's what you do to me. Every goddamn time."

He pulled back before he could come, chest heaving, and hauled her up—his mouth on hers before she could say a word. She melted into him, breath ragged and wanting.

He carried her to the bed and laid her down gently, crawling over her like he couldn't get close enough.

"You're not just my forever," he whispered against her collarbone, kissing a path to her jaw. "You're my everything."

Then he slid inside her, slow and thick, filling her in one deep, claiming stroke.

Her gasp turned into a moan as her back arched, legs wrapping around him.

"Jesus, Ali," he choked out, forehead pressed to hers. "You feel like fucking heaven."

He didn't rush it. Not this time.

He moved slowly, reverently, kissing her face, her jaw, her hand again—never letting it go. The ring glinted under the hotel lights, and every time he caught a glimpse of it, it drove him deeper.

"Say it," he begged softly.

"I love you," she whispered.

He dropped his forehead to hers, breath ragged. "Say it again."

"I love you, Dylan. I love you, I love you…"

Her words fell apart as he brought them over the edge together, his name breaking from her lips like a song.

Later, they lay tangled in the sheets, his arm under her neck and her hand resting on his chest, fingers tracing the Tritons logo inked just above his heart.

"Still want wall things?" she teased, drowsy.

He chuckled, kissing the crown of her head.

"Yeah," he murmured. "But tonight I just wanted you."

And he had her.

They didn't sleep.

Not really.

Just pauses in between—her head on his chest, legs tangled, breath coming back to center—before one of them reached for the other again. It wasn't just desire. It was years of longing, of almosts and what-ifs, finally finding a home in skin and sighs and whispered *I love yous*.

She rode him slow, her hands braced on his chest while his thumb traced lazy circles over her clit.

He bent her over the back of the hotel couch, kissing her spine while she shook from the second orgasm in as many hours.

She begged for him to stay inside after, to keep her full and warm while they curled together, and he did.

She was boneless in his arms, lips swollen, legs shaking, still gasping from the last round when he scooped her up and carried her to the wide floor-length mirror beside the closet.

"Dylan," she murmured, already breathless again. "What are you—?"

He turned her gently, their bodies flush, her front against the cool glass and his chest warm against her back. One hand curved around her hip, the other trailing up her arm to lace their fingers together. Their eyes met in the reflection.

"Look at us," he said roughly, his voice dark and thick with emotion. "Look at you."

Ali's eyes flicked away, a self-conscious flicker, but he brought their joined hands to her chest, holding her there.

"You're so fucking beautiful," he whispered, pressing a kiss to her temple. "Every inch of you. This body. This skin. This heart. All mine now."

She trembled as he nudged her legs apart, dragging the head of his cock through her folds. She was slick and sensitive and still aching for more.

"Dyl…"

"Watch, baby," he whispered, lining up and pushing in slowly. "I want you to see how it looks when I love you."

He filled her in one long, thick thrust, and her eyes fluttered closed again.

"No," he rasped, brushing her hair back from her shoulder. "Eyes on me."

She forced them open, biting her lip as he began to move—slow and deep, grinding into her in long, deliberate strokes.

"You take me so good," he breathed, watching her reflection unravel. "Every single time. My perfect girl."

Her hands reached for the mirror for balance, but he caught them, holding them in place against the glass.

"Can't go anywhere," he murmured. "You're mine now. My fiancée."

That word. That word lit her up like fireworks.

Ali moaned, her body clenching around him as he fucked her slow and hard, hips smacking against her ass.

"You feel that?" he groaned. "That's how I'll always come back to you. Like I was made for it. For this."

She was shaking now, her breath turning to sobs of pleasure. Her release built slowly, then consumed her all at once, her body clenching so hard it dragged him under with her.

He let go inside her with a guttural moan, their eyes locked in the mirror the entire time.

They stayed like that—tangled, trembling, breathless—until her knees gave out and he caught her.

Then he carried her back to bed, tucked her close, and kissed the ring on her hand one more time.

By the time morning hit, the suite smelled like sex and room service, and his back was sore in the best possible way.

Ali was curled under the blanket now, hair wild, cheek pressed to his bare chest.

Dylan smiled at the mess they were, kissing her temple.

"I'm pretty sure I can't feel my legs," she murmured sleepily.

He chuckled. "I take full responsibility."

"You should." She turned her face into his skin, sighing deeply. "That was...a lot."

"Best win of my life," he said, stroking her back. "And I don't mean the ring."

Ali peeked up at him, lashes still heavy with sleep. "What time's check out?"

"Late. Kallie made sure of it."

She grinned. "Of course she did."

They stayed in bed until noon, ordering waffles and fruit and enough coffee to caffeinate a small nation. Ali wore one of his oversized Super Bowl shirts, the hem barely brushing the tops of her thighs. Dylan couldn't stop touching her—couldn't stop looking.

She was his. Finally. Forever.

And he planned on spending the rest of his life showing her what that meant.

We Are Never Ever Getting Back Together

Ashley

The Georgia sun was already punishing, but Ashley didn't slow her pace. Her oversized sunglasses shielded her eyes and her ponytail bounced with every step. Her go-to lavender latte was waiting for her when the run was done.

AirPods in. Volume up. Confidence on.

The screen lit up—

AliKat, FaceTime Incoming—

Ashley grinned, breathlessly answering as she slid her sunglasses to the top of her head.

"Okay, first of all—the proposal post?" she said, before Ali could even get out a hello. "Literal chills! Brant cried."

Ali blinked on-screen, hair damp and coffee mug in hand. "Wait. Y'all were talking?"

"Keyword: *were*," Ashley replied, flicking her wrist with flair. "We're done. I mean it this time. I boxed up his sneakers and everything."

"No," Ali said slowly, brows rising. "You didn't."

"I did. Even the fancy ones that he never wore." She sighed dramatically. "I finally figured it out—I don't want someone who texts me when it's convenient. I want someone who looks at me the way Dylan looks at you."

Ali's expression softened. "Damn right."

Ashley hesitated, biting her lip before dropping her voice. "I actually...might have agreed to go on a date next week."

Ali perked up immediately. "Oh?"

"Yeah, the oldest son of the Rise and Grind family—it's fun. Light. No strings."

But then her gaze catches on a too-familiar figure in a fitted gray athletic tee, cutting across the path with a perfectly smug smirk

Damon Scott.

The District Attorney. Her sworn nemesis. Satan's spawn in running shoes.

She mutters into her phone, "Shit, I gotta go. The spawn just showed up."

Ali snorts on the other end. "Tell Damon I said 'hi'."

She ends the call just as he falls into stride beside her, effortlessly matching her pace.

"You stalking me now, Damian?" she asks, voice syrupy-sweet and venom-laced.

The annoyance flashes in his eyes, sharp and immediate. "You know it's Damon," he bites. "And if I were stalking you, I'd at least bring coffee."

"Try holy water next time."

He smirks again, unbothered.

She doesn't give him the satisfaction of a longer conversation. She picks up her pace, tossing a breezy, "See you in court, Scott," over her shoulder.

And just like that, she disappears into the trees, ponytail swishing behind her.

Baby...let the games begin.

The Bonus Sessions

Magnolia Ink

The Bonus Sessions

♥

Wish List

Ali

Ali's leg bounced beneath the table, her hands twisting together in her lap. She was nervous. Anxious. Honestly, a little scared. She could barely sip her iced coffee, afraid she might throw it right back up.

Dylan noticed. Of course he did.

His hand settled on her thigh, stilling the restless movement. He leaned over and pressed a kiss to her temple. "I'm right here, sweetheart. As long as you need me," he whispered.

Ali drew in a slow breath, forcing herself to steady. She could do this. She had spent weeks tossing and turning at night, knowing this conversation had to happen. She wanted to do this. A little for herself, maybe. But especially for Dylan. He loved her in all the ways she had always deserved, and she could do this for him. For the fiancé she loved with her entire soul.

They sat tucked into a corner table at the back of Coffee for the Soul in Winter Park, one of her favorite local coffee shops.

Then the door opened, and Ali felt it immediately.

It wasn't tension exactly. Not sharp, not like before. Something quieter. Heavier. Anxiety. Apprehension. Grief dressed up in softer clothes.

She tightened her hold on Dylan's hand while the other woman stepped up to the counter to order. Ali focused on her breathing. In. Out. In. Out. She could do this. She would do this.

When the woman finally approached their table, she moved slowly.

"Hi." Her voice was tentative, nothing like the bubbly, confident tone Ali had once known by heart.

"Hey, sis," Dylan said, calm and gentle beside her.

Daisy glanced at Ali, then back down at the floor for half a second before lifting her eyes again. "Thank you for meeting me. I know this is difficult. But it means so much that you're willing to try, Ali."

Ali studied her carefully.

Daisy didn't look like herself. She had reached out to Dylan several times over the past few months, asking if she could please talk to Ali. Every time, Dylan had pushed back. They were civil at family functions now, but Ali knew how hard it still was for all of them. Hard in that quiet, exhausting way that never fully let anyone breathe.

Eventually, Ali had told Dylan she would try. She would meet Daisy. She would listen.

But she wouldn't do it alone.

She had been too scared of being triggered, too afraid of what Daisy might say, of how easily old wounds could split open if she faced this without him. She didn't know what Daisy needed from her, only that she couldn't walk into it by herself.

For a few strained minutes, they made small talk while the barista finished Daisy's cinnamon iced latte. Weather. Traffic. The wedding. Safe little stepping stones over deep water.

When Daisy finally sat back down with her drink, Ali noticed how tightly she cradled it, both hands wrapped around the plastic cup like it was the only thing keeping her upright.

And despite everything, empathy moved through Ali in a slow, aching wave.

This had once been her best friend. Her person. The one who knew almost as much about her as Ashley did. The girl who had slept in her dorm room, borrowed her clothes, cried over boys on her shoulder, made her laugh until her stomach hurt. Now they could barely sit across from each other without anxiety curling around both their throats.

Ali cleared hers first, offering the olive branch because somebody had to.

"Daisy," she said softly, "it was a long time ago. We can't keep letting it control both of us. Whatever you need to say...you know I'll listen."

Daisy exhaled, her shoulders finally loosening like she'd been holding that breath for years.

"It wasn't about you, Ali. It never was." Her voice wavered, but she didn't look away this time. "I was jealous. Upset. Hurt. You were my best friend...and then suddenly, you were his."

Her fingers tightened around her cup before she forced them to relax.

"I felt like I lost you without even knowing I had a chance to keep you. You hid it from me. And I know why now, I do, but back then…it made me feel stupid. Like a fool. Like I was the second choice."

She swallowed hard, her next words catching like they didn't want to exist out loud.

"And the worst part was…I think—I know—I had feelings for you." Her eyes flickered, vulnerable and exposed. "A crush. Something I couldn't tell you. Couldn't tell anyone. I didn't even want to admit it to myself."

A shaky breath left her.

"And then you were suddenly Dylan's. Just…like that. Gone. It felt like you chose him over me, and I didn't understand how to handle any of it." Her voice softened, cracking at the edges. "You were the only person I would've ever talked to about something like that. And I lost you."

Silence stretched for a beat before she continued, quieter now.

"I know it was my fault. The way I acted…what I said, what I did. I should've told you the truth. But I was young, and I was scared of who I was, of what I felt." She shook her head slightly. "So I lashed out. In every wrong way possible."

Her eyes finally met Ali's again, glassy and unguarded.

"You'll never know how sorry I am. How much I've regretted it." Her voice dropped to almost a whisper. "I'll always regret it, Ali. I'm so, so sorry."

Silence settled over the table, heavy and unfamiliar.

Ali didn't move right away.

Daisy's words lingered between them, soft but sharp, like something fragile that could still cut if handled wrong. For a second, Ali just… stared at her. Trying to reconcile the girl sitting in front of her with the one she used to know. The one who used to sprawl across her bed, stealing her hoodies and her Skittles and every last ounce of her attention.

Her chest tightened.

Because part of her understood now.

And that almost made it worse.

Ali's fingers curled tighter around Dylan's hand, grounding herself. She hadn't realized she'd stopped breathing until her lungs burned for it. A slow inhale. Then another.

"You don't get to say it wasn't about me," Ali said finally, her voice quiet but steady.

Daisy flinched.

Ali swallowed, her throat thick. "Because it was. Maybe not for the reasons I thought, but it still was. You said those things to me. You *did* those things." Her voice wavered just slightly before she steadied it again. "You don't get to rewrite it into something softer now."

Dylan's thumb brushed gently against her leg, a silent *I'm here*, but he didn't interrupt.

Ali looked down at the table for a moment, gathering herself, then back up at Daisy.

"I didn't hide it from you because I wanted to hurt you," she continued, softer now. "I hid it because I was scared of losing you. You were my person, Daisy. I knew how you were about Dylan, about...everything. And I thought if I just waited, if I figured it out first..." She shook her head faintly. "I thought I could protect both of us."

A humorless breath slipped out of her.

"Clearly, I was wrong."

Her eyes stung, but she didn't look away this time.

"When everything blew up...you didn't just push me away. You humiliated me. You made me feel small. Worthless." Her voice cracked on the last word, and she pressed her lips together, fighting to keep it together. "Do you have any idea what that did to me?"

Daisy's face crumpled, but Ali kept going. She needed to.

"I spent years thinking I deserved it. Thinking maybe I *was* the problem. That if I had just been better—prettier, quieter, less...me—then maybe you wouldn't have—" She cut herself off, shaking her head.

Dylan's grip tightened on her thigh just slightly, steady and solid.

Ali blinked hard, forcing the tears back.

"I hear you," she said after a moment, quieter now. "I do. And I'm...I'm really sorry that you went through that alone. You shouldn't have had to figure all of that out by yourself." Her voice softened, genuine, because that part was true. "And I hate that you felt like you lost me."

A pause.

"But that doesn't erase what you did to me."

The words landed gently, but firmly. No anger. Just truth.

Ali let out a slow breath, her shoulders rising and falling with it.

"I'm not there yet," she admitted, her voice almost a whisper now. "I don't know if I can just...forgive all of it and pretend it didn't change me. Because it did. It changed everything."

Her fingers tightened slightly in Dylan's, then loosened again.

"But…" she hesitated, the word fragile in her mouth, "I'm here. And that has to mean something."

Ali met Daisy's eyes, not soft, not hard, just…open.

"I'm willing to try," she said. "Slowly. Carefully. But it's not going to be what it was before. I can't go back to that."

A small, shaky breath.

"Not after everything. At least, not right now. Not yet."

Daisy nodded quickly, like she didn't trust herself to interrupt.

"I know," she said, her voice gentle, careful. "I understand. And I won't push you."

She paused, swallowing, her fingers tracing the edge of her cup like she needed something to hold onto.

"I just…I've wanted to say that for so long." Her eyes flickered up to Ali's, vulnerable but steady. "And I needed you to hear it. Really hear it."

A small, fragile breath left her.

"So…thank you. For being here. For listening to me." Her voice softened even more. "I know it doesn't fix us. I'm not expecting that."

She hesitated, like the next part mattered most.

"But maybe…one day…we can try again."

Not *what they were*. Not yet. Maybe not ever. But something.

The words settled between them, fragile but real.

Ali didn't respond right away. She just…looked at Daisy. Not the version she had carried in her anger for years. Not the girl frozen in that last, awful memory. But the one sitting in front of her now. Softer. Quieter. Unraveled in a way Ali had never seen before.

Daisy's hand shifted slightly on the table, like she wanted to reach across but didn't quite dare.

For a second, Ali's instinct was to pull back. To protect. To retreat into the safety she had spent years building. But she didn't.

Her fingers loosened from where they had been curled into her palm. Just a little.

Daisy noticed.

Slowly, cautiously, she let her hand move the rest of the way forward, stopping just short of Ali's. Close enough to feel the warmth, not close enough to assume anything.

An offering. Not an expectation.

Dylan went still beside her. Ali could feel it, the way his presence sharpened—not tense, not controlling. Just aware. Like he was holding himself perfectly in place, giving her the space to choose this moment for herself.

Her heart pounded, loud in her ears. This was the line. The one she had sworn she would never cross again.

Her gaze dropped to Daisy's hand. Then, slowly, she reached out. Not fully. Not intertwining. Not forgiveness wrapped in a bow.

Just the lightest touch of her fingertips against Daisy's. Barely there. But enough.

Daisy's breath hitched, her shoulders trembling with it, but she didn't move closer. Didn't grab. Didn't take more than what was given. Ali let the contact linger for a heartbeat. Two. Then she pulled her hand back, resting it in her lap again. Not rejection. Just boundary.

But when she looked back up, something in her expression had shifted. Not healed. Not whole. But open.

And for the first time in years, the silence between them didn't feel like something broken.

It felt like something waiting.

Eldest Daughter

Ali

They lingered longer than Ali expected.

Somewhere along the way, Dylan gently picked up the conversation, easing them into safer waters. He talked about the upcoming season, about training camp, about one of the rookies who had tried to microwave a protein shake and nearly taken out half the locker room. His voice was easy, familiar. Light where everything else had been heavy.

It helped.

Not in a way that erased anything, but in a way that gave them all a place to breathe again.

Ali found herself listening more than talking, her body slowly unwinding even as exhaustion crept in, settling deep in her bones. The kind that didn't come from lack of sleep, but from feeling too much for too long.

Dylan noticed.

But he didn't call her out. Didn't draw attention to it. He just shifted closer, his presence steady and warm beside her.

After a while, he glanced at his watch and gave Daisy a small, easy smile. "Well, we need to get going, sis. I've got to meet Kallie later."

He stood, reaching for his keys before adding, softer, "Thank you for driving down. I know it was a long drive, but...we appreciate it."

Daisy nodded, standing with them. "Of course." Her eyes flickered to Ali, something hopeful but careful lingering there. "I think I'm going to stay a little longer before heading back. Six hours is...a lot."

Ali managed a small nod.

"Drive safe," she said quietly.

It wasn't much. But it was something.

Daisy gave her a gentle smile in return. "I will."

And just like that, it was over.

Or maybe...just beginning.

The walk to the car was quiet. Not awkward. Not heavy. Just quiet. The kind that settles after something important has been said.

Dylan opened her door for her like he always did, his hand brushing lightly against her back as she slid into the passenger seat. He circled around to the driver's side, but before he could even start the engine, the first tear fell.

Ali didn't try to stop it. Didn't choke it back or hide it away. It slipped down her cheek, then another, and another, until she was just...letting them fall. Silent. Steady. Like something inside her had finally loosened its grip.

Dylan didn't hesitate.

He leaned across the console, one hand coming up to cup her cheek, the other pulling her gently toward him. His thumb brushed away her tears as they came, slow and careful, like he was handling something precious.

"I've got you," he murmured, his voice soft, anchoring.

Ali's eyes closed, her forehead resting against his shoulder as she breathed him in. Safe. Familiar. Hers.

"I'm so proud of you," he whispered against her hair. "You did so good, sweetheart. So good."

Her breath hitched, but she didn't break.

He pressed a kiss to her temple, lingering there.

"I love you," he added, quieter now. "More than anything."

Ali nodded faintly against him, her fingers curling into his shirt.

Dylan pulled back just enough to look at her, his hand still warm against her face.

"You can rest now," he said gently.

And for the first time since she'd walked into that coffee shop, Ali believed him.

<h1 style="text-align:center">This Love</h1>

<h1 style="text-align:center">Dylan</h1>

Dylan didn't start the car right away.

He let her cry.

Not loudly. Not breaking. Just quietly unraveling beside him. And he stayed exactly where he was, leaned across the console, one hand cupping her cheek, the other steady at the back of her neck like he could hold her together if she needed it.

He knew better than to rush this. So he didn't.

When her breathing finally evened out, when the tears slowed into something softer, something spent, he pressed one more kiss to her temple and pulled back just enough to look at her.

"You ready to go home, baby?" he asked gently.

She nodded.

That was all he needed.

The drive was quiet.

He kept one hand on the wheel, the other resting over hers in the center console, his thumb brushing slow, absent patterns across her skin. Grounding. Reassuring. There.

She leaned her head against the window, eyes closed, not asleep—but close enough.

Dylan didn't turn on the radio. Didn't fill the silence. He just drove.

By the time they got home, she looked wrung out. Not fragile. Not broken. Just emptied. Exhausted

And Dylan knew exactly what to do.

"Come on," he murmured, guiding her inside with a hand at her back.

He didn't ask what she needed. He already knew.

The shower was already warming by the time she stepped into their bedroom.

"Go ahead," he said softly, brushing a piece of hair behind her ear. "I've got everything else."

She hesitated for half a second, like she might protest. Then she just nodded. Because she trusted him. Because she didn't have anything left to give.

While she showered, Dylan moved through the house with quiet purpose.

He dimmed the lights.

Closed the drapes, shutting out the late afternoon sun until the room softened into something cocooned and safe. Private. The outside world held firmly at the door.

He pulled back the covers, then rebuilt the bed the way she liked it—extra pillows, piled high and surrounding, like something she could sink into and disappear for a while. Not hiding. Just resting.

In the kitchen, he grabbed a bowl, poured popcorn, added just enough salt and melted butter the way she always did. A box of Raisinets followed, tucked beside it without a second thought.

By the time she stepped out of the bathroom, wrapped in one of his t-shirts and soft shorts, her hair damp and her face scrubbed clean of everything except the faint trace of exhaustion, the bed was ready.

He crossed to her immediately.

"Hey," he murmured, his voice softer than before, like she might break if he wasn't careful.

She didn't speak. Just looked at him.

And Dylan felt it hit him square in the chest—how much she had carried today. How much she had *chosen* to face.

He reached for her hand.

"Come here."

He settled her into bed like something precious. Carefully. Gently.

Pillows tucked around her, covers pulled up just enough, the bowl of popcorn and Raisinets within reach on the nightstand.

The TV flickered on low, the familiar rhythm of the Food Network filling the room. Something easy. Something she didn't have to think about.

Background comfort.

He climbed in beside her, pulling her against him without hesitation, her back to his chest, his arm wrapping around her waist like it belonged there.

Because it did.

Ali let out a slow breath, her body finally, fully relaxing into him.

Dylan pressed his lips to her shoulder, lingering there.

"I've got you," he whispered again, softer this time.

Always.

He stared at the ceiling for a moment, listening to the quiet hum of the TV, the soft rhythm of her breathing as it evened out.

There was no meeting with Kallie.

He'd made it up without a second thought.

Nothing—no schedule, no obligation, no damn meeting—mattered more than this. More than her. The woman he loved.

His thumb traced slow circles against her arm as her breathing deepened, sleep finally pulling her under.

And Dylan stayed right there.

Holding her.

Guarding the quiet.

Like nothing in the world would ever touch her again if he had anything to say about it.

Acknowledgements

Writing this book was one of the most challenging, soul-stretching, and joy-filled things I've ever done—and I didn't do it alone. This story was more than fiction—it was **catharsis**. It was a way to untangle some of the pain I've carried and turn it into something tender and hopeful.

To my sister, Mandy:

Thank you for loving me through every writing spiral—and for *literally* forcing me to finally write a novel. You've always seen this in me, even when I didn't. I love you endlessly.

To my friend Becca:

Thank you for co-founding Shelf Indulgence with me and for being the one of the most thoughtful, honest, encouraging, and genuine people I know.

To my Beta Readers:

Thank you for believing in Dali the way I did and for helping me shape and perfect their "Love Story".

To my Dad:

Thank you for being my personal sports encyclopedia and football fact-checker. Your continuity advice kept the story grounded—even when your answers went a little long and I zoned out.

To my Mom:

Thank you for walking with me through the hardest chapters of life. Heather Presley carries so much of your pain, your fear—and your strength

To the real-life Shelf Indulgence Book Club:

You are my people, my soft place to land, and my favorite source of inspiration and laughter. Thank you for building this beautiful book-loving space with me.

<u>To my 8th grade Language Arts teacher</u>— *Mrs. Lamb*:

You were the first person to tell me I could write, and that simple encouragement planted
the seed for everything that followed. Thank you for seeing something in me.

<u>To my Creative Writing Professor at GSU</u>— *Laura Valeri*:

Thank you for the endless encouragement & belief in my writing abilities. It was the
empowerment I needed.

<u>To my therapist</u>:

Thank you for keeping me grounded and reminding me I'm allowed to take up space.

<u>To the amazing writers</u>

—especially indie romance authors—who were brave enough to share their stories first:

Your courage made room for mine.

And finally,

<u>To the readers</u>:

Thank you for choosing this story.

Whether you laughed, cried, dog-eared pages,

or stayed up way too late to finish just one more chapter...

you made it all worth it.

A Note from the Author

If you made it to this page, thank you—from the bottom of my heart.

Writing this book was deeply personal. As someone living with Borderline Personality Disorder and in recovery from self-harm and suicidal ideation, parts of this story were incredibly hard to write...and incredibly healing. There are pieces of my heart in these pages, and if you saw even a flicker of yourself in them—please know you are not alone.

Healing is messy. It's not linear. But it's possible.

If you're struggling, I hope you'll reach out. Talk to someone you trust. Call 988. Let the people who love you hold the light for a while.

To anyone who ever felt like Ali—too sensitive, too complicated, too "much"— you are worthy. You are lovable. You are *still here* for a reason.

"What a shame she's fucked in the head," they said. —Taylor Swift, *champagne problems.*

But you and I both know...she was never the shameful one to begin with.

With love,

Kennedy Layne

About the Author

Kennedy Layne is a romance author and storyteller creating interconnected worlds filled with love, friendship, healing, and second chances. She's a proud dog mom to the cutest Maltese on the planet, Prince Charming (Char, for short), and a wild, rambunctious mini Golden Doodle named Presley Grace (yes, like Elvis).

Deeply rooted in her community, Kennedy is active in several civic organizations and volunteers as a librarian at her church library. She lives in south Georgia, with her younger sister, just down the road from her parents and her childhood home.

Kennedy is always planning her next adventure, whether it's a beach getaway or a magical escape to Walt Disney World. She's a proud Swiftie who believes there's a Taylor lyric for every occasion, that iced tea with Splenda (because, you know...diabetes) can cure anything, and that there will never be a better show than *The Vampire Diaries*. She cheers loudest for the Atlanta Braves and her beloved Georgia Southern Eagles—Hail Southern!